LAKES HOCKEY TWO

# STRONG AND WILD

SLOANE ST. JAMES

Editing by Dee Houpt | www.deesnoteseditingservices.com
Formatting by CC | formatbycc@gmail.com
Cover by Sloane St. James

1st Edition 2023

# CONTENTS

🌶 One-Handed Reader Shortcuts

# PLAYLIST

Available on Spotify

1. **Shadow** - Macklemore feat. IRO
2. **S.L.U.T.** - Bea Miller
3. **Higher** - The Score
4. **Look Who's Cryin' Now** - Jessie Murph
5. **Sleepless** - Dutch Melrose
6. **Promises** - EMO
7. **Blind Spot** - Saint Chaos
8. **Breakfast** - Dove Cameron
9. **Slow Motion** - Charlotte Lawrence
10. **Miserable Until Ur Dead** - Nessa Barrett
11. **Fade Into You** - Mazzy Star
12. **Harder To Breathe** - Letdown
13. **Demons** - Marlhy
14. **Somebody I F*cked Once** - Zolita
15. **Ghost Town** - Layto, Neoni
16. **Can't Sleep** - K.Flay
17. **Flirt** - NEFEX
18. **Slow Down** - GRAE
19. **Fire Up The Night** - New Medicine
20. **Storm** - Honors
21. **Villain Era** - Bryce Savage
22. **Bad Things** - MGK with Camila Cabello
23. **Buzzkill** - MOTHICA
24. **Dark Side** - Bishop Briggs
25. **Over My Head** - Judah & The Lion
26. **Drinking with Cupid** - Viola
27. **Dandelions** - Ruth  B.
28. **Opposite of Adults** - Chiddy Bang

29. **Tribulation** - Matt Maeson
30. **Horns** - Bryce Fox
31. **Mad Hatter** - Melanie Martinez
32. **Kryptonite (Reloaded)** - Jeris Johnson
33. **Where's My Love** - SYML
34. **Easier to Say** - Grady
35. **La Di Die** - Nessa Barrett feat. Jxdn
36. **Serotonin** - Call Me Karizma
37. **Control** - Halsey
38. **Pull the Plug** - VIOLA
39. **Until I Found You** - Stephen Sanchez
40. **Someone to You** - BANNERS

# MINNESOTA LAKES TEAM ROSTER

### Left Wingers
#9 Lee "Sully" Sullivan (C)
#16 Jake "Jonesy" Jones
#89 Matthew Laasko
#77 Teddy Leighton

### Centers
#46 Camden "Banksy" Teller
#71 Shepherd Wilder
#28 Joey Broderick
#65 Colby Imlach

### Right Wingers
#33 Barrett Conway (A)
#18 Ryan Bishop
#48 Brit O'Callahan
#21 Reggie Daniels

### Left Defensemen
#5 Rhys Kucera
#39 Dean Burmeister
#20 Doug Elsworth

### Right Defensemen
#14 Lonan Burke
#52 Burt Paek
#3 Cory Dopson

### Goaltenders
#29 Sergey Kapucik
#40 Tyler Strassburg

# TROPES

Hockey romance, enemies to lovers, neighbors, close proximity, workplace romance, cam girl and her top subscriber, friends with benefits, rookie hockey player, situationship, praise and degradation, all the banter, asshole MMC meets feisty FMC, melt your kindle, happily ever after.

# TRIGGER CONTENT WARNING

This book portrays how difficult it is to love a drug user, as well as the challenges that come with loving someone who loves a drug user. It contains prescription drug use (not by MCs), detailed detoxing (including emesis and defecation), addiction, verbal abuse, and death. In addition, there is slut shaming, misogyny, sexual harassment, mention of cheating (no cheating occurs), a brief third-act separation, BDSM, rope play, breath play, restraints, impact play, praise, and degradation. If you are triggered by these situations, please skip this one.

For 24/7 help, please call the National Drug Helpline at (844) 289-0879 or reach out to the Substance Abuse and Mental Health Services Administration 1-800-662-HELP (4357).

*For those who think praise and degradation
go together like anal sex and aftercare.*

*This one's for you.*

# ONE

## Rhys

"Come on, Kucera. Let's see what you got." Sully knows what I've got. I've been running these same fucking small-area drills with them all offseason. I'm at the point where I just want to play. I've done all I can, but I need experience playing a live game. I've had some ice time in preseason, but tomorrow is my first game. My first real, legit NHL game—and I've got shifts.

Lee "Sully" Sullivan is a natural captain since he's, without a doubt, the *dad* on our team. We've got the nets spread about thirty feet apart as we skate figure eights around them. I work defense, he works offense. My game has improved since starting with the team last spring. Today, I've held my own against him, and I can tell he's pleased. Sully is huge at six feet, five inches and the classic blond all-American hero hockey player. He'd probably be a pretty boy if it weren't for his intimidating size. Dude looks like a damn Viking. There are a lot of talented guys on the team. I'm shocked this is my life now. I looked up to these guys in high school, and now we're running drills together.

Growing up, I had jerseys for Sullivan and Barrett Conway. They've played side by side for fifteen years, and their friendship goes back further than their playing careers. Both guys are bachelors, but from what I'm told, neither mess around nor party too hard with the fans. At least not anymore.

Nowadays, Camden "Banks" Teller is the Lakes' playboy. Banksy is closer to my age at twenty-four. He's a shameless womanizer and seems to enjoy picking fights. An absolute arrogant fuck but seems nice enough. Banks is one of those guys that grows on you, unlike Lonan, who I've liked since day one.

Lonan got married this past summer and won't shut up about it, he's always in a good mood. The rest of the team told me about his wife—that might have been the craziest story I've ever heard. Glad he's in love, but I'll probably run more with the Sullivan and Conway crowd. I don't have time for women.

Having just been signed, I need to make sure I have my shit together. I'm expected to earn my number every time I step on the ice, every game this year will be a tryout. As a rookie I get a one-year, one-way contract. Three hundred sixty-five days to prove I'm worth signing a second season. I can't let anything get between me and my career, not after I've worked so hard to get here. Being the best in high school, D-1, minors, it's all led me to this. I put endless hours on the ice practicing and don't have much of a personal life because of it, but I made it. I've always wanted to play for the Lakes—this is my dream.

It's why I need to keep my head down and stay focused—also why the only woman I plan to focus on is Queen of Tarts. She's perfect for me. Killer body, a sweet personality, and I have no idea who she is. She's usually wearing some '50s housewife apron around her waist and nothing else. For only ten dollars a month I can watch her bake almost nude and chat with her about her day. It gives me something to jerk off to, and I get a little social interaction outside of the team. She's guaranteed not to be a distraction since we're strangers, and I get to spend time with her whenever it works for my schedule. Could I go out and fuck randos? Absolutely. The guys would give me hell for paying for nudes, but I can't beat the convenience.

"Kucera, what the fuck?" Sully yells after I miss the puck. Shit, if a woman I've only gotten off to through a laptop screen has got me missing passes, there's no way I could handle bunnies. *Focus, Rhys.*

We run passes and line skate for the next half hour before it's time to wrap up. When I walk into the locker room, it hits me—the next time I lace up, it'll be for a game.

I log in to my Followers account and see her username on the side—Queen of Tarts. I click on the sexy redhead and scroll through some of her latest photos. Most are of shit she baked, which is surprisingly eye-catching. Some of her creations more closely resemble art than they do something one would eat. But if I could pick between the two, I'd rather eat from her pussy than her plate. I scroll through a few of her pictures— some tasteful nudes. She likes to get a little kitschy sometimes with whipped cream and melted chocolate covering her nipples. Her tits are unreal.

Last week, I overheard some of the guys talking about the website, *Followers*, and that you can subscribe to different people, some are athletes or Olympians, others are just everyday folks, and often you get access to nudes, videos, or live streams you wouldn't find anywhere else. A couple of the guys are thinking of starting their own accounts. You shell out a few dollars a month and in return get a private view into the life of whichever content creator you fancy.

I decided to see what the fuss was about. When I joined,

there was a list of the newest creators on the left side of the screen, and the username Queen of Tarts stood out to me. After clicking, she had me hooked. My wallet was out, and there I was signing up as her first subscriber. There was no need to continue window shopping after seeing the merchandise.

We chat a lot. We had a lot of one-on-one time as she grew her following. Thankfully, the distance keeps us apart or she'd be irresistible. She's cool as hell. But I rely on our "relationship" to be online only, this way she doesn't interfere with my job. We have good chemistry as friends, often there's flirting involved. And I almost always get off during her cam sessions. She doesn't show her face, it's only neck down. But it's one great neck down. I don't stalk her page every second, but she usually gives a cooking tutorial every Tuesday. And well . . . it's Tuesday. And I've got nowhere else to be.

A notification pops up saying she's live. I'm the first viewer. Until someone else joins, this is a private show. She moves around a kitchen wearing a frilly pink half apron with bright-red cherries. It looks like something June Cleaver would wear, which is why it's so hot. The flesh-colored sleeve on her right arm covers up tattoos, I assume. She explains that today she's making French macarons. I'm already salivating.

"Looks like it's you and me today, Hat Trick Swayze."

It's a stupid nickname I earned in college.

**HatTrickSwayze: Nice cherries. New apron?**

"Why, thank you for noticing. I found it at a thrift shop last week for a dollar! Can you believe that?"

God, she's cute. I send a twenty-dollar tip with the note: *Apron Fund.*

Her laugh plays through my laptop speakers—she has an incredible laugh—that's what I was hoping my twenty would buy, and it worked. I still don't quite understand why it does something to me, but it does. It's not like me to want to make a woman laugh or get her to like me. I couldn't care less.

"I'll be sure to pick one out just for you, then, thank you."

I can hear her smile, but I wish I could see it. I'm already attracted to her voice. It literally gets my dick hard. My cock strains against my zipper.

This is how I get off these days. It's better this way. Even if I gave a woman the time of day, I'm a shitty boyfriend. As soon as things start to get serious, I burn it to the ground. I'm not relationship material. Hockey is my wife, and I'm her faithful husband. There's no way I'm about to throw away this opportunity by partying and fucking it all up. I've made enough mistakes in life, and I've been known to self-sabotage. But that's what makes Queen of Tarts so advantageous. She keeps me on track but gives my mind something to indulge in on the side. It's intimate and feels more personal than porn.

Even if I found a girl for the night, I like things rough. I can get off in the missionary position, but I'd rather wrap my hand around her neck and whisper dirty things in her ear while I do it. However, when you grow up in a small town in Maine, most of those women want someone gentle and sweet. They want a rural boy next door that will bring them daisies and change the oil in their car. Someone they can bring home to mom and dad and take to church on Sunday. I can play the part, but that's all it is—an act. I'm done acting. Until I find a woman who can match my level of wickedness, I'd rather fuck my hand than go through that song and dance again.

"One time in college, my girlfriend and I had a final coming up, and we needed to ace our meringue practical. Our macarons were absolute shit. So we stayed up all night making hundreds of these little guys, and by early next morning, we had them down pat. They were divine. The trick is getting the consistency right. You want it smooth like honey, like this."

She holds up the beater attachment and shows the blush-pink batter drizzling off like . . . well, honey. She scrapes the side of the bowl with a spatula and transfers it into a piping bag.

As soon as she starts piping, her tits squish together, and the suggestive placement of her piping bag is enough for me to palm my erection. I grab the lotion and envision her down on her knees for me. What I wouldn't give to see her lips right now so I could add them to my fantasy. I do the best I can with my imagination.

"I got a new neighbor not long ago, so I'm making these to welcome them to the building."

*Lucky fucker.*

"Think it's too pretentious?"

I type with one hand to respond.

**HatTrickSwayze: It's definitely on its way to pretentious.**

"Yeah, you're probably right. But they're homemade, so I feel like that brings it back down a notch."

She turns around, facing her white bedsheet backdrop. Not sure why it's there, as if anything behind her could distract someone watching her fantastic ass. My hand pumps faster. I imagine taking her from behind, pulling her hair, and making her cheeks as red as the cherries on her apron as she begs for mercy. She does something different today, she bends a little more exaggerated and arches her back, giving me a quick shot of her pussy. *Fuck me.*

"Since it's just us . . . and because sugar daddies that buy me aprons get a little extra."

I'll buy her a hundred aprons if it gets me another shot of that. I type one-handed.

**HatTrickSwayze: Oh, I'm your sugar daddy now?**

"The position is open if you want to fill it." She laughs.
*I'd like to fill her in a few positions.*

**HatTrickSwayze: Nah. But, I like the way Daddy sounds on your lips.**

"That's going to be a tough sell. I'm usually the one in control."

**HatTrickSwayze: Oh, you're a little hellcat, huh?**

That excites me. The thought of another top submitting has always turned me on. Maybe she's a switch . . . She rests her elbows in front of the camera, giving me a terrific view. They aren't too big or too small—each one a perfect handful. She's curvy in the best way.

"Maybe. I don't know if you could handle me . . ."

She steps outside the camera frame, and cupboards are opening and closing. I presume she's gathering more ingredients. I close my eyes as her words replay in my mind until the pressure builds inside me. My balls draw up, and I grip my desk as I visualize shooting my cum into her open mouth. *Goddamn.*

Normally I feel like an asshole for making her play depraved roles in my fantasies. But her having a little kink herself has made for a much more guilt-free orgasm.

She's trying to bait me with that suggestive comment. And it works.

**HatTrickSwayze: Maybe you just haven't found someone who can handle you? Do you know your limits? How much could you take?**

When she steps in front of the camera again, I can tell she's reading my response. My head cocks to the side when I notice her breathing pick up. *Interesting*. She inhales like she's about to speak but then another user joins the live video, and her chest relaxes as she clears her throat.

"I was wondering when you were going to show up, BigGuy69," she says cheerily.

**HatTrickSwayze: Have a good afternoon, Hellcat.**

Closing out of the window, I send her the max tip for her time and jump in the shower to clean up.

Around seven o'clock, I receive a text from one of the boys.

JONESY

Heading out to Top Shelf around 9. You in?

I'm tempted. It's literally the bar below my apartment. But drinking can be a slippery slope. Instead, my fingers type out a lie.

Nah, still sore from drills. But thanks for the invite.

JONESY

You're going to have to party with us eventually, rookie.

He's right, but I will avoid temptation for as long as I can. Scrolling through the food delivery app, I pick out my dinner —tonight I'll be dining on Vietnamese takeout. With freshly washed hair and a pair of sweatpants, I flop on the couch and turn on ESPN to zone out until my food gets here.

When I hear the knock, I reach for my wallet on the table and pull out some cash. Opening the door, he gives me the heavy brown paper bag as I hand him the tip. I nod my thanks.

My stomach growls, and the warm paper bag feels like the promise of delicious MSG and chi. But before stepping back into my apartment, I notice something sitting on the floor outside my door. It's a rectangular bakery box with a Post-it Note stuck on the top.

*Welcome to the neighborhood! —1B*

It's French macarons.

# TWO

## Micky

H at Trick Swayze. *Swoon.*

We share a personal intimacy exclusive from the other men paying to see me naked. It always feels like there's something there, so, if I'm being honest, yeah, I may have a small crush. But I'll never admit it. Crushing on a subscriber seems sad, even for me. It's probably the result of me being lonely and trying to force that role onto him so he can fulfill the needs my life is lacking. It's like me masturbating to him, except I'm finger-fucking my heart, not my vagina. *I should schedule an extra therapy session this week.*

He could be anybody. It's ridiculous to become so attracted to an online personality I've never seen before, but I can't help it. I've gotten so used to chatting with him every time I set up a live feed. I still haven't made many friends since the move, unless you count bar regulars, and so my mystery follower has become a close friend.

Clicking my *Followers* stats, I check my incoming tips and subscriber counts. Oh my God, that last pay-per-view session earned $680! Not bad for my fourth baking show. These paid-per-views bring in almost as much money as the monthly subscription payout. The majority of my subscribers were earned by posting campy photos of me baking nude. But, let's be honest, it wasn't really baking, it was playing with caramel and wearing a micro apron. I could be building a car engine and as long as there's sugar on my tits, they'll be blabbering that my crème brûlée looks delicious. *And it is.*

To be fair, a lot of the money is thanks to Hat Trick Swayze, who sets the bar high at the beginning of every video. Men hate being outdone by one another, and everybody wants to be a teacher's pet. If I can keep the funds coming in, I'll be able to afford the commercial space even sooner than anticipated. I need about $150,000 to submit my proposal, make the renovations, and afford the first couple of months' rent. I would have gotten a business loan, but being fresh out of college with zero collateral doesn't get you far with the bank. *Who knew?*

The building I've got my eye on houses a dilapidated bar and grill that's on its last legs. The health inspector barely gave them a passing grade last month, and I suspect the owners will be closing their doors soon. I want it. But that means I need to get my cash together fast so I can swoop in before someone else does. The inside is a dump, but the location is phenomenal, and it's the perfect spot for my bar and patisserie mash-up —Sugar & Ice. Everyone rolls their eyes at trendy bars, but this idea has been in the works for too long, and I'm not giving up on it so easily.

My commercial space—and it is mine—shares a street with one of the most popular craft breweries in the city, Citra Brewing Co. Which leaves me with an opening for partnership opportunities on special drinks and themed pastries. I know they have a blonde ale that would pair nicely with a bright tangy lemon tart. If I could get some to-go items set up to sell at their taproom, then it might send some of their customers my way. My business plan is more focused on cocktails, but I'm not against tapping a few of their kegs behind the bar if it gets me in with Citra and their patrons.

In addition to the brewery, it's within walking distance of a theater and two enormous creative advertising firms—that's my ideal clientele. Upscale cocktails with handcrafted desserts on the side. They eat that shit up. *Location, location, location.* But for this to work, I will first need the capital to bring that dump up to the level of excellence required to succeed. It has to look expensive.

I close my laptop and put my clothes back on. Next, I take down the hanging sheet that serves as my backdrop—along with a cheap strand of twinkle lights—and turn the temperature in my apartment back up. The lower temps keep my nipples perky, and I notice it pays out better when I do. Although, there was a heated moment during today's recording session. Mr. Swayze really got to me. I'm probably just hard up for a good, solid dicking—or it's him. I've never gotten turned on while baking nude on camera for people, but there's something about him, and I get this weird fluttery feeling every time I see his username.

The mixing bowls clank as I set them in the sink with the piping bags to start on dishes. As I scrub, I look over at the yummy French macarons I just finished. They turned out beautiful. I can't keep eating all these baked goods by myself, but I can give them to whoever moved into 2B across the hall a few weeks ago. That's what good neighbors do, right? You're probably supposed to do this right after the person moves in, but whatever.

After pulling out one of the brown bakery boxes in my cupboard, I neatly arrange the strawberries-and-cream macarons with their flawless eggshell finish. Then I scribble a little welcome note and slap it on the top.

*Yeah, I baked them naked, but I wore a hairnet and kept my hands clean.*

So far, they are awesome neighbors. Quiet, no parties. Still haven't seen them in the hall yet, so they must keep a weird schedule. I quietly step into the hallway and set the box next to the doormat.

The pile of clothes I have folded is pitiful. I need to go shopping for some new items. I like fashion, but every penny needs to go toward my new venture. And a new sofa. Last night when I sat down, the whole corner gave out, the main board that runs underneath snapped in half. *In half.*

When I'm done bundling socks, I gather them in my arms and walk to the other side of the room so I can shoot them into the laundry basket one by one. Five out of seven is pretty good for me. Sports have never been a natural talent.

Walking to put my clothes away, I hear the snick of my neighbor's door open. Curiosity gets the better of me, I rush to the door and check the peephole.

*That's* him?

The guy standing at the door accepting a food delivery is shirtless, wearing only sweatpants. *Gray sweatpants.* They hide nothing—and homeboy is packing. If that thing was any bigger, he'd need it registered as a weapon. I'd let him beat me with it.

*Roll, roll, roll his meat gently down my throat.*

I'm gross.

He's tall with chiseled abs and could cut glass with that jawline. Damn, my neighbor is *fine*. I want to sit on his pretty face. He's gorgeous with a tiny bit of scruff, and paired with his hair cropped short, it looks like he just came off an Army deployment—or at least one filmed on a Hollywood set. He's too hot to be anything except a model or actor. He looks like trouble. Thick, throbbing trouble.

His steely, hooded eyes catch on the brown box I placed at his door earlier. *Ohmygod, ohmygod.* When he bends over, I get a peek at his back, there's some serious ink back there. He looks unimpressed when he picks it up. But when he opens it, his full lower lip drops, and he looks at my door like he's seen a ghost. *Odd.*

He takes a small bite from one of the cookies and then spits it back out into the box. Rude! I tried them myself, they're delicious, so what the fuck? *You're welcome, dick.* He stares in my direction again, and I swear I can feel his gaze through the wood door that separates us. My brain takes over and reminds me if things ever got weird, I would still have to live out the rest of my lease across the hall from him. Besides, if he won't even eat my actual cookies, he's not going to mess with the one between my thighs.

He's probably the next Dexter. Yeah, that's it. Only antisocial sociopaths would spit out my baked goods. Okay, let's be real, if he ever invited me over, I'd still look at him and say, *oh, I love what you've done with the place. The plastic sheeting really brings the room together.* I have horrible taste in men.

I'm awoken when a dull thumping and the muffled sounds of somebody yelling come through the wall. Are those sex noises? *What time is it?* I check my phone—6:48 a.m. I sit up and listen closely, it's the sound of a woman, but they aren't sounds of pleasure. It's the sound of someone who's been *wronged*, and it's coming from the outside hallway. What on earth is going on out there? It's getting louder. So much for my *quiet* neighbor. I stumble out of my bedroom and pad over to the front door. My palms press into my eye sockets as I adjust to the light, rubbing the sleep and smearing yesterday's mascara around.

Squinting through the peephole, I've got a great view of the drama. There's a woman out there raising Cain at Hot Neighbor Kucera. I figured out his last name from the mailbox. He's either not home or not answering his door. Is that his ex? I can't see her face, but from behind, she appears disheveled. Just-been-fucked hair? I bet that asshole kicked her out and is making her do the walk of shame. *Rude.*

*Been there, sister.* Except she's turning her walk into a parade. This person is banging on his door and screaming at him to open up. Aggressive is an understatement.

My internal clock thinks it's the middle of the night due to my second-shift schedule. I need sleep, I've got to work tonight. Hot Neighbor better not piss off his lady callers on a regular schedule. At least order her an Uber and get her out the door first. Don't leave her pounding on the door for twenty minutes.

But there's no way in hell I'm going out there and getting in her way. I know better than that. I'd be pissed if I was tossed out post-coitus, and let's face it, crazy recognizes crazy.

Tonight is the season opener, and Top Shelf, the hockey bar that's located directly below my apartment, will be swarmed with fans. It will be nuts. Over the past couple of months, I've come to know the menu, the regulars, and the bouncers well —and how they handle crowd control when the players show up.

My white button-down dress shirt is a size too small. It's tight all over, which I'm not mad about because it brings in the tip money, and every dollar gets me one step closer to Sugar & Ice. I throw on my black suspenders and roll my cuffs up my forearms. I like the way my colorful tattoos show against the crisp white shirt. My hair is a rich red at the roots that blends into a light-blonde ombre. As usual, I keep it in a ponytail while I'm working. My look is part of my branding, and it's served me well in the industry. I do one last check in the mirror. My crimson lipstick matches my hair, and my eyeliner is right on the mark.

"Time to drain money from the patriarchy," I say, adjusting my red push-up bra.

I walk out my door at the same time my neighbor does. I believe in a good first impression, so I'll forget him spitting out my macaron and give a friendly introduction.

"Hi! I don't think we've met. I'm your neighbor, Micky. I'm usually around, so if you ever need anything—a cup of sugar, someone to feed your fish, whatever, let me know!" *Flour, eggs, a blowjob . . .*

He raises his eyebrow at me and nods, then pulls out his phone as if he's already bored with my one-sentence introduction.

"Oh, I forgot to ask—"

"I'm not interested," he mumbles, scrolling his thumb on the screen.

"I'm sorry?"

His eyes meet mine, and I'm graced with the most obvious eye roll I've ever witnessed.

*Wow. This arrogant asshole.* I know this guy is hot, but it pisses me off that he automatically expects I'm trying to hook up with him.

"I forgot to *ask*," I repeat, "if you knew there was a woman screaming the house down at the crack of dawn this morning? If it happens again, do you mind taking care of it instead of letting her pound on the door for an hour? Just as a heads-up, quiet hours are between ten p.m. and eight a.m."

"Huh, that's weird. Usually, when they're screaming, it's because I'm the one doing the pounding."

Well, at least I don't have to worry about sleeping with him now. This guy's a fucking douchebag. He has a nice body, but I'm done falling for assholes.

I finish locking my door.

"Good for you, sport. Just—"

He returns his focus to his phone and walks down the stairs like I don't even exist. And he still hasn't given me his first name.

*The pretty ones are always assholes.*

# THREE

*Rhys*

*oly fuck.* I share a wall with Queen of Tarts. Is this really happening? The macarons left at my door last night can't be a coincidence. I've been in my apartment for a few weeks, but it's not like we've run into each other in the hall. I moved here because these lofts are set aside for new Lakes' rookies, it's a great deal on rent, and it's a lot of space. So, as soon as my old lease was up, I grabbed one. But how did she get the other apartment? I thought these were exclusively reserved for Lakes' players? It's possible she's dating someone on the team, but I don't know of any of the other guys living in that unit.

My microwave beeps, alerting me that my pasta has finished. I need to eat quickly and take a shower before I head to the arena. I take out the warm bowl, careful not to burn my hands. It's got to be her. *Damn. What are the odds?* How am I supposed to focus on this season knowing temptation is living next door? I shove a forkful into my mouth as I peer at our shared wall. She's probably over there right now.

The whole point of having the subscription was that she was supposed to exist only on the screen. It wasn't anything I could get wrapped up in. It's weird enough I enjoy talking to her. What if she's nothing like she is online? Worse, what if she *is*? It's one thing when our arrangement is through the phone or laptop. No risk. Transactional. Her distance from me was supposed to be my fail-safe.

I've got to keep her at arm's length and focus on improving my game on the ice. I need this contract to renew, show them I'm worth the big ass paychecks they're signing. I won't let myself find out if she's the same person online as she is in person because it's irrelevant. Which is why I had to spit out the macarons. Her baking skills are phenomenal, it only makes me want to know her more—but I still couldn't resist them; I've never had one before.

Even now, my dick is getting hard just thinking about her. In a couple hours, I have my first season game, and I need to pull myself together. No more dreaming Queen of Tarts, only hockey. Tonight I get to wear number 5 on my back and represent the Lakes.

After I finish my pasta, I walk into the bathroom and turn on a cold shower to clear my thoughts of the queen next door.

Walking in through the back door of the arena feels different today. I'm psyched, but also feel like I might vomit from nerves. I enter the locker room and notice the change here too. There's a big energy shift. I'm not the first one to arrive but not the last. I'm sure the rest of the boys will be here soon.

Our goalies are getting their eyes focused for the game—Kapucik is juggling tennis balls and Strassburg is bouncing them off the wall at close range. Ryan Bishop, one of our centers, is backed into a corner with his eyes closed, meditating. Jonesy and Banks, our wingers, are kicking a soccer ball back and forth in the hall. Barrett Conway and Lee Sullivan, the captains, are going through plays and talking with the coach. Everybody has their own thing.

I drop down to the seat in front of my stall and sit back to tape my stick heel-to-toe. As I wrap it, I think about all the drills we've run and try to manifest a win tonight. Imagining the sounds of goal horns and visualizing the puck. They wouldn't be starting me tonight if I wasn't ready. I've earned my sweater.

Lonan walks in shortly after on the phone. Conway tosses me a puck to scrape across my tape job.

"Nervous, bud?"

I furrow my eyebrows lightly. "Nah. I'm ready."

"You'll get out there and things will fall into place. The worst part is the build-up—especially since it's your first one. Once the puck drops, everything will settle into place, and your instincts will take over. You got this."

"Thanks, man."

I grab the tape again to wrap the stick knob and then put on my gear and continue my visualizations. After Coach goes over some video clips of plays and gives a speech, it's time to head out onto the ice for warm-ups.

The crowd is amped tonight. It feels nothing like the preseason games. This is wild. I mean, it's the first official game of the season, so of course they are. The team turns a lot more easygoing during warm-ups—singing along to the music playing over the sound system and cracking jokes while we stretch. As soon as some of the guys start doing groin stretches there's a whoop from female fans. I look out to the stands to see a bunch of camera phones recording and homemade signs unfolding, referencing "hardcore pucking" and "sticking it in their five-hole." I cock my head at Conway and mouth *what the fuck* while gesturing to the crowd.

He shrugs. "Booktok. It's a thing now."

Jones explains there's an entire romance book genre based

on hockey players. What a time to be alive. We make a few laps and then Banks calls me in.

"Rook, you're on pucks."

I skate over the net and line them up next to Strassburg. We fist bump our gloves, and I snap pucks for them to shoot as they skate by, collecting the deflected ones on my stick. I wonder how many years I'll be on puck duty. After a few dozen shots, Sully comes over and sends some out for me, and I get a couple in the net.

"Shit, Strass. Rookie might make you collect pucks next time," Sully hollers.

I laugh it off, but that comment is the added confidence I need to start the night. Coach calls us back into the locker room. We get our speech from the staff and then it's back out for the national anthem and puck drop. My knees are shaky, but I know I'll be solid during my shift. Lonan and I are partners tonight, our shifts will swap with Dopson and Burmeister.

Banksy heads to center for the drop, and Strass scrapes up the ice behind me. Banks crouches down into position, mirroring the Phillies' center. The ref leans over, and once the puck hits the ice, it's on. Like Conway said, everything falls into place. First period, I skate my ass off and protect my corner. I've knocked it off the boards more times than I can count, and after many shift changes, twenty minutes pass like nothing. We head into the locker room, some guys gear down while others walk around or hit the bikes. Some are relaxing, but my adrenaline is way too high for that.

Second period we have a corner faceoff, Conway gets in front of it and snaps it to me, I backhand it to Sully, and he sends it in. The horn screams. *Holy shit.* We got a goal on the faceoff, and I made the assist. Even though Sully made the goal, the guys all slap my helmet too.

"Atta boy, Rook!"

"Kucera, baby!"

This is the greatest feeling. *I love my job.*

We finish out the period with no more goals, but I don't let any pucks get past me.

By the third, I'm pouring sweat. Philly gets one in the net. It wasn't my shift, but it easily could have been, they made a good play. Burmeister, the other left defenseman, skates toward the bench, and I'm back on the ice for another forty-five seconds of speed skating. And speed stopping.

The puck is back in my corner, and after fishing around with the other guys, I'm able to deke it back and send it up to Conway. He makes a few plays with the other forwards and snaps it in about halfway through third period. I shift out and keep Philly from getting any by me before the buzzer sounds. We won 2-1. It's a great way to start the season. The energy in the arena is insane.

Making it back into the locker room, there's a lot of celebration.

"You're coming out tonight, Kucera! We're celebrating that assist!" Jonesy hollers as he unties his skates.

I grin back at him as I work on my laces. "Yeah, okay."

"Rookie's finally coming out, boys!" There's a few more hollers, and I use the rest of my strength to yank the skate off my foot. I pull my jersey over my head and untie my breezers. This must be the hockey player equivalent of taking a bra off. I jump on the stationary bike and pedal with low resistance to cool off from the game.

Lonan jumps on the one next to me and congratulates me on my assist. I had a blast playing defense with him tonight. I'm quieter than some of the rowdy guys, but everyone has made me feel welcome.

"Hear you're coming out with us tonight?"

"Yeah, why not. I don't have much of an excuse, since I live above the bar."

His lips turn up into a mischievous half smile. "Have you met your neighbor yet?"

"Yes . . ."

"That's my wife's best friend, Micky."

*Small world getting smaller.*

"Aren't those rookie apartments?" So what's she doing there? Please don't tell me she's dating another player. I couldn't deal.

"They are, but she did me a solid last spring, so I hooked her up with an apartment since she was having trouble finding one."

*Ah.* Wish he could have found her literally any other place to stay, but whatever. Lonan is a nice guy, it's not surprising he's helping out his wife's friends too.

"Gotcha. She bakes a lot, huh?"

He grins. "Yeah, what makes you say that?"

"She left some cookie things on my doormat."

"Are they macarons? Freaking love those. Not as good as Birdie's snickerdoodles, but a close second, for sure. I'd work that angle and see how many cookies you can get." He waggles his eyebrows.

"Nah, bud. Not interested."

"Oh, you skate for the other team?"

I laugh at that, considering the number of times I've gotten off to Queen of Tarts.

"No, but I want to get settled on the team. I just got here. I don't have the luxury of screwing around."

"You're a lot more mature than I was as a rookie, that's for sure. Same goes for most of the guys here. We were all dumbstruck by pussy when we joined the league. It's everywhere. You'll see. But damn, when you find the right one, it's heaven," he says, staring at a picture of his wife on his phone.

Walking into Top Shelf feels odd since I've walked past it so many times. The bar erupts in cheers, and I follow the rest of the team to an area in the back with booths. We're celebrities to people, it's so bizarre. And Lonan wasn't lying, as soon as we walk in, the girls are nipping at our heels. He beelines it for his wife. I recognize her from the picture on his phone earlier, she's sitting at the bar talking to . . . *sonofabitch. No way.*

She works here? It's like I can't escape her! Micky's my neighbor, my teammate's wife's best friend, and now she's the goddamn bartender at the bar everyone hangs out at. It's not enough that she's on my phone and laptop.

I'm so fucked.

It's one thing to avoid a neighbor, but how the hell can I avoid her when she's everywhere? I can't. I'll have to lean into it. She's a knockout behind the bar, especially since I know what she looks like under that shirt. I knew she would be pretty, but I didn't anticipate her to be so beautiful that I couldn't even look at her in the hallway today. God, those lips. Would her lipstick coat my entire cock? Would those green eyes sparkle like they do now if I were buried in her throat?

"Kucera, right?" A small palm rests on my shoulder.

"Yeah." I look down to a cute blonde gazing at me like I'm a winning lottery ticket.

"Oh my God, I've been wondering when you were going to show up!"

"Oh yeah? Why's that?" I wonder if this is why rookies go nuts for girls, it's like we're set up to fail. I admit, I'm a good-looking guy, but it's irrelevant because I'm here to play hockey, not women. My agent says to lean into it, it will help me get more sponsorships.

"Oh my God, you're so funny! You don't even know how hot you are. It's so cute."

*Jeeezus.* Lonan wasn't lying. I could literally take her upstairs if I wanted to.

Conway leans over to me and whispers, "Bob and weave, motherfucker. Bob and weave. Be polite but hold your ground."

I take his advice and remove the girl's hand from me. "I'm gonna get a drink, be back in a bit."

"I'll save you a seat!"

*Please don't.*

She probably gives decent head, but she's not my type. If I had to guess, I'd say she's probably passive, but she's not submissive—and there's a big difference.

I don't mind a little brattiness, as long as it comes with a little obedience too. It's nice being in control, but if she's not into it, then it's not enjoyable. It needs to be consensual, knowing she wants to be put in her place and challenging her is what makes it so hot. I belly up to the bar to face the woman who I wouldn't mind seeing turn into a pathetic puddle of tears in my hands. She has a spark in her . . . and it's fun to play with fire. *It's also an easy way to get burned*, my brain reminds me.

"Hey, neighbor, what can I get you?" she asks with a smile. Yeah, those eyes sparkle. *Ugh, she would be so fun.*

"Whatever's cold, bottle."

"Sure thing. Are you having a good night?" She's using her customer-service voice. It's the same voice she uses when she's doing a live stream and there's a lot of viewers. But when it's only me watching her, she sounds different. I assume that's the real Micky. At least, that's how I imagine it to be.

Playing up the assholery, I check her out instead of answering her question. It's loud in here. I can pretend I didn't hear her.

She hands me the beer; I snatch it from her and head back to a spot between two of the guys so I'm not a carrion for the vultures with cleavage on the ends. My eyes naturally fall back on Micky. She's looking at me too. But with a lot more disdain in her eyes. *It's for the best, darling. You don't want me, and I don't have time to give you what you deserve.*

But I'd be lying if I said I didn't want to.

# FOUR

## Micky

Always cut someone off one drink too early rather than one drink too late. No one has ever muttered the phrase *"Just one more"* and meant it—case in point, this middle-aged mouth-breather who won't leave. He's about half a beer from belligerent, and I need him to free up the bartop real estate so I can help literally anyone else. He's been bitching about his ex-wife for the last two hours. Honestly, I'm thrilled for her because everything out of his mouth has been pompous and insulting. It doesn't take a urologist to see this guy is a massive dick. Thankfully he's on his way out.

In my peripheral, a new person takes dicksnout's barstool, and I look up to see none other than . . . another dicksnout. Great, it's my new neighbor—who I have learned is the newest rookie on the team. That explains his body and his cocky attitude. That's fine. I'm not taking shit from anyone tonight, him included. Half the Lakes hockey team showed up an hour ago to celebrate their win. Most are sitting in the back, and we have a couple of servers that exclusively cover their tables, so I'm not sure why he even sat down.

"Congratulations on the win tonight!" I say, overly chipper.

"Still not interested."

Clearly, he didn't pick up on my peppy sarcasm.

"Bud, don't be a dick. Freya's practically my sister-in-law." Lonan slaps him on the shoulder as he walks by. *Why did he just use the F-word?*

Rhys cocks his head at me.

"I thought it was Micky?" he accuses.

"Micky's a nickname."

"How do you get Micky from Freya?" he asks.

"You don't. Micky comes from my last name: McCoy." *He never noticed while getting his mail?* Our last names are right next to each other. He's probably too busy staring at his own reflection in the chrome hinges. He raises his eyebrows and rolls his eyes, unimpressed. *What a fucking treat he is.*

"Do you prefer Rhys or Kucera?"

"From you? Neither."

"Great, I've got plenty of other nicknames I can call you instead. Did you need something? If not, you can go sit back down with your team, and Amy will be happy to take your drink order." With a forced grin, I nod to his corner, where the server is jotting down their requests as we speak.

I walk away from him and check on my other patrons. When I glance over, he's looking down at the bartop with a sly smirk. He's pushing my buttons for shits and giggles. He snaps his fingers at me and points in front of him. Like I'm some puppy he's trying to train.

"I'm sorry, did you just *snap* at me?"

"Yeah, you walked away. You're supposed to serve me." *Well, since you asked so nicely . . .*

I clear my throat, trying to summon patience for this "VIP." *Viscerally Irritating Prick.*

"What can I get for you?" I ask through clenched teeth.

"Cocktail. Surprise me," he responds, without making eye contact. His gaze is obviously checking out the ass of an attractive woman that walks by. I take a deep inhale through my nose.

He gives off strong fuckboy energy. I've had my fair share of guys like that, but those days are over. I'm ready for something more mature than just casual sex and hotheaded himbos. That lifestyle comes with too many consequences at my age.

I have no regrets about the men I slept with in the past. I refuse to regret the parts of my life that formed me into who I am today. I was happy fucking for fun rather than forever. However, it's lost its appeal. There is no room for games, negging, or any other bullshit. I want someone to come home to. I want someone who will look at me the way Lonan looks at Birdie. I want to be cherished. Loved.

I certainly don't want anyone like Rhys Kucera. Not sure he could love anything more than himself anyway; he thinks he's special. Even now, he's asking for something extra when he knows we're slammed. That's fine. Two can place at this game. Turning my back, I mix the ingredients and bust out the blender despite all the other orders coming in. He asks what's taking so long, and I respond by pressing the pulverize button on the blender while I imagine his hand bouncing around inside. I pour the frosty red concoction into a margarita glass and add a tiny umbrella.

"Enjoy." I set it in front of him. He doesn't look at me, doesn't tip, doesn't say thanks. Just walks away with the drink to sit down with the guys. While finishing another customer's Captain and Coke with the soda gun, I peer over and he's practically retching after taking a sip. *Delicious.*

He doesn't bother me for the rest of the night, but every so often I catch him staring, like he's keeping tabs on me. I hate that his stare has heat flooding between my thighs. *I know. Bad, bad, Freya.*

Seriously, what the fuck is with this guy? How can he get under my skin and still make my panties damp? I remind myself he's only doing it to annoy me, so instead of glaring back, I ignore him—while I secretly plot to spray his doorknob with PAM when I get off work. I turn around and tend to a nice older couple who just sat down.

My phone vibrates in my pocket. I snag it and see Hat Trick Swayze has sent me a random tip out of nowhere. A big one. With the note: *Hope you're having a good night at work.*

It's too bad I can't serve *him* at my bar. I smile and text him back my appreciation and tell him I miss him. It's true. Even though we text often, that extra distance can be felt between us. Though it hasn't stopped us from growing close.

# FIVE

## Rhys

I lie back in my hotel bed in Winnipeg and glance out the window. I can't believe this is my life now. I'm in the NHL. I've worked so hard for this. Every now and then, little moments like this catch me off guard, and it hits me that *this* is my new normal. It's so surreal. It feels like just yesterday I was trying to get scouted for a college scholarship. Now, here I am. What a crazy life.

I open up my laptop and see that Queen of Tarts is online. I ping her, and within five minutes, I have an invite to a live video.

It's private. *Interesting.*

Queen of Tarts—Freya—is my neighbor. My only neighbor. And she has no idea that the asshole she despises next door is her top follower online. This is something I'll never tell her.

Now that I know what her face looks like, watching her lower half on *Followers* is way more exciting. I'm a piece of shit. But I'll never have her, and she'll never find out. Her face and hair are as striking as the rest of her. That fiery look works for her. It really fucking works. She's a hellcat. I'd love to see her wild hair wrapped around my fist.

**HatTrickSwayze: What are we making today, Hellcat?**

She giggles. "I like that nickname. We are making crois-sants." She pronounces it *kwa-sons.*

**HatTrickSwayze: *hon hon hon* (french laughter)**

That gets a full-on laugh out of her—hearing it in person would send me over the edge. If I was at home, could I hear it through the wall? Would the smell of buttery, flaky croissants waft into my apartment?

**HatTrickSwayze: If you keep feeding your neighbor, they won't be able to leave their house.**

I'm careful to say house instead of apartment. She stands in front of the camera and reads my messages. Her neck is so delicate.

"That wouldn't be the worst thing in the world. He's kind of an asshole."

A smile grows on my face. *Tell me more.*

**HatTrickSwayze: Oh yeah?**

"Uh-huh. He's so rude. He came into the bar where I worked and even there, he was a total dick." Then her voice turns lighthearted. "He had asked me to make him a surprise cocktail, we were already packed two people deep that night. So I made him a strawberry daiquiri . . . with Scotch."

My laughter fills the empty hotel room. *That's* why my drink tasted like ass. I was curious to know how she would respond to making me any drink she wanted. I figured she would have just plopped a Budweiser in front of me and said,

"*Surprise! Enjoy your domestic beer. Bye.*" But the daiquiri is much more creative. *Well done, Hellcat.*

**HatTrickSwayze: He sounds like a dick. Don't give him those croissants.**

"That's what I'm saying! Anyway, I don't want to talk about him. What are you up to today?"

**HatTrickSwayze: I'm out of town, traveling for work, so I'm just hanging out in my hotel until it's time to catch my flight. Hey, I've been meaning to ask, what made you start a *Followers* account?**

I don't want her asking about my job; it's bad enough my username is hockey themed.

"The money. I thought it would be a good way to earn some extra cash."

**HatTrickSwayze: For something in particular . . .?**

She hesitates for a moment. "Nope. I just like money."

*That's it?* Ugh, that's what I was hoping she wouldn't say. This is what all the guys warn you about when you join. Even the NHL organization offers financial management seminars where they warn us about people hoping to exploit us for money, that includes intimate partners seeking an easy payoff. For some guys, they're okay with that. They like the exchange of a trophy wife or gold digger. Not me.

"What made *you* join *Followers*?" she asks.

Truthfully, I subscribed to her *Followers* account to find a release with something more personalized than porn but less personal than an actual person. That's not what I type.

**HatTrickSwayze: Curious to see what it's all about.**

"Do you follow any other accounts?"

**HatTrickSwayze: Just yours. I couldn't afford to
follow anybody else lol**

I don't know why I say that. It's not like it matters for
our situation, but I want her to know I'm not to be considered a source of income for her. The money thing sets off
alarm bells in my head. My stepmom was like that with my
dad. It put Anna and me in a tough spot after our father
died.

"If you had all the money in the world, what would you
buy?"

That's easy.

**HatTrickSwayze: Probably buy my sister a house. But
she's had a lot going on lately. I don't really need
much. Maybe a few more private lessons with the
Queen of Tarts. ;)**

"That's really sweet. I take it your sister's important to
you?"

I rub the back of my neck. Talking about Anna is tough.

**HatTrickSwayze: Yeah. When we were kids, we were
close. We grew up playing hockey together. Then
when I went off to college, she sorta got left behind. I
regret not being there for her more.**

She takes a few seconds to read through my text.
"That's a lot to put on yourself."

**HatTrickSwayze: Yeah, I know. It's just hard. What people in your life are important to you?**

"Probably my best friend. She recently reunited with her parents—long story—but witnessing her reconnect with them is like watching her get the happy ending she deserves. Family stuff is hard, man. I have a mom and stepdad that I love, but they live on the West Coast, so I don't see them as often since I'm in the Midwest now. My grandma was really special to me too. She passed away a couple of years ago. She was feisty and a big part of my life when I was little."

That must be where Freya gets it.

**HatTrickSwayze: I'm sorry she passed.**

"Thanks. She was a pretty cool lady. I want to be as cool as she was."

**HatTrickSwayze: I'd say you're pretty fucking cool already.**

"Do you have a girlfriend?"
*There's a change of direction.*

**HatTrickSwayze: No. Why? You interested? Lol**

I'm not offering. I have too much going on in my life. Casual is all I can handle, and even then, I prefer a screen between us.

She chuckles. "No, I couldn't do the long-distance thing. I'm too needy."

I bite my knuckles. She's not making this easy on me. She may not have meant it this way, but all I can visualize is sexual neediness. And there's nothing sexier than begging.

**HatTrickSwayze: Oh yeah? Needy can be good sometimes. Are you looking for a boyfriend?**

"No, but there are times when I watch my best friend and her new husband, and I can't help but feel a little envious of what they have. They are so happy and comfortable, and they share a closeness that I've never experienced. So, when I see that side, it looks nice. But who has time to find that person?"

She's talking about Lonan and Bridget. Can't say I didn't notice the same thing.

**HatTrickSwayze: Do you think you'll be ready for something serious when you meet the right guy or girl? Or do you prefer casual?**

*Why did I ask her that?*

"It depends on how compatible we are." She ponders my question. "I don't mind a little casual fun if the sex is great. But if they're a decent person in addition to that, I'd consider something more. I need to have good chemistry with them. Sure would be awesome to get laid on the reg, though."

**HatTrickSwayze: Yeah, same. It's hard finding a partner.**

"It is!"

Fuck, watching her strut around that kitchen naked, layering that dough over and over, is the strangest thing to ever turn me on. I need a subject change.

**HatTrickSwayze: Okay, new topic. What's something you want to learn or wish you were better at?**

"Oh my God! Falconry!"

I bark a laugh.

**HatTrickSwayze: LOL what? Seriously?**

"Yes!" She giggles. "I want to try falconry someday. I don't have a space to keep large birds of prey, but I would do anything to see them up close someday. I love watching videos of falconers on YouTube. It looks like such a rush."

Who is this girl? I don't know what I was expecting her to say, but it wasn't falconry.

"What do you want to learn?"

**HatTrickSwayze: Bread-making**

My mom used to make bread when I was a kid, and I remember how the smell filled the house, it smelled like home. I never learned from her; I wish I would have taken the time when I had the chance. I've been picking up some tips from Queen of Tarts, but I learn better in person.

"That's it? You can learn that on the internet. There are recipes everywhere."

**HatTrickSwayze: Or . . . you could teach me? Would you consider giving me a private lesson?**

"Really? Okay. I mean, if you're sure. I'm not sure how great a teacher I am, but I'll do my best. Hey, I don't know if this is weird, but . . . would you want to exchange numbers?"

*Don't do it.*

**HatTrickSwayze: Not weird 207-555-6767**

*Damn it.*

There's a pound on my door. "Yo, Kucy! Bus is downstairs. Get your shit."

**HatTrickSwayze: Great. Thanks. Hey, I have to head to the airport. Can we chat tomorrow?**

"Yeah." Her voice softens. "I'd like that." She sounds so sweet and demure; I have a hard time imagining her being a top.

As I walk out of my hotel room, I pull out my phone and max out the tip for the chat session.

UNKNOWN

You don't have to keep doing that.

I've got her number.

Air flowing out of the vents fills the aircraft cabin with white noise as we board the charter plane. I grab snacks from the basket as I walk down the aisle, choosing a seat somewhere in the middle. After the flight attendants perform the safety briefings, we are ready for takeoff.

I'm about to put my headphones on when Jonesy leans over to ask if I'm heading to Top Shelf when we get back. I decline. I know we just won the game against Nashville, but I'm learning that traveling requires some rest between.

"How come you never come out with us, bud? Girlfriend have you on a leash?"

"Ha, no. Traveling wears me out. And I definitely don't have time for a girlfriend."

A few guys chuckle, then Broderick, one of the centers,

adds, "None of us have time for a girlfriend, but you don't need a girlfriend to get some."

"Slippery slope, my man," Lonan clucks. It's hard to envision him being with anyone but his wife the way he obsesses over her.

"Did y'all see Shoshanna? Pretty sure she got her tits done over the summer."

"You still fucking that girl, Jones? Jesus, when ya going to buy her a ring?" someone from the front hollers.

"Whatever. She does this thing with her mouth, where—"

A few of my teammates groan. "Agh! Nobody wants to hear about your beef weasel, man. Spare us. Please."

"Puck bunnies ain't got shit on puck wives. Married sex is awesome," Lonan says.

"Fuckin' A, Burke. We get it. You got married. Now fuck off already, eh? Let the rest of us get our dicks sucked in peace."

"Yeah, I call bullshit," Conway says from the row behind me. "There are some cool ass bunnies out there. Remember Raleigh? That girl I fucked a few years ago? She was insane. God, what I wouldn't give for another night with her."

"And then she left without a trace," a monotone chorus answers. Apparently they've heard this story before.

"Look, all I'm sayin' is not all bunnies are created equal. And it's pretty fucked up that we hold a double standard for them. We sleep around just as much. And yeah, I'm still fucking sore that I didn't get her number. She's probably married now." He genuinely sounds disappointed, Raleigh must have been some lay. He continues, "But Burke's onto something. We aren't getting any younger, boys, and it would be nice to have a family and settle down someday."

"Good advice, grandpa." Jonesy rolls his eyes as he brings his headphones over his ears.

I do the same and tear into a protein bar. I try to get a nap in before we land, but all I can think about are a specific redhead's delicate fingers kneading into dough. I have to get this infatuation under control or I'll end up like Conway.

My Uber pulls up in front of Top Shelf, and I grab my bag and thank the driver. When I swing the door to the building open, the smell of fresh, warm chocolate chip cookies punches me in the face. *Great, now I'm hungry.* I hoist my duffle over my shoulder and jog up the stairs two at a time as she steps out her door. She's in a tied-off faded RUN DMC shirt, denim cutoffs, and knee-high tube socks. No shoes, she must be going to the mailbox. Christ Almighty. I've seen her naked already, so why the hell do those striped socks make me want to push her up against the stairwell?

"Hi," she says tightly. She's not my biggest fan.

The words are out of my mouth before I can stop them. "Nice socks."

I keep my head down, enter my apartment, and slam the door behind me.

# SIX

## Micky

Now that we've exchanged numbers, we've texted a couple times. In the name of safety, we've only exchanged first initials. I don't know why, but it's exciting knowing I have a direct line to him whenever I need it. Even if I'm not always using it.

What are you doing?

R
Thinking about you.

Lol no you weren't.

R
No, I wasn't. But I am now.

Oh yeah?

R
Had another dream about you.

Sleep dream or daydream?

R
No comment.

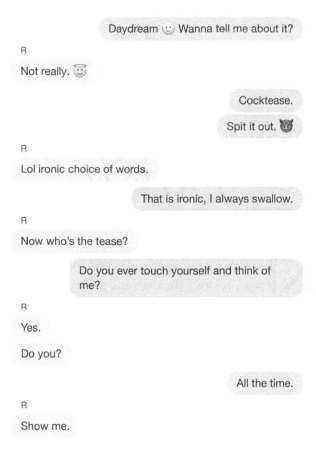

Daydream 😊 Wanna tell me about it?

R

Not really. 😇

Cocktease.

Spit it out. 😈

R

Lol ironic choice of words.

That is ironic, I always swallow.

R

Now who's the tease?

Do you ever touch yourself and think of me?

R

Yes.

Do you?

All the time.

R

Show me.

I don't know what makes me want to prove it, but I do. He's expecting a picture, but I can come up with a better way to surprise him. My impulsiveness takes over and I click the video icon in the corner of our text message. At least I have enough sense to not show my face and keep the camera aimed at my thighs.

"Hellcat." Hearing him speak for the first time makes my breath catch in my throat. Oh my God, that voice. It's intense. He sounds familiar, but I can't place it.

"Hat Trick Swayze," I answer with a smile.

He, too, has his camera facing away. But it's centered on the bulge in his dress pants. And what a fucking bulge it is.

"I like your tattoos."

*Shit,* I didn't cover them up. It's not like this was planned.

"I like your voice."

"Oh, yeah?"

"Yeah. It's sexy." It's making me fucking wet.

He chuckles, and I resist squealing. It's confident with a hint of arrogance.

Propping up against my pillows, I can't help reaching into my shorts. I like this guy. And his voice is killing me—death by arousal.

"You're trouble."

"Are you uncomfortable?" I'm so starved for attention, I need this, and I hope he's willing to give it.

He unzips and grabs the bulge over his boxer briefs. "In the best way. Push those shorts down and let me see."

"Are you alone?" *Does he have roommates? How do I not know how old he is?*

"Yup. I've got to leave for a meeting in a bit, but I'm all yours for the next . . . twenty-two minutes."

My fingers brush over my clit. He blows out a breath, and I love it. It's the most sexual interaction I've had in a long time. I'm taking it.

"Why don't you show me how it's done? You like to be in charge, right?"

"Stroke yourself."

He shoves his boxer briefs down and the most gorgeous cock is gripped in his fist. "Like this?" His voice lowers.

"Slower. Match my pace."

"You're gonna direct me, huh? What are you thinking about?"

"Riding you. Holding your arms above your head and

torturing you by slowly sliding up and down until your full length is buried inside me."

"Fuck, M . . ." He still doesn't know my name. He inhales through his nose and lets it out between clenched teeth like a hiss.

I slightly spread my thighs and quicken my tempo. "Is this going to make things awkward between us?" I ask, almost panting.

His voice is slow and sexy. "There's nothing awkward about the way you touch yourself. If this is what you need right now, then I want to give it to you. But I'm not paying for this session. If you rub your pussy, it's because you want it as bad as I do."

"It isn't about money. There's something about you."

I can't take my eyes off the screen, pre-cum slides down the side of his crown as his hand lazily rolls up and down the full length.

He groans. "I get that. Sometimes I think you were made especially for me to watch," he says. There's a smile in his voice, and it's contagious.

I swallow. His words are like a ball of warmth in my chest that expands out to the rest of me. I move my fingers lower and push them inside, my palm keeping pressure on my clit. A gasp slips from my lips.

"Christ, I can hear how wet you are." My hand moves faster, and his follows suit.

"Just like that, you're doing so well. Who's cock is that?"

The tendons in his forearm protrude as the tempo speeds up. He has nice hands. I imagine feeling them between my thighs, quickly strumming as I ride on top. I moan and my hips buck, wanting more.

"Yours."

"That's it, just like that. You fuck me so well."

"I never would have guessed you were such a dirty talker."

"Feels good, doesn't it? I want to see that big dick come just for me," I croon. "But not until I say so."

His breathy laughter is gruff, and it only heightens my arousal. Adjusting his seat, he fists himself harder.

I add another finger. "Oh my God."

"You have no idea how difficult it is staying quiet when all I want to do is throw you to the ground, spread you wide, and make you take every inch."

It sends chills down my spine, normally something like that wouldn't arouse me, if anything, I might be slightly disappointed since I like to be the bossy one, but I don't mind it when he says it. It makes me part my legs farther and pan the camera a little lower, giving him more of a show.

"Tell me how bad you want to come." I need to hear him say it.

"You've got me right on the fucking edge, I can hardly stand it."

"You don't get to blow until I do."

I watch him and how skilled his hands move. There's no denying how impressive his self-control is; most guys can't last while going at it the way he is. It's fucking hot. He must be so good in bed—his stamina tells me he's generous. I think about all the ways he could take me, fantasize looking down to his cock driving in and out of me. My climax builds, and I quickly pull out and focus my fingers on my clit, roughly working it the way I know will heighten my orgasm. I moan as my body rolls. He growls seeing me hit the finish line before him.

"Now, come with me."

A single grunt and he explodes. "Damn." As soon as he bursts, cum covers his fist and the growl he makes sends me over the edge. I'm done.

"*Fuck!*"

He's an incredible sight. I would give anything to have the real thing. We relax our bodies, and my knees close. I bring my hand out from between my thighs as he continues to lazily stroke himself. *It's so hot.*

I sigh happily, and he chuckles. Neither of us know what we're supposed to say now.

"That was . . ." As I start to speak, there's a stupid pounding next door. It's the fourth time this week. It just keeps getting worse. I can't deal with this anymore.

"Hellcat?"

"Ugh, I'm really sorry, I have to go take care of something. Can we text later?"

"Of course."

Now I'm pissed. She's interrupting my Hat Trick Swayze time. I suspect it's the same woman since the banging matches the pattern. It's gotten out of hand. I get dressed and wash up. I'm gonna say something. Obviously Kucera's done nothing to stop it. This has to end.

I crack open my door. "Hey, girl, no dick is worth this kind of commotion."

"Excuse you. Mind your business," she snaps.

She doesn't even turn around to look at me when she says it. If this is her shining personality, I don't blame him for kicking her out.

"Look, I don't know who you are, but I know you come around a lot because your knocking is loud as fuck. I'm going to give you some advice, that guy sucks and he's not worth it."

I shut my door and lock it.

Maybe that was a little rude, but I'm tired, and she started it.

---

"Cheers!" Birdie, Audrey, and I clink our glasses before taking sips.

"Shit, I haven't had a chance to do anything since before Liam was born. It feels so good to escape parenthood for a couple of hours," Audrey says on a sigh, beaming.

"You're my sister-in-law, anytime you need a break, call Lonan and me! We are happy to babysit. We aren't quite yet ready for our own, but we love the perks of being aunt and uncle to those kiddos," Birdie says.

Since Birdie has gotten to know her family more, she and her brother, Jack, and his wife have become a tight-knit group. Audrey is awesome. After meeting her, I knew she needed to start coming out with us during our girls' nights. We have become quite the threesome.

It took some finagling of schedules, but tonight we are hitting up the bars and painting the town. I finally have a night off, and the Lakes are out of town, which means my bestie is all mine. It's not that I can't see her when Lonan is around, but I don't want to take away from their time together when he's gone every other week. It's a running joke that we share custody of Birdie.

As if on cue, Birdie's phone buzzes with a video call from her husband. *They're so adorable I want to run into oncoming traffic.*

"Hey, baby."

"Hey! Congrats on your goal tonight! How's Boston?"

"It's good. My roomie and I are having a couple of beers before we call it a night. Early flight home tomorrow."

I peek over her shoulder, Lonan switches to a rear-facing camera to show off his room. There's movement in the corner, and it seems his "roomie" is my nemesis. Rhys holds up his beer, gesturing hello to the camera. *He sure can wear the shit out of that Lakes hoodie.* I envision his smooth abs naked underneath the soft material. He looks cozy. Like a hot, huggable bear. *I fucking hate him.*

Lonan switches back to the front-facing camera, but Rhys

enters the frame behind him when he grabs something out of the mini fridge.

"What are you gals up to tonight? Getting into trouble?"

"Micky and Auds and I are having a girls' night."

Birdie turns her phone to show us the screen, and we wave to say hi. Rhys peers at Lonan's screen, clearly able to see Audrey and me. "So, definitely trouble, then. One sec, babe."

Then Birdie thrusts her phone into my hand.

Lonan hands over the phone, and we hear a muffled, "Here, hold this, I gotta grab another beer."

"Oh, I see, you're parent-trapping us. That's cute. Very original." I roll my eyes at Birdie.

"Hey," he says, stealing my focus.

"Having a nice slumber party?"

It's hard to hear him over the ambient noise of the bar, but I can tell his voice is low and rough. "The best. Are you behaving yourself tonight?"

A warm blush travels up my neck, and I catch Birdie side-eyeing Audrey. *Super. This will be fun to explain later.* His voice is deep and sexy, it's similar to Hat Trick Swayze's but his personality is way off. There's a flicker of something in his eyes I'm not allowing my mind to entertain as anything more than him throwing some dominance shit back in my face. Little does he know I don't operate that way.

"Nope. Not that it's any of your concern. You aren't the boss of me, *sir.*"

"You know what they say about famous last words."

I'm about to open my mouth to dispense more snark, but he hands the phone back to Lonan before I get the chance. *Fucker. I hate when he gets the last say.*

Birdie wraps up with Lonan on the phone, and after she hangs up, she and Audrey stare at me.

"Micky."

"Uh-huh?" I respond, admiring the ceiling tiles.

"Want to share with the class what's going on between you and Rhys?"

"Yeah, I thought you hated that guy?" Audrey asks.

"I do. He's an asshole, and I loathe him."

"Oh really." It's more of a statement than a question, but I answer her anyway.

"Yes. If I was locked in a room with Stalin, Hitler, and Rhys, and given a gun with two bullets, I'd shoot Rhys twice."

"Oh, stop. He's way too hot to die. A man like that should be ridden hard and often, and denying us the chance goes against every rule of sisterhood. Oh God, think of how hot he'll get when he's older—*total Daddy*. You can't deprive the world of witnessing a glorious transformation like that." Audrey points at me.

Birdie and I gawk at Audrey in surprise.

"What are you talking about? You're married!" I laugh.

"Which is why I need to live vicariously through you! You need to fuck him for the rest of us married gals who can't." Audrey takes a sip. "He's a ten and you know it."

"Look closer. There's a decimal point between the one and the zero."

"Whatever . . . sounded like he might be into you," she teases.

I'm so over this conversation.

"If he was into me, he wouldn't ignore me in the halls when I say hello. He wants none of this." I circle my hand in front of me, gesturing to myself. "His anaconda don't. Now, can we talk about *anything* else? Please?"

"Fine. How's your *Followers* account going?"

"Good, it's picking up speed," I say happily, pleased we can finally discuss something not Rhys-related.

"How much have you made so far?"

"It's wild. Right now I'm averaging about three-k a

month, but subscribers increase every week. I'm so close I can taste the lease agreement!"

They put their elbows on the table and rest their head on their hands.

"What's it like?"

"Do you have any creepy guys that message you?"

"Is it weird to know so many dicks are jacking off to you at the same time?"

I shrug. "There's always a few creeps. Sometimes it's discouraging, but for the most part, my followers are pretty cool. Just regular men."

Birdie nudges her shoulder in Audrey and bites her straw. "Micky has a crush on one of her followers."

"Stop. I just enjoy talking to him. But . . . yeah, if I knew him in real life, I would probably try to fuck him." I smile, thinking about Hat Trick Swayze and the noises he makes when he comes.

"So, what's his deal? Is he hot?"

He has hot-guy energy. That voice and body are *very* appealing. Although, that might simply be my biased opinion. He's been a subscriber since the beginning, so we practically have history together. Before my followers grew, he had often been my sole viewer during live streams. It allowed us to get to know each other, and we've had a lot of fun conversations together. Sometimes flirty, sometimes platonic.

"I've never seen him. We just have good connection. A guy like *THAT* knows how to treat a woman. He would say hi to me in the hallway—that alone should tell you how big a shovel Rhys would need to raise the bar."

"Could you ever hook up with him?" Audrey asks.

"I dunno. I suppose it's possible, he travels for work."

"Yeah, so do circuses," Birdie mutters into her glass.

"Excuse me! Your husband also travels for work!"

"Shit. You got me there."

"Okay, okay. So what else?" Audrey gets us back on topic.

"I dunno. He's just . . . cool. He's funny and seems genuinely interested in what I have to say. And unlike Rhys, he's a good tipper."

"Oooh, sugar daddy, perhaps? Is he local?"

"I've never asked him, but I definitely don't want a sugar daddy."

"She gets weird when it comes to making her own money," Birdie says to Audrey.

"I like being independent."

"Well, if you like the guy, see if you can get his name or a video chat sesh so you can see what he looks like. No photos! You don't want to get catfished."

I pause a moment, not sure if I should tell them. "We had phone sex." I leave out the FaceTime part.

Their eyes light up. "You have his number? Seriously?! When? Today? Was it hot?"

"Oh my God, it was so hot!" It bursts out of me, and I drop my head into my hands.

"You have to get him on a webcam! Now it's serious."

"Actually, he did ask me to teach him how to make bread."

"Is that a euphemism for something?" Birdie asks.

I lift my head and grimace. "No, you pervert. He wants to make actual bread."

"Well, that's perfect!" She claps. "Set up a video chat with him!"

I contemplate it. It's a good idea. But what if it's weird.

"Then get his name and what state he's in. We'll run a background check. Go through criminal records. The works."

"I suppose it would be nice to put a face to the name or whatever. But honestly, he's just a cool guy that's fun to talk to. I don't have any expectations to take this any further than what it is. His area code is Maine."

"Well, if he's cute and travels to Minnesota for work,

maybe you could get a hookup. Take care of that dry spell." She winks at me.

It would be worth the plane ticket.

*If there is a Goddess up there, please let Hat Trick Swayze be hot, available, and not a creep so I can get deep-dicked before this vagina between my legs withers to dust.*

*Amen.*

# SEVEN

## *Rhys*

"So, I assume you're a hockey fan based on your username?"

"Yeah, I follow it every year. I played in college, that's where the nickname came from."

I kick my feet up on the desk and open a bag of M&Ms to snack on while we talk. Hearing her voice triggers an oral fixation. *I wonder why.*

"You're not a Lakes fan, are you?"

Ha! Looks like I've pissed her off enough to hate the entire Lakes organization.

"Hell no, I especially hate that new rookie they have. Hear he's a douchebag. Checked my favorite forward into the boards last week, and nearly busted his wrist." It's not a lie, Grellinger used to be one of my favorite players, and I fucked up his arm last week. "Speaking of douchebags, how's your neighbor?"

I chuckle to myself and grab another handful of chocolate.

"Ugh. He pops up everywhere like a fucking groundhog. He always shows up while I'm working. I think he enjoys needling me."

*Only because you make it so much fun.*

"Maybe he likes you."

I'm attracted to her, like every other straight, red-blooded man in her vicinity. She's gorgeous. But mostly it's 'cause she's so reactive. She's a firecracker, and as long as I remember to keep my distance, I can keep having my fun without getting my hand blown to pieces.

"Ugh. I'm so tired of people saying that. It's such a cop out. Just more boys-will-be-boys bullshit. We need to stop saying it to little girls too. It makes them grow up to think violence is some form of affection."

"Never thought of it like that. Touché. So, he's clearly a jerk, but are there any other guys at work you like?"

I don't even want to know why I asked her that, but I'm pretty sure I know the answer.

"My coworkers are cool. I get along well with the other servers and bartenders. And there's a lot of nice guys on the team that come in sometimes."

"Nice guys aren't any fun though, are they, Hellcat?"

"Usually not, but you're nice and fun. You're my favorite follower."

Hearing her say that makes me smile, but it also annoys me. We can't have anything between us. But God, I wish we could. Hearing her go all *dommy mommy* on the phone kicked everything up a notch. Not because I'm a sub, but because topping a top has always been my biggest fantasy. Unfortunately, I'll be keeping that bucket list item unchecked. I have a career to focus on, plus my family drama. Anna called four times this week.

I laugh. "I'm also probably your favorite tipper."

"Eh, I like you even if you didn't tip as much. Not once have you said, 'Hey, Sweet Tits, show me your pussy.'"

I mean, I kinda did during our little FaceTime encounter.

"Shit, I haven't?! I meant to! Hey, Sweet Tits, show me your pussy."

"Funny, funny. Hey, when are we setting up our bread-making date?"

"It's a date now?"

"Sure, why not?"

"Hang on, let me look at my schedule." I put her on speak-erphone and check my calendar app. "How about Wednesday afternoon? Two o'clock your time?"

"You know, the best way to do this is if you have your camera on too. Maybe we could show our faces this time."

*Fuck.*

I sit up straight and push the bag of M&Ms away from me. Now what? I have no excuse.

"You want to see me, huh?"

"I've been curious . . . Like I said, you're my favorite."

Welp. It was fun while it lasted. This little tryst of ours had to end eventually. I figure I have three options here: One, ghost her. That's a pretty dick move. We've had great conversations over the last several months. Even though we met through a monetary-exchange platform, we've gotten to know each other well enough to take ghosting off the table. Two, show up on camera. Surprise! She'll never talk to me again and will swiftly disconnect the call. Game over. Three, show up in person. Surprise! I might be able to explain myself before she slams the door in my face.

"Okay. See you Wednesday," I say reluctantly. "Hey, one thing. Promise you'll still talk to me after you see what I look like?"

"I don't care what you look like."

*Oh, I bet you will, darling.*

We say goodbye and my phone drops to the desk. I form an O with my mouth and blow out a big exhale. *Wednesday.*

This ought to be interesting.

There's nothing going on tonight. No game. No guys asking to party. Nothing. I pace around in my living room. Normally, I'm happy being a homebody. But not tonight. There's a certain redhead pouring drinks beneath my living room floor. I'm almost positive she's working, but I don't know her schedule. *Why can't I shake this fixation on her?* I pace back and forth again. I could go downstairs to see if she's working. *No. Don't be an idiot. Find something else to do. Leave her alone.*

My apartment is quiet and still. The dim lamp in the living room makes the space warm and inviting, but regardless of how cozy it is, there's somewhere else I'd rather be. What is with me tonight? A slight thump of bass on the floor from whatever party is happening at Top Shelf below is a steady reminder of her. I can't ignore it. Just like I can't ignore her. Walking into the kitchen, I look for something to do. I've already done all the dishes. My palm slides across the counter, raking crumbs into my other hand. That's probably enough to take out the garbage.

I jump in the shower and get in a quick tug to relieve this hard-on that won't seem to go away lately. That minx sure knows how to get a fuckin' rise out of me. I throw on some jeans and a Henley. Spritz some cologne, I don't know why— *yes, I do*—I'm just taking out the garbage. It's not like I'm going down there to impress anybody. *Oh, no? Ya sure about that?* This doesn't involve you, Brain. Stay out of Dick's business.

I grab my wallet, lock the door behind me, and head down the stairs with my barely full trash bag. I'm a masochist. Why else would I want to see her bartending and flirting with other men? She's a great girl, her only downside is the way she makes her money, and only because I'm suddenly a possessive motherfucker.

In the alley, I fling the lightweight bag into the dumpster and turn to head back inside. I'm right here. Wallet's in my pocket. What's one drink? It doesn't even need to have alcohol. I'll order a pop just to be social. That's all this is, being social. It's not about her. *You're so full of shit.*

I open the door to the bar and am met with the rumble of people talking, boisterous laughter from somewhere off to the side, clinking glasses, and music playing. And she's there like I knew she'd be.

Looking hot. As. Fuck.

It's not even her outfit, she's simply wearing an old band tee and shorts. Same outfit from the other day, but she's swapped the tube socks for fishnets. She looks like Eddie Vedder's wet dream. Or maybe mine. I hover near the door and just watch her for a minute or two until a barstool frees up.

*It's open if I want it.*

She glances toward me and makes eye contact. I hold her gaze for a brief second.

And then I walk away.

# EIGHT

## Micky

It's busy tonight.

"I need four Michs, two Coors, and six shots of rail vodka ASAP."

"On it."

"Behind!" Amanda calls, squeezing around me with stacks of clean drinkware.

I've been on the clock for four hours, and according to my pedometer, I've already walked five miles. The bar is filled with the low rumble of conversation, barstools being scuffed around, glasses clinking, and the faint sounds of Lakes post-game commentary coming from the televisions. Another win tonight, people are happy, and the bar is full of good energy. It will be a fun night!

Birdie is hanging out at the bar. The place is filled with fans who've finished watching the Lakes beat Dallas 5-2, and now they are waiting around to see if any players show up. According to Birdie, Lonan and a few others will be showing up any minute now. She's sipping on a gin and tonic, and I'm working on a cucumber and basil sour ale from Citra—it's tart, refreshing, and delicious.

"Ready for another one, Gary?" I ask my regular. He's an

older guy in his sixties and is one of my favorite customers. He bought me a beer after I gave him one on the house.

"Yeah, why not. How ya doing tonight, Micky?"

"I feel almost as good as you look."

"Hey now. I've told you I've been happily married for thirty-eight years. You gotta quit hitting on me, lady."

I laugh and grab a new bottle, swapping it with his empty one.

"You going to bring her down here one of these days so I can size up my competition?" I toss the empty bottle in the recycling, and it adds to the cacophony of sounds.

"Yeah, if I can drag her away from her book club. She's from Seattle, too, ya know?"

"Well, I'd love to meet her. Us West Coast gals have to stick together. You tell her I'll give her a free drink when she comes in."

He nods his baseball cap in reply.

A collective "Ayyy!" booms when some of the Lakes boys walk in. The crowd joins in singing the local hockey anthem to congratulate the team on their win. I still haven't learned all the words to that song, but I probably should, considering it's a hockey bar. Hopefully I'll be out of here and working on Sugar & Ice before I get it memorized.

Behind the bar is a cheat sheet with the players' usual orders, so I begin popping bottle caps and pouring shots to get it ready for the server to pick up.

"See ya later!" I call to Birdie right before Lonan wraps his arms around her waist from behind. The smile on her face grows, and her eyes sparkle as she turns to face him. They are such a great match—and their story of a childhood crush to all-grown-up marriage makes me reel.

"Micky! How's it hanging tonight?" Lonan asks.

"By a thread." I grin. "How many of your boys are coming in tonight? Is this everybody?"

"Kucera should be right behind. He used to never come out with us preseason, but lately, he's been coming to Top Shelf with us regularly. You happen to know anything about that?"

"Nope." But I'd almost put money on him coming around just to find new ways to piss me off.

"Kid's doing great so far. Keeps to himself a lot, but he's smooth on the ice and has good intuition. And he's got hands—I like him."

*That makes one of us.*

"Good to hear. I'll send your drinks out in a sec. Want me to get a food order put in?"

"Nachos!" Birdie shouts. "Love you, Micky!"

"Love you more!"

I smile and enter her order on the touchscreen register as they walk to their corner. And automatically add extra jalapeños for her like a good best friend.

A group of four college boys are at one end of the bar. They have been cracking jokes and making me laugh for most of my shift. It makes me miss my college days.

"How's everybody doing down here? Need anything?"

"I'll take your number."

"All right. I'm going to think of a number between one and one hundred. If you guess the correct one, I'll give it to you."

"Seventy-three."

"Fifty-eight."

"Fourteen."

"Ninety-nine."

"Twenty-five," a deeper voice shouts from behind them.

I'm faced with the one and only Rhys Kucera. *Goody.* What's better is he actually guessed the correct number.

"It was twenty-five, but you're still not getting my number."

# RHYS

My ass parks right in front of where she's pouring. She looks up to me and does a double take. The bottle she's holding slips from her fingers. Hockey reflexes are a hell of a thing. I train at least five days a week to improve my reaction time, so reaching across the bar and snatching up the bottle before it drops is a lot easier than tracking eighty-mile-an-hour pucks.

"Thank you," she says.

"Anytime."

This might be one of the last times I get to speak with her after she finds out that Hat Trick Swayze is her asshole next door neighbor.

"Can I get you something?"

"Club soda with lime," I mumble.

"Do you ever order the same drink twice?"

She's been keeping tabs on me.

"I like to switch it up."

She finishes pouring the beers for another customer, and after setting them in front of the man, he checks her out as she walks back toward me. I glare at him until he realizes he's been caught. I'm not much better, I've already scoped her ass twice in the last two minutes. But I have a different relationship with her.

As she fills my glass with the soda gun, I attempt small talk.

"You behaving yourself tonight, Freya?"

She sets the drink in front of me and narrows her eyes.

"No."

I smirk. She loves pushing my buttons as much as I love smashing hers. She's the kind of trouble I'd like to take home and tie to my bed. I should be throwing money down and leaving. Better yet, I should've never shown up in the first place. This woman has a pull on me I can't explain. It makes me crazy. Why is it so hard to walk away from her? I think I know the answer to that. Because she's Queen of Tarts. And Queen of Tarts is the object of my obsession.

This tattooed, tough-as-nails woman has a gentle side. And I'm the only person in this whole fucking bar that's seen it. She can be sweet and silly. She's beautiful. Smart as hell. She's scrappy; she likes a little fight. And so do I. No matter how many times I try to ignore her and this thing between us, the attraction sits there. Like a stubborn ball of sexual attraction that won't budge. It's impossible to leave her alone. I want to test her limits and see what she's like when all her complex layers are pulled back.

"You really think you can rattle my cage with that?" she asks.

"I know I can."

"You won't. I eat boys like you for breakfast."

"What time is breakfast?" I ask with a half smile. She's probably a demon on her knees. All the blood runs to my dick when I imagine holding a fistful of her blazing-red hair, watching those dark lips slide up and down my cock. Her bright eyes gazing up at me. *Damn.*

She straightens and steps back from the bar. She feels the attraction, but I'm the one with the guts to say it first. But I needed to say it before she closes me out forever. At least, let her have that thought in her head. It might be enough to tempt her to give me a chance when shit hits the fan.

She leaves me to my soda and tends to the others. I'd rather stick my dick in a beehive than watch her flirt with other men. But more than that, I'm annoyed that I'm annoyed. It's irrational, but most infatuations are. Despite how much I try to oppose my attraction to Freya, it only seems to grow. The more I push her away, the bigger the temptation is to make a move. And seeing her laugh and joke with other customers makes me surprisingly jealous—I've *never* been a jealous guy—

there's never been a reason to be. Usually, other men worry about me.

I'm out of line for assuming I have any claim on her. But my feelings don't give a fuck if I'm being unreasonable, it still pisses me off every time she flashes that smile at another man. I don't get them on camera since she doesn't show her face, the closest I've come is hearing it in her voice. They'd probably be envious I've seen her naked, but those smiles are priceless. They should be mine.

Even though I suspect she's mostly smiling because she's a great bartender, it still makes me twitchy. She's terrific at her job; she knows how to work the room and make people happy. Now that I see her in her element more, her passion for entertaining and creating a fun atmosphere is obvious. She's busting her ass back there, but she's doing it with an upbeat attitude, well, except for when forced to interact with me. I take full responsibility for her contempt—this was the idea, right? Everything is going according to plan. So why do I have all this pent-up aggression whenever she's around?

The team is back in the corner, as usual, but I can't seem to move from this barstool. Witnessing her work is weirdly captivating. The way she moves between customers and juggles orders is flawless, every transition is smooth from one task to the next. It's satisfying to watch in the same way seeing someone power wash an old patio on YouTube is.

I'm having a good time until some smarmy fucker pulls up the barstool next to me. I already don't like the way he's leering at her.

"How are you doing tonight?" she asks, placing a cardboard coaster in front of him.

"I'm great now. How are you?" he replies, staring at her chest with zero shame.

*How does she deal with this shit daily?*

"Excellent. What can I get you?"

"I'll take a redheaded slut."

My ears perk up. I stare straight ahead and pretend to watch the TV behind the bar while I eavesdrop.

"Do you want that in a drink or a shot?"

"Hopefully, in you."

My eyes dart to hers. She's not impressed. I'll give her the opportunity to rip into this guy herself, but if she doesn't, I will.

"Classy."

"Ya know . . . I notice you every time I come in. You gotta boyfriend, baby?"

I hate this guy. I sit up taller, hoping my size will intimidate him into shutting the fuck up.

"Nope, *aaand not your baby*. We have two-for-ones on bottles tonight. Let me know if you decide what you want." She steps away to check on other patrons.

"Alright, alright," he acquiesces loudly. "Let's do the two-for-one. Heineken."

*Gotta love a good stereotype.*

"You got it."

My shoulders relax.

After setting them in front of him, he reaches for her wrist, but she snatches it out of his grasp.

"I didn't give you permission to touch me," she asserts.

"Yeah, but if you did, I bet I could make you *really* happy."

She swallows but quickly covers up any fear in her eyes. This guy is a fucking predator. Seeing her uncomfortable makes me furious. Her gaze bounces to me for half a second, she probably sees the anger on my face. This asshole is at the top of my shit list.

I'm about to say something when Freya's demeanor changes. Her back straightens in defiance, and she presses her tongue into her cheek, smirking at him. *Good luck, champ.*

This dude is about to get annihilated. There's something ferocious behind her eyes.

*Atta girl, give him hell.*

I've pissed her off in the past, but she's never given me that look before. She's *big mad*.

"The only way you could make me happy is by leaving. Unfortunately for me, I have to wait for you to nurse those two Heinekens first. And I'm guessing it's gonna be a while."

I grin into my beer as I take a sip, refusing to look over at her or the piece of shit harassing her.

"Oh, she's sassy." He seems pleased. "Ya know, I like it when they have a little fight in them."

I'll be kicking this guy's ass in the parking lot just for that comment alone.

"You get that a lot from women, I suspect."

He points at her. I want to rip his whole hand off.

"That's what I'm talking about. Where have you been all my life, Red?"

"Busy hiding—like every other woman in proximity to you."

His jaw clenches. He's zeroed in on her like she's some injured prey, but he'll soon find out she's the hunter in this scenario. She has a sweet side, but there's a reason I call her Hellcat. I monitor her carefully to read her body language. The twinkle in her eye tells me she's having fun sparring, and I'd be lying if I wasn't amused watching her knock his dick in the dirt. She's clearly been hit on many times because she's got a response for every single one of his sleazy lines.

He looks left and then right. "Looks like you're not very good at hiding, huh?" His reply comes out slightly aggressive.

"Everyone makes mistakes." She gestures to all of him. "Seriously, give it up, dude. I'm not interested. This isn't going to end in your favor, I promise you."

"Normally, when a girl gives me lip, it's because I pull

down my zipper." He leans over and whispers, "Is that my dick I smell on your breath?"

Setting my beer down, my hands turn into fists.

She gets right back in the dude's face, throws her thumb over her shoulder and leans toward him to reply softly, "If you do it's 'cause I just ate out your sister in the bathroom."

I'm caught midswallow and aspirate on my beer, sputtering and coughing like an idiot. *Did she just tell that guy he fucks his sister?* I'm chuckling along with everyone else who caught her little retort.

The red on his face proves she hit her mark. He's embarrassed. *He should be.*

"Jokes on you, my sister's dead!"

"That explains all the dirt," she mutters.

Freya doesn't fuck around.

"You know, if I wanted a bitch, I would have bought a dog. By the way, how much is your cunt going for these days, Queen of Tarts?"

And that's my cue—I'm going to kill this motherfucker. The sound of my chair scraping against the floor draws attention away from her as I insert myself between her and this misogynistic shitbag.

"You're done talking to her. Get the fuck out."

He has the audacity to smile at me.

"Why? You want her for yourself, Kucera?"

"Let's go outside."

"Hey, man, I'm cool. I have no issue with you." He's wrong on both counts.

"I disagree. Let's go."

She reaches over the bar and grips my arm, it sends a shockwave through me. Must be the adrenaline.

Her voice is low and calm. "Rhys, don't. This place is packed tonight. Every single person in this bar has a camera in their back pocket and would love nothing more than to upload a video to Twitter of you beating some guy to a pulp. As much as I would enjoy seeing you make a fool of yourself, take a minute and think about what you're doing. This shit always ends up on the news. I'm fine, really. Don't screw this up for yourself and do something you regret."

*I don't know what I will do to this guy yet, but whatever it is, I'll have zero regrets.*

I relax my tone. "It's fine, we're just going to talk. Right, buddy?" I slap him on the back.

"I have nothing to say to you." He chuckles.

"That's okay, I have plenty enough for the both of us. I'll grab your coat."

I grasp a fistful of his jacket from between his shoulder blades to not-so-nicely escort him outside.

Before I take two steps, Freya grabs a flashlight from behind the bar and aims it at the bouncers. When they turn around, she drags her finger across her throat to signal he's cut off and points at me and my new friend. I really would prefer to see this guy out myself, but it seems she has saved this asshole's life instead.

*See?* Sweet side.

# NINE

## Micky

"Hey, Amanda? Can you cover for me? I'm gonna run to the restroom."

"For sure. You good?"

"Yeah, just need a minute."

"That guy was a twat, don't let him get to you."

"Girl, that's an insult to twats everywhere," I mutter as I walk toward the back hall.

I glance back and Rhys and that jerk have met the bouncer at the door. Rhys leans over and whispers something to Justin, our biggest security guy. Justin's eyes find mine. I mouth, *I'm fine*, then finish my beeline for the bathroom. Unfortunately, there's a line about six girls deep.

I feel guilty for having Amanda take over, it's a madhouse out there. Thankfully, most of my customers are good, and I haven't stepped out from behind the bar since I clocked in. Tonight started so well, but that last guy got under my skin. Especially when he said my username. This is the first time I've been recognized off camera. I don't know what I'd do if my info was leaked at my workplace. Or to Rhys.

Walking farther down the hall, the loud sounds of conversation, laughter, and music dampen with each step. I reach the stairs that lead to the apartments and duck around the corner to hide in the dimly lit stairwell. I'm safe here. I slink down to sit on the steps with my back pressed against the cold brick wall. My shoulders relax and I close my eyes. *Breathe in for four, hold for four, out for four.* I just need a minute to collect myself.

Deep down, I know it wasn't the guy throwing insults that got me worked up. It was that Rhys was right there to witness the whole thing. The last thing I want is for him to know my secret or come across as weak. But clearly, I did a poor job of that, because he stepped in when he thought I couldn't handle myself. I wanted to get the last word in. Instead, it made me look like I needed to be bailed out. I don't need some man to save me.

I hate he got a front row seat to watch some jerk try to humiliate me. If Rhys hadn't been sitting there, I would have been fine, but I felt his eyes burning into me the entire time. But why does it even matter he saw? I shouldn't care what he thinks! I rest my forehead on my knees. Why is it always the assholes I gravitate toward? Probably because despite being an arrogant, rude human, he's one of the hottest pieces of man meat I've ever seen, and I still can't purge the image of him in gray sweatpants from my brain.

I will give myself thirty more seconds to get my shit together and then I'm stepping out there bright-eyed, as if nothing ever happened. Heavy footsteps are headed my way, probably some college kids looking for a place to hook up. I stand, prepared to tell them they need to find a new make-out spot, when the last person I want to see turns the corner.

"Hey."

*You've got to be kidding me.*

Sighing, I ask, "Why are you everywhere?"

"Are you okay?" His voice is gentler than usual.

He takes a step closer.

"What are you doing back here?" I demand.

"Honestly, I have no idea." Another step.

"Great. Can you have *no idea* elsewhere?" Another step.

I stumble on the stairs behind me, but he grabs my arm so I don't fall. Before I know it, I'm standing on a step with my back against the stairwell wall, holding the handrail to keep from losing my balance.

"Do *I* have permission to touch you?" His voice does something to me.

"Depends on how you plan to touch me."

"You have quite a mouth on you, don't you? Maybe it's time somebody teaches you how to use it."

"Oh, are you offering? Fuck off. I can handle myself, thank you."

"Freya, that guy was twice the size of you. You kept egging him on. If I hadn't been there—"

"You're right; this is all my fault. I was asking for it. Do you think it's what I was wearing?" I squish my boobs together to increase the cleavage.

"That's not what I said."

"Why don't you go back and sit with the rest of the team? I didn't ask for your help."

He snakes his hand up the side of my neck until his fingers are buried in my hair. His thumb gently brushes my temple. I hate how good it feels. He leans in until his lips sweep over the shell of my ear and his warm scent surrounds me—I shove him backward.

"Jesus, you're so fucking frustrating. Do you always lash out like this when someone tries to help you or is your mouth something special you reserve for me?"

I roll my eyes. "Please, I would never give you my mouth, much less *reserve* it."

"I like seeing you stand up for yourself. You're kinda hot when you talk back . . . You're like a fireball nobody can touch." He chuckles. "This ridiculous hair definitely matches your personality." He thumbs one of my locks and ever so gently tugs as it runs through his fingers. The edges of my vision blur with the overflow of nerves firing. *I'll never let myself go more than a week without an orgasm again.*

"What the fuck do you think you're doing right now? Is *this* your version of hitting on women? Does this actually work for you?" I glare at him.

He smiles. "Sometimes."

"Hate to break it to you, but whoever was willing to fuck you was just too lazy to jerk off."

He shakes his head. "You're just begging to be put in your place, aren't you?"

This is the most he's ever spoken to me, and even though he gets on my nerves, part of me wants him to keep talking.

"Fuck you. God, I hope you choke on all the shit you talk."

He pushes me back, pinning my arms to wall with one hand and cupping my face with the other. He levels his eyes with mine.

"Look, goddamnit. Next time, when someone talks to you like that asshole back there, and I'm not here, you're not going to provoke them. You're going to call Justin over and make him deal with it." The fury in his voice is so contradictory to his gentle caress on my face. "Promise me."

This motherfucker . . . he enrages me. But he also gives off this fluttering feeling that I can't get a handle of. *Why does he have this effect on me?*

"No. I don't owe you shit. That call is mine, not yours."

He's not going to tell me how to do my job. Besides, I like walking out the big mouthy ones, it makes my balls feel bigger.

His thumb stops moving and lowers down to my neck, and he searches my eyes. I tilt my chin up, daring him to try me. He doesn't back down, showing just how far he can wrap his fingers around my throat. My lips part, it's a strange new feeling of power. I'm not usually in this position. My mind quickly catalogs every sense I'm experiencing so I can log this moment in my memories to appreciate later.

Someone could walk around the corner at any time and find him pressed against me, but the sounds from the bar seem miles away. I'm surrounded by the scent of his clean cologne. And best of all, the feel of his rough, masculine hands holding me in place. If I didn't hate him so much, it would be nice. His furrowed eyebrows and intense glower confirm he's picturing the same things I am. He looks at my lips, studying them.

"And what about all the creeps from *Followers*? Huh, Hellcat?"

Without warning, he drops his hand and backs away. The loss of his body heat sends a chill through me, but not nearly as much as his words.

When the name registers, I freeze. Did he just say what I think he said? *He didn't* . . . the blood drains from my face.

*"What did you just call me?"*

He looks away for a quick moment, and his jaw tics. When his eyes meet mine again, they look guilty. It's a coincidence, it has to be.

I shake my head. "No . . ."

"Yeah."

"No. No, no, no. You hacked my Wi-Fi or something, right? Right, Rhys? Tell me you just hacked into my network, got my password. Anything."

"It's me."

It can't be. I stare at him while every ounce of my dignity shatters at my feet. My heart is hammering in my chest. This isn't happening.

"The FaceTime thing?" I choke out.

"That was me."

I can't breathe. My mind replays every thing I ever said to

him. Every flirtatious comment. Every sweet remark. He's seen the most private parts of my life. He's seen *my actual* private parts.

I told him things I would never want Rhys to know. It wasn't supposed to be like this. God, he's probably been laughing at me this whole time. My chin wobbles. It's one thing for him to see me naked, it's another for him to get a glimpse at my inner thoughts. He doesn't get that part of me. Those privileges belong to people who care about me, who treat me with respect. I told him things I never would have if I'd known it was him. I have never felt so humiliated.

"Why me, Rhys?"

"I didn't know it was you at first."

*At first.* The shame climbs up my throat.

"How long have you known?"

"I figured it out after those pink cookies were left on my doorstep. I had no clue it was you before that." *They're called macarons, dickface.*

My eyes are burning. I want to cry, but I'll be damned if I let this motherfucker ever see me shed a tear.

For weeks now he's let this go on. He let me have phone sex with him! Knowing full well I believed he was someone he wasn't. He had plenty of opportunities. But no, he's been watching me, leading me on in conversations, manipulating my feelings. Making me share my secrets. Meanwhile, treating me like I'm less than during every in-person encounter. I've been played so hard.

I'm so stupid. It was a website. It was only ever a website, money for nudity. How could I have imagined finding anything more than men who wanted to view me naked? I've never been made to feel so cheap. And now he wants to know if he can get the real thing. That's what the phone sex was about. *That's what all of this is about.*

He could have told me before. He could have canceled his

subscription like a decent human being and backed away. But no, he thought it would be more exciting to break me in person and see my reaction. See how bad he hurt me up close.

Well, *fuck that.*

"Get the hell away from me."

"Wait—" He holds out his hands, like he's going to somehow explain himself. *The nerve.*

"No." As if I'd listen to anything he has to say.

"Can I defend myself?"

I push him away. "I cannot believe you. You're sick."

"Why? Because it's me?"

I swallow the feelings down. My face is on fire. "I didn't deserve this."

"I should have said something sooner. I'm sorry."

*Who has he already told? The whole hockey team?*

He looks like he's about to say something, but his mouth just opens and closes, unable to find the words. There are no words.

"Don't ever speak to me again. Don't sit at my bar. Don't watch my videos. Don't even look in my *fucking* direction," I seethe.

"Freya—"

I turn my back and walk to the bar, wiping my face to make sure no tears are present.

"You okay?" Amanda asks, her brow furrowed. "That guy was a prick for hitting on you like that. Justin kicked him out. Things are slowing down if you wanna take off? I'm sure I can get Brandon to step in."

"No, no, I'm fine. I'm good."

Even for somebody like Rhys, this is low. The worst betrayal. Why wouldn't he tell me? And how many people has he told? Maybe the whole fucking Lakes team has been watching me.

I did everything I could to protect my privacy. He could

have found someone else to beat off to. Did he even masturbate to me? Or was he only getting off on debasing me? Building up to the moneyshot of my humiliation. And possibly damaging my reputation in ways I haven't even grasped yet. Did he record me? My tattoos were showing when we were on camera. Should I worry about videos of me being leaked? This could affect Sugar & Ice and my chances for making a name for myself in this city.

He was a close friend.

Another sadness aches, I have to reckon with the hurt that someone who I trusted so much doesn't even exist. I liked him, really liked him. That's rare. It was pathetic to entertain the idea that I could find someone like him on a site like *Followers*. What did I think would happen with someone who literally paid money to see me waltz around my kitchen naked? Ever since Kyle died, I've been careful to not let anyone in. Until *him*. I didn't mean to do it, but I let my guard down. The connection I felt wasn't based on physical attraction. There was chemistry. It felt so *real*. I'm mourning something that never existed.

*It was never real.*

I play back everything he's ever said on *Followers*. All the ways his words made me feel and the warmth they gave me are replaced with humiliation. I've never been more ashamed, but I refuse to cry over somebody like Rhys. Fuck him, he's the one who lied.

The night passes in a blur as I take orders and fill them on autopilot. Amanda knows something's up, but she probably suspects the other customer got to me. I place an order for a dozen soft pretzels and a vat of cheese sauce before the kitchen closes. I may not cry over him, but I sure as hell will be putting away some carbs tonight. Some people run when they're hurting. I eat. And I'm no bitch when it comes to soft pretzels.

Once I clock out and step into my apartment, I go straight

to the bathroom to scrub the makeup off my face and throw on an old flannel shirt, not even bothering to button it. Opening the first Styrofoam container of pretzels, steam rises from the white box and the smell of salty soft dough fills my nostrils.

I turn on my "*Men Ain't Shit*" playlist and plow through each pretzel one by one. Now *this*, this is real. This is all I need. Chewy pretzels and cheese sauce, baby. There's no way any man is better than this deliciousness.

*Things are gonna be okay.*

Today was hard, but I don't have to go through it again. I can move on with my life like he never existed. Because he didn't. There is no Hat Trick Swayze. But someday, I'll find somebody *like* that person, and when I do, he'll be real. He'll treat me well. He won't lie. And he'll have a gigantic penis.

*Keep your chin up.*

Eventually, I'll make more friends here. I have my regulars, and they like me. My coworkers. I have Birdie and Lonan and Audrey. I'll learn from this and be safer with my *Followers* account. Maybe I should consider myself lucky. He could have been a serial killer. Though, truthfully, I can't decide whether I'd prefer a murderer to Rhys Kucera.

I don't have to decide today. I crack open another beer, and between my collection and the shots bought by a couple customers tonight, I've lost count. I rinse the beer down with another giant soft pretzel.

Rhys's door slamming causes mine to rattle, so I creep over to the peephole.

There's a note taped over it. *Asshole.* I open the door and focus my drunk vision on the scribbled words.

**207-555-6767**
*(IN CASE YOU DELETED IT)*

# -HAT TRICK SWAYZE

*Fat fucking chance.* I rip off the note, wad it up, and chuck it at his door.

# TEN

## *Rhys*

P retty sure she's blocked me based on the way my calls aren't going through. One of the guys said she was throwing them back hard last night. She's a bartender, so she probably has a decent tolerance. But either way, I need to see her. Even for a minute. At least make sure she's okay.

I knock on her door. When she opens it, I'm tempted to laugh. She's a mess. She's wearing an oversized flannel with no pants, every button is mismatched by one or two holes, and there's something hanging out of her pocket, *is that a pretzel or a churro?* I try hard to keep it together, she's the most adorable trainwreck I've ever seen. *Fuck, I miss this girl. It's been less than twenty-four hours, but I miss her texts and the anticipation of her videos. What does that say about me?* She's the only woman who could look like this and smell like . . . *cheese sauce?* And I still want to fuck her brains out.

"Wild night?" I ask with a raised eyebrow.

She starts to shut the door on me, but I shove my foot in the doorway.

"Too soon. You're right, I'm sorry."

Her weight shifts from one foot to the other. "For what? Commenting on my presentation or something else?"

I squint my eyes to look closer. "What's on your face?" I reach out to the smear on her chin, but she slaps my hand away and brushes it off.

"Um . . ." I point at her shirt. "I think you have a soft pretzel hanging out of your pocket."

"I know! It's there on purpose!" she snaps, slapping my hand away a second time.

I hold up both my hands as a ceasefire and have to steel my face to keep from laughing.

"What do you want?" She snarls, like a pissed-off raccoon.

I take a deep breath. "I owe you an apology. A lot of apologies."

"Did you record me?" She wraps her arms around her waist and looks at the floor. There's so much shame in her voice. It guts me.

"What?"

"The cam video. Did you record it? There are laws—"

"Jesus. No. I wouldn't do that." *Does she believe I'm trying to blackmail her?*

"There's a lot of things I thought you wouldn't do." Her eyes look wet.

*Ouch.* I can't fault her. Any trust she had in me has been obliterated.

"I just wanted to check on you. To know you were okay."

"Never better," she deadpans, throwing her arms open wide.

She seems checked out from me and this conversation.

I don't know what I expected, but it wasn't this. I want feisty Freya back, but this version looks brokenhearted. I purse my lips and nod toward the floor. I shouldn't have come over, she's not ready.

"I'll see you around, Freya Girl."

"Don't call me that." Her eyes glaze over even more, and that sweet voice I love comes out defeated and hollow. "And Rhys?"

"Yeah?"

"I meant what I said about staying away from me."

I want to reach for her, but she slams the door in my face.

I fucked up.

# ELEVEN

## Micky

It's Sunday night, and I'm finishing the final closing chores at Top Shelf. It's been a long shift. We had the hockey game on tonight, the Lakes played in Chicago, and it went into double overtime. Anytime that happens, people start ordering drinks and food to quell their anxiety. Other than that, tonight ran smoothly, but I'm coming off a six-day work week, and I'm looking forward to my bed.

Thankfully, and surprisingly, Rhys has been respectful of giving me space. He's only shown up with the team once in the last two weeks, and even then, he didn't sit at the bar. He placed his order with the server, same as the rest of the guys. We've not spoken one word to each other since *the incident*. Well, that's not true, he's spoken one word. He said hi in the hallway about a week ago. I didn't acknowledge it.

When the last of the glasses are washed and restocked, the ice bin drained, and the soda gun disassembled and sanitized, I walk around the bar to straighten the barstools and tidy up the floor.

"Do you want me to wait for you?" Amanda asks, putting her coat on.

"No, I'm good. Almost done. Just need to grab my tips

and clock out. You can head out, I'll lock up. Do you want me to walk you to your car?"

"No, that's all right, Justin's outside, he's going to walk to the lot with me. Have a good rest of the night!"

"You too, drive safe!"

I pick up my stack of tips and stuff them in my back pocket. I made almost $300 tonight, which is awesome for a Sunday night. As I turn off the lights and lock the front door, I decide I'll run a nice hot bath and maybe even shave my legs, just so I can rub them together like a cricket when I climb into my bed with clean sheets. Tomorrow's my day off, so I can sleep in as late as I want.

*Fate, however, has different plans for me.*

When I climb the stairs, I hear knocking. As I make it to the top step, I recognize the woman, she's back. She's not pounding on his door like before, but she's not giving up even though it's almost two in the morning. If she's so obsessed with him, why doesn't she realize they played an away game tonight? I will not let this woman's issues interrupt my sleep again.

"He's not home," I say dryly, pulling out my keys to unlock my apartment.

When she turns around to look at me, I almost flinch.

I know that look. The pale face and hollow cheekbones.

*He looked just like her.* But I had to go to work. Our bills were behind, and the electricity was about to be shut off that week. I'm done blaming myself for his choices, but it still doesn't heal the memory of seeing Kyle's once-sparkling eyes glazed, dull, and staring right through me.

That relationship started so great. He was funny, smart, and kind. He was supposed to be "the one." I loved him. But after being prescribed pain pills for a twisted ankle—a fucking twisted ankle—he was hooked. That was all it took for him to turn mean and angry. He was a jerk. I continued to care for him, but the only thing he cared about was the high. The doctors kept writing the prescriptions. Until they didn't. And then he was forced to find them elsewhere.

I tried so hard to keep him clean, but it was like trying to bail out a boat already submerged underwater. There's not a person on this earth that could have made him stop craving the drugs. I was powerless against his addiction. Opioids and I were in constant competition for his attention, and in the end, they won—and I lost the person I loved more than anything. It's why I refuse to go back to Seattle. I can't go back there without being reminded of him. It's too painful.

Everything in me says to get in my apartment, shut the door, and pretend I never saw her. I promised myself I wouldn't ever get involved with someone with addiction issues. Platonic or otherwise. I can't go through that again. It reminds me so much of everything I went through. There's an anger in me that still hasn't gone away.

But I can't ignore her. She's dope sick and craving.

She sneezes.

"Do you need help?" I ask.

"You got any money?"

*Color me surprised.*

"No." Suddenly it feels like there's a neon sign pointing at the wad of cash in my back pocket. I can't let her see it.

"Do you know when my brother is getting home?"

*Shit.*

"Wait, Rhys is your *brother?*"

"Yeah."

For the first time, I feel some sympathy toward him. Loving an addict is a fucking nightmare. It's a burden impossible to let go of. Your heart is tethered to a sinking ship. I guess this goes to show you never know what someone else is going through. Maybe that's why he's always such a dick. If so, I can't blame him. During those dark years, I was miserable.

Constantly stressed out and worrying. Wondering when he would get home and how long he would stay for. Never knowing whether he was safe or even alive.

"Do you have his phone number?"

"I sold my phone."

My eyebrows shoot up. Besides drugs, that was Kyle's most prized possession. It was his connection to his dealer. It's practically a lifeline for addicts. She sneezes again, and seeing how runny her eyes are makes me wince. I'm thrown into my past when I notice she's sweating through her shirt. She stinks. I can smell her from ten feet away.

I don't know anything about this girl, she can't be over twenty years old, and she's in a bad way. Detoxing alone can be deadly, and I know she'll run if I even mention calling 911. I have to ease her into it. When I take inventory of her symptoms, I know I've already chosen to help her. I've done this before; I can do it again. *Just this once.* I've been in enough therapy to know I need to set boundaries. I'm not responsible for her. She's not my sister.

But she is Rhys's, and I can't let his sister die on his doorstep.

"What's your name?"

"Anna," she rasps.

"Are you on anything right now? Taking anything?" She looks at me nervously, probably suspicious I'm a cop.

*Paranoia? Check.*

"Are you?"

"No. If I was, do you think I'd be like this?"

*Irritability? Check, check.* This is gonna go down like a rat sandwich.

"Come on. Let's get you cleaned up." I turn the key in my deadbolt and push the door open. She doesn't want to trust me.

"Look, you and I both know you're about fifteen minutes

away from either shitting your pants, or puking up bile. I don't want to deal with cleaning it up out here. Just come inside, and I'll let you use my bathroom."

She hesitates, but eventually shuffles into my apartment. *Thank God.*

"Where's your bathroom?"

I point down the hall. "Middle door on the left."

She heads toward the bathroom, and I quickly go to my bedroom to hide the roll of cash in my back pocket. I stuff it under my mattress, along the edge of the elastic pad and the fitted sheet. If she lifts the mattress, she won't be able to see it. I change out of my bar attire and get into some comfy clothes. Then I grab four sets of pajamas for Anna, *if that's really her name.* Four sets will get us started. I've never been so thankful to have a washer and dryer in my unit. After grabbing pajamas, I go to the linen closet in my hall and grab all of my towels.

As I predicted; I can hear the diarrhea from out here. She probably made it just in time. She flushes, and I knock on the door.

"I'm not a professional. We should have you looked at by a doctor."

"No! I don't need a doctor. If you call somebody, I'll leave . . . And then I'll come back to shit on your doorstep."

She opens the door, and a wave of stink penetrates the hallway. My bathroom will need a deep cleaning tomorrow, thanks to the biological warfare that is her anus. Regardless of how I feel, I don't let it show on my face. Letting her maintain a little dignity will go a long way. But I gotta get this girl in the shower, like yesterday.

I grab the first of many pairs of pajamas she will go through tonight and a couple of towels and enter the bathroom.

"What do you take?"

She scoffs at me.

"If you're gonna be here, I need to know what I'm in for."
She rolls her eyes. "Oxy."

"Do you snort, shoot, or swallow?"

"Swallow. I'm not fucking stupid."

I look up at the ceiling, when she follows my gaze, I place my hand under her chin so I can see up her nose. It's red, raw, and looks fucking painful.

*Apparently lying runs in the family.* "When was your last hit?"

"Couple days ago."

"How much do you usually take?"

"Fuck, I don't know. Sixty?"

It's a relief. This is doable.

"That's good. I know you feel like shit, but detoxing from one-twenties would feel a lot worse."

"Oh good, that makes me feel so much better. Thanks."

"Have you been tapering down?"

I know she's getting annoyed, but I need to know what the risks are.

"Only because I'm broke."

"Where are you getting money?"

"Lady, I don't know you. Why're you asking so many fucking questions?"

"Hey, if you want a safe space to detox, you need to help me out, or I'm calling the police. You don't have a car, and you're not going to make it far in the condition you're in."

"Rhys gives me rent money."

"Do you still have the apartment or are you couch surfing?"

"Surfing." Based on her condition, she's either squatting or crashing at dope houses.

"That's nice."

"Fuck you too."

*That's fair, it was a low blow.*

"Sorry." I hold out my hand. "Here, give me your clothes."

"Uh. No, thanks."

"Seriously, I'll wash them and give you something clean to wear. My clothes will fit you."

A child's clothes would probably fit her. Mine will be baggy, she's thin as a rail.

"Have you got the strength to take a shower?"

"I don't know."

"'K', I'll help you." The handheld showerhead I bought will pay for itself tonight.

The bathroom slowly fills with steam as the water heats up. As soon as she steps in, the water around her feet turns cloudy with dirt and who knows what else. Then the water turns brown. *Shit brown.*

"Wait!" she yells, realizing what's happening.

She's lost control of her bowels. Fuck, I wish Rhys were here to help me. You know it's bad if I'm wishing for his presence, but it's true. I could use another set of hands.

"I'm sorry. Fuck, I'm so sorry, I can't—"

"It's okay. Don't worry about it. I hated that shower curtain anyway. It's fine. Really."

"Oh my God," she sobs. "This is so gross."

"Don't think about it."

Tears stream down her face, and my heart breaks for her, and for Rhys.

"Hey, how old are you?" I ask, trying to change the subject.

"Nine—" *Sniffle.* "Teen."

Jesus, she's a teenager. Once she's stable, I start with her hair. My expensive deep conditioner works wonders to help get out a few matted sections of hair. Then I shampoo her hair, then another round of conditioner.

"That smells good," she mumbles, barely above a whisper.

A brief window into the sweet girl locked inside her frail, addicted body. Jesus, I could cry.

When I'm able to run my fingers through her hair without snagging, I grab washcloths and help wash her back, arms, and legs. Everything on her front and her ass is on her to handle.

After the water is off, I wrap her in a towel and sit her on the toilet so I can work on drying her hair.

"I'm going to throw up."

I help her to her knees and open the lid to the toilet so she can vomit. And she does. She has nothing in her stomach, so it's mostly dry heaves. I pray she doesn't get diarrhea while throwing up, forcing us to go through this whole process again.

"You're doing good. I'll be right back." I run to the kitchen and fill a large cup with cold water from the faucet. When I return, her eyes are bloodshot, and the capillaries under her eyes are broken from all the dry heaving.

"Chug this."

"I can't."

"Yes you can. Hold your breath and chug. It will give you something to throw up so you're not gagging. Cold water feels a lot better coming up than anything else."

She takes my advice and gulps. She hands me the empty cup, and I refill it. Within a couple seconds, she's throwing up all the water. I hold back the clean, wet hair from her neck. I'll be surprised if her hair ever dries, she hasn't stopped sweating.

"Thanks," she says, spitting into the toilet.

We go through a couple more rounds, and I make sure the glass stays full and rub her back as she heaves. When her bout of nausea wanes, she sits on the floor and leans against the bathtub.

"So, you're my brother's neighbor, then?"

"It would appear so."

"Are you fucking him?"

"No."

"Do you want to fuck him?"

"No." Not one hundred percent true. I wouldn't mind taking that dick for a spin, but I loathe the person it's attached to.

"Then why are you helping me?"

"Because I didn't want you to die. And I didn't want you to shit or barf in my hallway."

We stare at each other for a minute and then both chuckle a little. She must feel a bit better.

"'K'." She pauses. "I think I'm done throwing up for now."

I hold out a clean set of pajamas. "Put these on. Let me get you a toothbrush." I'll be impressed if she actually brushes her teeth, I'm sure every tooth aches.

The taste in her mouth must be pretty bad, because she does it. She's tender with her gums but brushes every inch of her mouth. Under her tongue, over her tongue, the roof of her mouth, inside her cheeks. It's probably been a while. Poor kid. As she cleans, she begins shivering, and her cold sweat intensifies.

We spend the next four to five hours switching between hot sweats, cold sweats, chills, vomiting, and diarrhea. She's being put through hell, and her body is barely holding it together. I've had to do a load of laundry since we've gone through so many changes of clothes and towels. She's fighting it, and I want to hope that this time will be the last, but the only reason she's detoxing is because she hasn't been able to buy anything. I don't know if that's because she's pawned her phone and can't reach her dealer, or if she's out of money.

"Think you could sleep?"

"Not really." Kyle used to detox all night. He was exhausted, but the insomnia was no joke. "But could I lay down and rest?"

"Yeah, let me get the bed ready." The guest bedroom doesn't have any furniture, so she'll have to rest in mine.

I grab extra sheets for my bed, in case we have any bodily fluids go rogue. As I add the sheets, all I want to do is climb into the bed myself. The birds are chirping outside, and the sun is coming up. It'll be a while before I can fall asleep again. She stands around my room while I get it ready. I was hoping she would have stayed in the bathroom so I could move the money from under my bed, but I can't get it out now without her seeing my hiding spot. I usher her into the bed so she can stretch out, then I go back to the bathroom and start cleaning. Once everything sparkles again—and doesn't smell like death—I change my clothes.

Now that there's finally a lull, I need to get a hold of Rhys. If it were my sister, I'd want to know. Unfortunately, I don't have his number. Because I deleted it and threw away his note. Like an idiot.

When I walk back into the bedroom to ask Anna for his number, I'm stunned to see her sleeping. At least her eyes are closed. I can't wake her, that would be cruel. She needs rest. I'll have to reach out to Lonan.

> Hey, can you give me Rhys's number?

LONAN

Good morning to you too. Somebody hungry for a Rhyses Pieces? Why do you need his number?

> Yup. I want to bang him.

*In the face. With a chair.*

LONAN

Fine. Don't tell me.

207-555-6767

Here goes nothing. I save his number in my phone and shoot off a text.

> Hey. It's Micky.

RHYS

Hi Freya.

*Asshole.* I let it slide. The next thing I text him will make him feel bad enough.

> Sorry to do this over text, but your sister came around looking for you. She's coming off of something pretty heavy. You'll want to check on her when you get in, but I'm keeping her at my place till then. Text me when you land and I'll unlock the door.

RHYS

Fuck. We're boarding the plane now.
Should be home in 2 hours.

> I'm sorry.

I lock my phone, and sprawl out on the floor. *Just two more hours.* I'm so tired, but I can't fall asleep. I need to hear if she throws up, and truthfully, I don't trust her, not because she's Rhys's sister, I don't trust any addict. I brush my teeth and get ready for bed, even though it's eight o'clock in the morning. Today is my day off, I was hoping to go to IKEA. I need a desk and a new sofa. *And a new shower curtain.* Lonan helped me get my broken couch into the dumpster last week, and I miss having somewhere to sit.

My plans to sleep half the day will have to be postponed.

# TWELVE

## *Rhys*

F *uck.*

After I throw my bag overhead, I pick a spot and pull the seat belt tight on my hip. The faster we can take off out of Chicago, the better. My stare burns a hole into the headrest in front of me. With a bouncing leg, I clench my fist over and over. I want to punch something.

Don't lose your cool in front of the guys. Don't panic. It will be fine. *That's a load of bullshit.* It won't be fine. I can't believe Anna showed up. I always tell her when I will be out of town. If there was something she needed, she was supposed to ask me before I left. She has my schedule.

Moving her with me to Minnesota was supposed to be good for her. I thought if she got away from those assholes back home, got sober, maybe she'd straighten out. It hasn't done shit. If anything, she's gotten worse. Times like this make me happy our parents aren't here to see this. They'd be disappointed in me. It's my fault she's addicted. But I don't know how to help her, nothing seems to work. And now Freya's with her . . .

The *Followers* thing was messed up, but I was prepared for that fallout. If Anna came around, there's no telling what condition she was in, and what Freya has had to deal with. What's she going to think of me now? God, she probably thinks we're a family of fuck-ups. She wouldn't be too far off either. Doesn't matter. I'm sure any chance of forgiveness is long gone.

Now I'm the one that feels humiliated. This is karma. Anna showing up—and likely asking Freya for money—is a rotten game of *I'll show you my shame if you show me yours.* Something neither of us wanted to play. *Fuck!*

"You good, man?" Lonan asks, brows furrowed.

"What?" I snap. My eyes soften, and I shake it off. "Sorry. Yeah. I'm fine."

"Well, if it makes you feel any better, Micky texted me for your number. You're into her, right?"

I almost laugh, he has no clue how far off base he is right now. But he hasn't mentioned my family, which means Freya probably didn't divulge why she needed the number.

"Yeah. She say why she wanted it?"

"I asked, she said she wants to bang you. I assume that's a lie. No offense."

"None taken."

I owe her. If the league organization found out about my family drama, it wouldn't look good. Anna can be a liability, but I love her. She's my baby sister, we're each other's only family. I couldn't be there for her then, but I can try now. Although, damn, she makes it difficult sometimes.

I wonder if she was high or detoxing. Based on the text, she's detoxing. I hope she's not doing drugs in Freya's apartment. Shit, should I have warned her? I check my watch again. It feels like time is standing still. *Let's get this fucking bird in the air already.*

"You sure you're okay?"

"Just tired, wanna get home."

"Same, I miss Bridg. Gonna go home and fuck my wife," he says as he makes his way toward the back.

I'm envious. I know I'm not supposed to be involving myself with anyone, but it can be lonely. Regardless, it's my rookie season, a time to keep my head down and prove myself. Thankfully, our game against Chicago went well. We won, and I got another assist, but any joy from last night's game was sucked out of me when her text came through.

When I get off the plane, I all but sprint through the airport. I have to get home and see what I'm dealing with. *What Freya's been dealing with.*

On my way.

FREYA

K.

The eleventh letter of the alphabet has never looked so callous.

When I reach the front door, I fly up the stairs and throw my bag down on my doormat. After gently knocking on her door, I enter her apartment, and Freya meets me at the entryway and holds her index finger over her lips.

"She's sleeping, I'm trying to let her rest."

"Freya, I'm—"

"The cold washcloths on her forehead helped, but she's still getting the chills on and off, so she's wrapped up in a blanket. She's been throwing up, had diarrhea. I've made her drink as much water as she's willing to, but she's probably still dehydrated. Make sure she gets a lot of fluids today. Her last shower was just before I texted you. We got her teeth brushed, and she seems to be doing a bit better, but she's had a long night."

"Sounds like you both have."

She nods at the floor; this woman is fucking exhausted. I

94

don't know what she's been through, but it makes me regret every time I was a dick to her.

"I'm sorry I wasn't here. You shouldn't have to deal with this."

"You don't have to apologize, I understand." She shrugs. "Ex-boyfriend."

*Shit. That's rough.*

"I don't know how to thank you for taking care of Anna."

"Based on how she's doing now, she should be out of the woods by sometime tonight. But she might be riding the struggle bus today." She turns to walk farther into the apartment, and I follow. *Where's her couch?*

"Um, so I've still got a couple of her items in the laundry, I'll bring them by tonight or tomorrow."

"Okay." *How is she so on top of this?* I'm usually a mess after a night with Anna.

She steps out of the bathroom with a stack of clothes. "Here's some underwear and comfy stuff for her to put on after she wakes up. She's probably going to want something clean. Here's her toothbrush. Here's two rescue kits with some naloxone—Narcan. Make sure she keeps one on her, but you should hold onto the other one. Just in case."

"Fuck, I don't even know what to say."

I'm speechless. She's shown me mercy when I gave her none. There's not a shred of judgment in her eyes. Not toward me or Anna. She spent the last six hours tending to my dope-sick sister with nothing but compassion and kindness. She's giving and selfless and . . . *and I royally fucked up with this woman.*

"Well, I'm hoping you'll say you'll take her to your apartment so I can get some sleep."

"Yeah." I take a big inhale. "Yeah, of course."

I follow her to the back bedroom and wake Anna up to

walk back to my apartment. She shuffles behind me, groaning about her aching muscles.

Once she's tucked into my guest bed with all the extra sheets like Freya showed me, I set the pile of clothes on the dresser. Including Freya's underwear. *Dude, don't be weird.*

Anna agrees to drink a glass of water before she goes back to sleep.

"Your neighbor is cool."

"I know."

"I shit in her shower." She chuckles.

I give a pregnant blink. "You *what*?"

*She can't be serious.*

"It was so fucking awful. I felt terrible."

"You shit in her shower? Does she know?"

"Yeah, she was there when it happened."

"Oh my God. *Anna.*"

"She washed my hair and it smells really good. Here, smell it." She holds out a handful of hair, and it's Freya-scented.

"I still can't believe you shit in her shower." My hand scrubs over my face.

Anna finishes telling me about her night. She looks like hell, and she's still sniffling and sneezing. Yawns every other sentence. Has a headache. And I swear you could measure her sweat in a fucking rain gauge.

> Anna told me about last night. I hear I owe you a new shower curtain. If there's anything else that needs replacing, let me know.

There's a lot I owe her. She doesn't respond. I tell myself it's because she's already fallen asleep, but I know it's more likely because she's still not talking to me. Can't blame her, I'm no longer on thin ice, I've fallen through.

# THIRTEEN

## Micky

After being awake for almost twenty-four hours straight, I hurry to my bed. When I pull the sheets off, I look for the cash I stuffed under the mattress. My shoulders slump. It's gone.

*Goddamnit.*

I look around my room for anything else I hold of value—just the cash.

Right now sleep is more important than the money. I can figure this out another time. I can make the money back. I'll do an extra live stream this week. Besides, I'm not about to get into it with Anna. I've had enough run-ins with theft and addicts to know how that's going to go. If she's anything like Kyle, she'd fight me on it for hours, talking in circles. I could find the wad of money between her ass cheeks, and she'd still say someone else put it there. I don't have the energy.

I'm out cold before my head even hits the pillow. I only planned on sleeping four hours but snoozed until after four o'clock in the afternoon. I needed it. Last night was brutal.

I have to get moving because Birdie's dad, Ken, will be picking up his truck tomorrow morning, and I still need that new sofa and desk from IKEA. I throw on a sweatshirt and leggings, wrap my hair in a messy bun, and get my ass in gear. While getting dressed, my eyes land on the last of the laundry I need to return to Anna.

*Which means I have to see Rhys. Ugh.*

I gather up the items, along with a couple more sets of loungewear for her. She's probably sweat through the others by now. I hope Anna hasn't fled yet. I imagine it would be cathartic to see someone overcome their addiction after everything I went through with my ex. I wouldn't want anyone to experience that.

When I knock gently on his door, the footsteps on the other side alert me that Rhys is home. There's no way Anna would have footfalls that heavy. She barely weighs a hundred pounds soaking wet. When he opens the door, it annoys me how good he looks. Especially since I'm sort of slumming it, but I'm in a time crunch, and I don't care what I look like to him.

"Hi, just returning Anna's clothes, and here's a couple more in case you need them."

"Thanks. You didn't have to do this. Do you want to come in for a bit?" He steps back, holding the door open wider. *Hard pass.*

"No, I'm on my way out, just wanted to give these to her before I left. How's she doing?"

"Better. I think she's coming around. Still itchy, says her skin is crawling. And I swear to God, the sneezing fits are making me fucking nuts." He rubs his forehead.

"Give her an antihistamine. It might let her sleep a little too. Imodium also helps with some of the other side effects."

"I'll do that. Thanks. She said she's going to stay a few weeks and get clean."

*Oooh, wouldn't hold your breath on that.* I internally cringe at his hope. I don't doubt Anna has the strength to work through her addiction, but the odds of her doing it alone without rehab are slim. And the fact she's already making promises—*while detoxing*—probably means she's already planned her escape. As soon as he turns his back, she'll bolt. She's never wanted to get high more than she does now.

"That's good. I wish her luck." I turn to leave. I don't have it in me to break his heart.

"Freya—"

"Yeah?"

"Thank you. Really."

All I can do is nod, then get my feet moving down the stairs and out the door. I'm running out of daylight as it is.

IKEA is a dreamland for a girl like me on a budget. I've already furnished most of my apartment, modestly, but I need a desk. And now that the sofa broke, I need to get something to sit on while I binge *Second Bite*. So, here I am, land of flat packs and self-assembly, ready to pimp out my place with a few necessities.

I freeze under a hanging sign that reads *SÖNDERÖD*. I hate these ugly rugs; they remind me of Kyle. He was lying on one of these the day I found him. Would I have noticed them if I hadn't spent the night babysitting Anna? I've put in a lot of work in the last five years trying to move on with my life. I sought counseling early on, but the best thing for me was leaving Seattle behind. His friends and my friends were all the same, it was easier to break ties with everything and everyone.

Vancouver was a new start for me. I made friends quickly —I met Birdie. We both were going through our own traumas. Her with her narcissistic adoptive mother and me with my demons surrounding Kyle. Especially the blame I had put on myself. After enough counseling, I realized I had no control over him or his addiction.

I have to force my body to physically turn away from the rugs. *Focus, Micky. You have stuff to do today.* The sofas at IKEA are similar in aesthetics. The IKEA aesthetic. I wish I'd taken measurements before I left the house. Who forgets to measure their room before they buy a couch? I haven't lived in the apartment long enough to confidently say how much space I have. Can I fit a L-shaped couch in that area . . . maybe? My ass jumps from cushion to cushion seeing which one makes it happiest.

The winner is a boring gray one with a low back and storage underneath. There. Decision made. I write down the number code so I can pick up the pieces when I get to the flat-pack warehouse.

On the way to the desks, I pass the shower curtains and grab a new one, plus a couple of new liners. Rhys might need a new one too.

The desk options are more abundant than the sofas. Shit, I'm going to need a desk chair too. Meh, I'll use a chair from the kitchen. I hope I can fit all this in Mr. Hayes's truck bed. A light pine rectangle desk with a long drawer along the top catches my eye. Again, I write down the number and keep moving.

Normally, I'm not one to splurge, but I decided on the way over I would buy a plant today. Plants always help make things better. There are shelves of them looking for loving homes. Two will be adopted by me today. Lucky little guys. I swap my small cart for a flatbed and transfer my pile of goods so I can collect the furniture from the warehouse. An announcement from above alerts shoppers that IKEA will close in thirty minutes. I made it just in time.

While standing in the checkout line, my eyes land on the chocolate bars. I look away, but my gaze slowly returns. Damn it. I swipe a few off the shelf and throw them in my bag like it's their fault I'm so hungry.

It is not an easy task for someone of my size to load up all these boxes into the truck bed. Luckily, everything fits and I don't need to strap anything down. But I need to get home soon because it looks like it might rain. The last thing I want is to have to deal with a bunch of waterlogged sofa cushions. Thank God I have the truck to get all this stuff home, or I'd be in serious trouble. But getting them home and carrying them up the stairs are two very different things. Should be interesting.

Twenty minutes into the thirty-minute drive home, the rain hits.

Out-fucking-standing.

A little rain is okay, I can deal with this. I just need to get home and hope the rain doesn't turn torrential within the next ten minutes. Besides, the plants that got wedged in the back are getting a nice drink of water. *Look at me seeing the glass half full and shit.*

After pulling up to the apartment, I quickly hop out and start pulling flatpacks out of the truck and hauling them inside the door. I'll get it up the stairs in a minute, right now my priority is getting the cardboard out of the rain before it disintegrates on me. By the time I get the desk in, each box seems heavier than the last. *Lack of sleep and food will do that to a person.* I break a sweat moving as fast as I can, but the clouds open up and downpour as I get the last two boxes in. The cardboard is slippery, and my hands keep losing grip as I pull it out of the truck bed.

Finally, the last box is carried inside the small entry door now crowded with IKEA cardboard. I look up the long straight stairway and cringe. Time for a break. And a chocolate bar. I sit down on one of the boxes and plow through what's left of my candy. Rain streaks down the windows, and it's strangely soothing. I'm surrendering to the day. The night with Anna. The interaction with Rhys. The thoughts of Kyle. The wet cardboard. I'm having a bad day.

Once the chocolate is gone, I stuff the wrapper in my pocket and get to work. Tugging one box at a time up the stairs and into my living room. The open space where the couch used to be will be filled with flatpacks in no time. I'd be annoyed by how many trips I have to take, but if the boxes were any bigger, I probably wouldn't have the strength to pull them up the stairs. I'm really out of shape.

As I grab my next box, the other apartment door opens. *No, no, no,* I whine. Dragging boxes up stairs is not the smoothest of techniques, but I was still hoping it was quiet enough to not draw any attention to myself. I keep my head down but can already hear his footsteps heading toward me.

# FOURTEEN

## *Rhys*

H er clothes are drenched. She's halfway up the stairs, struggling to haul soggy cardboard boxes into her apartment. Somehow she makes it look sexy. Especially those frustrated little grunts.

"Can I help you with that?"

"No, I got it!" Her words have bite. Just when she finishes snapping at me, the box slips from her arms and almost goes careening back down the stairs. Luckily, I get a hold on it. This is the second time I've had to catch something she's dropped. It's not clumsiness, this box is almost as big as she is. Besides, I've seen her balance pretty impressive trays of drinks in the past.

"I can handle it." She's glaring at me like she'd rather put out a campfire with her face than let me help her.

"Go open your door, and I'll carry in the rest for you."

"I can do it!"

*She obviously needs help, and her tough-girl routine is getting on my nerves.*

"Goddamn it, Freya! Will you stop being so stubborn, and just let me do something for you?"

"That's rich," she says under her breath.

Huffing up the stairs in squeaky, waterlogged shoes, she opens the door. *That wasn't so hard, was it?* She shoves aside the pile of boxes in her entryway to make room for this one. I set it on the ground and go back to get the remaining flat-packs. This is a lot to assemble for one person. I have no doubt she can do it, but it will be a pain in the ass.

When I get into her apartment, I actually have time to take in everything. Last time I was here, I was so focused on my sister I didn't have the chance to look around. Her decor is industrial. The apartments are a tad industrial with the exposed brick, high ceilings, and black windowpanes. So it's an easy leap. Still, it's very masculine for someone with curves like hers. The space smells like her perfume and shampoo.

"Okay, well, thanks for helping me move these boxes. And, um, here." She thrusts a shower curtain in my arms. "In case you need it."

"That was very thoughtful of you."

"I'm a thoughtful person," she snaps. It's such a contradiction to the sentiment that a small laugh rises from my throat. Her voice calms, and she glances behind me. "Well, you know where the door is."

I will not leave her here in this mess. "Where's your box cutter?"

"What?"

"*Where-is-your-box-cut-ter?*"

"I heard you, dickhead. Why are you asking?"

"We'll need it to open the cardboard boxes." It comes out slightly more condescending than I mean it to, but I'm aggravated.

"We?"

"You helped me, now I'm helping you."

She bites the inside of her cheek and narrows her eyes. Scrutinizing my face like she can't tell whether I'm serious. I suppose that's warranted.

"Fine . . .The box cutter's in one of those top drawers, be careful cutting anything, I don't need my couch ripped before it even gets put together." She gestures to the far end of the kitchen counter. "Be back in a sec, I'm going to put on some dry clothes."

"Can I help?"

"Fuck you," she singsongs, walking down the back hallway toward her bedroom, holding up her middle finger. My amused grin grows wider. *Shit, she's grumpy tonight.*

Kind of wish she meant it, because even looking like a drowned sewer rat, I'd tap that *so hard*. Walking into the kitchen, I open the first drawer. It's her aprons that she wears on her live streams. This one on top with the cherries brings back lots of happy memories. I vividly recall jerking off to the image of her in this, not only the time she wore it on camera, but also every time I was in the shower for the whole week after.

She comes out of the hallway in dry yoga pants and another baggy sweatshirt, wrapping her hair into a messy bun. "Did you find the—what are you doing?"

"These cherries were the hottest," I say, matter-of-factly.

"Don't talk about my fuckin' cherries! I'm still mad at you."

"For what? I apologized."

She rolls her eyes. "For making me trust you. For watching me naked after you found out who I was, and for leading me to believe you were . . . different. I really liked you. And if you recorded our phone . . . session, that could ruin my reputation."

"Pretty sure I was there jacking off with you. How do I know you didn't record me?"

"There was nothing showing that would identify you. I've been very good about trying to keep my identity hidden. All of my tattoos were visible in that shot."

"Would it make you feel better if I gave you a video of me getting off?"

"Are you crazy?"

"Do you want to find out?"

She purses her lips, trying not to smile, and her eyes flicker with something sinful. If we ever get to move past this resentment and do something about the tension between us, I will take my time reminding her how much we once liked each other.

"You're ridiculous. This doesn't get you out of giving me an actual apology for being such an asshole. Or for lying to me."

"You're right. I'm sorry."

She watches me expectantly with one raised eyebrow. If she's looking for more than that, she'll be waiting a long time.

"Anything else?" She prods.

"Nope."

"Wow. You suck at apologies."

I shrug. I'm not all that sorry. Getting to know her was worth it.

"I don't know what kind of point you're trying to make here. You're really gonna spend your Monday night putting together furniture with me?"

"If that's what it takes to knock that hard-as-fuck chip of your shoulder."

"My chip is valid," she mutters as she pads into the living room among the forest of cardboard. "I don't understand what's happening here. Is this you trying to be friends, or do you just want to clear your conscience so you can sleep at night?"

"Can't it be both?"

"I have no idea who you are. Is this Jekyll or Hyde? Hat Trick Swayze or my dickknob neighbor?"

"Can't it be both?"

"No! It can't. Give me that instruction packet." She waves her hand toward the sofa.

"We don't need instructions." I ignore her request and remove the upholstered pieces from some boxes.

"I want to make sure you're not doing it wrong."

I throw the instructions at her. *Gah, she's annoying.* I remind myself this is the same woman who cleaned up my sister's literal shit last night, and take a deep breath. *Well, well, well, if it isn't the consequences of my actions.*

She unfolds the assembly manual until it's a map bigger than she is. Behind the paper, she grumbles, "I can put together my own furniture, you know."

"I know you can, babe. But I've also put this sofa together once before, so I can tell you from experience, it's a lot easier with a friend."

"There's that word again . . ." she says on a sigh, turning the map of instructions around.

I throw up my hands. She's insufferable.

"God, talking to you is like pulling teeth. Fuck, you're guarded! How come you were so open with me when we chatted online?"

The flash in her eyes tells me she's ready to fight now. Makes me wonder what the hell we were doing before. *Yikes.*

"You pulled the rug out from under me! I don't know who you are at all! In person you barely acknowledge me, and when you do, it's just to provoke or cut me down. You're an asshole. I wish you never would've subscribed to me."

*Oooh, she's bad for my blood pressure.* I clench my jaw.

"I'm an asshole because I don't want to be involved with you!" I bark.

"Wow, fuckin', Dick Tracy, everyone." She scoffs and shakes her head. "I'm *well* aware you don't want involvement with me. You have made that very obvious at almost every interaction. Which brings me back to my question: Why.

The. Fuck. Are. You. Here?" She punctuates each word with a clap.

"I didn't mean it like that. I can't stop this attraction for you. But I wish I could," I say, yanking out more boards and sending the empty cardboard box sailing across the room.

Her face scrunches, and she rubs the wrinkle between her brows. "Oh my God. We're going in circles. Nevermind." Her attention returns to the two boards she's putting together.

"You're impossible to stay away from. Everywhere I look, there you are. So I'm done fighting it. I'm throwing in the towel. Let me get to know you more."

Maybe we'll never get what we had on *Followers* back. Online, she's a dream. She's sweet, charming, and funny. In person? She's a fucking trip. Yes, some of that is my doing. *Okay, a lot of it is my doing.* But she gets on my nerves too.

Her stomach growls. *When was the last time she ate?*

Since meeting her, it's like I'm in a sea of men throwing money at her. *Followers*, at the bar, everywhere I go. I refuse to wait in line and beg at her feet with the rest of them. If I'm to have something with Freya, there will be no sharing her. She was too casual about doing it for side money. I don't believe that. There's only two reasons women go online to show off their bodies: One, they desperately need the money, or two, they genuinely love doing it. I suspect it's the latter for Freya, and she just doesn't want to admit that she relishes all the attention. It's possible there's more to it, but I'll never find out because getting close to her is damn near impossible. The walls she puts up around her are thicker than the Hoover Dam.

I get she's pissed, but Christ Almighty, put the playlist on shuffle. It drives me insane. I don't want *just* the feistiness, but I also don't want *just* Queen of Tarts. It's the combination that's so irresistible. At the moment, she's only giving me the wild rebel.

"I miss the Queen of Tarts."

She keeps her focus on sorting through one of the plastic bags of bolts, screws, and washers. Her stomach growls again, this time louder than before. "There's a million other content creators on *Followers* willing to show you their tits. Have at 'em."

If we're going to argue all night, she's going to have to eat some food first. Besides, I could eat. I open a meal delivery app and pull up one of my usual places. I feel her eyes boring into me, and she clears her throat a couple times like she's getting impatient with me. If she has something to say, she can come out and say it. None of that passive-aggressive bullshit. When I don't respond, she begins what I can only describe as rage-Allen-wrenching. I finish typing in her apartment number instead of mine when she throws the tool down.

"I didn't mean for you to look them up now. I thought you were here to help me."

I'll let her assume whatever she wants. I toss my phone on the rug and stare her down while grabbing the two big pieces sitting next to her.

"Come here. Hold this at ninety degrees while I screw the side in."

After hesitating, she eventually gives in and sits next to me to hold the parts as I instructed. Her scent is different from before. It's not the soft floral scent she wore earlier. Whatever she's wearing now is more seductive. She's dangerously close, it would be so easy to sink my fingers into her sides and pull her into me.

"It's sexy when you do what I say," I mutter.

"You're the worst." Her voice has softened. Finally, the friction in the room is dissipating.

"Alright, I'm going to flip it up on its side, so you're going to have to use your big-girl muscles and hold it steady while I attach the hardware."

"'K'."

That's the first thing she's said all night that isn't laced with animosity, and it's not even a full word. I feel her eyes on me. My ego can't resist peeking at her. Sure enough, she's checking out my arms with zero shame as I hold up one end of the sofa. Our eyes meet, and she averts her gaze immediately.

My lips curve into a half smirk. "Saw that."

We finish building the rest of the sofa in silence. The desk comes together easier, until I fuck up the drawer rollers and accidentally install them upside down. If that's the biggest mistake I make tonight, I'll be in good shape. Unfortunately, all my mistakes have to do with her. And based on her hostility this evening, they'll take a lot longer to fix.

As I'm finishing adding one of the last parts, the food arrives. She pads over to the door and stands on her tiptoes to look out the peephole. If she hadn't been spitting venom all night, I might actually think it was cute. She opens the door.

"Sorry, I didn't order—"

"Aye!" I push off the floor. "Yeah. Yeah, that's for us."

I hand him a cash tip and take the tall, warm paper bag from his arms and thank him before kicking the door shut behind me.

"I wasn't looking up new *Followers* earlier, I was ordering food. I could hear your stomach growling from across the room," I tell her, laying out the food on her kitchen island. "Get over here, I know you're hungry."

She drops the pieces in her hands and tries to coolly walk over to the kitchen. It's obvious she's starving, but she's too proud to say anything.

"What did you order?"

"Thai."

"I'm allergic to peanuts."

The container in my hand freezes in midair. "Are you shitting me?"

"Yes." She gives me the first real grin of the night. It's small, but it's a start.

I shake my head. *Didn't anyone ever teach this girl not to joke about allergies?* She's been poking this bear all night.

"For future reference, do you have any allergies I should know about?"

"I'm not allergic to anything. You?"

"Nope." I hold out a plastic fork for her.

"Thanks."

She hoists herself on the countertop and pops the top off her steaming plastic container of pad Thai.

"You eat on the counter often?"

She looks at me like she didn't even realize it was an odd thing to do.

"Sorry, I'm not used to having people over. Birdie and I always ate on the counter. I guess I never broke the habit after she left. Feel free to sit at the kitchen table I never use, or there's bar stools around the island." She nods at the chairs.

"Hell no, scoot over."

She hides her smile by looking down into her food.

"Wait! First, how much do you weigh?"

"First of all, that's rude," I say, hiking my ass up next to hers, we're practically touching. "Second, these are granite. It could probably hold three of me."

We eat in silence, side by side. She doesn't say another word. Watching her wrap those pouty lips around her fork is making my dick twitch. I grip the container of food tighter. I don't want to take my eyes off her, but if I don't, my zipper will snap. I take a deep inhale and breathe out. *Change of subject, Kucera. Think.*

"Want to hear a joke?"

"Sure."

"How do you make an old lady say fuck?"

"How?"

"Make another old lady say bingo."

She smiles a little more and even gives a small receptive chuckle. Cracking her hard shell feels like such an accomplishment. I want to pump my fist.

"Reminds me of my grandma."

"The one that passed?"

"Yeah, she swore like a sailor. And *loved* Bingo."

I nod, and we return to quietly stuffing our faces. Though, this time the silence isn't as cold. It's almost pleasant. Comfortable.

"So . . ." I begin. "When do I get that bread lesson?"

I see the moment she physically locks back up again. *Too soon.*

"Never. We're not friends."

"Wanna settle for frenemies?" This woman is such a pain in the ass. *Come off it already.* I'm probably wasting my time trying to get closer to her. But I can't dismiss the magnetism between us, and my brain keeps holding onto the nugget that before she knew I was *Hat Trick Swayze*, every single one of our conversations had chemistry. That seems to all have gone out the window when my identity came to the surface. But it has to still exist somehow. If only she'd stop fighting it.

# FIFTEEN

## Micky

I wake up the next morning to a text message. When I grab it off my nightstand, I see it's from Rhys.

RHYS

I'm trusting you not to post this, but here's some insurance for you to hold on to.

He didn't. A second later a follow-up message comes through. It's a video clip. *Did he seriously send me a sex tape?* My fingers fumble to close my messages app and lock my phone. I place it next to me on the bed. Then pick it up again and go back to his message. I squint at the video thumbnail to see if there's anything visible. I'm curious. It's for me to keep and use if I need it for blackmail. But I kind of want to use it for my own purposes . . . This situation would be so much easier if physical attraction was not a factor. I'm constantly horny these days, it's fucking ridiculous.

I could just watch it once to make sure it's what he says it is. This could be a video of anything. He watched me plenty of times on *Followers* after he knew it was me. That's basically the same thing. I keep my eyes closed against the light filtering through the curtains.

*"Are you crazy?"*

*"Do you want to find out?"*

Without thinking, I press play.

The video opens to him setting up his phone on a bench at the end of his bed that faces a tall mirror. I roll my eyes. *Of course he's one of those guys with a huge mirror at the end of his bed.* He's wearing his jersey for added identification, but it's not long before that's being tossed on the bed behind him and he stands there unbuckling his jeans and pushing them lower —he's hard and not wearing any underwear. In the mirror's reflection, he stares down the camera lens. It sends a chill up my spine. Taking a seat, he slowly strokes himself base to tip. I had more of a top view when we had phone sex, but this is something else entirely. If Rhys ever got an injury, he could make a killing as a porn star. Maybe *he* should start his own *Followers* account.

"Freya, I'm trusting you to be a good girl and not share this with anyone."

I smile at the way he says my name. This video is custom-made for me.

*Holy shit, this is hot.*

My hand creeps into my sleep shorts. My eyes stay fixed on his body, away from his dumb handsome face. I tell myself I'm mastur*hating*. It's all lies. Secretly, *I'm loving this.*

This is top tier amateur solo porn, I'm impressed. Is this how Rhys felt when I would give him private videos on *Followers*? No wonder he tipped well.

*Focus.* While he fists the thick erection, I rub small circles to the same rhythm, paying notice of the way he gets himself off. He switches up his rhythm every now and then, like he's edging himself. During our FaceTime session, I told him what to do, but here he's in control of himself, and I love it.

"Fuck, Freya."

Shit, he was thinking about me during this. Does he

imagine me on my knees or my back? Is he taking me from behind in his fantasy? I trace my opening and slide two fingers inside. His muscles flex as he speeds up, and his throat bobs as he leans back on one elbow. He quickly pumps himself. The thick muscles in his thighs twitch, and he lets out a groan. He's about to finish. *Jesus Christ.* It's an incredible view.

Suddenly I'm aware of my heavy breathing. Giving the attention back to my clit makes my back arch, but I keep my eyes on the screen, I don't want to miss a second of this, and I'm getting close. All of his muscles are pulled taut. He's completely falling apart to the thought of me.

All at once he stops, braces himself with a hand on either side of him, his still-hard cock pointing toward heaven. He growls something low, but I can't hear it. I frantically turn up my volume and back the video up a few seconds. It's barely audible, but it's there. "*That's my good slut, Freya girl.*" Every muscle in his body seems to flex as he comes hands-free.

My mouth drops open.

*I can hardly think, I'm so turned on.* Being degraded has never gotten me off before, but hearing it in his voice? It's exactly what I need to finish. His rumbled moan when he comes is my undoing. I curse and my hips buck as the orgasm rolls through me.

That video is the hottest thing I've ever seen.

As soon as my orgasm fades, I wait for the feeling of shame and regret to creep in and take its place. But they don't.

I'm fucking freezing. Perhaps I should stand on a heated blanket. Sure, my nipples look happy, but at what cost? Besides, this live stream isn't as entertaining now that Hat Trick Swayze isn't here. Despite finding out he and my nemesis are the same person, my eyes were still jumping to the queue of viewers to see if he joined. I miss seeing his username there. It was something I looked forward to because it usually spurred some fun discussion later on.

It also means I'm not bringing in as many tips as I normally do. He consistently started early by dropping down a Benjamin, and it always triggered more from other members vying for attention. The biggest tip I've gotten today is twenty dollars. Not complaining, money is money, but it's slowing down my progress. If the rest of the streams are like this, it will set me back at least a couple months. There's a domino effect of Rhys and the impact he's had on my life. How can someone I despise have such a big influence?

I was anticipating to close on that rental space sooner. Might need to up my video quantities, or post more-revealing content, which I'd prefer not to do. Not that I have anything against the other creators who post explicit videos—get that paper, ladies; rob them blind—but it was a boundary I set for myself in the beginning, and I plan to stick to it. I get enough rude messages as it is. I don't know how the other women do it.

Besides, I've been so tired lately. Which is why I'm phoning it in today with chocolate chip cookies. They're damn good, but I'm usually making something more involved than drop cookies. I'm not in the mood to be "on" for everyone today, but the more engaging I am, the better the revenue. *Fake it while they spank it, right?*

I make a few jokes and interact with some of the other viewers, but none are him. I used to tell myself it wasn't him that made me swoon, it was only the familiarity between us. But BigGuy69 is in the room, he's been a loyal subscriber and has always been kind and sweet. So why don't I get butterflies for him the way I did every time Hat Trick Swayze showed up? It added excitement to filming live streams, knowing he was there. He became part of the reason I did it. I loved the stirring anticipation that built all week as I waited for the flirty conversations I'd been accustomed to. Now everything is dull. Even the twinkle lights behind me don't seem to glow as bright.

It's funny, the whole time that flutter in my stomach was happening he was typing on the other side of my apartment wall. I want to believe Rhys genuinely has the capacity to be the person I knew on *Followers*. Maybe I should cut him some slack. I've lashed out at him at every opportunity—and my anger was warranted.

If I ease up on him, it will only be as a probationary period. I'm holding him to Hat Trick Swayze standards going forward.

We aren't at bar capacity tonight, but there's been a steady stream of customers for the last couple hours. Now that the weeknight happy hour crowd has filtered out, things are slowing down. The lull allows me to get caught up on some behind-the-bar housekeeping. Amanda and I wipe down the counters, bring out the clean glasses from the dishwasher, check on garnishes, and chop up a few more limes.

I'm pulling out a new sleeve of cardboard coasters, busy dreaming about Sugar & Ice, when my thoughts are interrupted by Amanda clearing her throat. She nods to the end of the bar. Sometime in the last thirty seconds, Rhys sat down near a group of older college boys. He fits in with their age group, wonder how old he is, anyway? Can't be much older than any of them, I've probably got at least five years on him. *There's an easy way to find out.*

"What can I get for you?"

"Whatever I had last time, thanks."

I lean over the bar. "Can I see your ID?"

He stalls for a moment.

"You've never carded me before."

"You've got an innocent baby face. I have to check."

He most certainly does not, and his eyes narrow at my remark.

After handing me his license, he looks over at the group of college boys nearby. "She card you?"

All of them shake their heads.

I hand it back. He's twenty-four, I was close.

After popping the cap, I slide the beer in front of him.

"Interesting that you remembered what drink I ordered last time."

"Bartender brain." I tap my temple and grin. That's not entirely true. He's ordered something different almost every time, but somehow, I remember them. What a waste of knowledge. I could have filled that space in my brain with something useful. Like the migration pattern of whales. Or the capital of Kentucky.

"Hey, sweetheart, can I get another one?" one of the other guys asks.

"She's not your sweetheart." Rhys chuckles, staring straight ahead as he takes a swig of beer.

"Don't listen to him. I'll be your sweetheart." I say pleasantly. "Lemme get you that beer."

Annoyance radiates off him. I stealthily peek in the mirror behind the bar. His eyes are already on me. His tongue pressed to his cheek, and he shakes his head. Those usually light-hazel eyes seem much darker. I peer back at him while swapping out an empty bottle for a new one.

I chat with the boys; they are all heading into their final semester. We discuss their majors and what they are into. Rhys keeps cutting eyes over to us. Eventually they cash out. They are heading over to Citra Brewing, safe from Rhys's death glares, and they invite me to check out some live music with them after my shift. I give them a lukewarm *maybe* and then we exchange information.

Rhys grumbles something as they sign their receipts, and I try to act hospitable enough to make up for his dickery. He's intimidating our clientele. After waving goodbye, I turn my focus on him.

Bracing myself with open arms against the bar, I lean in. "What are you doing?"

"Enjoying this delicious beer and the lovely company of my hellcat."

*My* hellcat.

"Don't you have some skates that need sharpening? Or a stick that needs taping? Perhaps a toaster that needs a bath?"

"Nope, I'm right where I'm meant to be." His lips turn up in a cocksure smile. He leans back, relaxed, his threaded fingers resting comfortably behind his head. Pleased with himself.

"Didn't I make myself clear the last time you interfered? If I need your help, I will ask for it. How do you expect me to make any money if you keep scaring off my customers?" I whisper-shout.

"Oh, I could think of a few ways." *That sly smirk.*

If he wants to be obscene, I'll call his bluff.

"I'd *love* to hear your ideas."

"I mean, I'm still waiting for you to teach me how to bake bread."

*This shit again?*

"I told you! YouTube!"

He quickly leans forward so we're practically nose to nose. "I don't want to learn on YouTube. I want to learn from you." He jabs his index finger on the bartop. *Fuck.* I forgot how rough his voice becomes when he's angry.

I'm so exasperated with him and this damn bread lesson thing. I study his face. "Fine. But it's going to cost you."

"Name your price."

"A thousand dollars. Take it or leave it." If he takes the offer, I'm a grand richer, and if he leaves it, I won't have to listen to him ask about bread ever again. *Win-win.*

"Done." *What?*

"I want the money up front," I add as a clause.

"I'll drop it off tonight."

My head tilts to one side. He's being ridiculous. "Rhys, why are you doing this?"

"When is my lesson?"

My mouth doesn't move. I can't fathom somebody paying a thousand dollars to learn something so simple. *Hat Trick Swayze wanted to learn how to bake bread, this is him showing himself.*

"Wednesday at four. If you're a minute late, the lesson will be canceled, I keep your money, and you'll owe me another thousand just for wasting my fucking time."

His smile says he won. And maybe he did.

Rhys pays his tab and heads back upstairs through the rear stairwell. Still no tip for drinks. He's paying enough for the dumb bread lesson, I don't care if he never tips for his drinks again.

Two hours later, I clock out. I don't go to Citra to watch live music. I go home to snuggle up in bed and watch a movie. Alone. My pillow is tucked into my side, my arms squeezed around it. Maybe I should get a dog if it's the loneliness that's getting me down. But dogs cost money, and deep down, I know it's not just that. I want human companionship. Someone who I can come home to and who'll ask about my night at work. Against my leg, my phone vibrates with a text message.

RHYS

How was the rest of your night at work?

## SIXTEEN

*Rhys*

My trainer has me sprinting back and forth on the green turf in the Lakes' athletic room. Every couple sprints, he changes the distance at which I need to decelerate. Charging at a dead run and stopping at the drop of a hat is a bitch. I'm relieved when we wrap up. I still have another hour of strength and conditioning after this.

The coaches say that my technique is getting better, and I'm hitting all the benchmarks, but there's a few things I need to improve upon. Thankfully, we'll work through them next time. A few of the other guys are in their own lanes running drills. It's crazy how fast they are. *Do I look that fast when I run them?*

I squeeze my water bottle, shooting water into my mouth after my last squat jump with the second trainer. My muscles burn, but they go harder on us whenever we get a few extra days between games. The music coming from my earbuds motivates me to keep my reps up and pace each lift. It's easy to zone out, but unfortunately, every time I do, it strays to Freya or Anna.

Between Freya coming around and Anna getting clean, it's

an upswing. Spending time with my sister while she's sober gives me so much hope. She's turning a corner in her life. I don't remember the last time she hung around for two weeks straight. Granted, she said her apartment is having construction done and it's been noisy, so that might account for her recent occupancy. I don't mind, it's nice to have someone around, we usually have dinner together when I'm home. She's been staying at my place and trying to find a new job during the day. I'm proud of how hard she's working.

Freya has tolerated me well in our last few interactions. I wonder if she watched the video I sent her or saved it for when I eventually fuck up. For now, I'm making headway, though I still don't know what the hell I'm doing with her. After everything with Anna, it was like something snapped in me. I didn't care about my no-dating rule anymore. Life will pass me by either way. When Mom and Dad died, I became numb, but when I'm with her, I feel something. I don't want to lose that.

She gives me a rush the way hockey does. Like she's someone I could devote myself to. And dominate. I've seen the guys take home any women that saddles up next to them at the bar, and it's just not my bag. Avoiding women was easy when it was other women.

*But Freya* . . . She's my dream girl. How often does that come around? When we're not at each other's throats, we're like hot chocolate and snowy mornings. Unfortunately, I had committed myself to ignoring her so much that switching gears has proven challenging. Yesterday I went out and picked her up some things as a thank-you for her help with Anna, just some items that needed replacing. Like her cleaning supplies and a few clothes. I mean, she loaned Anna her underwear. *I don't want to check her out and wonder if she's wearing the same underwear my sister had on.*

I wrap up a set and grab my water bottle, wiping my brow with the hem of my shirt. What are the odds that I ended up next door, in the only two apartments, to Queen of Tarts? I don't believe in fate, but if I did, this would be damning evidence. Do I feel guilty for not exposing my identity immediately? A little, but I was still getting my head out of my ass.

She just needed some time to cool down. Hell, we put furniture together. Pretty sure assembling IKEA furniture and remodeling a kitchen are the top two ways to find out if you can actually work together. We got in each other's face a few times, but it was mostly her getting all that pent-up anger out of her system. I wouldn't mind getting that aggression out another way . . . but this isn't the place to start daydreaming.

I picked up some Dilly Bars from Dairy Queen on the way home. It's a nostalgic thing for us; Mom and Dad would stop by after church every Sunday, and we would each get one. I haven't had one in ages, but today seemed like a good day for it. Balancing the box of ice cream and my gym bag, I shoulder the door open and throw my duffel down.

"Yo! I brought home DQ, if you want a bar before it melts you better get your ass out here."

Walking into the kitchen, I toss some of my stuff down. I expect to hear her run out, but I'm met with silence. She's probably out looking for a job or something. Walking to the kitchen, I start unwrapping one for myself and notice a note on the counter: *Went to get groceries. Lasagna night!*

Sweet, I haven't had homemade lasagna in forever.

After a shower, I climb into bed for a nap. Today's workout kicked my ass.

When I wake up, I check my phone for the time. Damn, I was out for a few hours. Guess I needed the sleep. Stepping out of my room, I don't see any sign of life. I check her room. Empty.

> Hey. Where are you?
>
> What happened to lasagna?
>
> Anna
>
> Dude, just text me back.

She ran. *Goddamn it.*

I thought she was finally getting it together. I walk across the hall and knock on Freya's door, just in case she came over here. My mind considers all the places she could be. Things were going so well.

Light footsteps get closer as she pads toward the door. There's a pause, she's probably checking the peephole. Thankfully she opens.

"Hey. Is Anna here by any chance?"

I hand her a Dilly Bar. Freya tilts her head to the side with pursed lips. She side-eyes me and gingerly takes the ice cream as if it's a bomb that's about to detonate.

"Thank you?" She looks cute in her skirt paired with a Biggie Smalls tee. I don't quite understand her fashion, but it works. "No, sorry. She's not here. Did she take off?"

I rub between my eyes with my thumb and forefinger. "Yeah. I think so."

She must see the disappointment on my face because she invites me in. I take a seat on the couch she and I assembled. It looks good in the space. Comfortable. Though it does little to comfort me right now.

"Want something to drink? I've got sparkling water, ginger ale, beer, or we can bust out the heavy stuff . . ."

"Sparkling water's fine. Thanks." I don't drink when I'm angry.

"Any specific flavor?" she asks.

"Surprise me."

"Didn't you learn your lesson the last time you asked me to *surprise* you with a drink?" she says, opening the can with a hiss and pouring it over ice. "Did she tell you where she's living?"

"I know where she lives, I pay the rent. It's more so that she's not responding to my texts."

"Do you pay the rent or give her money for rent?"

I'm smart enough not to fork over a couple thousand a month in cash.

"Her rent is on autopay out of my account, I don't give her cash or checks for rent if that's what you're asking."

"When was the last time you were there?"

Why is she asking me all these questions, does she—*oh no. No . . . Anna wouldn't sublease it. Would she?* "You don't think . . ."

She cringes and pulls up her shoulders. "She told me she's been couch surfing, which probably means she's staying with friends or crashing at other houses."

She means drug dens.

"Shit." *God, Anna. Why can't things ever be easy with you?*

Leaning forward, I rest my elbows on my knees and rake my fingers through my hair, I need to figure something out.

"Are you giving her any other money?"

"No, not really . . ." I'm so annoyed at her for taking advantage of me. *Again.*

"Not really?" she prods.

I don't appreciate her tone. I'm doing the best I can.

"I gave her some money for groceries." She said she wanted to make dinner. She used to love cooking. I was under the impression she was trying to get back to her old self.

"Do you want my advice?"

"No, but it sounds like I need it."

If she's telling me not to take care of the only family I have left, she's wasting her time. Anna is my responsibility. She got into pills because of me. I'm all she has. There's no one else looking out for her.

She tucks a strand of hair behind her ear and meets my gaze. "I'm going to tell you this from experience, you need to set some boundaries. For your sake and hers. You cannot give her money anymore. None."

"What am I supposed to do? Let her starve and be homeless?"

"Okay, first rule of dealing with addicts is that you have zero control over her addiction or actions. That's her baggage. If she's homeless or hungry, that's not on you. You set boundaries, if she breaks them, there are consequences. She'll see it like you're giving her an ultimatum and will likely try to use it against you, but you gotta stay firm.

"For example, she can come to your house, but she can't bring drugs or friends that use drugs into your home. If she does, the consequence is that she's no longer welcome. If she decides to play fuck around and find out with the police, you will not pay her bail or any of her legal fees. You rented her an apartment, she chose to sublease it and take the cash, so she no longer gets the money. If that's indeed what's happening, reach out to whoever's living there and have them pay you directly. Get the idea? But the most important thing is that you follow through with the consequences or she'll walk all over you."

Jesus. She doesn't know Anna, she won't go along with any of that.

"Why do you know all this?

"Told you, I dated an addict."

I lean back into the couch and groan, scrubbing my hands down my face.

"Why can't she ever seem to get her shit together? I

shouldn't have to jump through so many hoops for her. I've made it so easy. Her only requirement is to stay clean."

Freya looks at me, there's sadness in her eyes. Like she's ashamed *for* me. "I know, it sucks, but she's not in the driver's seat. Any money she gets is going straight up her nose."

I narrow my eyes, it sounds so depraved when she says it that way. "Don't say it like that."

"Why? Does it make it sound too dirty? Addiction is ugly, Rhys. And you need to start questioning her motives—especially when things are going well. She's going to break your trust over and over again. It's exhausting. I'm sorry to throw all of this on you at once, but I don't want you to sink like I did." She stares off into space like she's trudging up old memories. After blinking a few times, she takes a sip of her water and furrows her brow. "Has anyone in your family gone to a Nar-Anon meeting?"

*What family?* I take a sip of my bubbly lime sparkling water, and it fizzles on my tongue. "No, it's just us."

She purses her lips and nods toward the floor. "Shit, I'm sorry. That's really hard, but it doesn't need to fall solely on you . . . If you can get yourself to a meeting, it might help with some of the stress. Give you some support. Setting those limits is really, really important for your own mental health. It doesn't mean you *can't* help her, but you need to protect yourself too."

Her logic makes sense, but one is easier said than done. I'm afraid if I push Anna too hard, she'll leave for good. Growing up, our parents told us we were to watch out for each other when they were gone, so that's what I'm trying to do.

"Your ex ever get better?"

"Nope." She pops the P. There must be a story there because she turns and walks away after saying it. Maybe she's still hung up on the guy. He'd be a dumbass to let go of a girl

127

like her. Either way, it's obvious she doesn't want to talk about it.

She clears her throat. "So, there's something—"

"Oh! I have some stuff for you. One sec, let me grab it."

Back in my apartment, I call out Anna's name one more time, just in case. As expected, no answer. My hands wrap around the bag handles and piles of clothes, and I haul them into her apartment.

"Whoa. Rhys. What's all this?" she asks, her eyes wide.

"These are your pajamas." I stack them on top. "No offense, some of your pj's could use an update, and after what they went through that night, I took some liberties and picked up a few things. If you don't like them, the gift receipt is in the bag. I got your sizes from the tags, so I hope everything fits." I check some of the other bags. "Um . . . here's cleaning supplies, since I'm sure you went through a lot of it that night." *I sure as hell did.* "A shower curtain . . . some new bedding—"

"You bought me sheets?"

"I'm just replacing some things that might have been damaged," I explain.

"Rhys, this is a lot. You didn't need to do this. I was a human taking care of another human. That's it. It's not a big deal."

"It is a big deal. After everything Anna told me, I'm still coming out ahead here. I'm grateful you were there that night. Please, let me do this."

"Well, thanks. This is really nice," she replies sincerely.

Her response is so heartfelt I almost do a double take. She possesses a gentle softness that balances all her hard parts. *The side of her she hides.* The one I've only witnessed when chatting through a computer screen. Replacing some of her items is the absolute minimum. She may have saved Anna's life that night, all I did was run some errands.

Also, there are items hidden at the bottom of the bag I hope I get to see her wear before I die. I walked by that damn high-end boutique four times before finally giving in. Even if I don't get to see them in person, knowing she is wearing them under her clothes will make me smile.

# SEVENTEEN

## Micky

was so close to telling him about the money she took, but even after I started bringing it up, I wanted to take it back. It was a relief when he interrupted me. He looked so downtrodden that she left again. I'll bring it up eventually, but the timing wasn't right.

Wow, I can't believe he bought all this. There's enough cleaning supplies to last me through the apocalypse. I should give all this shit back to him, but these sheets are Egyptian cotton. And I want them.

Most of the pajamas are nicer than what I would buy myself, some a tad more revealing, but nothing out of the ordinary as far as sleepwear goes. I rifle through the bags more until my eye catches something black. And strappy. *What in the . . . this motherfucker—*

> Did you buy me lingerie?

RHYS

Doesn't sound like something I'd do . . .

> Yes, it does. It absolutely does. Where are the gift receipts for these? They aren't in the bag.

RHYS

No receipts? So weird . . .

Look, you're not supposed to share
underwear with strangers. I wasn't going to
give you back the same ones. They're just
replacements for what you already had.

Yeah, I don't remember giving your sister
any thongs.

Or this black strappy thing.

Garters. Wow.

This lace bodysuit is pretty though . . . I don't even know
how to begin putting this other thing on, it crisscrosses
everywhere.

RHYS

Made me think of you.

Why's that?

RHYS

Because they're dark and complicated to
figure out.

And really fucking sexy.

I'm thankful he can't see the blush on my cheeks.

RHYS

If you don't want it, I'll take it all back . . .

I'll keep it. I've been looking for new ways
to boost my revenue on Followers.

RHYS

No. You aren't going to wear those for other
men.

> It's a gift, so I can do whatever I want with it.

RHYS

What did I say about behaving?

> I forgot.

> Don't be late tomorrow.

I login to my *Followers* account wearing the exact outfit Rhys told me not to wear. If he wants to buy me lingerie, I'll do whatever the hell I want with it. Today I'm making lemon-blueberry scones. I've swapped the apron for this crisscrossing black strappy lingerie that I had to look up online to figure out how it's supposed to be worn. To be fair, he nailed it with this one. Once I tried it on, I loved it. It's very much my style: a little sex, a little rock and roll. And not gonna lie, I look damn good.

**Excellent_Cut1200: No apron?**

**DarkhorseTX: my pacemaker's gonna be working overtime today**

**BCKeeper5: Whoa, Black Betty Rocker**

**SuccaMuhMeatballs: How is this hotter than when you're naked?**

**Kimmy1223: ^^ this**

"Just thought I'd try something different for everyone today. It was a gift. Glad you approve."

I read through some comments and laugh. I'm chatting back and forth with my more engaging followers when my eye snags on the list of viewers. My breath catches when I see his name. It's the first time he's logged into a livestream since I told him to stay away. I wore this lingerie as my own little act of rebellion, but now that he's here to witness me doing what he specifically asked me not to, it makes it all the more enjoyable. *Eat your heart out, Rhys Kucera.*

**HatTrickSwayze: Does the person who bought that for you know you're wearing it for a crowd? Better hope they aren't watching or you might have to face some consequences**

."They know I'm wearing it. But I once heard them say that they like it when I'm their good slut."

Perhaps that's jumping in the deep end, but I've missed flirting with him in the chat so much. My thumbs run under a couple of the straps as I do a little spin to model the outfit. I imagine him sitting there stewing, he's gotta be so annoyed with me right now. *I love it!*

"Okay, let's get down to business. Today, I'm going to show you how to make lemon-blueberry scones," I announce. "I almost decided to make pumpkin scones, but I figure since it's fall, there's enough basic white-girl shit going around, we don't need to overdo it. Anybody can make these, they are stupid easy."

After doing an overview of what supplies and items are needed in this recipe, I work to slowly combine ingredients. Scones come together pretty quickly, so I'll need to stretch this video as much as I can. I pick up my frozen stick of butter and make a provocative show of my hands sliding up and down the hard block, trying to be as explicit as I can, then I carefully unwrap it and begin grating with reckless abandon.

**BCKeeper5: Jesus, that took a left turn.**

**JohnnyCoxville: Lorena Bobbitt has entered the chat.**

**S0niQz: I need an adult.**

I chuckle. "The key to success here is using frozen grated butter. Refrigeration isn't going to cut it, you want it harder than your dicks right now. Ladies, you should be able to key your ex's car with that butter, 'k'? Frozen like my father's heart when he left for cigarettes and never came back . . . just kidding. It was groceries."

It's a true story, but it's such a classic stereotype, it's hard not to crack jokes. He couldn't even come up with a creative way to abandon us. We were so much better off without him. My mom eventually married my stepdad, and there's not a better match for her. He treats my mom like a queen, and she deserves it. My subscribers are used to my sense of humor by now, but I can tell which ones are new, based on the few condolences messages that come through.

**FullyStacked_92: She's always like this. You'll get used to it.**

It's sweet when my OG followers help out the new kids, sometimes it feels like we're a big family. If we were . . . Hat Trick Swayze would be Daddy.

*Pull it together, Micky.*

"Okay, moving on, you want to work the cold butter into the dry ingredients to create crumbs. This allows the butter in those crumbs to melt as the scones bake, which is going to release steam and create those delicious little buttery air pockets."

The longer this video goes, the more obvious it is how quiet Rhys is. Normally, we chat a lot back and forth. For a split second, I regret not saving this for him but then I remember I don't owe him shit. He relishes getting under my skin, and I'm happy to administer a dose of his own medicine. Tit for tat.

As much as he pisses me off sometimes, the back and forth brings a smile to my face. We drive each other mad, but beneath the games, it feels like we have this magnetic pull. Opposite poles. No matter how hard we try to distance ourselves, neither of us can resist the attraction that continues to pull us together. The closer we get, the harder it is to stay apart. It's equal parts right and wrong. Even now, as I stand here and zest these lemons, all I can think about is if he's getting off to me.

I hope he is. I'll tuck that notion in a box and save it for a rainy day when I feel like shaming myself.

# EIGHTEEN

## Micky

He better not be late. I have no clue whether he will show. Rhys is a wildcard. He's crazy enough to pay a thousand dollars to learn how to bake bread, but he's also a big enough dick to spend a thousand dollars to stand me up solely to push my buttons. It's fifty-fifty.

I'm wearing black jeans, a black scoop-neck tee, a black apron, and I took extra time on my makeup. I will not let him be prettier than me in my own apartment.

12:58. Two minutes. I've been pacing by my front door for the last five. Careful not to smudge my mascara, I look through the peephole. I'm startled to see him standing outside the door. What is he waiting for? I get the jump on him and whip the door open.

"What are you doing out here?" I startle him enough he jumps.

"It's great to see you too." A confident smile overtakes his face. "You said one o'clock. It's twelve fifty-nine." He taps his watch. It doesn't look like an expensive one. The way he seems to throw around cash, I'd expect him to wear something flashier.

He follows me to my kitchen, and I hand him an apron, the one with cherries. "You said it was your favorite."

"It is. Would have enjoyed seeing it yesterday," he muses, tying the strings around his waist with one hundred percent confidence. His eyes burn into me, but I refuse to acknowledge his little comment. Instead, I shuffle around the sourdough starter and bags of flour like there's a purpose to it.

He stands next to me, and I peek at him from the corner of my eye. His shirt spans his chest just right, it's like it was custom fit. Hard pecs, broad shoulders, thick-as-hell thighs. He kicked off his shoes at the door like a gentleman. And seeing him pad around in socks makes him seem more human. It sets the tone, making this feel more casual and intimate. I like it. Usually we're verbally sparring, but this feels like two people hanging out together. Who knew socks were the great equalizer?

Previously, I struggled merging Rhys with Hat Trick Swayze, and now it's becoming harder to separate them. Today feels reminiscent of the date I was so looking forward to until he ruined everything. Technically, *it is* happening now, and this time it's in person. He doesn't seem affected by the shift between us, but it's taking a lot of effort to disregard my attraction to him.

That attraction becomes exponentially harder to refute once we mix the ingredients and I show him how to knead the dough.

*Holy fuck.*

This is so bad for me. His skilled fingers sinking into the soft dough, working it over in his huge hands is . . . *pornographic*. I should have never taken the money.

I clear my throat and do my best to concentrate on actually teaching him something. "This dough has a higher hydration, so it's going to be sloppy in the beginning. You can use your dough scraper if you need to."

"I like using my hands. And I prefer sloppy. And knead-iness." He winks.

"Have I mentioned I hate you?"

The heel of his hand stretches the dough over the counter, he folds it back on itself, turns it ninety degrees, and repeats the move. Again. *And again.*

"Like this?" His voice drops down into something sexy and deep.

*Fuck.*

"Uh, yeah. That's great. There's a two-handed method you can use as well." I swallow and take the warm dough from his hands to show him. "Basically you use both hands, first use the heel of one hand to push it this way, then cross over with the other and push it in the opposite direction. Here, you try."

His forearms and biceps flex and bulge. *Heaven help me.* The way he manipulates it, grips it—squeezes, presses, and strokes it. The man's a natural. He must be on the same wave-length, because when he slaps—no, *spanks*—the dough and then jiggles it under his palms, my knees want to give out. Luckily, I'm still standing, but the nervous laughter that slips from me couldn't be more obvious.

It's unnecessary, but the salacious part of my brain shows him the slap-and-fold method. Picking up the ball, I smack it against the counter. When he swings and slams the dough down with a loud crack, it's like I'm in some war movie with a flashbang, all I can hear is a high-pitched ringing as he punishes the ball of dough with his massive hands.

*This is so hot.*

He does it a few more times, I lost count, but it's enough to drench my panties. Even if I wanted to be mad about it, I couldn't. He's technically doing the correct movements—and honestly, I could watch a full nine seasons of this man fucking up some gluten. I'd camp out a week early to see the premier.

"Hey, so . . . can I apologize?"

My cheeks heat with embarrassment. I don't want to discuss that, why can't he knead the dough and leave me to my ogling?

"I didn't mean to betray your—"

My trust? *Spare me.* I'm over it, I want to move on. Watching him knead this dough is satisfying, but I need a break. *And maybe a cigarette.* In fact, he's probably overkneaded by now.

"Okay, that's probably enough for today. We can let this proof overnight in the fridge, and we can bake it tomorrow morning if you're around. Sound good? I can clean up."

"Do I get to wash my hands before you kick me out in a hurry?"

"Oh, ha! Yeah, you can use the sink to wash your hands. It's over there." I stupidly direct him to the faucet.

"Yup. I see that."

I keep myself busy by scraping up the bits of dough stuck to the granite slab while he washes his hands.

"Thanks for the lesson. Tomorrow around ten okay?"

"Sure. Good. Yup. Fine." I nod like a lunatic, dropping my scraper and ushering him out the door. He's far too attractive. It's obvious I am kicking him out when he doesn't even have time to put his shoes on. He leans down and picks them up, then walks backward across the hall with a big shit-eating grin on his face. He knows he got to me. I couldn't have made that more clear if it was painted on my forehead.

"This was fun." He beams. *He has nice lips.*

*Say goodbye and shut the door, McCoy.*

"K. Bye," I say, standing at the threshold of the door before promptly shutting it.

Once he's gone, my arm drapes over my forehead and I close my eyes, looking toward the sky. Good God, that man.

*Yes, hi. I'd like to make a deposit into my Jill till, please.*

# NINETEEN
## Micky

Today, I'll be ready for him. As I run the conditioner through my hair, I finish my pep talk. Rhys will probably be back to his normal stir-the-pot self, but I'll be unaffected now that I don't have to deal with the simulated gluten porn from yesterday's lesson. We're literally just slapping some flour on it and throwing it in the oven. There's nothing sexy about watching a timer.

I finish washing my hair and getting ready. By 9:45 a.m., I'm standing in my kitchen, staring at the swollen ball of dough like it offended me.

"You know why you look like that, don't you?" I say to the ball. "It's because you let him grab you and toss you around like a damn ragdoll. How about you show a little self-respect today, huh?"

It stares back at me.

"Stop looking at me like that. This is about you. Not me."

No response.

"No, I'm not saying you were asking for it!"

My reprimand to the dough is interrupted by three knocks at the door. My stomach flips. He's ten minutes early today. I open the door, and he doesn't hide his eyes roving over my body. *Stay strong.*

"How big is my ball?"

"Excuse me?"

"The dough."

"Your ball is fine. Average, at best."

"That's a first."

I roll my eyes. "The oven is already preheating. It takes a while because the cast iron dutch oven needs to get up to temp as well. I'm going to give it another fifteen before we pull it out."

"So . . . do you think all this preheating will get you hotter than you were yesterday watching me work the dough?"

"Ya know what?" I shove the bowl of dough into his chest and push him toward the door. "You can take this back to your apartment. Cook it for twelve hours at thirty-six hundred degrees. Bye."

"No, no, no, no." He chuckles. "I'll stop. Promise."

"Be nice to me," I threaten, stabbing my finger into his stomach. It bounces right off him. Those are some fierce abs.

"I'll be real nice to you," he whispers.

Shaking my head at him, I stick my tongue into my cheek to mask my amusement.

*Don't respond. Don't give him ammo. Ignore it.*

I don't want to smile, but it's my stupid fucking physio-logical response to grin at attractive men. He knows exactly which buttons to push. I hop on my counter and try to start a conversation as a distraction.

"Where are you from originally?"

"Outside of Bangor."

"Maine, right?" I've always wanted to see that part of the country.

"No, Hawaii?" *Tool.* "What about you?"

"Seattle."

"Huh. We're from opposite corners. Feels a little weird."

"Feels a little *appropriate*," I correct.

"Do you have any family that lives there?"

"Yeah, my mom and stepdad."

"You close with them? And what was that stuff about your bio dad the other day?" he questions.

"Yeah, I'm close. My dad didn't treat my mom well when I was younger. Then one day he just left. Early on, things were hard, but life got so much better for all of us, my mom was much happier. Before I moved to Vancouver for college, she started dating Rich, my stepdad. He's a really nice guy, fell in love with my mom and is good to her. Smart dude too. He's an astrophysicist. How fucking cool is that?"

"Pretty fucking cool."

"What about you? Are you close with your family?"

"Well, you already know about my sister. My parents and I were close. My mom died of cancer when I was in middle school. Then right after I started college, my dad had a heart attack. I was already here at the U of M. There was some money left for Anna and me, the rest went to my stepmom. I used mine to move Anna out here with me. My sister blew through her inheritance, as I'm sure you can imagine. She was using back home. I thought if I could distance her from the people who influenced her, then she might get better. But you know how well that turned out."

"I'm sorry you went through that. That's a lot of pressure for a kid."

"Sounds like both of us dealt with some pretty high-pressure shit when we were younger."

"Yeah, I guess so."

He leans back on the upper cabinets. "Are you still in contact with your stepmom?"

"No, after Dad died and she got her settlement, she was out of the picture."

That's cold. Rhys seems tight lipped, so I'm not going to ask more.

The timer goes off and I hop down to pull out the heavy dutch oven radiating heat.

"This is my favorite part." I let out a small squeal. "You're going to do what's called punching down the dough. You're essentially just deflating it. This releases carbon dioxide and helps relax the gluten. Then when you're done, fist the dough —"

His eyebrows raise, and he gives me a suspended blink. "I'm sorry, what?"

"Rhys." I stifle my laugh. "Fist the dough and form it into a ball."

He holds his hands up, palms facing me. "Just wanted to clarify."

He presses the bloated, puffy ball, and the airy dough fills in around his fingers.

"Oooh, I see what you mean. That is satisfying."

"Right!?"

He forms it into a loaf like I instructed, then we transfer into the dutch oven and place it back in the oven.

He joins me on the counter and claps his hands together. "Okay, serious question, ready?"

"Lay it on me."

"Tacos, pizza, pasta. You gotta fuck one, marry one, kill one. Go."

"Oh, wow." I chuckle, considering my options. My brain runs through the different scenarios. "Um . . . Fuck tacos. Marry pasta. Kill pizza."

"You're going to kill pizza?!"

"Well, I'm certainly not going to kill pasta or tacos."

"I need justification."

"Tacos are spicy, sensual, they're going to give you a wild time. You never know what you're getting with a taco, they'll keep you on your toes. They can be hot enough to make you sweat. Stuffed with whatever meat you're in the mood for. Guacamole may be involved. You can't have boring taco sex. Pasta will always be there for you, it's the carbohydrate ride-or-die. Bad day? Pasta, baby. Good day? Still pasta. You can throw in some spice, but overall, it's safe. That's who you marry. Ideally, you want pasta on the streets and tacos in the sheets. And pizza is the fuckboy of foods. Fine at a college party or late at night, but he wasn't going places, and eventually, you had to leave him behind."

"Damn. You came prepared," he says wide-eyed. A tentative smile grows on his lips.

"My turn, ready?"

"Let's hear it."

"Cinnamon roll, bagel, donut. Go."

"Fuck donut, marry bagel, kill cinnamon roll," he rattles off.

"Holy shit. Just like that?"

"Just like that."

"State your case . . ." I hold out my arm, gesturing to the pretend panel of people.

"Obviously, I'm fucking the donut. It already has a hole. It's sweet and glazed. Sometimes they squirt, they're messy and sticky—I mean, there's nothing better than fucking a messy donut. Bagels are wholesome; you can have them for breakfast, lunch, or dinner. They still have a hole, but they're tougher than a donut so you can fuck them harder and put them into more positions without breaking. They are down for whatever: peanut butter, cream cheese, tomatoes, eggs, bacon, salmon. You know what, I'm marrying AND fucking the bagel. And kill cinnamon rolls because they make my teeth feel like they're wearing tiny sweaters." He runs his tongue over his front teeth.

My head slowly turns ninety degrees to look at him.

"I am *never* letting you near my bakery."

"Nah, you'll be begging for me to come inside your bakery." He nudges my shoulder.

I'm getting wet listening to this guy talk about fucking baked goods. What is going on with me? It's not my fault, this is purely physical. I swear he looks sexier than he did yesterday. *Holy hell, he can fill out a tee shirt.* After he leaves, I'll take care of myself and dissolve all this sexual energy.

We play a few more rounds of Fuck, Marry, Kill, then we are interrupted by the beep of the timer. Bread is done—and I'm oddly disappointed that our time is almost up. I was actually having fun.

It's a beautiful sourdough when he pulls the loaf out. He transfers it onto a cooling rack. I show him the underside, have him knock on it to hear the hollow thump. Despite me having him overknead it for my own perverted enjoyment, it looks good. Great crust. When it's cooled, I hand him a serrated knife to carve a few slices off the end.

The second the warm slice hits his tongue he groan-growls. *Jesus.*

"It's just bread. Stop making it sound so explicit."

He swallows his bite and licks his lips. "If I like what I'm eating, I say so." He holds my gaze when he says it, and a flush creeps up my neck. His eyes follow the warmth on my face.

"You're wondering what noises I'll make when I eat you, aren't you?"

Nonchalantly admiring the slice of bread in my hand, I sigh. "I don't have to wonder. I know I'm delicious."

"Maybe. But I bet I could make you moan before I do."

*What?*

I turn to face him with a smirk. "You think I'll moan from your tongue before you moan from my taste? What are we betting?"

He licks his lips again, and my thighs clench. I can't tell if he's leading me on to screw with me or if he's serious. Either way, I refuse to back down to him.

"If I win, I get to take you out."

*Well, that was unexpected.*

"Like on a date?"

"Uh-huh."

I hesitate.

"Okay . . . if I win, you cancel your subscription on *Followers*. And you have to be nice to me."

"Wow, way to reach for the stars." He rolls his eyes. "Okay, what are the ground rules? Can I use my fingers?"

After seeing his dexterity work over the dough last night, my vagina is begging for me to say yes. But my brain reminds me I'm trying to win this thing.

"No!" I answer too quickly. "No fingers."

"Like a pie-eating contest?" His lips curl into a mischievous grin. "You won't last two minutes."

"Oh, please. You're getting creamed, Kucera."

"You better."

I purse my lips trying not to laugh. *Goddamnit, I walked right into that.*

*There's no way he'll win.* Oral sex has never gotten me off. It's too gentle, never feels like anything. "Where do you want to do this?"

He pulls out a chair and points at the kitchen table. "Get on. You eat your meals on the counter, I eat mine at the table."

*Fuck.*

I'm waiting for him to backpedal and say he was kidding, but he's serious. *Am I really letting him go down on me, stone-cold sober, before noon on a Thursday?* This could be my chance to put a dent in his ego. I've had some very enthusiastic lovers, but none have made me come with their mouths. He looks sure of himself, and I'd love nothing more than to knock him down a peg or two.

His jaw clenches, and I swear his nostrils flare when I unbutton my jeans. I leave my panties on to not appear too eager and perch myself on the round black table. When he takes his seat in front of me, I suddenly feel like Little Red in front of the big bad wolf. *All the better to eat me with.* His pupils dilate, darkening his eyes as if he's stalking prey, it reminds me of that night in the stairwell. I hope I'm not making a dire mistake with this stupid bet. He must sense my apprehension because he grabs my calves and pulls my ass to the edge of the table, directly in front of him.

"You good with this?"

"Uh-huh."

"Say you want me to eat your pussy."

"I give you *consent* to eat my pussy." *Like hell am I using the word* want.

He slips his thumbs under the sides of my underwear and drags them down, I lean on my elbows and raise my ass as he pulls them off. He drops them to the floor.

"Spread your legs for me. Show me." His voice is low and commanding. *It's not helping.*

"Can you stop talking? The point is to be silent." If he doesn't stop speaking in that gravelly voice, I'll lose. It's audio porn.

I part my thighs, and he stares for an uncomfortably long moment. I can't tell what he's thinking. He urges me back so I'm lying flat on the table, then massages his palms up and down my inner thighs.

"No hands," I rasp.

"You said no fingers, I'm going to touch you with my hands." The air is cool on my wet flesh; I hope he doesn't see how turned on I am. If he would have stayed quiet, I might've still had the upper hand.

"That doesn't even make sense, y—"

"You know what else doesn't make sense? How wet you are already. Freya, you are—" *Damn it.*

"Shut up." I keep my eyes fixed on the ceiling. "First one to make noise loses."

The atmosphere is heavy with sex and neediness.

"I'm going to make sure everybody downstairs knows what a good little slut you are," he growls.

My breath catches, and his mouth is on my body before I get to retort. I seal my lips shut.

He starts slow with the tip of his tongue, applying feather touches to my center. *This will be a cake walk.* The delicate feel of his mouth on me is a welcome reminder that oral sex does nothing for me. I suppress a grin.

Propping myself up on my elbows, I raise an eyebrow, trying to look as bored as possible. He pierces me with his gaze, flattens his tongue, and licks from slit to clit. The feeling is meh, but the visual? *Whoa.*

My back settles on the table again. *New rule. No watching.* I swear I feel his lips pull into a smile. He's so conceited. To distract myself, I try to list all the types of flour.

*All-purpose, whole wheat, pastry, coconut . . . almond . . .*

His pressure increases and he yanks me closer to his face. *Shit.*

*Coconut . . . wait I already said that. Gluten-free . . .*

The noise in the room pulls me from my thoughts. *The sound of his mouth on me. His breathing. My breathing.* It's not loud, but it might as well be rattling the walls.

He takes a break to nip at the soft flesh on my thigh, and I hold my breath to stay silent. His nose slides up and down the apex of my thighs, giving both an equal amount of attention. Another bite. He's touching me everywhere but where I want it.

Okay, he's *maybe* decent at this.

I feel his eyes on me, but I keep mine locked on the black industrial ceiling.

*Semolina . . . 00 . . .*

His tongue is back with an increased pressure, and my breathing becomes more shallow. If this was real foreplay and not some competition, it might get me off. Right when it starts to get good, he reverts to the feather touches from the beginning, but this time it's not as easy to ignore. It's this out-of-control feeling I'm not used to.

*Rye . . . self-rising . . .*

Normally I'm the one calling the shots, directing my partner what I like and how I like to be fucked, but in this moment, I'm forced to stay quiet and surrender to him. Endure all the sensation while I try to ride out his storm. I've never been submissive. I don't know if it's Rhys or the new experience, but this power exchange is exhilarating. I lift my feet a centimeter off the table to prevent myself from grinding against his mouth. The urge is there. He gently guides my calves to rest over his shoulders. The soft little flicks of his tongue turn into firmer, stronger licks. *Rougher.*

The alternating speed and pressure was premeditated. He's becoming slightly aggressive, and it's clear that everything until this point has been him laying the groundwork for building up my orgasm into something torrential. My lips part, and I throw my arm over my eyes, trying to focus.

*Self-rising . . . self-rising . . .*

He's applying the perfect amount of tension and pressure on me. He knows exactly when to push me and when to pull back again. This feels *really* good. His tongue sweeps along the inside of my thigh, and he nips. Then repeats on the other side. The small bites make me tremble. When he returns to my center, he latches onto my clit and sucks.

*Fucking fireworks.*

My body twitches, legs jerk, there's nothing that will stop

it. He's not letting go, he doesn't ease up. When I grab the edges of the table and squirm, the sucking builds stronger. My confidence wanes as the inevitability of my orgasm comes to light. It's purely biological, I don't know why I thought I could outsmart it. Everything in me is telling me to forget the stupid bet, lean into it, and milk this orgasm for everything I can. It'll feel so incredible when it hits, just give in. If I'm gonna lose, then I'm gonna have my world rocked with a mind-blowing consolation prize. The stubborn part of me says to fight for my life and win. His tongue has to be getting tired.

Without thinking, I lean on my elbows to watch him again. His hazel gaze locks on mine, and those massive hands lift my legs off his shoulders and lay them back on the table, holding my thighs open wider. He looks so fucking hungry.

He closes his eyes again, and it gives me the opportunity to appreciate how distinctive and masculine his face is. His strong jawline, those sharp cheekbones, and the way they tense and release as his mouth moves against me. The coil inside me winds tighter, my body clenches to combat it, which doesn't seem to work in my favor. It only brings me closer to the edge of nirvana. *Relax. Relax!*

His hands glide down the inside of my thighs and pause just above my knees. When he looks up at me again, he pushes them open wider and unleashes the full force of what his mouth can do. He sucks hard, pulling at my clit with his lips. His fingers dig into my thighs while his thumbs stroke over the painful stretch. It intensifies every sensation. I'm practically panting, but I can't look away. The corner of his eyes crinkle, and his eyes dance with gratification as he notices how affected I am. I only have seconds left before I combust, but I'm no coward, if he makes me come, I will look him in the eye while it happens.

His expression turns menacing when he sees how hard I'm fighting this and that's all it takes to break me, I whimper and immediately slap my hand over my mouth and look at the ceiling, just in case he didn't notice.

*He did.*

I try to stop it, but I can't. I've already lost, and the floodgates of pleasure burst open now that I'm no longer holding back. My legs shake under his grip, and I cry out. My climax is violent.

He doesn't stop, but he doesn't hold back his own sounds anymore either.

"That wasn't easy for me either." He groans against my clit and the vibrations make me moan. "Fucking hell, Freya. How can someone so feisty have a pussy this sweet?"

The game is over. He won, I came. This should be the end, but he's not stopping, and I'm not going to ask him to. There's a strange high from losing to him. Why does the idea of him defeating me make my skin buzz? It's turning me on all over again. *What is Rhys doing to me?* I like being strong and in control. I get off on being bossy and making others submit, so why am I loving this so much?

The noise he made tasting that bread can't compare to the sounds he's making now. This man is *verbal*.

"You want another one, don't you?"

"Uh-huh." I nod like an idiot. I don't even try to stand up to him anymore. "Make me come."

"Ask me nicely."

"Please." I can't believe I said please. To Rhys.

"You want my fingers this time?"

More nodding. I don't care, I need to get off.

He slides in one finger. I moan, it's the penetration I've been needing. He adds another, and his thick digits fill me up.

"Of course you're this tight, I knew you would be." He grazes his teeth over me, as if he's itching to bite down. "One of these days, I'm going to fuck this sweet, tight cunt, and you're going to drench my cock with your cum."

I'm struggling to breathe, unable to repress every gasp of pleasure that escapes my lips. I can't stop watching. I want more. "Do you have a condom?"

"Yes, but that's not happening today. When I fuck you, I'm taking my time." He continues. "And I've got a flight that leaves in a few hours."

My head lolls back to the table, and my jaw tics. The disappointment on my face only seems to entertain him. He casually smirks. "Yeah, I know your secret, Freya. You act big and bad, but deep down, you're so fucking desperate and needy. You want someone who's strong enough to put you in your place." He chuckles.

His fingers crook inside me, and I sob. I reach up and grab the edge of the table behind my head, holding on as the second orgasm swells.

Then he actually laughs at me. "Look at you, I can already feel you locking up. You want to come so bad, don't you? Just do it, you're too weak to fight this. We both know you want it."

I use the leverage of my arms against the table to grind myself on his hand.

"That's it . . ." He tilts his head and smiles, he's so fucking smug. Then uses his other thumb to press against my asshole. My need is overwhelming, it's the sweetest agony. His mouth returns, licking and sucking, working in tandem with his fingers.

"Oh my god," I moan. *I want to scream.*

A growl rips from his throat as I teeter on the edge of climax.

Legs quaking, my body attempts to curl in on itself. The orgasm crashes into me. I try to force my thighs together, but he doesn't allow it.

"Rhys!"

My breath turns ragged as pure pleasure takes over my body.

"There she is," he drawls as I come on his hand. "So pretty."

After he extends the last of it by stroking my G-spot, his chair shoots back across the floor, and he stands up and undoes his belt.

"Get on your fucking knees and show me you deserve my cum."

*Fuck yes.*

I scramble off the table and drop to the floor. He frees his cock, and it bobs out, he's so hard. I might hate Rhys, but I don't hate his dick. I could hate-fuck him for hours. Staring up at him, I plead with my eyes for him to take me. I open my mouth, but he grabs my jaw in one hand and traces the head of his dick around my lips with the other. He glowers at me like this is a punishment, but it feels like a reward. He gives a tight slap to the side of my face, and I shiver. *Why does that turn me on?*

"Suck."

I salivate when the first drop of pre-cum hits my tongue. He hisses and grips my hair with one hand, cupping my face with the other. His thumb softly brushes away the sting on my cheek as he pushes himself into my throat. I gag once but recover. He guides himself in and out. His gaze moves to my lips and then back to my eyes again.

"You are such a sweet slut," he whispers, and it's endearing on his lips. I moan around him. I can hate myself tomorrow. Right now, I love it. I *want* to be his slut, and I'm relishing every second. His movements become sporadic, and he taps my cheek twice with his thumb, letting me know he's about to finish.

"Stick out your tongue, Freya." He says it so calmly, but

his jaw clenches when he retreats from my mouth. I can finally catch my breath.

Keeping a hold on my chin, he pumps his erection with the other hand twice before pressing it against my tongue to catch the spurts of cum. I curl it upward to keep from spilling and he releases a puff of air.

I look as doe-eyed as I can, knowing it's killing him seeing me on my knees with my tongue out, his cum on display.

He tenderly cups my cheeks, stroking my temples as we hold eye contact. I'm waiting for permission. I don't even mind that this is Rhys, I wish I could freeze this moment to remember how thrilling it feels to submit for the first time ever.

"Swallow."

I do, and his lips part.

"Did I do good?" I don't know where that comes from, because why the fuck do I care?

*But I do.*

He smiles, and something flashes in his eyes. "So good, darling."

# TWENTY

*Rhys*

My infatuation with Freya started when I would jack off to her on *Followers*. Then it grew as I got to know her as we chatted online. I can deny it all I want, but we had something before I even knew she was the girl across the hall. When I found out she was my new neighbor, my plan to avoid her only backfired.

I don't know what to make of her anymore. Her taste is still on my tongue as I board the plane. The sweet glimmer in her eye as I came on her tongue made me melt. This confusion is exactly what I was trying to avoid. I had every intention of only baking dough when I went to her place this morning, but now it feels like we're on the precipice of something much bigger.

If we didn't hate each other, the conversations we had today might be considered agreeable and friendly. It was easy, like we were still hiding behind our usernames and being our true selves, complete honesty. What was I doing making a game out of oral sex? Not only that, but I bet a date I'd win.

*A date.*

I'm not supposed to be dating, but this could be my chance to make things right. Pretty sure that's why it flew out of my mouth without even thinking. Truthfully, I'm shocked I even won that dumb bet. The second she spread her legs, I knew I'd have to focus. She smelled sweet, tasted sweet, and goddamn, did she ever behave sweet. That's what really got me off.

She's under my skin now, and I don't know if there's any way to go back to the way it was before. Not now that I've seen the fiery, tenacious Freya turn soft and pliable in my hands.

"Kucera, you're up!" Coach yells. I stand, ready to take my shift. We're in the second period, and I've gotten more ice time than I ever have before. Los Angeles is playing well tonight, but we're playing better. The puck is staying on their end for the majority of the time, until they get a breakaway. Their right winger takes off, but I get in his face until he dekes. *Shit.*

He takes a shot from the far corner, Kapucik is in the net, he steps out to block, LA dekes again and passes it. That last fake-out made him lose track of the puck. They have a wide-open shot now, and the crowd is losing it. He's not going to block it in time.

"Block the shot!" Sully screams.

I do the only thing I can and drop my body as he shoots. The puck flies toward me like a bullet and it punches me right in the side. I grunt and let out a curse. It hurts like a mother-fucker, but I clamber back up again and pass to Lonan.

"You a'ight, Rook?" Kapucik shouts.

I wince from the pain.

"Good." I get moving, Banks pushes it back over the blue line into their end. And I follow. I block a couple more attempts on our goal before my shift is up, then I'm back on the bench.

I spit and then squirt water into my mouth. Coach and the boys give me a slap on the helmet before Jenny, one of the team's orthopedists, checks out my side.

"How's the pain on a scale from one to ten?" she says, prodding my side.

"Two?" I say. It's probably closer to a six, but I doubt anything is broken.

"You gotta lie better than that, at least give me a four or five. The bruise alone tells me you're hurting."

"Yeah, it hurts, but I can play. I'm fine."

"Okay, see me in the locker room before third period," she says, laying my pad back down.

"D-man playing goalie." He laughs. "Kap is never gonna live this down. Hope it makes the highlights tonight." A clap hits my back. "Way to go, bud."

I nod but feel a pang of sadness that there isn't any family to watch it on ESPN if it indeed does make the highlights. I would have loved for my parents to see that. For Anna to see it, we'd probably laugh about it, and she'd give me a hard time. Well, the old Anna would. I shake off the somber feelings and get my head back in the game. That's the mental stuff that will mess with my energy tonight.

During second intermission, I head over to the med office so Jenny can inspect the *injury*. That word seems to be a little generous, it's just a big welt.

"Shit, this is going to be one ugly bruise. I don't know how it didn't break your rib," she says, pressing her hands along my side. She prods a few different areas, asking if it hurts. A few spots are somewhat tender, but nothing serious.

"I can give you something for the pain to get you through the rest of the game, but you're going to want to go easy on it for a bit, and I want you to go in for an x-ray when we get back home." She pauses and side-eyes me. "Don't look at it until after the game."

It must be ugly. "Are you going to let Coach know I can play third period?"

"Yeah, but I'm going to have him limit your shifts."

At least I get to play.

During my first shift in third period, I'm checked into the boards by Duchamel, the same prick that threw the slapshot into me. I'm too busy defending to throw gloves. And I don't want Coach to think I'm out here picking fights for the hell of it, or lose even more ice time. After my last shift change, I hit the bench and take a breather.

There are a few unwritten rules about hockey. One of them is when you do something bad, you pay the consequences. If a player crosses the line between physical and dirty, he must answer for it, and ninety percent of the fights are usually one player having his teammate's back. I've played enough hockey to know the sound of a stick thrown on the ice. The noise grabs my attention, and when I look up, Banks's gear slides across the ice while he charges barehanded for Duchamel, who shucks his gloves. *Oh fuck.*

It's no secret Banks is our enforcer. The boys on the bench whack their sticks against the boards as he takes swing after swing for me.

*Aw, I'm touched.*

All jokes aside, the warm feeling hits me in the chest. First, Lonan was eager for me to make the highlights reel, and now Banks is out here beating the shit out of some guy for checking me into the boards. Meanwhile, Jenny's checking my bruise again, like a den mother, making sure I'm not hurt.

They've claimed me as one of theirs; this team is my family. It will never be the same as having my actual parents here, or Anna sober enough to watch my games, but having this—this kind of support—is a close second best. They have my back. I was always putting everyone else on a pedestal, but now I'm feeling like I've earned my spot on the ice with them.

Back at my apartment, I drop my duffel and hang up the expensive-as-fuck suit. It's the nicest outfit I own. Thankfully the Lakes have a small team of people in public relations to make sure we all look put together and meet the dress code. One admin, Holly, insisted she take my measurements herself. Barrett Conway told me to keep my wits about me, and he wasn't wrong, considering how many times she had to "check my inseam."

There's only one woman I'm interested in these days. And I'd much rather spend my money on her than fancy suits, like bribing her for bread-making lessons. Which might have been one of the best investments I've ever made. Though, a dangerous one. I'm not sure where this leaves us. It was one thing when she was on my laptop screen, but it's another now that my dick knows how good the inside of her fucking esophagus feels.

The guys want to go out tonight, so when I get out of the shower, I put on jeans and a Henley. It'll be a while before they get to Top Shelf. I flip through television channels to pass the time, stopping at ESPN when I see they're rolling hockey highlights. *Sonofabitch.* The next one up is me taking a puck to the side. My hand rubs over the tender bruise—it's a good thing Jenny told me not to check it out during intermission. It's gruesome, but it looks worse than it feels. After getting bored with sports, I go back to channel surfing. There's nothing on. I'm scrolling through a list of movies to stream when my phone dings.

We're downstairs. Wanna beer?

Down in a minute.

The second I walk through the doors, my eyes find her. She's chatting with a group of women sitting at the bar— looks like a MILF convention. When she moves to the other side to help a new customer, my eyes catch on her ass in a mini skirt.

*Freya. Maneater. McCoy.*

I'm not the only one who notices. About eight other men and one of the MILFs have also noticed her assets.

I don't know why it annoys me. She can dress however she wants. This feels awfully similar to her *Followers* live cam from the other day, purposefully baiting me and trying to make me jealous. *That still pisses me off.*

I make my way to the team's corner and choose a spot with them that keeps Freya in my line of sight. *Why do I keep doing this?* Brit's forehead wrinkles, he's in a deep conversation with Sully, only pausing long enough to hand me a beer, but that's about it. The rest of the seats are loaded with players and bunnies. No surprise, Banks is enjoying two women in his lap, while Barrett seems like he'd rather be anywhere else. I take a swig of beer and join in the conversation about how well we did in the last few games and a couple of bad calls made by the ref.

Banks whispers to one of the women on his lap and points at me, and before long, the bunny straddling his left thigh comes over and sits on mine.

"You looked lonely over here by yourself," she coos.

She's attractive, *very attractive.* But still, my gaze stays locked on Freya. When she makes eye contact and notices the woman with me, she scoffs and shakes her head before looking away—*jealousy.* It's kinda sexy. And the perfect opportunity for a little payback.

"Yeah, I could use a friend." I put my arm around her waist and pull my eyes from the woman I really want. "What's your name?"

"Reese."

"Well, what a coincidence, I'm also Rhys."

"I know." She has a sinister smile. "You're number five, right?"

I nod, and we make small talk. Every now and then I glance up and Freya is checking on me and the woman seated on my leg. I stealthily slide my phone from my back pocket and text her.

> How's your night going?

FREYA

It's great, getting lots of tips.

*No shit, with her ass looking the way it does in that skirt. Everyone with a front row seat is drooling all over the bar.*

FREYA

Happy to see you're making new friends.
☺

Her attempt at being flippant bombs horribly. *Payback's a bitch.*

> Her name is Reese, isn't that funny?

FREYA

Hilarious.

> Want me to introduce you?

FREYA

No thanks.

> Why? She's funny and a very pretty girl. I'm kinda into her.

FREYA

Good for you.

> Wait, you're not jealous are you?

FREYA

No. I think it's a little strange that you asked me out on a date, but now you're telling me you're 'into' someone else. Generally, it's not wise to flaunt other women around the person you're interested in.

> I don't remember saying I was interested in you. I didn't ask you on a date, I won a bet.

FREYA

Message received. I can't text while I'm working.

> Do you remember talking to me about boundaries and consequences?

FREYA

Yes.

> The lingerie I bought for you was for you. I asked you not to wear it in front of other men or women. That was a boundary.

> It made me jealous. Seeing me with Reese tonight, is the consequence you face for not respecting my boundary. You disobeyed me

She looks up at me, and I sink my hand into Reese's hair, pressing a kiss to the side of her neck while I lock eyes with Freya. The woman puts her arms around me while she continues her conversation with some of the other women nearby. Freya laughs, but it doesn't appear genuine. She peers down at her phone and the three little dots blink along the bottom of my screen. My heart rate picks up. I move my phone to my other hand so I can continue my text conversation behind Reese's back. Literally.

> FREYA
>
> I'm not jealous, if that's what you're getting at.

>> Yes you are. Ask yourself why it bothers you Reese is getting my attention?

> FREYA
>
> First of all, you can stop saying her name. Secondly, if you want to fuck her so bad, go ahead and do it. Walk the walk, Kucera. Better hurry up though, you don't want to miss your turn.

*Walk the walk, Kucera. Goddamnit, she's infuriating!*

>> It should be you on my leg. She might have her arms around my shoulders, but it's your pussy I want around my cock. You're who I want. It's always been you.

>> You want me to. It's what you need isn't it? For me to call you my good little slut and take over so you can let go. Work your body over until you're a pathetic, blubbering mess. Aren't you curious what it would feel like to be the weak one for once? Even hellcats bow to the devil, Freya Girl.

I hit send and watch her read the text. Her teeth trap her lower lip, and a glass shatters behind the bar. She startles, and one of the bartenders moves toward her with a towel as they clean it up. When she stands, she sinks a flustered hand into her hair like she doesn't know what to do with herself. I have a penchant for rattling her, especially when it comes to sex. She straightens some bottles behind the bar and checks her phone again. My eyes are trained on her every movement. She says something to the other bartender and crosses the room toward the hallway, cutting her eyes at me for the briefest glance.

I make an excuse about using the restroom and slide Reese off my lap. When I turn the corner, Freya is in the shadows near the back stairwell. It's dark, but her face and body are bathed in red light from the EXIT sign above. We lock eyes, and I pull her around the corner. My hands pin her to the wall, and she rushes to lift her skirt. I drop to my knees, pull her panties to the side, and throw one of her legs over my shoulder.

No words are exchanged, but she's telling me exactly what she needs. Her free hand finds purchase of the handrail behind her as I lick and bite her inner thigh. She pants and trembles above me. *I fucking love it.* Those dark eyes peer down at me, and I can't look away. I want to watch her every reaction. I dive in, dipping my tongue in her center before directing all my attention to her clit. She stifles a moan and leans forward like she's going to fall, but I catch her with my palm, firmly holding her in place while I devour her sweet, delicious cunt.

When she regains balance, she claws and marks the nape of my neck. If I didn't know any better, I'd say she was doing it to send me back to what's-her-name covered in her scratches. Claiming me. She whimpers when I spear two fingers inside her. I narrow my gaze as a warning, and she bites into her lip. I fuck her with my hand and use my tongue to massage the small knot of nerves. Then I suck. She holds her breath, and her body tightens and writhes before she gasps and surrenders to her orgasm.

She pulses and jerks her hips. Standing, I move to kiss her, but she turns her head away from me.

"No kissing."

She doesn't want to kiss me? *Fine.*

But she will open up.

I push her chin down to part her lips. My Freya-soaked fingers paint her tongue, she closes her lips around the base, sucking as if it were my cock. I'm straining against the zipper of my jeans, my body begging to fuck her right here on the stairs. I think she's about to ask me when she pulls her panties off, but instead, she stuffs them in my pocket, straightens her skirt, and walks away without saying a word.

I brace my arm against the wall, catching my breath, willing my dick to deflate.

*No fucking chance.*

Taking a deep breath, I jog up the back stairs two at a time to my apartment, throwing the door open and loosening my belt before I even get to the bathroom. I wrap her drenched, silky underwear around my fist and slide them up and down my shaft. Still tasting her on my tongue, I pump my dick less than a dozen times before I'm coming.

"*Fuck!*" I shout into the emptiness, the only sound is the bass from the bar below.

Out of breath, I pray for some post-nut clarity, but it never comes.

*I want Freya McCoy.*

# TWENTY-ONE

## *Rhys*

L onan Burke is in the Maldives for his honeymoon. Lucky bastard. Since the trip was something he won at one of the Lakes charity auctions, he gets a pass. Despite me having to partner with a different player, we are killing it tonight. Our passes are connecting, communication is good, and our pacing is right on the mark.

Burmeister jumps on the ice as I come back in.

"Way to skate, way to skate!" Sully slaps my helmet as I get back on the bench. "Good shift, rookie, yeah?"

"Yeah," I pant. Had a couple shots at the goal. Unsuccessful, but we kept the puck safe, which felt good. Would have felt better hearing that buzzer ring, but whatever.

Banks leans behind one of the guys and shouts, "Hey Kucy, they're always coming around that net and trying to hit the middle. Your sticking looks good, just make them go outside."

I nod. He got in a fight about halfway through the last period, one of the other players has been chirping at him all night. Dude loves attention. He's arrogant, conceited, and acts like the world is his playground. Anytime I've tried to ask Conway or Burke what his deal is, they just mutter something about "Edina" and "cake-eater." Whatever that means. I get the impression he comes from old money. He looks like the kind of guy who would pay someone else to fight his fights, but that's where he goes off script. On the ice, all that pretty-boy privilege goes out the window and he becomes this alter ego. You piss him off, and he'll quickly collect retribution. Banks is wildly protective of the team. Not sure if that's because he's passionate about backing his boys or if there's something else going on in his life.

We're sitting at 4-0 in the third period, and there's only a few more shifts remaining.

I get a couple more pointers from the guys before I'm up again. My brain recalls their advice. I push them away from the goal and hammer them into the boards wherever I can. Sometimes all you need is another player's viewpoint to make sense of what's happening right in front of you. This is a team I can learn a lot from.

Back in the locker room with our win, everyone is celebrating. I hit the bikes after the game with a couple of the other guys, including Banks.

"Hey, man, have you decided whether or not you're doing a player initiative?"

Player initiatives are special projects that some pros take on, usually for charity. Many start their own organizations, others set up hockey clinics and camps for underprivileged kids, and sometimes it's just writing a check.

"Yeah, a little. What's yours?"

"Domestic violence."

"Oh, yeah, didn't you open up a women's shelter?"

That's right. I remember hearing about the grand opening of a housing project he set up for families before I was signed. His protective mentality makes more sense now.

"Couple of 'em."

Seeing Anna struggle so much, I've been trying to incorporate addiction and sobriety into my charity. There are several rehab centers that other players donate to, I could do something like that.

"I've thought about doing something with addiction."

"That's a good one. There's a lot of that in the pros. Team docs overprescribing pain meds and such. What makes you choose that? Something close to home?"

"Yeah."

*Very close to home.* Anna finally texted me back this week. She apologized, something about a friend needing her. *Uh-huh.* She makes it sound like everything's fine, but I know it's just a matter of time before she needs something. And now that I'm traveling all the time, it's harder to keep tabs on her. She says she's getting better, and I have to believe that. The fact she's responding to my messages is a good sign.

"Is that why you never get drunk?"

"Huh?"

"Whenever we go out, like Top Shelf, you get one, two beers, tops. Then you get a pop or some shit."

"Yeah, I guess. Not a big partier."

I don't like feeling out of control, and after seeing Anna struggle so much, it's better to play it safe.

"Speaking of drinking, what's the deal with you and the bartender?"

"Freya?"

He raises his eyebrows and smirks. "I thought her name was Micky."

It's hard not to envision her without smiling. "Yeah, Freya, Micky, whatever. She's my neighbor."

"You fucking her?"

"No, not fucking her." I chuckle.

*Not yet anyway.*

"Yeah, but you want to."

"Taking the fifth."

"I tried to set you up with that bunny the other day, and you did nothing with it. I took her back with me and another girl, and we had a lovely evening together. There's definitely something between you and Red. Are you serious about her or just messing around? Because Burke might kick your ass if you're just looking to get your dick wet. You know how he gets when it comes to family shit."

Yeah, I'm aware of the way Lonan gets. He's already given me a few stern glances at Top Shelf. If he wasn't on his honeymoon, there's no way in hell I'd have let Reese sit on my lap. Not that Freya is into me, but he knows there's something going on between us. And now, apparently, Banks has picked up on it too.

"I'm not looking for anything serious, per se, but I wouldn't mind exclusive fucking."

He thinks I'm joking and laughs, but it's the truth. I don't need to be in a serious relationship, but I wouldn't be opposed to a *situationship*.

"There's a rumor going around that she's on *Followers*."

I feel the color drain from my face. It's bad enough that other randos get to see her, but having guys on the team get off to her makes my blood boil. Lonan is the only other guy on the team that knows, but I can't picture him saying anything. I swallow and try to sound casual.

"Like, the camgirl website? Who said that?"

"Yeah, man. Bishop's brother plays for Vegas. He was in town a few weeks ago."

I remember that. Pretty sure his brother's name is Paulie. That guy was a major douchebag, which is why I didn't go out to the bar with the team that night. "Micky was working when we went to Top Shelf, his brother asked her about it, she laughed him off. But he said her voice was dead on, and I guess her nails had the same design that was in the video he was jerking off to."

*Fuck.* I know what nails he's talking about, she showed them off to the camera. They were unmistakable. She's been getting popular on *Followers*, but I didn't believe any other NHLer would be keeping an eye on that kind of thing with all the pussy around all the time. What would they want it for? I mean, I can't imagine anyone who *wouldn't* want to see her body. But I've never been good at sharing.

"Crazy . . ."

"Yeah, Burke says it's not true though. Said he would have heard if she had a *Followers* account from Birdie." I appreciate him lying to shut that down. I'd do the same.

"Bishop's brother say what the username was?"

"Nah. He was pretty trashed, I don't think anybody was really listening to him."

I nod and change the subject. Relieved.

*Only three more days until I get her alone.*

# TWENTY-TWO

## Rhys

"Yᵒu guys watch *Emily in Paris*?" Jonesy asks.

*The fuck?* We're running defensive drills, and I'm learning that Jonesy is hands down the most endearing, weird-ass motherfucker on the team.

"The chick show?" Sully asks.

"Chick show?" he yells. "How about a little affirmative action?"

"What's it about?" I ask, flipping pucks to the guys as they skate by.

"It's about this girl, Emily. She lives in Paris. This season, she gets bangs."

*Wow, dude.* I spin on my skates to look at him and raise my eyebrows, waiting for him to say more.

"I know, man. It's good! You gotta watch it!"

A few months ago, I'd say he was fucking with us—or *really* high—but after getting to know him more, I'm confident he's dead serious. A few of us laugh and shake our heads. He seems completely unfazed.

"If anyone wants to come over for a watch party tonight, text me, so I know how much pizza to get."

"Dude, nobody is coming over to watch that," Banks hollers from the other side of the net.

"Sorry, bud. Can't tonight," I say.

"Hot date, eh?" Conway asks.

"Actually, yeah." I can no longer hide my smile. I've been in a great mood for the last couple days. At first, I blamed all the nice weather we've had lately, but it probably has more to do with the exquisite green-eyed redhead I'm having over tonight. It's not the date I owe her from the bet, but I invited her over to hangout, and surprisingly, she said yes.

"Ooooooh, you owe me fifty bucks, Cake-eater!" Jones shouts to Banksy. *Is my social calendar so bare that they're taking bets on me?*

I haven't been able to stop thinking about Freya since, well, since I found out she lived next door, but it's been especially bad now that I've gotten a taste of her. Our stairwell rendezvous has been replaying in my mind over and over again. The urgency in her eyes as she pulled up her skirt for me will forever live rent free in my mind.

Freya is a sweet girl with sharp edges. She reminds me of those caramel apple suckers I loved as a kid. Once the caramel was gone, my tongue would get sliced up by the razor-sharp air pockets in the tart green apple. *Whoever decided it was a good idea to aerate hard candy is an asshole.* But those suckers were too delicious to leave alone—like now. Except Freya is even more fun to lick.

"Ah, shit!" Conway shouts to the guys. "Father Kucy's breaking his vows!"

I laugh. "What's that supposed to mean?"

"It means you never take home any ass. Why do you think the bunnies all want you? Every girl wants to be the one to break you in. We were starting to consider maybe you were on O'Callahan's team."

Brit O'Callahan came out a few seasons ago. He's had his

own player initiatives setting up welcoming environments for LGBTQ hockey players and donating to various organizations that help communities form teams around the US.

"Hell no. We don't claim him." O'Callahan chuckles.

"Fuck you too!" I laugh. "You should be so lucky!"

She arrived as I pulled the bread out of the oven, dressed casually in black jeans and a loose, cropped green sweater. It makes her emerald eyes even more pronounced than before.

My gaze roves from her toes to her blazing-red hair. "You look nice." *She's drop-dead gorgeous.* It's been too long since I've had my eyes on her.

"I know." That attitude makes my dick twitch. "Did you bake?"

"I did. Wanna check my work?" I walk toward the kitchen and proudly present my lopsided loaf. "It's ugly, but I believe it's edible."

"You know, the last time bread was involved, things got out of hand . . ."

"Why the fuck do you think I'm making sandwiches?"

She carefully flips over the still-hot loaf and scratches the bottom with a knife. "Looks good." Her eyes follow me around the kitchen as I pull out ingredients. I'm not the greatest cook, but I make one hell of a dagwood.

She pulls up a barstool and makes herself comfortable. Elbows on the table, she rests her chin on her hands sweetly and leans forward. "What is it we're doing on this date?"

"This isn't a date. It's hanging out. I'm making you something to eat."

"That's even more confusing. Like, we're fuck buddies, but now you're making me food . . ."

"Everybody's gotta eat. And why do we have to put a label on it? You're fun to hang out with. I enjoy your company."

"A label." She snorts. "So, it's a booty call with a sandwich? I'm fine with that, just wanna know what the expectations are."

"First, I expect you to eat this sandwich and say *thank you*," I say.

"And after that?" She looks up at me through her lashes, and I'm immediately sent back to last week, the image of her down on her knees, gazing at me with those stormy-green eyes.

"I told you, it's whatever you want to do tonight. Actually . . . I have a surprise for you."

I leave the room to grab the toy I bought her and return with both my hands behind my back.

"What's this?"

"If you want to watch a movie and relax tonight, choose my left hand. If you want to practice handing over control, choose my right hand."

Her eyes pan back and forth, but it doesn't take her long to tap my right arm. I smile, satisfied with her choice, and hand her the small black box.

"Can I open it now?"

My chest thumps at her asking for permission. Her fingers tear into the wrapping, and I watch as she curiously opens the box.

"A flower? What is this? Wait . . ." She presses a button and the silicone toy comes to life, she raises her eyebrows and laughs. "Is this one of those vibrators that show up in ads all over my social media?"

"I'm the only person that gets to use this on you." I won't even let her take it out of my apartment. "And look, I even got it in your favorite color." I wink. *Black*.

"So what was in your left hand?" I hold out the package of

microwave popcorn, and she raises her eyebrows. "I figured it would have been empty, knowing your ego."

*She's not wrong. I considered it.*

I stand opposite her on the other side of the kitchen island. "I'm not going easy on you tonight."

"You underestimate how much good little sluts can take."

"It's not about how much you can take, it's about how much you can give of yourself. And just so you know, when I call you that, it's to make *you* feel sexy. As soon as it stops bringing pleasure—it's over. Don't confuse my degradation with disrespect . . . And the side of you that loves being a slut" —I stab my finger in my chest—"that belongs to me."

She tries to act unaffected, but her throat bobs on a wary swallow.

"The feeling you have right now, the one that's quieting all the busy thoughts in your head? Lean into it. Tonight, you're going to leave the attitude at the door. You can be big and bad for the rest of them, but not me." I skim my hands down her arms and goose bumps rise under my palms. "For me, you'll submit."

I move behind her.

She blows out a puff of air. "In your dreams."

"Stop." My voice is firm but softens when she tenses, and I turn her around. "You chose the box that allows you to relinquish control. Do you still want that?"

She nods. Her eyes turns soft and meek. I could stare into them for hours.

"How's that feeling now?"

I appreciate her contemplating her answer. "A little nervous."

"You want to keep going?"

"Yes."

Her shyness is the sexiest thing she's ever worn. My gaze drops to her lips. I want to kiss her, but kissing is too intimate for Freya. She wants to keep this sexual—it's the smart choice, it's safer. Kissing would cross a line.

"If you're coming up on a limit, say *yellow*. Just before we hit your limit, or if you need me to stop for any reason, you say *red*."

"It's cute you think I'll need a safeword."

My brows draw together, and I cock my head to the side. *Has she never used safewords before?*

"Everyone should use safewords, and I expect you to use yours if you need them. We should have established communication earlier, but going forward, they will always exist between us. They help build trust."

"Okay."

I squeeze her sides, enjoying her flinch, and return to my side of the counter. Once I'm done stacking the ingredients on our sandwiches and top them with another slice of toasted, fresh-from-the-oven bread.

"Hope you're hungry." I slide the plate in front of her.

"I need leverage to eat this thing." She grunts while smashing the sandwich down to a size that's somewhat manageable. She'll need the sustenance. Her moans around a mouthful of food go straight to my dick. "This is the best sandwich I've ever had."

After we finish eating, she wanders around my living room and peruses my bookshelf. She goes up on her tiptoes, and I check out her ass.

"I'm going to snoop."

I stuff both hands in my pockets and rock on my heels. "Be my guest."

"You read a lot, huh?" she comments, skimming her fingers across the book spines.

"It helps me come down after a game. Sometimes the adrenaline takes a while to drop off. Do you read?"

"Yeah, but I haven't had time to indulge for a while, pretty busy with work or the *Followers* thing." At the mention of the website, my nostrils flare. It never bothered me before, but now that we've gotten closer, it's hard not to be more protective of her. Possessive.

When she reaches up to pull out a book, I reach around her and touch the exposed skin at her belly. *What is the point of a cropped sweater?* Her breath hitches, and she leans into me and reads the cover.

"*Winnie-the-Pooh*?"

I tighten my arm around her and pull her against me.

"It's a classic."

"I cannot picture you reading this."

"'Pooh was delighted with the rather pleasurable new use he'd found for his honey pots.'" I quote A.A. Milne while sliding her hair off her shoulder. I lick a line from the base of her neck to her ear.

"This is the creepiest foreplay."

I laugh. "Wanna roleplay instead?"

She puts the book away. "Dibs on the honey pots."

I take her hand and lead the way, snatching the small box off the table as we walk by. As soon as we pass the threshold to the bedroom, she spins me around and pushes me against the wall, attempting to unbuckle my belt. There she goes again, trying to control the scene.

I fist her hair and pull at the base. "What did I say about you trying to lead?"

"Habit." She smiles.

*Brat.*

Leaning down, I whisper in her ear.

"Get on the bed."

I let go of her hair, admiring how her pupils dilate and her lips part. She scurries over and climbs onto the oversized mattress, her knees digging into the plush comforter and blankets.

"You finally going to fuck me tonight?"

"Do you deserve it?"

"Yes."

"Prove it."

Kneeling, she pulls her sweater over her head, showing off the black strappy push-up bra I bought her. Slowly, one at a time, her hands work to undo the vertical line of buttons on her jeans. She's wearing one of the sets I bought. Even if other men have seen her wear this, I'm the one that gets to fuck her in it.

"Good girl." I twirl my finger, motioning for her to spin.

She stands and does a wobbly three-sixty on the uneven surface, showcasing the lingerie.

"Very nice."

I pull off my shirt and undo my belt buckle, and her eyes light up at the clank of metal. That's as far as I get before I need my hands on her. She's still fixated on my zipper. When I walk to the bed, she drops to her knees again and reaches into my boxers. A delicate fist wraps around me, and a soft sigh leaves her relaxed lips. I love those sweet noises she makes. Such a juxtaposition to her tart exterior.

Wrapping my hand around her, I pinch her ass before slapping it.

"You're leading again."

She throws up her hands. "What am I supposed to do? Just lay here?" She scoffs.

"Exactly."

I'm stunned when she actually does what I say instead of doling out some other saucy comeback. I kneel on the bed and peel the thong off her body.

Nodding at her to continue, she spreads her legs. Glistening.

"Freya, Freya, Freya . . ." I muse.

"Why don't you do something about it?" she pouts. More impatient than irritated.

I massage the wet flesh and roll one of her nipples between my thumb and forefinger. She whimpers. "Such a sweet little whore when you make those noises." My dick is screaming to fuck her, but I already told her my intentions, this is about submission. I want to give her feelings no other man has before. And I want her to grant me this first experience.

I press the pad of my thumb to her clit and make small tight circles. Every time she tries to grind against my hand harder, I pull away. Then I skate my fingertips over the sensitive skin between her legs, lighting up the nerves at the junction of her thighs. Her muscles twitch and I return to massaging her clit again. I alternate between the two sensations until she's frustrated and squirming. Her breaths grow shallow, and the pulse in her neck is pounding.

The next time my thumb applies pressure, I slide two fingers inside. She's overly snug. *Jesus* . . .

"Are you about to come already?" I laugh.

"Don't make fun. It's been a while."

I smile, it's barely been a week. "You have such a needy cunt."

Her channel narrows as I work her over, taking my time. She lifts her hips to rub against me, but I hold her down with my arm pressed across her stomach, then drop my head between her thighs and gently blow over her center—just to piss her off.

"Rhys . . ." she grumbles.

Being nice, I curl my fingers and revel in her gasps.

"How's that?"

Her mouth drops open, but she doesn't respond. She doesn't want to like it as much as she does. I understand.

The smirk on my face disappears when I suck her clit into my mouth in time to feel her clench. I will never get tired of feeling her fall apart on my mouth and hand. When she starts to come, we make eye contact, and I see her. *Really see her.* She regards me with the same intensity. *Wow. What was that?*

"Like that, yeah," she says in a hushed voice. Her thighs close around my head, and I use my only free hand to push a leg open so I can hear the sounds of her climax. *Those moans.*

I don't stop fucking her with my fingers.

Her muscles relax. "The first one was free, the rest you're going to work for," she quips. That's cute.

Tonight, she'll pay for every snarky comment that's ever popped out of her mouth. I turn her on her side and bring my palm down on her ass with a sharp clap. She startles. Her skin pinkening from my hand is so gratifying.

I lay her back again and close my mouth around her pulsing clit. This time she jolts.

"Wait, wait—I'm not ready. It's too much." She's hyper-sensitive.

*I don't give a fuck.*

As she thrashes and pushes against my forehead, I relentlessly lick and suck. She screams, and I wrap my arms around her thighs, pulling her into me. Our gazes meet, and her mouth drops open. I close my eyes and return to feasting on her. She tastes so sweet. This is the third time I've eaten her pussy in the last week, and I hope to keep it a regular staple in my diet.

She groans through gritted teeth and tries to lift her ass. I force her down again, unwrapping one arm from her thigh so I can fill her with my fingers. She hisses. When I decide she's had enough, I sit up and grip her chin, opening her mouth so she can taste herself. I push them toward the back of her throat. She relaxes to keep from gagging.

"You think you get to decide when you come?" Reaching for the black silicone flower on the bed, I set it next to her.

When I retreat from her mouth, my thumb pauses on her

plush bottom lip. I stroke it back and forth. God, she's beautiful.

"You're going to withhold orgasms?"

"No. I'm not going to stop giving them."

She searches my eyes. "Do you use that thing on other women?"

It seems to come from a place of possessiveness, which I appreciate. I bought this for her. *For this.*

"Only you."

With my free hand, I reach behind her back and unclasp the strappy, crisscrossing bra. She shimmies out of it. While spreading my knees in front of her, I pull her closer, wrapping her legs behind my back. My eyes rove over her naked body.

"Unreal."

She blushes, and it only makes me harder. I trace the vibrating toy over her hard nipples. Her breasts subtly jiggle with the pulsations. Her chest rises and falls with each breath. I glide it down until it's settled between her thighs. She sighs and relaxes, closing her eyes and getting comfortable with the sensation. But I didn't buy this for the vibrations, I bought it for the suction. I've seen what it does to her.

"Look at me." She peers up, her expanding pupils are rimmed with the penetrating green ring of her iris. I press another button and the sucking begins.

That full lower lip trembles, and she flinches. "Oh my god, Rhys."

She can't refuse looking between her legs, and I use the opportunity to slide my fingers back in. She gasps and whimpers. She's finally letting go and enjoying herself. I love it.

"That's a good girl."

"I need more." It's a start, but I want her to communicate beyond more.

"What do you need?"

"You know."

"Say it."

"Fuck me," she begs. "Show me how you fuck me."

I tuck my tongue in my cheek, pleasantly surprised by her plea. Her submission is so natural. Her knees squeeze against my sides, quivering.

"Rhys . . ."

I crook my fingers and fervently tap the spot that makes her shake. She surrenders to her pleasure and cries out, her chest heaving. The strong, choppy twitches from her legs reverberate through me. Gorgeous.

"Okay, you can take it off my clit now," she says on an exhale.

"Use your safeword."

Her eyes pop open, understanding my plans for her tonight. "What?"

I press the button on the flower to kick it up to the next level, and her back arches. Her legs unwrap, and she tries to scramble backward, but I use my knees to press down on her thighs, not enough to bruise her, but enough to keep her spread open for me. "Oh, fuck . . ." she mewls as another orgasm rolls through her.

Once she's finished, I retreat and reach into my nightstand for a condom. Eyes shut and mouth open, she brings her quaking legs together, knees knocking, while she catches her breath. She opens her eyes to the image of me rolling on the condom.

"You want to know how I fuck you?"

She nods, a relaxed smile on her lips.

I tease my cock along her seam, feeling the short pulses from her most recent orgasm. After covering my length with her arousal, I grip her thighs as I sink into her. The first time I tasted her, I knew it was over for me. Now that I'm buried inside her, I'll never stop wanting this. She doesn't know it yet, but she's mine now. The way her eyes go wide and her mouth slacks when I enter will forever be burned into my memory. My chest warms at her reaction.

My shoulders cave, and suddenly it's difficult to breathe.

"Christ. You are"—*everything I've ever wanted*—"so tight, baby."

I struggle to move, it's like I have tunnel vision, and I'm in awe of her. We adjust to the feeling of her body hugging my erection, and I groan. Her lips transform into the most wicked grin. "Take me."

*Hellcat.* Her words snap me out of my stupor. I pull out until the head of my cock sits at her entrance and slowly thrust back inside, driving into her with long strokes. I fan my fingers across her stomach. My palm continues its path between her breasts, they rise and fall with each inhale and exhale as she anticipates my hand climbing to her throat. I collar her delicate neck in my hand. So rewarding.

"Rhys."

"You love being my obedient little fucktoy, don't you?"

"Yes," she moans. Her enthusiasm makes me pump into her faster.

"You are stunning, Freya Girl." I push my thumb across her lush lips. "This pout . . ."

She draws in a breath.

"This delicious pussy." I glance down to where our bodies are connected, and she curses. I return to her throat and firm up my grip. "Watching you choke and squirm while I fuck you . . . God, you are so perfect."

She clenches around me, and I see it in her eyes, the submissiveness. She's giving me permission to tame her, at least for a moment. Lifting one of her legs over my shoulder, I increase my tempo. One hand grips her side to hold her steady. Her muscles tense—*that's my girl.* She's right on the brink, and I bring the vibrator back to the tight bundle of nerves, and she bucks against me.

"I love watching you come," I say over her moans.

My name leaves her throat on a ragged wail. I pull all the way out and drive back in, extending out the orgasm. Her thighs quake while her clit throbs under me. After she comes down, her eyes have a strange nervousness about them at the realization that we aren't done yet. I won't stop fucking her. I won't slow down. I won't give her a break. She needs this, but she dreads it.

"I can't come again."

I chuckle. "Don't lie to me."

She swallows and blinks. "I'm spent. I'm not one of those people that can come like five times in a row."

I enjoy a challenge. "Is that a dare or a double dare?"

She shakes her head, her eyes are piercing, and a frustrated rumble releases through gritted teeth. She's trying to intimidate me. It's adorable.

My laugh only makes her angrier.

"You can't make me do it."

"Sass me and I'll make it worse, darling. You know what you're supposed to do. Now be a nice slut and give me another one." I reach up and gently slap her cheek. Fire flashes behind her eyes.

My free hand slips down to her swollen, overworked clit. She pleads with me to stop, but not enough for her to say her colors. I slow down, needing to edge myself so I don't explode the next time she does.

She whines, and her gasps turn to moans. Louder and louder. She's building up that foundation, and I can't wait to knock it down. I want to come so bad. Fucking hell, this is difficult. As she lifts her ass, I spank her sharply, then rub the spot with my palm. She almost falls back to the bed after her punishment, but I pull her against my pelvis as I fuck her over and over again. Grasping the sheets, a cry catches in her throat as she succumbs to another round.

Her slick pussy locking down on my shaft as if she owns it. *She does.*

"You come on my cock so well."

Like before, I have to force her legs apart. "Tsk, tsk, tsk. These legs stay open for me." *When will she learn?*

"Oh my god. I can't go again. I mean it. I can't. I physically can't do it." She's almost in tears. *How can she look even more beautiful?*

"You can and you will, Freya," I threaten. I'll get her there.

"Fuck you." There's that fire; I resist grinning at her brattiness.

"Watch your mouth," I warn, grabbing her chin.

Deep strokes slide in and out of her wetness. I pull out, the tip kisses her opening and then plunges back inside. A never ending, relentless rhythm. Leaning down, I bite the soft underside of her breasts, and she makes a breathy squeak.

"You're the one that likes watching it," she snarks.

"Good one." I lap at the bite marks with my tongue.

I have to keep concentration. I'm overstimulating her and edging myself at the same time. It's a fragile balance. I distract myself by naming off the goalies in the western conference. When I gain control of my impulses again, I push her body even harder and she groans. Her abs flex. Another groan.

"You're such an asshole," she seethes.

"Aw, come on, baby. Why don't you sit on my lap and tell me all about it while you ride this dick." Grabbing her arm, I haul her up and pull her onto my knees while I force her up and down on my erection.

"I hate you," she moans. Her words contradict the sounds she's making.

She's so cute when she's pissed off. I pinch her clit, and she actually snarls at me.

"Okay, Hellcat." I smirk. "I'll make you a deal. You look me in the eye and come up with five things you hate about me.

If you make it to five, I'll stop. But if you drop eye contact or fumble your words, I get to slap this pretty pussy. Ready?"

She consents. I'm starting to worry I won't ever get to come. I let her fall onto her back again while I grip her sides and impale her on me. She wastes no time getting started.

"You ignore me."

"One."

"You spit out the French macarons I made you." *She saw that?*

"Two."

"You let that g-girl sit—" She inhales. "Sit on your lap." She looks away, bracing for the impact. I spread her wide for me and slap as I thrust. Her surprised mouth pops open and the lovely raspy moan has me doubling down on my focus.

"Three," I grit out.

"You . . . you . . ." It's as if she's forgotten how to speak.

"What's wrong, baby, can't think straight? Don't be impolite. Answer me."

*Slap.*

*Gasp.* "You don't tip me at the bar!"

"Four."

She moans and slides herself up and down my cock while lying on her back. *Well, this is fun.* Does she even realize she's fucking herself on me?

"That was only four. Focus, Freya. Give me one more."

Her eyes bounce between mine, but nothing comes out of her mouth.

"Need help? How about I didn't tell you I was Hat Trick Swayze . . . Or that it pisses you off that I'm able to get you off with my tongue when no one else can . . . What about that I watched you on *Followers* even after I knew it was you, stroking myself every time you told me about your boring day —I'll never stop rubbing my dick to you . . . Come on, Freya, say it. Tell me why you hate me. I'm arrogant . . . I get off on your anger . . ."

She hisses again, still grinding against me.

"That's what I thought. You're not going to give me number five. Because you love it when I make you come, don't you, Freya?" She worries her raised eyebrows and nods as if she's ashamed. I continue gripping her hips and driving into her. Leaning down, I bite below her ear. "Say it out loud," I whisper the command, slowing my strokes and gripping my dick to fight my release.

She mumbles under her breath.

"Speak up."

"I love it when you make me come," she whimpers.

"Fuck . . ." She's killing me.

Her rhythm becomes choppy as she attempts to keep up.

"You are the sweetest fucking slut, baby." I shake my head in disbelief. "Okay, give me one more. I know you have it in you."

I feel her up, toying with her nipple.

"I-I don't!"

"Then why didn't you say number five? Why didn't you give me a color?" I growl.

She gets up on her elbows and kegels around my shaft like a vise, trying to get me to come first. Sighs and gasps and moans leave her hoarse throat. Freya makes the most heavenly noises when she's overcome with pleasure, even when she's doing it to manipulate me.

"Remember talking about those limits way back when? Tonight we're finding yours."

I know she's not lying. Her body is tired as fuck. Her limbs are heavy, she's exhausted and her eyes are glazed. It's taking every bit of energy for her to keep going. I'm so proud of her.

I pull out and bend her knees, forcing her back so I can spit on her asshole.

"Shit," she gasps.

Sitting on my heels, I bring one of her legs over the other, maneuvering her onto her side, so I can plunge in and out. Tip to base. Base to tip. Those long strokes that drive her crazy.

"I know you're tired, but I need you to hold your leg for me."

She does because she's no quitter. My girl is a shaky mess and has never looked sexier.

I use two fingers to lift her chin to look at me. "You can do this. You are doing such a good job. Just one more."

She gazes back with the most trusting eyes, and it's the submissive Freya I'm staring at. Sweet and subdued. She's transformed from grizzly to gummy bear.

I press gently against the knot between her cheeks, covered in my saliva. "Consent, Freya Girl."

She blows the air out of her lungs, preparing for another round. "Green."

Fuck, I want to take her here too. She's incredible.

Slowly, I press my middle digit into her tight ass, add more spit, and finger her ass while I fuck her cunt. Her breaths stutter.

"Don't drop your leg," I warn.

I bring the vibrator to her clit.

There's worry in her voice. "Rhys . . . I don't—"

"Deep breath."

She gulps air, and when I turn it on, the delicious torture rips through her. I watch in awe, fulfilled from sending her into oblivion one more time. I'm putting her through the wringer tonight, and the pleasure on her face is breathtaking. I can't hold back anymore. I need to come so bad it hurts.

I fuck her harder. When she shakes and cries out my name, I explode, filling the condom up with my release. A roar climbs out of my throat, the relief is overpowering. Her thumping walls squeeze tighter than ever. She absentmindedly drops her leg, and the soft skin over her stomach wrinkles and contracts as another one tears into her, back-to-back. She's coming so hard. She gave me *two*.

And then I feel it.

She gushes around my cock. *She's squirting.*

With my name on her lips, her eyes snap open, and she appears more surprised that it's happening than I am. *Is this her first time?*

*It is. And I'm the one to give it to her.* My heart pounds. My energy is zapped, but getting this from her is reenergizing.

"Ohmygod, ohmygod."

As she slows, I match her pace, bringing us back to earth in slow thrusts.

"You did so good, baby," I soothe. "Look how much you came."

She sobs, completely overwhelmed. Hopefully she's not embarrassed, but I'm prepared to keep her with me all night until she's regulated back to her usual sassy, rebellious self.

Letting go of the vibrator, I wipe away her tears, then lie next to her, tucking her body into mine. I don't care that the bed is soaked. My lips caress her shaky shoulders as she lets all her pent-up emotion out. Before long, she calms and her breathing slows—melting into a puddle after the adrenaline rush.

She sucks in a breath and sniffles. "I think . . . I think I ruined your sheets."

"You didn't ruin anything. You were incredible, Freya."

After a minute, I stand and walk to the bathroom, turning on the water for the tub.

From the corner of my eye, I see her come up behind me.

"What are you doing?"

"Running us a bath."

"Oh." Her eyebrows raise. It's like she's never seen a bathtub before. Did she believe I'd put her through the paces, fuck her savagely, and not take care of her afterward? I may be an asshole, but I'm not a monster.

Without turning on the lights, my hands fish around in the cupboard and set out two fluffy towels. I step into the water and offer my hand to help her into the deep tub. I'm guessing these are specially built for the athletes that use the apartments. Probably for ice baths or heat therapy.

As she lowers her body into the steamy water, she inhales through clenched teeth but then sighs when she settles herself between my legs. I lather up some soap in my hands while her trembling hands quickly work her hair into a top knot. I press a kiss to her shoulder before I wash her body. Neither of us says anything. Nothing needs to be said. We're exhausted and depleted. When I wash her arms, she's finally comfortable enough to lean into my chest and let her head loll back on my chest. It feels . . . right.

My hands drifts lower, and I'm extra gentle between her legs, where she's, no doubt, the most tender. She exhales softly, I love the sound of her relaxing in my arms. Without thinking, I reach for her chin and turn her head to face me.

My lips brush hers, and I pause, waiting for her to object. I glance at her eyes before my gaze falls to her mouth again. Does she need this as much as I do? Threading my fingers into her hair, I tilt my head and steal her lips. Our first kiss. It's charged and electric and wild. Like her.

Fuck, even her mouth is sweet. Trapping her subtle sighs on my lips while our tongues twist and glide together, she turns into me more, sliding a hand behind my neck. I feel alive. This kiss breaks one of her rules of friends with benefits, but I'm ready to break every other rule that goes with it. I've never wanted a woman as much as I do Freya.

She's everything.

She gave so much of herself tonight. Not only her body but opened up and gave me a sacred piece of her. Trusted me with her vulnerability. I felt it in my core. It's the most meaningful connection I've ever felt during sex. It scares the hell out of me. But it doesn't scare me enough to stop.

My lips slow, and she turns her face away from me. Dipping down, my lips graze over her shoulders. She takes the soap from me and lathers up my arms and legs as I bracket her between them. Tomorrow we'll be back to fighting like cats and dogs, but for tonight, we are letting ourselves have this.

After climbing out, we dry off with soft cotton towels, and I return to the bedroom to change the sheets. She walks out of the bathroom and goes to put her clothes back on.

"You can stay here tonight."

She bites the bottom corner of her lip and shifts her weight.

"It doesn't have to mean anything," I reassure her. I'll say anything to get her back in my bed.

She flattens her lips together and hesitates. I take her hand and pull her back into the fresh bedding. I wrap her naked body in the downy comforter. She snugs her back to my front, relaxing in my arms and molding herself to my chest. I don't let myself think about how perfect our bodies fit together.

"Thank you for showing me," she rasps, barely above a whisper.

"Thank you for trusting me. How are you feeling?"

"Relaxed." She sounds like she's about to fall asleep.

I smile, tracing my fingertips under her breasts.

"And . . ." She pauses, contemplating her words. "And confused. I've never done anything like that before. Being submissive, squirting, all of it. I didn't know it would feel like that."

"Did you like it?"

"I loved it."

Our breathing blends into a peaceful rhythm as we fall asleep.

I don't know what time it is when I wake to a dull pounding coming from the front door. I don't want to move. There's a warm, tranquil Freya still dozing in my arms. I never get her like this, and I don't want it to end.

*What is that noise?*

Reluctantly, I drag myself out of bed, make it to the front door, and look through the peephole.

*Shit.* I open the door.

"Can I borrow a couple bucks?"

Her eyes are like black holes.

"Are you high?"

"That's a rude thing to ask."

I turn around and squint at the clock on the microwave. "It's four in the morning, Anna. What the fuck?"

"I know, I know. I just got a new job, and I need some money for gas. I work the third shift."

"You don't have a car."

"I know. But my Uber driver needs money for gas . . ."

I rub my forehead. "That doesn't make sense."

"Okay. So, can I have it?"

"Where are you working?"

"Well, I don't have the job yet, but I need the money. If you're not going to give me money, then I need a place to crash."

I try to remember what Freya said about boundaries.

"Anna, you can't be here when you're high."

Just then, Freya comes around the corner wearing my robe. Seeing her in something of mine makes my heart hammer.

"Rhys? What's going—"

"It's just my sister."

Freya heads back into the bedroom, and Anna's face contorts. She looks pissed.

"*Just?* Wow. Thanks, *bro*." Anna sneers.

When Freya returns, she's dressed.

"I'm going to head home. Thanks, uh, for dinner."

"Freya, you don't have to go."

"It's fine. You have to get up early anyway."

"Oh! She doesn't have to go, but I do? She has a bed already, it's across the hall!" Anna shouts. *How is she this amped at four in the morning?*

I was hoping I could get a decent goodbye from Freya. I was looking forward to kissing her again, but instead, she steps between Anna and me and slips back into her apartment before I can even respond.

And just like that, the private bubble we were in bursts.

"That's fine, if you don't want to give me a place to stay, I'm sure there's plenty of other men that will happily take me in and let me earn some money. Jesus, my own brother plays in the pros and won't even give me a cent of his million-dollar signing bonus."

"That's fucked up. And fuck you for putting that on me. This is your choice." I'm pissed at her for giving me an ultimatum and for waking up Freya and ending our time together early.

"Well, right now, it's your choice." She holds her arms out wide. "What'll it be?"

I'm tired, and I can't tell if she's bluffing or not.

Damn it, I don't want to deal with this. "Guest bedroom." I hate it, but at least now I know she'll be safe tonight. "Take a shower first, you stink."

# TWENTY-THREE

*Micky*

It's five in the morning, and I can't go back to sleep.

*Fuck.* I'm in trouble.

That was the best sex I've ever had. There's fucking and then there's what he did. It was more than sex, it was a whole experience. I've never let go of my inhibitions like that. He completely took over, and I let him! That's not something I give up easily. Honestly, it's not something I do. But it was based on trust and respect and care—three words I never imagined using to describe Rhys Kucera.

He's one of the most fascinating men I've ever met. He's dominant and aggressive. He's intense. But he's also very down-to-earth when you get to know him. In a crowd, he's mostly quiet and keeps to himself, but during those times he's observant and protective. When we're alone, he's charming and funny, and he confides in me. And I like what he has to say, especially the things he says when he's between my thighs. But he's not looking for anything serious, he told me himself.

They say if you're not dating for forever, you're dating for heartache. *But what if I just want to date to get my vagina licked again?* I was hoping to get him out of my system. A little *rock-my-*

*box-and-change-the-locks* action. But I let him do things I haven't let anyone do before. What would cause me to put that confidence in him so early? What does it mean if I trust him that much already? To surrender myself like that? It sounds like heartache.

It's hard to sleep when those questions keep bouncing around inside my head. I've got to work tonight, and if I plan on getting any rest before my shift, it's gotta happen now. The Lakes play tonight, I can't be dead on my feet.

Four hours later, I awaken from my second sleep. More of a power nap. I slept so soundly next to Rhys—another thing that hasn't happened in a long time. After returning to my bed, it felt kind of empty.

I'm not surprised Anna came back. It's the cycle. Take, leave, come back, take, leave, come back. Wash and repeat. There's never any giving. I used to think Rhys wasn't giving but he's proven me wrong. Especially when it comes to orgasms. He excels at it.

I pad into the kitchen and turn on the coffee maker before getting into the shower. It was less than twelve hours ago that Rhys had a bath drawn for the two of us. That was the part I was most apprehensive about. Not the degradation, no. He can call me his good little whore all night long, but the second he wrapped his arms around me and held me . . . that was something I wasn't sure I could handle. The aftercare scared me.

*The aftercare.* It was so . . . unexpected. He was considerate and attentive. He pressed the lightest kisses to my shoulder. He held me and whispered sweet things. I don't know if I've had that . . . ever.

Certainly not after aggressive sex. Rough sex is fun, I like it, but usually during hookups it's just that. A hookup. It doesn't come with aftercare. It comes with a high-five and an Uber. But he asked me to stay the night. *And that kiss?* That kiss terrified me, it brought back feelings I didn't know still existed. It was spectacular.

I work the shampoo into my hair and scalp and rinse it out. Then glob on some conditioner and let it soak in while sudsing up a washcloth with soap to scrub his scent off me, the smell of his soap from our bath. It's sexy and intoxicating, which is exactly why I need it off my body.

What would have happened the next morning if Anna hadn't shown up? Probably would've been awkward as hell. And what now? Do we fall back into our old pattern of hating each other? We have fun together, but I'm not sure I can be fucked like that and keep a boundary with my emotions.

After I get out of the shower, I throw on some leggings and a sweater. The delicious aroma of coffee wafting through the apartment is inviting. Weather is beautiful outside. I open the window to breathe in the invigorating fresh-autumn air. There's just something about a crisp fall day and a warm cup of coffee the morning after a night of intense gland-to-gland combat.

The knock at the door startles me from my daydreaming. I look through the peephole and am surprised to see Rhys on the other side. When I open it up, he's holding matching to-go cups of coffee in his hands.

"Hey." He looks down and sees the mug in my hand. "Looks like I'm a little late. I didn't want to come over any earlier and wake you."

"Thanks . . ." I open the door wider for him to enter. "You didn't need to get me coffee." We had a good time, but this wasn't necessary. Maybe I scrambled his brain with my amazing vagina.

"I wanted to apologize for last night."

My shoulders slump. *He regrets it.* Of course he does, this was never part of the plan. He won't see that it bothers me. Because it doesn't. Not even a little. I couldn't care less.

"Yeah, no worries. Just a one-time thing, I get it. Shouldn't have let it go that far."

"The fuck?" His brows come together. "No. Whoa! No, no, no. That part was great. I'm apologizing that Anna showed up. Our night together got interrupted."

Oh. *Oh.*

"I never meant to spend the night. I mean, it was nice, but we both know what this is." We're sexually compatible. We fuck well together. No more, no less.

With an icy stare, he stalks closer, stepping into my personal space and backing me into the wall.

"And what *is* it, Freya?"

I look down at my mug. "You know, a hookup. Getting it out of our systems . . . Dusting off the entertainment center."

He lifts my chin but doesn't respond. It makes sense he's a bit surprised. I mean, what woman would freely kick themselves out of his bed? Who wouldn't want to have a round two? *If you had any sense, you would.* I try to ignore my conscience. His lips press into a grimace, and his jaw clenches.

"What did you think it was?" I ask.

"I thought it was the best sex I've ever had, and I want it again."

# TWENTY-FOUR
## *Micky*

I'm glad I got a small break after sex with Rhys. My clitoris was straight up bruised after he used that toy on me last week. The time apart has also given me more opportunities to contemplate what it is we're doing.

I told myself I was done with fuckboys and wanted a relationship, something real. Like renting an apartment versus buying a home. For some people, renting works great for them, they can do it for their whole lives. It certainly has its perks. There's more independence. Other people rent for a while until they feel like they've settled down with a career and then they are ready to put down roots and make an investment. A commitment. And there's the last group. They'll jump right into home-owning because somebody once told them it was slutty to "shop around." Fuck that noise.

It seems like casual sex is the only option for us. But . . . a few more times wouldn't be the worst thing in the world. He's right, we have off-the-charts bedroom chemistry . . . And kitchen chemistry . . . And stairwell chemistry.

And I've changed my outfit four times. Four. It's not a date, it's sex. *He doesn't care what you wear; it's your pussy he wants.*

RHYS

You're late.

> Had to finish up a few things, I'll be there in a sec

RHYS

Don't make me wait any longer or I'll come over there and get you myself.

> Don't tempt me with a good time. 😉

My hair and makeup look fine, but the clothes elude me. I don't want to appear too eager. What's wrong with me? I don't get nervous for dates.

*This isn't a date.*

I can't help that something about Rhys makes me want to put in the extra effort, which is why tonight I'm going in there with my body groomed and primed. I'm prepared for anything.

I can't change my clothes a fifth time, I hate being late. Especially after all my threats to him about tardiness, the last thing I want to do is give him a reason to retaliate. It's a short sundress with a floral print. I had to dig it out of the back of my closet. I'm used to wearing a lot of black. But figured, what the hell, he might get a rise out of seeing me in something a little more feminine and innocent. He likes me sweet. And the more he likes me tonight, the harder he'll work. Pretty sure my math checks out.

I hustle the short distance between our front doors. He swings it open before I can even knock.

"Sorry I'm late. I didn't want to come."

"Don't lie to me. That's the whole reason you're here, Hellcat." He grabs my arm and yanks me inside, kicking the door shut and pushing me up against it. This is the shit I showed up for. He boxes me in with his arms.

"What the hell are you wearing?"

"My tuxedo?" I should probably cool it with the sarcasm or he's really going to get me tonight. Oh well.

He grabs my jaw while he appraises me. "You look very pretty in this dress, Freya Girl."

I let my eyes roam over his body. Freshly showered, tight shirt, nice jeans. No socks this time. Ugh, he's so handsome.

"I hope you're ready to behave tonight."

My thighs press together. "No."

"No?"

"You want me to play nice? You first."

He sweeps my hair off my shoulders and lifts my chin up so he's gazing in my eyes. His lips move to my shoulder, and he skates the tip of his tongue up my neck and behind my ear. Opening his mouth, his teeth graze over my skin back down again. *Chills.* The restraint he exhibits makes me feel warm and wanted.

"I plan to be very nice to you, Freya Girl." A small shudder rolls up my spine.

His mouth brushes over mine, and he coaxes my lips apart for our tongues to meet. It feels like we are healing old wounds and making up for all the harsh words we've hurled at each other until this point.

"You're staying the night," he mutters, dropping a kiss to my cheek. "Don't argue."

He takes my hand and pulls me down the hallway. We pass the guest bedroom, and I consider asking where Anna is but don't want to take him out of the moment.

He pulls me close when we enter his room. The space is beautiful, similar to mine. High ceilings, exposed brick, black sash windows, and a huge metal bed with a steel canopy. The massive mirror at the end of the bed doesn't annoy me like it used to, now it's a bonus.

"Be good so I can use you, because tonight you're mine,

understand?" The words make my skin tingle. "Do you want to be degraded?"

"I thought you'd never ask . . ."

He studies my face while toying with the side zipper of my dress. He pulls it up, down, up again. Like he's deciding whether he wants me to keep it on. Goose bumps spread across my skin. When he tells me not to take it off, it makes the extra time I took picking it out all worth it. This time, I'm wearing one of the thongs he bought me, something I haven't shown off in front of other men.

"On the bed . . . You're such a sweet fucktress." The anticipation is overwhelming. "Bend over, let me see you."

Kneeling on the soft bedding, I do as he says and drop down on my hands. I smile, knowing full well this dress is too short to cover my ass when I'm bent over. I subtly stretch to pull the fabric higher. His warm palm glides up the back of my thigh and under my dress.

"I can see right through your thong."

"Isn't that why you bought it? To see my pussy?"

His index finger hooks underneath, pulling down, then snaps it. I close my eyes, living in the moment and loving his foreboding nature. He chuckles and drags the thong down my thighs. Lifting one knee at a time, he removes it and tucks it in his nightstand. This time when his large hand slides up the back of my thighs, he spreads my cheeks. I mentally high-five myself for the anal prep I did this afternoon. I know he's staring at my ass, and it's making me wetter by the second.

"Fuck," he groans.

*Please, yes.* I'm already descending into that submissive neediness, less inclined to talk back to him and be sassy. Doesn't mean I'll ever fully stop, but it's fun to switch things up.

Strong fingers dig into my backside as he keeps me open for him to view. His thumb slips through my arousal, and I suck in a breath. He moves up to my asshole where he adds pressure. I arch my back as my body begs for his touch.

"Are you going to let me take you here?"

"Please?" *Jesus, it's like I'm not even trying anymore.*

"Freya, did you just say *please*?" I'd answer, but I can't find the words. "Be careful, you don't want anyone finding out how much you love to beg."

I suppress the eye roll.

He continues to press against that spot, and heat pools in my belly. "Remember how hard you came the last time I was here? How much do you think you would come if I were inside your tight round ass?"

My inhales come faster with each breath. The sound of his voice, the anticipation, it's killing me.

"There's only one way to find out."

Walking to the side of the bed, his belt buckle clinks as he loosens it. That sound makes me shiver. He reaches into the bedside table and pulls out a small bottle of lube and a vibrator, this one different from before, but in new packaging. I'm turned on that he's specifically buying sex toys to use on me. For us. I like knowing he's surfing the internet and deciding which toys will bring me pleasure while he fucks me.

"You can use this, or I can, whatever's most comfortable." The way he says it feels less personal, and all the excitement from before feels less special. A small ache in my chest forms, but I ignore it. I don't know why that stings. This is only sex, right? I should be grateful he provided a toy.

I position myself in front of him, sitting up on my knees to unzip his jeans, freeing him. He has a gorgeous cock. He's the prototype for dildos everywhere.

"May I?"

"Make it wet. I want to see you sloppy."

He guides my mouth, and I send him to the back of my throat, where the slickest saliva is. With his size, I'll need all the help I can get. I lube him up and don't hold back. My blowjob is wet, sloppy, and loud.

"Mmhmm, just like that. Keep going, sweetheart."

He cradles the back of my head, rubbing small circles at the nape of my neck. As I take him in and out of my mouth and listen to his praises and small groans of approval, he brings one knee on the bed and moves the vibrator between my legs. My back arches.

"Turn around and show me how wet you get sucking my cock."

When I pop off him, he wipes the bit of saliva from the corner of my mouth. I spin around, and he chuckles darkly.

"You're dripping."

After kicking off his heavy denim jeans, he pulls his shirt over his head. His thumb outlines the perimeter of my center, drawing out my arousal and spreading it around, from my clit to my opening and up to my ass.

"You remember your safewords?"

"Red to stop, yellow to slow down."

He brings his other knee up on the bed and traces the pulsing silicone up and down the back of my thighs, over my cheeks. I squirm, wanting to feel it on my clit. The longer he teases me, the wetter I get.

"Rhys, please . . ."

"Polite whores are patient."

His thumb swipes through me again, and this time he easily slides inside, there's hardly any friction between us, the sensation is intense. I almost choke on my inhale.

"You ready?" he asks. I appreciate how often he checks in with me.

"Mmhmm."

He adds some lube to my ass and presses his middle finger into me.

"Just stretching you out." I gasp as he preps me. My core

wants to contract, but I try to relax and take deep breaths. He pushes in the crown, pressing himself deeper inside.

"Yellow."

"Good, Freya. That's so fucking good." I adore the praise as much as I do the degradation. He coats his erection in more lube. Dramatically slower this time, he continues to penetrate me, it's much smoother this time.

"Green."

He kneads my ass cheeks and spreads my thighs apart. It's been so long since I've felt this, the electrifying rush that pounds in my chest.

"You choose the pace, Freya," he says, "I'll match it."

*This guy knows how to anal.*

Even though I'm thoroughly lubed up, I need to let my body acclimate to his size. I pause with my head hanging between my shoulders. After a slow breath, I relax my muscles, then take him inch by inch in shallow thrusts.

"Freya, this ass. *Jesus Christ* . . . How are you doing?"

I exhale. "Good. Just need a second." He feels so good.

"Fuck, I feel like *I* need a second."

After administering a small, sharp spank, he moves his palms up and down my back before settling them on my hips, they're warm and protective.

He picks the vibrator up again. "Don't fight it, don't think, just feel." He's being so careful with me. I appreciate it but am concerned the intimacy is crossing a line. Sliding it up my legs, he rests it at my entrance, and I continue to rock against him. With each stroke, the pull inside me grows.

"This is what you need, isn't it?"

God, yes. I needed him.

"Uh-huh," I pant.

His hand travels up to my neck and wraps around my throat, palming me from behind. My body reacts quicker this time. Everything tightens, and I think I might come. He chuckles, and I hear the gratification in his voice. "I love the way you melt for me. As soon as my fingers covered this sweet, sensitive neck"—he gently strokes me with his thumb—"I felt your body flutter around my cock." I can only moan in response.

I am so close to coming. I pick up my pace a little, and the buzzing silicone is placed where I need it. I grind, pushing him deep into my ass and pulling off until I reach the tip. I catch his reflection in the mirror off to the side, his head falls back, and he groans. He's putty in my hands. It brings me more satisfaction than it should. The constant stimulation is making my legs quiver. I'll soon lose control.

My abs flex and my back arches.

"There you go."

He releases my throat only to wrap his arm around me and pull me to my knees while he's buried to the hilt behind me. I cry out.

Sliding back up to my neck again, he grips my jaw and presses a soft kiss to my temple. When he lets go, he gives a tender slap to my face and returns to gripping my neck.

I form an O with my mouth and blow out. Keep it together. My feminism takes a backseat while my kink rides shotgun. I relish those small swats.

"Does my slut need me to take over?"

I can't even think straight, much less be in control. I'm stuck in this blissful fog of euphoria. Every nerve is sparking and wanting more, but I'm too raptured to do anything about it. It's a paralysis of the best kind.

"Please, Rhys."

"You beg so well, baby." He nips behind my ear.

He takes me again, and at this angle, I feel him everywhere, it's pure pleasure. One hand around my throat, the other pushing vibrations into my clit.

"How does it feel?" he whispers.

"So good," I moan. "It's always so good." His hold on me turns possessive, and I grip the back of his neck and shoulder to steady my balance while my body shudders. "Harder."

He sets the vibrator down to grab more lubricant. Once he's ready to continue, his controlled drives are determined, rougher. I cry out with each drum of pleasure that rips through me as he pounds from behind. I'm overwhelmed, my pulse is whooshing in my ears, but underneath the noise, "Be mine, Freya Girl" slips from his lips. Did he really say that, or did I imagine it? Probably side effects of all the oxytocin.

He gently lowers me back onto all fours and fucks me down from my climax with languid strokes. Ever so slowly, he pulls out, and it's like I could come all over again.

Forcefully gripping my hips, he flips me on my back and feasts on me. He has a taker attitude, but this man is all giving. This is what I found so attractive during our long chats—when he's in, *he's all in.*

He shoves my dress higher and looks up at me from between my thighs. "You are the most beautiful whore. And you're mine, understand? I can't stay away from you."

My body trembles, his words sparking another orgasm. *His fucking words.* He extends his arm to grab my throat again while licking and sucking, and I fall over the edge. He brings one leg back down on the floor, pulling me to the edge of the bed in front of him, still writhing from the last one.

"Relax. Deep breath, babe."

I exhale and concentrate on relaxing my lower half.

"Ready?"

I've never had anal sex in missionary. His firm grasp pushes up my calves, he spits with impressive accuracy and then slides the head of his cock back inside me. Fuck, he's huge. The angle shift makes it all new. He fills my ass and holds himself there. I'm adjusted to him, but I need more movement. I want to feel him gliding in and out. He senses my frustration and simply smiles, enjoying my misery.

"You better start fucking me."

He barks out a laugh but remains steady.

My cheek gets another slap. "Don't try to top from the bottom, Princess. It's very unbecoming."

He leans down to kiss me, and my stomach erupts with butterflies. *No, it's too much.*

"Red."

He pulls back and raises an eyebrow at the use of my safeword. I don't want to hurt his feelings by recoiling, but I don't want my feelings hurt either.

"Red for kissing you?"

I nod. "Use me. Make me your slut, Rhys. Fuck me, mark me with your cum, and turn me into a mess like you do every single time."

"Move an inch and you won't be coming tonight." His voice sounds colder than before.

I bite my lip and do as he says.

The way our bodies move together. It's *everything*. He sets me free. I'm dizzy and tired, and another orgasm hovers on the brink. I know I'll be sore tomorrow, but it'll be so worth it. His eyes are locked on mine, and I want to look away, feeling exposed. His stare is too intimate. If it was anyone but Rhys, this would be heaven. It's the way I've always wanted to be looked at. But this is just sex.

"Why can't I kiss you?"

"Let's talk about it later."

"No. Now," he growls.

"Y . . . you're going to make me feel things."

"Good. Because there's plenty of things I feel for you." I dig my fingers into his back. "I was thinking about all the times I sent you money on *Followers*. Every time I paid you to let me jack off to your body. Darling, I could drain my bank account and it wouldn't be enough. You would still be the most priceless thing I've ever fucked. You are so much more than anything—"

"Red." I can't handle hearing this. "You can't say things like that when you're inside me." I'm embarrassed to pull the safeword again. I should be able to handle a few flattering comments and not take them to heart, but it's him. For me, those words hold significance. There are consequences if I misinterpret his praise for something deeper than sex.

His jaw clinches when he swallows. We watch each other, battling to stay in the moment. Without warning, my legs are pushed off his shoulders and he drops to his forearms and sinks those strong fingers into my hair. His lips move over mine, and I don't fight it this time. The way he grips me is tense and full of frustration, but he's kissing me like I'm the most treasured thing he's ever held.

At this moment, nothing else matters. Our kiss is emotional, packed with apologies and longing for more in equal measure. It's a truce. *I'm willing if you are.*

My pussy clenches as he thrusts. He presses his forehead to mine and catches his breath.

"That's it, baby." It doesn't sound as arrogant as it usually does, it's encouraging, like he wants to stroke my pleasure, not his ego. *This is Rhys, unfiltered.*

"Where do you want me to finish?"

"Mark me."

Pumping a few more times, that familiar tightening pulls at my inner walls. Then Rhys withdraws from my ass and straddles my stomach. He strokes his slick cock a few times while maintaining eye contact and then spurts cum on my chest and neck. The act itself is degrading, the look in his eyes is filled with lust and possession and . . . devotion. Kneeling over me and panting, he looks like a god. We're both speechless. Whatever arrangement we had when tonight started no longer exists. That line in the sand washed away.

This wasn't just a hookup. His gaze tells me he feels the shift too.

After pressing a small kiss to my temple, he carefully backs off me and climbs out of bed, bringing back a wet washcloth to clean me up. Afterward, he leads me into the attached bathroom. Like before, he runs a bath for us, this time adding Epsom salt. I unzip my dress, and it pools at my feet. After climbing in, he takes my hand, ushering me between his muscular thighs.

"You did so well tonight."

"I didn't do anything, you did all the work." I sigh happily.

"You did, Freya. You put a lot of trust into me, and you had no reason to after I lied to you. I'm sorry. I don't take your trust for granted. I need you to know that."

*Wow.* I'm not sure how to respond, so I look down at the water and nod.

"Are you sore?"

"It's a nice sore."

He pulls my back to his front and wraps arms around me in a bear hug. I relax against him, and we settle in together, matching our breaths. After what must be ten minutes of silence he asks, "Tell me why you're on *Followers*."

*That came out of left field.*

"What do you mean?"

His feather touch skates up and down my arm. The warm water trickles off his fingertips and drips down my cold, pebbled flesh. "I once asked you, and you told me it was just for money. Tell me what the money's for."

"A commercial space."

He doesn't say anything, so I continue.

"I want to open a patisserie cocktail lounge mash-up. It's

been my dream for a while. But fresh out of college I couldn't get a business loan, and there's this spot I picked out that's going to open up any day now. The location is impeccable. I joined *Followers* to make extra money so that when it becomes available, I can swoop in and make a cash offer."

He exhales, and it sounds like relief.

His lips press against my temple. "Why didn't you tell me before?"

"I dunno, it's personal. Something I've kept to myself, except for Birdie, she's known about it for years."

"You've had this plan for years?"

"Yeah, it began in college and grew from there. Eventually I wrote up a business plan and ran it by a few people who checked my homework. I had to adjust it again when I moved here, but it's solid. As long as I get the location I want, that's the most critical part. It's near Citra Brewing, a few ad agencies. A theater. The clientele is beyond ideal."

"That's really impressive. I'm proud of you. Thank you for sharing it with me." Dropping his chin to my shoulder, he inhales.

"Thanks." I smile, feeling proud of myself too. His approval is important, it also makes my heart thump.

His fingers continue dripping water over my chilled skin. "What are you going to call it?" His lips move back and forth across my shoulder, warmth radiating from his kisses.

"You can't make fun of it."

"I won't," he promises.

"I was thinking of Sugar and Ice."

His lips curl into a small grin against my skin.

"Very fitting. Icy and sweet, just like you."

My elbow finds his ribs, and he chuckles, twining our fingers together and wrapping his arms around me again. I turn my head and kiss his lips. Then his gaze falls to my shoulder and he smiles big.

"What?"

"Hold still, I believe I got some cum in your hair."

I fall back against his chest laughing at the unexpected transition. He very sweetly attempts to rinse the strands. Eventually I move to the other side of the tub and dip my whole head underwater and work my fingers through my hair. When I come up, I find him relaxed with both arms resting on the sides of the tub. He observes me thoughtfully as I wring the water from my hair.

I angle the side of my head toward him. "Did I get it all?"

He pulls me back into his arms and water sloshes up the sides of the tub.

"All of it."

We sit in silence together until the water chills. He gets out before helping me step out of the tub and wrapping me in a towel. I'm definitely feeling some aches now.

After drying off, he climbs into bed and holds up the sheet for me to climb under. I look between him and my dress on the bathroom floor.

"I told you, you're staying the night."

*What about his sister? Anna was not pleased to see me last time I was caught leaving his apartment.*

"But—"

"Get your sweet ass in this bed. Now."

I follow orders. I'm tired of thinking. When I slide in next to him, I release a content sigh and rest my head on his chest. I'm soothed from my head to my toes. His fingers slip through my hair, and it lulls me into a serene trance. My body is exhausted. If I was smart, I'd pull back and continue to safeguard my heart, but denying our connection is futile.

And I can't bring myself to leave his arms.

# TWENTY-FIVE

## *Rhys*

I can't get this woman out of my head.

> What are you doing?

FREYA

Nothing . . .

> Wanna get food?

FREYA

Right now?

> Yeah. I'm bored and I'm hungry. And I kinda miss you.

FREYA

Where do you wanna go?

> Let's go to that shithole you wanna buy.

FREYA

They got a C on their last inspection, we aren't eating there. Btw I checked the public notices and they filed for bankruptcy last week.

Well, then we better celebrate, darling.

I typed and deleted *darling* three times before deciding to go with it.

FREYA

How about fajitas?

Meet me downstairs in 10.

"Mmmmm." With closed eyes, Freya does a cute shimmy as she savors a bite of peppers and chicken. She's not wrong either. These are hitting the spot. I don't know how she's been here only a few months and already knows which restaurants have the best food.

"Now who's making sex noises when they eat?"

"These aren't sex noises, they're food noises."

"Sometimes they're both." I wink at her.

I wipe my mouth with the napkin and sit back in the booth to observe her. She's sexy when she eats. It's not something she does in particular, it's her nature. Everything she does is sexy.

"So, tell me more about Sugar and Ice."

"What do you want to know?"

*Everything. And I have no idea why.*

"I dunno, what do you picture it looking like?"

She finishes chewing her bite and takes a sip of water.

"The best part about it is the front." Her eyes track outside, and she points out the window.

"Wait—*that's* it?" I see now why she wanted to come here. She wanted a good view of her future establishment.

"You're right. It's incredible. Wherever did you ever find such a place?" I ask sarcastically, rolling my eyes. The front is a big metal door, there's a small window, but that's it. The sidewalk is in disrepair. I figured she was downplaying it, but I was right on the mark when I called it a shithole.

"I know, it looks bad, but have you ever been somewhere that looks like a dump on the outside and then you walk through the doors and it's like you're entering a completely different world? It's magical! That's what I want. Granted, it's rundown on the outside *and* the inside, but I plan on changing that. It has so much potential. High ceilings, brick archways, I suspect there might be wood flooring underneath the warped commercial tile. I just need to finish getting the capital."

"How close are you?"

"About three months away." Her eyes fall in disappointment. "I was hoping they could hang on a little longer. I might be able to get rent for a couple months, but without my full amount, I'm not sure if the landlord will let me have it without proof I can get it cleaned up. They've made it clear they're hesitant to keep it a restaurant. I'm not sure what condition the kitchen is in, so I have to be prepared for purchasing new commercial ovens, which would take a larger percentage than what I originally allocated for appliances."

"Tell me about your vision for the inside."

"Why do you want to hear all this?"

I shrug. Truthfully, it baffles me too. "I find it interesting. And it's important to you."

"Okay, so when you walk in, there's this big arch I'm pretty sure is brick if you tear down the hideous plaster mural painted on it."

"What's the mural of?"

"Richard Nixon."

"No, it isn't." I stab more food with my fork.

She grins around a bite of food. "He's not even smiling."

"Oof."

"Right? Anyway, if the brick is anything like the stuff on

the adjacent wall, it's gorgeous. Can you imagine the brick archways? I want it to mimic a prohibition-style speakeasy. Maybe even have a password at the door." Her eyes are twice the normal size when she describes it. I've not seen her so passionate about something before. "It's a decent-sized space, but there's a step-down area on the west wall, so I'd love to have a U-shaped bar in that area." She's drawing out an invisible map for me on the table. "Then over here, there's some awkward structural columns, but I thought it would be cool to turn them into three-sixty seating around the load-bearing posts."

"Clever."

Her fingers continue their explanation over the invisible floorplan. "Over in this section would be a great spot for some grab-and-go desserts. Then I would have lounge seating across this area, intimate sections for business deals or small parties, couples on first dates. You know, like this."

"Like this? What do you mean?"

"Isn't this the date?"

"No."

I haven't had the chance to take her out and do something special. I suppose that's on me. I need to make that right. When was the last time I was on a real date? I can't fuck this up, it has to be something good.

"Isn't it? You're buying me lunch and asking about my dreams for the future. Sounds like a date to me."

"I was bored and wanted to get food. You're fun to hangout with, so I invited you to come with me." I gesture between us. "But, I see your point. I'm enjoying your company. You seem to be enjoying mine. I plan to kiss you afterward . . ."

I waggle my eyebrows at her, but she responds with the classic Freya eye roll.

"If you want this to be a date, it can be a date. But it doesn't count as the one I owe you from our bet."

"You're crazy."

"So are you. That's why we're great together."

# TWENTY-SIX

## Rhys

"Where are we going?" She leans forward in my truck, looking around.

"If I told you, it wouldn't be a surprise."

She turns and narrows her eyes. "Maybe I hate surprises."

"If you did, you wouldn't say *maybe*. Also, you told me on *Followers* you liked them. And even if you did hate them, *maybe* I don't give a fuck."

"You should. I could make your life a living hell."

"You already make it a living hell. Being around you is like having a migraine and an erection at the same time."

"Fuck you." She laughs and pokes my shoulder. "I'm lovely."

The last couple weeks have been a breeze. Being with her is so easy. Most of the time, we spend our time together laughing and making jokes. When that's not happening, we're tied up in the bedroom or wherever else I feel like having my way with her.

"Speaking of surprises . . ." I clear my throat. *I don't know why I'm so nervous to ask her.* "I've got an extra ticket for Thursday's game. Will you come?"

"To watch you play?"

"Yes, I thought that was implied when I offered a ticket to a hockey game."

"I can't, I work Thursday."

"Quit. It'll be worth it."

She smirks at me.

"But . . ." She shrugs casually. "Maybe another time?" If I didn't know any better, I'd say she sounded hopeful.

I smile, satisfied with her answer. Reaching into my wallet, I pluck the spare ticket from my billfold and hand it over to her. "In case your schedule changes or you decide to come and see me instead of flirting with other customers."

"That's tough to beat. It's pretty fun flirting with other customers."

"I bet it's more fun watching me work up a sweat."

"Yeah, but I don't need a ticket to your game to do that."

I reach across the console to squeeze her thigh. I hope she likes this date. I told her to dress warm since we would be outside. We already have some snow on the ground. This season is flying by so fast.

"Are you taking me skating?"

I shake my head.

"Are you taking me camping?"

I look at the empty backseat of my truck. "With what gear?"

"Are we going to the zoo?"

"No. Stop guessing."

She slumps back in her seat and groans.

When we enter the parking lot, she sits up again and searches for something familiar. I park next to the facility sign, and she reads it aloud.

"Bradley Raptor Center?" I see the moment it dawns on her what we're doing, and her face lights up like Christmas morning. Her bright-green eyes sparkle, and she covers her mouth.

"Oh my God. Rhys. No way! Are we?"

I chuckle as I turn off the truck. "Something you've always wanted to try, right?"

"I get to meet falcons?!" She grips my right arm with both hands and makes an enthusiastic high-pitched sound. Seeing her happy makes my heart swell.

"A falcon, a hawk, and an owl. And feed an eagle a fish head." It sounds disgusting, but her eyes are dancing. *Wait, is she . . .* "Freya, are you going to cry?"

"No!" She swipes under her eyes. "I'm just excited!"

She's so cute, getting all worked up over rotting fish heads.

# TWENTY-SEVEN

## Micky

We get inside in time for the eagle feeding. A nice woman guides us back to one of the smaller raptor rehabilitation rooms. Inside is a giant bald eagle. The poor thing has a hurt wing, but he happily takes a fish from me. Rhys shudders and gags in the corner. I have to fight the fit of laughter climbing up my throat. Seeing him disgusted is hilarious. Even though it's not his favorite part, I still catch him taking a video of it.

Afterward, we go outside and an instructor shows me how to hold my arm steady for the birds. The strength of these mighty winged creatures is incredible. A peregrine falcon flies above us, and when the man gives the signal, I forget to blink. Powerful blue-black wings come barreling toward me. I hold my breath, all of my senses heightened. The magnificent raptor swoops in and gracefully catches onto the glove I'm wearing. It grips my forearm with its massive talons and eyes me curiously with those deep-black eyes. This is so fucking cool.

We go back inside and meet a hawk that was rescued last year, and after that, an owl. The barred owl's beautiful brown-and-white mottled feathers were fluffed up in the outdoor facility. It watched us carefully as we came upon it. Silent, calculating, a natural hunter. It reminds me of Rhys. And I'm like a mouse he swallows whole.

I've never been on a date like this before. I feel connected to these fierce birds of prey, I admire their strength and grace. My heart somersaults. I can't believe he set this up. Goose bumps wrap around the back of my neck, and suddenly I've never felt more present. I see things so clearly. I'm falling for Rhys Kucera.

*Would that be the worst thing?*

Rhys is so different than I predicted he would be. He's got this hard, quiet exterior, but on the inside, this man is so sweet and thoughtful. I cannot thank him enough for this unforgettable experience. He keeps brushing it off like it's no big deal, but I know this couldn't have been easy to organize.

After a morning of falconry, he takes me to lunch, my pick. I choose a cute little bistro on the corner. It's warm and cozy in the space, a welcome respite from the chilly morning outdoors. The server brings by a few glasses and a carafe of water, and I fill our glasses.

"So . . ." he says.

"So . . ."

"I have a couple things I want to ask you about."

"Hit me." We're approaching the soul-baring stage. I'm ready for whatever he wants to ask. I'm an open book for this man.

"Your *Followers* account."

"What about it?"

"Just wondering what the plan is there?"

He tenses up every time *Followers* is mentioned. It's no secret he's uncomfortable with me stripping for men on camera. Can't say I blame him. It's not easy to see other women fawning over him all the time either. I knew if we kept seeing each other that this conversation would happen eventually.

"Rhys, come out with it. The only way this will work is if we have open communication. I'll tell you whatever you want, just ask me."

He takes a sip of water and sits back, taking me in. Being under his scrutiny makes me feel subconscious. I tuck some of my hair behind my ear and wait patiently for him to speak.

"I met you on there. The attraction we have was built off those conversations. I guess I'm feeling a little jealous, maybe nervous. I don't want you to do it again with someone else. I like you."

*Seriously? He's worried I'll meet someone else?*

"What we have is different. It started early. We had a lot of private conversations on the side. I don't have private conversations with anyone. The only time I talk with my subscribers is during the live feed in the group chat."

He breaks eye contact and nods. His eyes fixed on the scenery outside the window.

"Do you trust me?"

"Yes . . ." He brings his gaze back to mine. "But I'm still uncomfortable with it. It's one thing to have other men watch you naked and seeing you flirting with them—"

"But—"

"No, I understand. You're doing it for the tips. It's part of the gig. I get it. But I don't have to like it."

"The person I am online is not who I am. I don't want you to view me and that person as the same. Queen of Tarts is a fake version of myself, she's a role I play, catered to people who pay to view me as a sexual object. Do you remember the first time we chatted?"

"Yeah, you were weird."

"Exactly. I have no idea why you kept talking to me."

He smirks. "You know how much I love a challenge. I

knew it was fake, but I wanted something they didn't have. I think I knew you were mine even then."

My heart has melted into a puddle. I hate I am causing him so much concern. I don't want him to feel like what I have with him is anything even close to how I am with those other people.

"You should know . . ." This is scary to say in the light of day. "I would do things for you I would never do for any other man. Do you want me to shut down my *Followers* account?" My live streams bring in more money than my bartending gig, it would be so hard to turn down, but I will if he asks me to.

He blows out a breath and looks out the window. "I mean, of course I do, but I would never ask that of you. It's tied to your dream. I just wish there was another way."

"Me too. It won't always be like this. I just need some more time. Did I tell you I called someone about the property?"

"Your commercial space?"

"Not mine yet. *But* I'm meeting with an inspector to do a site survey this week. I need to move quickly. I've registered the name and gotten my license. I'm so close I can taste it." I reach across the table and place his large hand in both of mine. "I'm so close, Rhys. I can't stop now."

"I know. Forget I brought it up. I don't want to add to your stress." A little late for that. I hate seeing him like this. He seems more hurt than anything.

"Will you come with me?"

"To your inspection?"

"Yeah, I want you to see it." I want him to be a part of this. Sugar & Ice is important to me. And so is Rhys. I like the notion of combining the two.

"When?"

"Two weeks. That's the soonest they could get me in. You

don't have a game. I already checked. But if you don't want to go, it's okay. No hurt feelings. It might be boring."

He squeezes my hand. "I wouldn't miss it, baby."

There's still a forlorn look in his eyes. It's obvious we aren't done talking about this, but I can't end just before the finish line. This is the first time I've made money like this, *good money.* I can't show up emptyhanded when it's time to make an offer, they're expecting me to *show them the money.* This deal won't happen without collateral.

I want to change the subject. "Have you heard from Anna?"

*Why the fuck did I ask that?* Of all the things to ask. Am I purposely trying to sabotage this date by bringing up another sensitive topic?

"I dunno. She called a few days ago. She's doing okay. She sounds good."

"That's good." I try to sound upbeat, but it's difficult to mask how I'm feeling around this man.

"You don't sound convinced."

"It's just . . . I've been there before."

"Tell me about him. Is he still using?"

Kyle's face flashes in my memory for a split second. "He OD'd, Rhys."

The air is heavy with silence.

"Hi! I'm Sheila! I'll be your server today, are we interested in any appetizers this afternoon?" She's not at all affected by the change in atmosphere.

Emotion clogs my throat. I cough to clear the uncomfortable heaviness and paste on a smile.

"We need a few more minutes," Rhys says, keeping his eyes focused on me. The bubbly server nods and bounces off to another table. His gaze remains on mine. He waits a beat before asking, "Do you want to talk about it?"

Not really. But it might help him understand why I'm so adamant about this. I blow out a breath. Here goes nothing.

"I loved him. Fiercely. I thought he was it for me. He was supposed to be the one."

I hear Rhys swallow from across the table. I don't have the strength to look at him when I tell this story, so I stare at my drink and gently spin the chilled glass of water. My fingerprints create little windows in the condensation at the base. It gives me something to concentrate on while I drudge up the ugly memories.

"I thought he had been doing better, he seemed better. He was happier and work was going well. He was promoted twice and had these exciting business trips. I was so proud of him. Then a friend texted me that she saw him in a weird part of town. He was supposed to be at a seminar in Salt Lake City. I questioned him about it, and he became overly defensive. It was like a switch flipped in his brain. He started yelling at me, accusing me of not trusting him. He was paranoid. I let it go, but the next time he had a business trip, I tracked his phone."

"And?" He says it almost rhetorically and takes a sip of his water.

"It was all a lie. He was staying in a rough area, just outside of Seattle. What's crazy is I remember thinking, *please just be cheating on me.* Isn't that terrible?

"I immediately went online to look at our bank statements. It was full of cash withdrawals. He was spending all of our money on drugs. The only deposits were from my two recent paychecks. He had been fired from his job, those "business trips" were just nights he spent on a bender. Once his facade was pulled back, he wasn't Kyle anymore. He wasn't a person."

I continue to spin the glass, more condensation pools on the table. Rhys takes my free hand, but I don't look at him.

"I felt frozen. I was devoted to him, but he'd been living

this double life. I tried to help him so many times. But he didn't want it for himself. I thought I could want it enough for the both of us. It doesn't work that way. He started sleeping around, one time I walked in on a girl blowing him, she had been snorting lines off his dick. He lied to me, he stole from me, and he gaslit me within an inch of my sanity."

"Why didn't you leave?"

"The same reason you can't say no to Anna. I loved him, I trusted him, and assumed deep down he cared about me enough to leave it behind. The man I knew would have never done those things. *He must still be in there somewhere, right? I know the real Kyle.* I couldn't see what was happening right in front of me. Or maybe I didn't want to. I couldn't compete with drugs for a place in his life. He loved the high. I didn't stand a chance.

"Anyway, one day a letter came in the mail, our power was about to be turned off, all of our bills were overdue. We had almost fifteen grand saved up, which was a lot of fucking money for a couple of twenty-some-year-olds. Our savings account was empty. I lost it. I spent that night crying, yelling, begging him to stop using, trying to get him into a program that we couldn't even afford—we were so fucking broke, Rhys."

My stomach is tight, it's hard to breathe. Other than my therapist, I haven't told anyone the whole story before. Even after he died, I was still trying to save his reputation.

"He turned everything back on me. *He could quit—he just doesn't want to. It's to help him sleep. He's not hurting anyone. He's too scared to quit.* Then he hit me where it hurt, he looked me in the eye and said, '*You will never make me feel as good as this does. I will never love you like this.*'"

Tears brim my eyes as I recall the look on his face when he said it, he meant every word. That was the moment I knew I'd lost. I spent the night crying myself to sleep.

All of the air in the restaurant feels like it's being smothered as I relive the memory.

I clear my throat. "I had to go to work the next day, and that morning, the light under the bathroom door was on. I don't know why it stood out to me, but it did. I knocked on the door and told him I was leaving for work. He said he loved me, which only reminded me that he loved something else more. I didn't say it back. I felt numb. When I got home that evening, the light in the bathroom was still on, and I knew."

I press my fingertips to my eyes and take a deep breath. My stomach is in knots.

"I opened the door and saw him on the floor. His eyes were open and there were these bruises under his skin. He was cool to the touch. The room smelled like vomit and shit. I just curled up next to his stiff body and lay there, sobbing into his chest . . . He bought the drugs with the money supplied him. I loaded the gun for him and then went to work without even saying *I love you* back."

Swiping under my eyes, I compose myself. *How did we end up this deep into the story? And before lunch?* When I look up, Rhys is staring at me wide-eyed. I spit out the ending, wanting to finish the conversation. "His drugs had been cut with Fentanyl, and he overdosed."

Rhys says nothing. He just walks to my side of the booth and hugs me. I let him hold me. I take a deep shuddered breath. *I'm not going to cry here. Today has been so nice. Don't ruin it.*

I need to say one more thing, so he understands. "Being with Anna during her detox brought back so many memories. I promised myself I wouldn't allow it back in my life. There's no strength left in me to go through that twice." His hands caress my arms, leaving chills in their wake. "I'm worried about you, Rhys. I can see how much you care about Anna, and I don't want you to go through the same hell I did. You've been through so much already. It's been five years and I'm still working through it in therapy. For years negative thoughts echoed in my head, *I could have saved him*, or *I could have done more*. But with support groups and my therapist, I've learned that they are unreasonable and illogical lines of thinking. The hardest part is knowing they are going to die and having no choice but to wait for the phone call or the light under the door."

"Freya . . ."

I know what's coming. A *but*.

"I can't just abandon her. There's no one else who will watch out for Anna. I'm all she has."

"You can love her *and* set boundaries. It doesn't have to be one or the other." I touch each of my fingers and list off examples. "Don't let her show up high. Don't give her money. Don't let her borrow your truck. Don't let her manipulate you. Offer her rehab whenever possible, but protect yourself too . . . Don't light yourself on fire to keep her warm."

He swallows down whatever response he has loaded, instead he answers, "Okay. I will."

He won't.

"I didn't mean to get into all that. We were having a great date and I . . . I'm sorry." I chuckle nervously. "We should decide what we're going to order before our server gets back."

He wraps his arms around me tighter.

"You're an incredible woman, Freya Girl. Don't apologize for sharing yourself with me. You know I care about you, right?"

Hearing him say that dissipates some of the sadness at our table.

"I care about you too." *More than you know.* "So, what are you hungry for?" I pick up my menu, trying to lighten the mood.

He brings his lips to the shell of my ear and nips. "You."

I give him a shove. "Get back on your side of the table, freak."

"I'll show you how big a freak I am."

"Pinky promise?"

After talking about the darkest thing that happened in my life, the rest of lunch was light and easygoing in comparison. I'm not sure if I'm supposed to go back to my place or his after we get to the top of the stairs outside our doors. He unlocks his door and holds it open for me.

"I didn't want to assume—"

He nearly cackles. "What-the-fuck-ever. Get in here." *I like it when he's bossy.*

"How about a *please*?" I say.

"I'd love a please." He grabs my side.

After shaking my head at his stupid joke, he drags me back to his bedroom, and I peel off my shirt. He kicks off his shoes and hops onto the bed, crossing his arms behind his head to watch.

"Why aren't you getting naked?"

"Why *are* you?"

"I figured because—"

"Oh, you figured right. But first I want to cuddle."

I think he's fucking with me and finish removing my top and climb into bed topless next to him. He doesn't seem to notice, he simply tucks me into his side and pulls out my hair tie, gently running his fingers through my hair and then presses a kiss to my forehead. I close my eyes and focus on his touch.

"I want to see you."

My eyes pop open, and I turn to look at him.

"My face?"

He grins. "No, smartass. I want to *see* you. And I want to see *only* you. And I want you to see only me."

A giggle slips out. "Are you asking me to go steady?" I tease.

He grips my ass, and I yelp.

"Yeah, maybe I am." He beams. "I like you, Freya . . . I really fucking like you."

He tucks his chin down, and I taste his lips. I'll never get enough of his kisses.

My voice softens, and a blush rises to my cheeks.

"I like you too."

He closes his eyes and exhales, relieved that we both feel it. "Say yes."

I bite my lip and hold my breath for a second, relishing the moment. I like the idea of us being exclusive.

"Yes."

We've done aftercare together, but that was always after sex. There was a reason for it. Now I question if it was always more than that, but I was just too mad to see it.

"Good." He kisses my forehead and snatches the TV remote off his nightstand. "You want to watch something? I DVR'd *Second Bite*. The new season isn't streaming yet. I thought you might like to see it."

*I've fallen so hard.*

# TWENTY-EIGHT

## Rhys

"**L**ucy! Who's in your seats?" Conway nods to the stands.

"What?" They are usually empty unless I give them away to other players for their families or charities. *Or Freya.* Crouching on the ice, I adjust my skates. When I stand and spin around, I look to see my girl in the stands.

"That the bartender from Tops?"

"Yeah."

He smirks. "Nice."

I can't look at her without smiling. She's my girl. It's official now. I didn't mean to tell her I wanted exclusivity so soon, but it slipped out the other night, and I wasn't about to take it back. I'm falling. She has to feel it too.

My eyes connect with hers, and she raises a timid wave. *Shit, she's cute when she's uncomfortable.* Then she turns her hand and the "cute" wave transforms into a middle finger, a reminder of who I'm dealing with. I snatch it from the sky like an air kiss and bring it to my lips.

I'm amazed she showed up. And I appreciate it. A lot. It's a big deal for someone with a work ethic like Freya's to take a night off and come to one of my games. Especially when she's trying so hard to save up enough money for the commercial space she's got her eye on and the deadline drawing near. It's too bad I'll be traveling for the next few days. As soon as I get back, she will get a big fat reward for being here tonight.

We're playing one of our best games this season. I'm skating the best I have yet. We all are, everyone is in tune with each other, and I have a sense of oneness with the team, like I've hit my stride. I've found my place here.

Conway passes the puck to Jones, it bounces off the walls a few times, but they gain control as we keep the pressure on, sending it back to the opponent's end of the ice. Lonan and I cross the blue line as the boys engage in a puck battle up in the goalie's face. Banks is at the ready, awaiting a pass to flip it in. I'm headed toward the corner in case we need to send it around the back.

There's a feeling of static in the air, it's electric, we all feel it right before a goal is made. No one talks about it, but it's there. As soon as their goalie is wrapped up on the left side of the net, I expect Conway to pass to Banks, but instead, he dekes it to me along the boards. I rush to capture it. Instinct takes over as I sweep by and make a snapshot to the open right side of the goal. The puck sails through the air in slow motion, their tender is still searching the ice, it's got a clear runway. When the net takes a hit from the black rubber, it billows.

*Holy.*

*Shit.*

My first one.

Time seems to stop, but the blaring horn of our goal brings everything back up to speed again. The crowd roars, but the announcer can be heard above it. "A first NHL career goal for Rhys Kucera!"

The boys slam into me, piling on and slapping my helmet with their gloves. The ones on the bench pounding their sticks. I can hardly make out what the guys are saying over the roar of the crowd. All I know is that at this moment, it's the most support and love I've felt in a long time. This team is my family.

"Atta' boy, Kucy!"

"Whatta fuckin' play!"

"Kuuuuucera!"

"Yeah, baby!"

"You want the puck?" Conway shouts.

"What?" *What does he mean?*

"Hey, ref, grab the puck!" Burke yells behind him.

The ref comes over, and Lonan stuffs it in my glove. "First goal, bud! This one's yours!"

*My first puck.* There's no way I'm gonna cry, but I definitely could right now. Strangely, one of my first thoughts is how happy I am that Freya was here to see it. I search the stands and find her staring at me in astonishment. When our eyes meet, I wink at her, and she presses steepled fingers to the big, beautiful smile on her face. Her eyes crinkle at the sides and her smile grows. She's the bright-red cherry on top of it all.

After my shift, the coaches, Sully, and the rest of the team give me slaps on the back. My heart is pumping, and the adrenaline rush of scoring is nearly overwhelming. I wasn't sure it would feel different than goals I've made in the past, but it does. It's *so* different. *Fuck, this feels good!* One of the assistant coaches takes the puck for me so I can return my focus to the game.

The rest of the night passes in a blur. We win 3-1. My goal is the last one of the night, and it feels damn good, especially since the team we played is ranked well. We exit the ice and start stripping gear. I find the puck sitting on the shelf in my locker, right next to my name plate. I tuck it safely in my bag and fish out my phone. The guys are excited, giving me a few more congratulatory cheers. My face is stuck grinning ear to ear, I might stay like this forever.

FREYA

OMG!!!

I'm so proud of you, Rhys! That was amazing!

Her words hit me right in the chest. I've been craving that.

Thanks, gorgeous. Don't leave yet. Stay in your seat, I'll have someone come get you. 😘

When I step into the private back hall to the locker room, she's there waiting for me. She lets out a squeal and jumps into my arms. I tuck my head into her shoulder and breathe her in. I don't remember the last time I was so at peace. Freya does that.

"That was an awesome goal." I bite my lip, enjoying that sentence. "So, how do you feel?" she asks. I set her back down.

"Incredible." I think back to the sound of the buzzer and the guys slamming into me with back slaps. Their padded arms wrapped around me. I drop my head between my shoulders and shake my head. "I can't believe it."

Pulling the souvenir out of my bag, I show it to her. "Check it out. My first NHL puck."

"Wow!" She holds it in her hand, turning it over before she hands it back. "This is so cool. Where are we going to celebrate?"

I wrap my arms around her. "My bed."

She gives me a playful nudge. "I'm serious! Are they going to Top Shelf or somewhere special? I'm going to buy you a drink."

"I am being serious. You're coming home with me." And I'm not drinking tonight, I want to be sober because I'm ready to put in the work with Freya.

And that same heady buzz I felt on the ice before my goal is the same one I feel when I look at her.

# TWENTY-NINE

## Rhys

S he's wiping down the bar and the other barback splits up the cash in the tip jar. She's got three more minutes on the clock, and I know she will work all one hundred eighty seconds of them. That's how Freya is. I won't rush her. I take my time checking her out in that tiny black top.

The last several weeks have been wonderful together. Whenever I can, I meet her at work, hangout with the boys or at the bar until her shift ends, then I get to take her upstairs where we spend as much time as we can together before I have to get back on a plane for another away game. It's hard being apart. I find myself missing her more and more. She's become such a part of my life that sometimes it's hard to remember there was ever a time she wasn't there.

She taps the touchscreen monitor and glances toward me. I wet my bottom lip. I'm wrapped around her finger. She waves to her coworker and grabs her envelope of tips before making her way to our booth. Every step closer makes my heart race faster. I can feel the guys' gazes on us, but a train wreck couldn't make me peel my eyes away. Let 'em look.

Usually she greets me with a bratty little remark. Not tonight. The gleam in her eyes tells me everything I need to know. Without saying a word, I take her hand, stand up, and lead her into the dark hallway we know so well. Only this time, we aren't stopping. At the top of the stairs, she unlocks her door, and I follow her into her apartment. As soon as I cross the threshold, I kick the door shut, hold her neck with my palm, and pull the hair tie from her hair. The delicious smell of her shampoo releases as I sink both hands into her thick locks.

Towering above, I walk her backward until she hits the wall, locking my lips on hers. It's all I've been able to think about. Her mouth drops open for me, and she sucks in a breath. Her tongue darts out to lick my lips, and she swipes her tongue over mine.

"Goddamn, I've missed you," I growl under my breath.

"I smell like stale beer and work. Can I take a shower first?"

"Can I watch?"

"Sure." She smiles.

She walks away, and I stare at her ass strut down the hallway. No sane person could turn down that invitation.

She turns on the shower and before long, the glass doors fog with steam. I lean against the bathroom doorway while she strips. Facing away from me, I'm rewarded a second helping of the view I got following her here.

"See something you like?" She doesn't turn around; she must feel my presence.

"Yes."

"You're welcome to join me."

"Raincheck." If I go in there, we'll end up fucking before she flips the top on her shampoo bottle. I'd rather take her in bed where we have more room to play.

"Suit yourself," she says, opening the shower door and slipping inside.

Something tells me I will regret turning down her offer to

step behind those glass walls. She takes time soaping up. She's doing it to tease me. It's working. I just want to admire her for a few minutes with no distractions. The fear of mixing hockey and women doesn't exist anymore. I don't care about the consequences. Whatever they are, she's worth it.

Freya turns off the shower, opens the door, and wrings out the water from her hair. I'm standing on the rug, waiting with her towel. Most of her makeup has washed off, but I swipe under her eyes to clear some of the leftover mascara. It's unbelievable how green her eyes are. I wrap her up in the towel and turn her so she can see herself in the mirror while I dry her off. Starting at her shoulders and arms, working my way down her back, over her breasts and stomach, her waist, hips, ass, thighs, calves, and feet. Every inch of her glows. She smells fresh and clean. The scent is all Freya.

She raises a hairbrush to her strands, but I slide it out of her hand and brush her hair, starting at the ends and working my way up. She swallows. It might be the most intimate thing I've ever done. But intimacy feels so natural with Freya. Our gaze meets in the mirror, and I notice a small dose of apprehension in her eyes. She looks like she's about to say something but then stops.

When I'm finished, I pick up the hairdryer on the counter and turn it on. I want to take care of her tonight. I tousle her hair, running the warm air over it. I feel her watching me in the reflection the entire time. When I'm finished, I give it another quick brush. I can't help but run my fingers through it. This time, I'm watching her. Her eyes close and every once in a while, a small shudder runs up her back when my touch grazes her neck.

"Thank you," she murmurs.

"You're welcome."

I bend down to kiss her warm, bare skin, and she pauses for a moment again, her eyes fixed on mine. She opens her mouth to speak, but quickly purses her lips and drops her bare shoulders back down.

"What do you want to say, Freya Girl?" My brow draws together, and I smirk at her. This isn't like her. *What is she thinking?*

She doesn't deny it, so I wait. After a moment, she sucks in a breath and holds it. This little stalemate of hers has me anxious. Finally she exhales and clears her throat.

"I'm in love with you."

My mind goes blank for a moment while my heart hammers. Now I'm the one holding my breath. It's as if she has struck a match and lit a fire in my chest. The way I feel about Freya is illuminated, it can't hide in the darkness anymore. I'm being swallowed up by emotion. Slowly, I spin her around and bury my hands into her soft, silky hair.

A sense of clarity falls over me.

I'm done fucking around. Losing her would kill me. I've been telling myself for years that relationships will always come second, they can wait, women are for someday. But what if there's no someday option? Sometimes it's now or never. Refuting it won't lessen my feelings, I'm already in too deep.

I've got two choices here: dive in or run away. If I walked away from her, I'd never forgive myself for not finding out what could be . . . or telling her how I feel. If I dive in, my only regret will ever be trying to push her away in the first place.

"I love you so goddamn much," I whisper.

She pulls me out of the bathroom and into her bedroom, dropping the towel on the way. She sits in the center of the bed. I grab my shirt at the nape of my neck and yank it over my head. Then wrap my palms around her ankles and tug hard, dragging her to the edge, her bright hair is fanned around her like a starburst.

Falling to my knees, I spread her legs. I love this pussy. My lips press to the inside of her thighs. She's bracing herself on her elbows, watching my every move. I groan when I get my first taste of her and flatten my tongue to lap up her arousal. I hear a small sniffle, but she sighs and gets comfortable. My hands move up her stomach to grope her breasts and tug on her nipples. I flick my tongue over her clit, eliciting another moan.

When my lips seal over her and suck, she comes alive. Her back arches, and she whimpers. I spear two fingers inside and feel her tighten around them. Red fingernails scratch my scalp, and I grip her hips to force her deeper into my mouth, letting her grind against my face.

*That's it.*

"Wait . . ."

I look up.

"Make me come on your cock first." That's about the only thing that could persuade me off her. "Please."

I take one last taste and rise to my feet.

Cradling her neck, I lick the corner of her lips. She cups the sides of my face, pulling me closer and tangling her tongue with mine, tasting herself. Her eagerness makes me smile against her mouth.

Her hands drop to my jeans, and she unbuckles my belt and shoves down my pants. I do the rest of the work and kick them off, along with my boxers. She scoots up the bed and rests naked against the pillows. Her legs are open, and she pulls me between them, reaching down to stroke me.

*Fuck.* I would let this girl crash my truck if that's what she wanted. I'd toss her the keys without thinking twice.

She places her delicate hand on my throat and speaks softly.

"Rhys?"

"Yeah, baby?"

"Don't degrade me tonight, 'k'?"

I pause for a moment before returning her kiss and suck her bottom lip into my mouth. "Anything you want."

Usually our sex is kinky and frenzied, tonight we're laying our hearts bare. There's a connection that's different than what I've experienced before with Freya. It's still hot as hell, but it feels like tonight is meant to explore the depth of our love. I've said the words, but now I'm going to prove it.

"You are so fucking precious." I pull each of her nipples into my mouth and graze the peaks with my teeth. She writhes as I work the pad of my thumb over her clit. I've gotten to know exactly how she likes to be touched.

"I'm on birth control."

My gaze snaps to hers, taking in the significance of what she's saying.

The old me would never trust a woman to go raw, in fact I'd probably insist on using my own condoms.

I bring myself back to her mouth and kiss her, our tongues swiping gently. Her legs open wider, and I line my length up with her entrance. I brace my forearms on each side of her and study her face. We're locked into this moment.

*Just us.*

I sink into her and blow out a breath. She inhales a small gasp, and with it comes a twinge of emotion I feel in my chest.

"Rhys . . ." She's slick and warm, and stretches around me so well.

Every slight movement causes my body to twitch. She was made for me.

"You're fucking breathtaking."

Her eyes flutter closed when I move inside her.

"Eyes on me, baby."

When she opens them, they are filled with trust and compassion. Heat creeps from the base of my neck, burning its way to my core. Long, slow strokes make her pulse quicken, and with each downstroke, I pick up speed. Her sweet, raspy moans are so perfect. I'm drawing out each and every one.

She wraps her smooth, quivering legs around me, and I sit up, unable to resist getting more control. My fingers dig into her thighs.

"Fuck me, Rhys."

"No."

Her body tightens, and I stretch my large hands over her torso, keeping her still while I work her over. Her mouth drops open, and she grabs my forearms to hold on. She props up on her elbows to watch our bodies connect. I lean down to spit on her clit and massage my thumb over the soft bundle of nerves. A tear slips down her cheek and her back bows. I love watching her come apart.

Feeling her so fully, so closely, is incredible. Nothing's between us. She coats the entire span of me as I fill her to the brim.

"Let me take care of you."

*Not just tonight.* I adore caring for her, and having someone do the same in return. Having each other's back and watching out for one another. I don't want to lose what we have. I'm not sure when it happened, but she's become my best friend.

Her shallow breathing slows, and she interrupts my thoughts.

"I loved seeing you play," she says in a labored sigh.

"What?" I chuckle and sit up, holding her knees apart. What is she talking about? I continue lazily sliding in and out of her.

"Going to the game, sitting in your seats. It was thrilling to watch you skate so aggressively and predict passes. You're pretty captivating out there, number five."

My mouth curls into a half smile. "Why are you telling me

this now?" My thumb finds her swollen clit, priming her body for another round.

"I dunno, you're incredibly talented. And I'm proud of you." *Fuck.* "Just wanted you to know that."

I freeze, unsure how to respond. Instead, I lean down and conceal my face in her neck, suppressing the pang of emotion rising up my throat by swallowing it down. My parents told me they were proud of me, but I haven't heard that in years, not until Freya texted me the night of my goal.

I clear my throat and give in to her, sucking on her neck and nipping at her earlobe, masking the overwhelming feelings. My teeth slowly skim down her neck, I bite the top of her left breast and then the right, and there's a sharp intake of air from her with each one. Her fingers cradle my head, and she holds me to her. It's so comfortable. She rocks against me, urging me deeper.

My head rises, and I graze my hands over her body, admiring my two bites on her flushed chest and the desire in her eyes.

"I won't apologize for marking you up," I mutter.

"I never asked you to."

Her hands bracket each side of my jaw as she brings my mouth to hers. The kiss is greedy and insatiable. I grip her chin and part her lips for me. Her tongue licks against mine. We're consuming each other. She leaves me breathless, and I pause to rest my forehead against hers while I catch my breath.

Keeping a slow pace is difficult. She tries to lift her hips, wanting more from me, and I don't give it to her. Wriggling beneath me, she tries to speed me up, but I stay steady. It's worth the wait when I sink every inch inside. Her face relaxes and her lips part. I get a rush seeing her like this. Enraptured and quiet. It's so rare of her character. *And I'm the one to make her feel this way.* The only man who will ever see this beautiful, meek side of her. I've experienced nothing like Freya before, everything about what we have feels fresh and new.

With each thrust, her moans grow louder and more desperate. My hand descends on her throat, and she smiles.

"Jesus Christ, you're pretty when I'm taking you."

She tucks her tongue in her cheek and blushes, still preoccupied with rolling her hips under me.

"What do you need, baby?"

She nods, her big eyes hazy. "Make me yours."

*Damn, what those words do to me.*

She wraps her arms around my neck, her ankles lock behind my back. I sit up on my heels and pull her into my raised lap. My fingers dig into her supple ass and hips as I slide her up and down my cock.

"Who do you belong to?"

"Fuck," she cries.

"Answer me, darling."

"You." There's pure hunger etched on her face, and those emerald eyes are full and bright.

"So sweet." The corners of my lips curl up into a smirk. "I love how well you take me."

My teeth nip at her neck again.

"Rhys, I'm close." *Me too, love.*

Her legs shake, and she digs her nails into my shoulders. I drive into her, tits bouncing with each plunge. She shudders and her body squeezes my cock like it's trying to strangle me. I get my hand between us and rub her clit, which pulses wildly under my fingertips. She screams my name as she comes. *Fucking hell.* If I had to pick between the sound of a goal buzzer or hearing *that*, it would be the latter. Every time.

She peaks so beautifully. Her pussy throbs in a strong, steady rhythm.

"Take it all, Freya Girl." *Take all of me.*

My lips capture hers, and all I feel is this crazy love. It sends me overboard. That fuse that's been burning finally hits dynamite, and I explode.

*Freya is mine.* It's the only thought that runs through my head when I empty inside her. I've never come in a woman before. It's intense. I'm dizzy and spent. I fall backward onto the bed and pull her with me, she releases a cute little shriek, and I wrap my arms around her in a bear hug. We lie in silence, hearts pounding in our chests.

I shift to the edge of the bed and stand. She locks her ankles behind my back, and I carry her into her bathroom, depositing her onto the countertop. I kiss her neck and slowly pull out, all the tension in her body loosens. I already miss the warmth of being inside her.

"Spread your legs."

Her eyes darken, and a sinful grin appears on her face. That look alone could destroy me. When I bring my gaze between her open thighs, it's hotter than I imagined, seeing my cum leaking out of her tight cunt. Dipping my fingers inside, I'm constricted by her still-spasming pussy. I show her my index and middle finger covered in a mix of us.

She grabs my wrist, taking both fingers between her lips, sucking them clean from the base to tip. I grab her chin again and gain access to her mouth, slipping my tongue inside, needing to know how we taste together. It's salty and sweet. She's so damn sexy.

After we get cleaned up, I lightly slap her ass, and she races back into bed. There's no hesitating whether we spend the night together anymore. Lying on my back, she nuzzles into my shoulder. I press my lips to her temple and draw lazy patterns up and down her spine. Her skin is silky smooth, I can't stop touching her. Her index finger does the same on my chest. She leaves two soft kisses along my biceps, and it does me in.

I love her so much.

# THIRTY

## *Micky*

fter getting a rare Saturday with both of us not working, we went over to Lonan and Birdie's for lunch. She cooked this amazing homemade pasta and we both ate more than our fair share. After we came home, I insisted we sleep off the big meal. Rhys may be used to putting away that many calories in one sitting, but I'm not. When I wake up, there's a light blanket draped over us and the sun is setting. It's a bright winter sunset of brilliant reds, oranges, and pinks that reflect off the walls. It's beautiful and quiet. His breathing is still steady and relaxed, so I snuggle in, curving my back into his bare chest during our daytime nap.

A leg wraps around mine, and he pulls me into him deeper. *Butterflies.* He's grown on me. Like a thick vine taking over. Or a hot-as-fuck barnacle.

It's like my bones turn to butter, this is the most comfortable I've been in a long time. His hand slides to my front, fingertips trailing back and forth over my stomach. A soft smile blooms on my lips. My exhale comes out as a passionate sigh, and I can feel his soft chuckle on the back of my neck.

"You're my new napping buddy." He sounds gruff and sleepy in my ear. *Ditto.*

His muscles flex as he tries to stretch without moving his arms from my body, and he lets out an adorable, exaggerated groan, as if he's a big bear coming out of hibernation. It's seductive.

He adjusts his leg, and I'm able to feel how hard he is. The stiffness of him sparks a fire low in my belly. Flames licking at my core. My mind is focused on one thing. I grind against him, and a rumble escapes his throat. The last sex we had was something else entirely. Deeper, compassionate, weighty. *It wasn't fucking.*

Though, tonight, I want to be fucked. I want to be owned and made small and helpless. I want the thrill of his commands and control. And afterward, I want to be kissed, touched, and cherished. I enjoy the juxtaposition of the two. I reach to scratch my nails up his side.

"I need you. How about we go back to our regularly scheduled programming."

His slow breaths stop. The groan against the back of my neck is dark, making the hair there stand on end. I told him what I want; why isn't he saying anything? The mood feels different, but his touch remains the same feather-soft brushes. I guess that wasn't enough to provoke him. He buries a hand into my hair. Then he kisses me. I love the taste of Rhys. The initial caress of his lips elicit a soft whimper, but after a minute, it's still too soft. I try nipping his lower lip, but he doesn't take the bait. His lips are almost hesitant. I want him to show me he owns me.

"What do you mean by that?"

"I dunno, last time you were *reallllly* vanilla."

Instantly the atmosphere changes. The air crackles.

"Come again?" he growls.

"I'd like to. I just don't understand why you're always being so gentle with me," I say in my most innocent voice. My nipples are aching. I need this.

247

"Let's see where this little show of yours is going to take you," he says, amusement in his gravelly voice. "You think you're in charge tonight?"

"Somebody should be."

His chuckle is dark.

My breaths come faster. Talking back to him like this is exhilarating. And also frightening.

"No, darling. You are *my* fuck toy, and I'll use you however I want. Now apologize."

This is the Rhys I want tonight. Just out of curiosity, I consider how far I can push him . . .

I giggle. "Bitch, you won't do shit."

*Welp, that should do it.*

Everything happens so fast when he flips me onto my back and glowers with hooded, dominant eyes. *Uh-oh*. His strong hand crawls up to my neck where he grips my throat, and I try to hide my simpering, but it's useless. I've hit my mark, and it feels good to win.

He tsks me with a sly grin. *There he is.*

"That was the wrong answer."

*Oh, I disagree.* It's triggering the exact response I'd hoped for. Standing from the bed and shedding his jeans, I get the opportunity to ogle his taut muscles. His body is a machine. He works quickly to unbutton my pants.

"Bra and panties stay on," he growls.

I smile to myself, happy I wore more of the lingerie he bought me and knowing it's turning him on. He tosses a pillow on the floor.

"Kneel. You're gonna be there a while."

*The circus is here!*

I slide off the bed and do as he says. My pulse is pounding with anticipation. I've never bratted this hard before, I don't exactly know what's going to happen.

"I know how much you love rubbing your pussy when

you take my cock." *It's true.* I move my hand between my legs, eager to begin.

"Hands behind your back."

I fold my hands behind me, and he wraps a belt around my wrists. Crouching down to eye level, he brushes his thumb over my wet lip, nudging it down. "Next time be better about restraining your words too."

He reaches behind me and snatches his car keys from the nightstand, placing them in my restricted hands.

"These are your safewords tonight. I don't want you speaking with your mouth full, and you're not going to be able to tap me when your hands are all tied up. Instead of yellow, you jingle the keys. For red, you drop them on the floor. Understand?"

"Yes."

"Yes, what?"

*Hmm . . . I wonder if he's a daddy or sir kind of guy.* That's a stupid question.

"Yes, sir."

"Look at you, using your manners." He regards me with stormy eyes and I shiver. He takes the hair tie from earlier to swiftly braid my hair. I'm slightly annoyed, knowing he's clearly had practice doing this with other women.

He leans down to my ear. "Before you get any doubts, I used to braid Anna's hair before school. Wipe that sour look off your face." He's gotten *really* good at reading me.

It's terrifying and oh-so thrilling.

He stands to his full height and pulls down his boxers just enough to give me access. I'm salivating.

"Lick."

I can't stop my smile as I stick my tongue out and lick him base to tip, paying extra attention to the crown, making sure I keep my eyes trained on his.

"Open."

My lips part for him, and the keys dig into my palms when I clench them tight. He grabs my jaw and widens my mouth. He slides himself to the back of my throat and doesn't stop. I stop short of a gag, I've been mentally preparing. When he pulls out of my throat, I take a big gulp of air. He cups my cheeks and enters my mouth again, moving me over his shaft. I moan around his length. The taste of his smooth, hard flesh makes me wet.

Every nerve ending seems to buzz with hypersensitivity. I'm so turned on by this man taking control of me. He's using me and doing whatever the fuck he wants. It's exhilarating to experience the things he wants to do.

His pace quickens, and he grips the nape of my neck, thrusting himself down my throat. My eyes grow wide, tears building in the corners. *Fuuuuuck.* I delight in the helplessness of it all. When I reach the base, he holds me there. My throat wants to reject him, but I concentrate on relaxing my muscles. The oxygen is burning up, my brain says to jingle the keys, but I don't want to. Not yet. He pulls out and rubs my swollen lips with the crown. I pant, saliva still strung between us.

"So lovely."

I groan for more, and he gives me a soft slap on the cheek. My mouth goes slack in surprise, and he gives me what I want. The way he grabs and urges himself into me is delicious. I moan again.

"Does it feel good to be used?"

I whimper in response. *It feels so fucking good.*

"Like a mindless plaything, obeying and pleasuring me while I ignore your whining. I bet that soft pussy is so wet right now."

*You have no idea.*

"You look so innocent with those big angel eyes. Tell me why a good girl like you loves to be used and degraded." He fucks my mouth harder with tears streaking down my face. *Goddamn.* It's such a gentle, trickling sensation in comparison to the punishment he's giving me.

The ache between my legs grows. I squeeze my thighs together and wiggle my ass, trying to grind on the pillow under me. I need it so bad. Just when I get purchase and feel the friction against my clit, he pulls out and gives me another gentle smack on my face before gripping my jaw and rubbing his thumb over the sting. He bends over and roughly tilts my face up.

"Knock it off," he growls. "You don't get to come. You're here to give me what I want and do what I say. And right now, you're going to gag on my cock like a good little slut until I'm done with you."

*Holy shit. I never want to top again.* My heartbeat surges in my ears. He continues pushing down my throat. My eyes shut tight as I focus on taking him.

"Don't close your eyes, those tears belong to me."

I bring my gaze to his, and he bites his lower lip. I'm powerless here. *Unless I drop my keys, that is. Do I want to drop the keys?* Not yet.

His pace slows to a crawl, propelling me to the edge of choking with each slow advance. It's easier when he's fucking my face. It's rhythmic, I can anticipate what's happening. But when it's this slow, there's fewer breaks for air, and it's harder to know when I'll get oxygen again. The curiosity in his eyes dances as he sees how my body reacts to this new tempo. My spit coats him, but he's so mouthwatering excess dribbles out of the corner of my mouth. He pulls out, and I cough. He repeats the process. It's delicious torture.

"You are so gorgeous when you're choking on my cock."

He pulls out slightly, and I'm able to get in a deep breath. The oxygen is cool and welcoming, soothing the burn in my lungs. Before my pounding heart can relax, he picks up speed again, this time more forceful. I can feel the dribble on my chin.

"Oh, baby, you're drooling everywhere. Messy girl."

His force is strong enough I jiggle the keys.

He eases up, and I see the subtle concern behind his commanding eyes.

"Feeling sorry now?"

I nod.

"You're doing such a good job, darling." I think he knows there's not too much more I can take. But I don't want to be done yet either. My body is twitching with need. His thrusts demand more from me than I'm able to give, and I shake the keys again.

"If I untie your hands, are you going to be good and not touch yourself?"

"Mmhmm." Before I know it, there's a snap of the belt, and my hands are free again. He gently tilts my chin up.

"Almost done. Keep your hands nice and pretty on your thighs." I hold them still as he enters my mouth again.

He curses under his breath, he huffs, and his breath catches. *He's close.* I double down on my sucking and lean into it. I've earned his cum. I want it.

"Swallow," he orders. His hips jerk while his thumb strokes my neck as the salty spurts glaze my tongue.

His words come out calm and heavy on his breath. "Fuck. Just like that. Take every drop." He does that sexy low chuckle and stares lovingly into my eyes.. "You're such a fucking cum slut, aren't you?"

*Good god.* I'm dripping down my legs.

He continues to praise me as I finish him. When he pulls out, one final spurt lands right on the corner of my mouth. He uses the head of his cock to paint it over my lips like lipstick while I find my breath. It's so fucking possessive.

I take his hand for balance and rise to my feet, leaving behind rosy crescents from my fingernails on my thighs. His strong arms slide under mine, and he pulls me to his mouth, kissing me like I'm the only woman in the world.

# THIRTY-ONE

## Rhys

*Who the fuck is this girl?* I want to give her the world.

I was rough with her. Rougher than I've ever been with anyone. "Are you okay?"

"I could be better . . ." she says, wanting to get her own release.

"Where's my apology?" I ask. Playing with her swollen rosy lips. *God, these lips.*

"I'm sorry," she says, batting her lashes.

I grip her thighs and flip her back on the bed with a bounce.

"Oh, yeah? Why don't you spread your legs and show me how fucking sorry you are."

Quickly she drops them open and whimpers, her eyes desperate. She's starving for this. I hook my thumbs into the underwear and slowly pull the lingerie I bought down her legs.

"Do you have any idea how sexy you are?" I kiss the inside of her knee. Her legs tremble already. "I want to give you everything."

She sucks in a gasp of air, and my mouth drops onto her

sex. I groan at her taste. She moans, gripping the sheets, almost thrashing, desperate for release. *Hellcat.*

I pull back and let my teeth scrape over her sensitive thighs. She shudders and twitches.

"Please, please, please . . ." she begs quietly. Suddenly that refractory period is getting *real short.*

Scooting her closer to the center of the bed, I climb on top and kneel between her legs to keep them apart. One hand on her neck, I force her to keep eye contact while I finger her drenched pussy. Hardly any time passes before she's coming. It's such a burst of energy that explodes from her, she squeezes me as tight as I've ever felt. I remove my hand from her neck long enough to give a sharp love tap on her cheek.

Her legs quake, and she whimpers something about coming again.

"How are you going to handle my cock if you can barely handle my fingers?" Just then she clamps down on me again, and I laugh. Fuck, she's got orgasms stacked up inside, and I intend to wrench out every single one.

When she focuses again, her eyes almost look frenzied as she begs me to fuck her. I can't say no to that. Christ, no man could. I pull her hips close and slide myself up and down her wet seam. She gulps air as her chest rises and falls. The antici-pation is burning up all the air in the room. I tease her opening with the pad of my thumb, tracing around the edge, on the verge of penetration. I push my index and middle finger in, and when I rub the top of her vaginal wall, she contracts. Then I surprise her by entering underneath my hand, massaging her G-spot while my cock drives into her.

There's nothing better than that first "Oh, fuck" that slips from her lips.

"Is this what you need?"

She bites her lip and nods. It's not enough for me, she needs to be set loose. I remove my fingers and wrap my arm behind her back, rolling us so she's on top of me. She rides me, closing in on another orgasm.

"Show me how good you can be. Don't stop, darling." Her breasts bounce in the black lingerie as she gyrates on top of me. This whole room reeks of sex. *Goddamn, she knows how to work those hips.* "But no coming until I say so."

"Rhys, please. Don't do that."

"I love you needy, but I've spent the last half hour controlling you, so let's see how well you can control yourself . . . Slow down."

Reluctantly she reins it in and leans back, supporting herself by gripping my thighs as she rolls her body—the view is unreal. I reach around and release her bra. She lifts her hands only to pull them out of the straps.

"Damn." I grope her breasts and tug on her nipples.

"Thanks, I grew them myself," she pants with a half smirk.

My palm connects with her ass on a loud crack. "Smartass."

Gripping the flesh on her hand-printed cheeks, I help drag her body up and down my cock, adding to her momentum. Shallow breaths tell me she's getting there, but I remind her of the rules. "You're so fun to fuck. I can fill you up and play with you all day. That's what gets you going, isn't it? Me using you to get off?" My hand slaps the other side of her ass and then kneads the sting away.

"Oh my God." Her eyes shut; she's in ecstasy.

Before she opens them again, I push her off me and onto her stomach. I reach down and grab the belt from earlier, wrapping it around her waist. She grinds into me, her needy sounds grow more desperate.

"Please, may I come now, sir?"

*Well, look who decided to play nice.*

"Not yet."

Hiding the sharp buckle in my fist, I grip it near her sides, making sure it's not too tight before yanking her body up with a *humph*. I line myself up with her entrance, then grab the belt like a harness as I fuck her from behind. It gives me some added control so I can keep taking her at the speed I want, to give it to her the way she likes.

She gasps. "Oh fuck, Rhys."

"This the rough you want, darling?"

"God, yes. *Fuckfuckfuck . . .*" she mewls.

"You're taking it so well."

"I'm going to come, I mean it."

"No, you're not. Good little sluts wait to come until they're told."

Her body tenses, and she groans, trying to hold on. She's fighting it with all her might, but her body is right on the cusp. I feel the drum of her pulse growing in her core. It makes me want to come right along with her. I reach around and massage figure eights into her clit.

She whispers something, but it's inaudible.

"I'm going to countdown from ten, and when I hit zero, you're going to come on this cock."

As I countdown, I don't go easy on her, I'm railing her, listening to her sobs of pleasure. Her arms are wobbly as she tries to hold herself up. I pinch her clit between my fingers.

". . . Seven . . . Six . . . Five . . . so good, Freya. You're almost there . . . Four . . . Three . . . Two . . . One. Come for me, baby." I slap between her thighs, and her back bows as she spasms around me. My balls draw up before I fucking detonate. She moans my name as the orgasm overtakes her, and she throbs around me, making me delirious.

Slow relaxed thrusts draw out her climax and help us transition down before collapsing. She's spent. I slide my hands up and down her smooth back as we both come out of the sex haze, then I unbuckle the belt from her waist and rub the red marks where it bit into her soft skin. The smile on her face makes me feel better.

"You okay?"

"Better than okay. You are the most incredible"—she swallows—"man I have ever met. Have I told you how much I love you?"

"I'll never get enough of it."

There's a tinge of emotion in her eyes when she stares at me, which is to be expected after the orgasm that just rocked her body, but the twinkle she's looking at me with is hitting me in my chest and rendering me speechless. I do the only thing that feels natural and kiss her with all I have.

# THIRTY-TWO

## Rhys

"Hey, babe, can I get another one?"

"Not your babe," she reminds the guy for the second time.

These motherfuckers have been flirting with her since I walked in. It's not necessarily their fault for doing it in front of me since nobody knows we're a thing. No, not *thing*. Mine. But she shouldn't have to correct someone twice.

She pours me another soda and puts a cherry in it.

"Because you love my cherries." She winks. Imagining her in that cherry apron still gets my dick hard.

I suck it off the stem and chew it with a slight grin. She bites her lip like she's envious of a piece of fruit, and it has the exact response I hoped it would. She steals the stem and puts it in her mouth. She places her elbows on the bartop in front of me and rests her chin on her hands innocently as she ties the cherry stem in no time, then drops it back in my glass. *That girl is anything but innocent.*

"Licky Micky," some asshole says, walking into the bar. I turn to look at who the hell said it, and it's some older regular I've seen around.

"Douchey Brucey," she responds.

I hate feeling like I'm sharing her. Whether it's between men online or at the bar, it's difficult for me to watch anymore. I know it's pretend, it's for tips, but that doesn't make it any easier.

The guys tease her, and she throws it right back, she can handle it, but I can't. I finish my drink and walk behind the bar.

"Rhys, you can't—"

I grab her neck and place a bite where it meets her shoulder while locking eyes with the men attempting to flirt with her. I'm staking my claim. She draws in a sharp inhale. It's just firm enough to leave a mark on her for the remainder of her shift.

"I'll see you in our bed after work."

A smile crawls onto her lips. "Yes, sir."

I see the envy on their faces, which is ironic, considering I'm the one who's jealous. A few have the decency to look away, ashamed for speaking about her in front of me. They should have been ashamed when they did it without me here. *Dicks.*

My conscience reminds me it was less than a couple months ago when I was literally sending her money to jack off to her naked body. But this is different. We weren't what we are now. As soon as she told me I had her heart, she became mine. I think I was hers from the beginning.

---

"I heard they're looking at expanding, taking over some hole-in-the-wall place that just went under."

My ears prick up. We're on our way to Nashville for a game tomorrow evening. Banks is sitting in the row in front of me, chatting with Lonan.

"Who's expanding?" I question him.

From between the seats, he tilts his head up to answer me. "Citra Brewing. They're putting together a proposal to take over that shitty restaurant that just closed down the street. Something about turning it into a separate tasting room for private events."

*They can't. That's Freya's space.*

"When did you hear that?"

"Few days ago, my buddy's one of the investors."

*No. No. No.*

How on earth am I going to break the news to her? She will be heartbroken. There's no way she's got the capital to compete with whatever Citra is putting in on their offer.

Feigning boredom, I toss a puck up in the air and catch it.

"Oh yeah, I've seen that place. It's a dump, Citra will probably get it for a steal. Your buddy mention how much they offered?"

He turns around and looks at me. "Why? You have something you want to share with the class, Kucy?"

"Nah, I just like their beer. Thought maybe I could invest in something like that too. Just curious how much money I would have to put up." It's half true. I do like their beer.

"I'm sure they would be down for some connection to the Lakes. I'll get you in touch with my guy."

Conway pipes up from across the aisle. "Do it. I've invested with a couple local start-ups and it's been great. Property is always a good investment. I've got a place in Hawaii I rent out year-round, it's terrific passive income. Someone else manages it, I don't have to do a thing."

I hate it when lies turn into bigger lies and start involving more people. Now I will probably get stuck listening to some business pitch or going out for drinks to network and "discuss opportunities." Fuck that.

"Thanks, man."

"For sure. Hey, been meaning to ask, are you still hooking up with that bartender or is she available?"

"She's not available."

He turns around and kneels on the seat.

"Oh, I see how it is. Does she fuck as wild as she looks?" He's trying to get a rise out of me. He should know by now she and I are involved.

Out of respect for her, I keep my mouth shut, but I can't help the smirk that curls on my lips.

"Oh, shit, you must really be getting it good. Lucky bastard."

"We're seeing each other."

"For real? Like exclusive?"

My gut twists. That's a loaded fucking question. I wish we were truly exclusive, but that's not true. Hundreds of men are seeing Freya. I remind myself some things are mine. I know what her face looks like. I know what it feels like to have her trembling under me. I know she bites her lip when she's turned on. The way she sounds when she comes. Those are mine. And above that, I have her heart.

"Yeah."

Lonan laughs in the seat ahead of me, and he mutters something like *fuckin' knew it*.

Next Lonan turns around and looks down to face me. "You guys getting serious?"

"I mean, kinda. More serious than anything else I've had before."

That's an understatement. It's never been like this with women. They've always been there, standing on the sidelines and trying to get my attention, but I've remained focused. Freya's the only one that's made me look, the only one who could pull my focus from everything else in my life. She's given me a life outside of hockey. Being with her brings balance to my world. She doesn't see me as a hockey player, she sees me as a person—and that's something I've lost sight of over the years. My worth comes from more than my athletic abilities. The things I feel for her . . .

"Kucy . . ." Lonan drawls all sing-songy.

"Huh?" My mind is too wrapped up in her. *There she goes stealing focus again.*

"Be good to that one. I like you, man . . . but if shit hits the fan, I'll be forced to take her side. She's practically a sister-in-law to me."

*Wanna have a new brother-in-law?* The intrusive thought pops into my brain and partially stuns me. A couple months ago marriage never crossed my mind. But a couple months ago, I didn't know Freya. Not that I'm anywhere near ready for a proposal. But she makes life so fun, I wouldn't be opposed to spending a significant portion of my life with her by my side. I *hope* she becomes a permanent fixture in my future. She'd make a good partner.

*Fuck, how did I even get here?*

Needing a distraction, I open my email and see my agent has sent me a six-month sponsorship gig for some energy bar thing. Pretty sure I've eaten one of those before, it tasted like a carpet pad. I scan through the email and whistle under my breath. *Shit. More carpet pad, please.* I shoot an email off to my financial adviser. I've got a couple things I want to discuss. It's probably time I start diversifying, and this is going to put a big dent in that signing bonus.

# THIRTY-THREE

## Rhys

M y phone dings and I smile when her name appears on the screen.

FREYA
Congrats on your win!

Thanks 😊

FREYA
How's Nashville?

I snap a photo of the view from my hotel room and send it off to her. It's pretty.

Not a bad view. What are you up to tonight?

FREYA
Hanging out, watching Second Bite. Thanks for letting me steal your DVR 🙂

What are you wearing?

FREYA

Wouldn't you like to know . . .

Send me a pic

She sends me a photo of her in one of my old college shirts I left at her place. No makeup, hair tied up in a messy updo, natural freckles showing, her colorful floral tattoo sleeve on display, and those delicious, creamy legs I want to spread apart with my tongue. She's so beautiful, sometimes it's hard to believe she's real. I tap the download button to save it to my phone.

FREYA

It smells like you.

*Fuck.* Seeing her so relaxed in my clothes makes my heart clench. I don't know what it is exactly, but it does something to me. It's part sensual, part domestic, part possessive—and all Freya. Just the way I want her. Knowing she likes the scent of the shirt, that she's missing me, makes my dick twitch. If it's the scent she wants, I'll happily put it all over her when I get home.

Damn, your view is much better than mine.

You just made front page of my phone. I like how you look in my shirt.

FREYA

This old thing? 😊

This gorgeous photo of her will live as my phone background forever.

Ya know, you're pretty cute when you're being nice.

FREYA

What am I when I'm not nice?

> Hot as fuck.

FREYA

😂 😅

When do you get home?

> Flying out Wednesday, should be back
> around 6 pm.

FREYA

Looks like the next four games are
home . . .

> Somebody's been checking out my work
> schedule.

FREYA

You do remember I work at a hockey bar,
right?

> I'm ignoring that. You looked at my
> schedule.

> I think you like me.

FREYA

☑ Yes ⬜ No ⬜ Maybe

> One of these days I'm putting you in the
> WAGs box.

I stare at my screen. I don't know how this stuff is supposed to go, it's new to me. But I want to lock her down. After about a minute, three little dots show up on the bottom of the screen. Then disappear. Then appear. This goes on for what feels like forever. Hope I didn't cross a line with my *Wives-and-Girlfriends* text. My toe taps on the floor, and I get up to pace around my hotel room. What, is she writing a novel? *Spit it out, woman.*

FREYA

K.

> Did you misspell 'K' a thousand times? You know I can see when you're typing right?

FREYA

Anna just showed up.

# THIRTY-FOUR

## Rhys

"I hear they're hiring a Zamboni driver." Reynolds, winger for Seattle, chirps at me after dekeing me again. That's the third puck to get by me tonight and into the net. Kap is in the net and counting on me to keep the rubber out of his area, but I can't steal for shit. I should have had those. What the fuck is wrong with me tonight? I can tell my teammates are frustrated. Lonan's given me a couple funny looks. It's freaking me out. We're getting spanked 3-0. All three should have been prevented by me. This is horrible. I haven't anticipated one pass correctly tonight.

When they've had enough of my bullshit, I'm pulled and benched for the rest of the period. Dopson takes my place with Lonan. During intermission, Coach follows us back to the locker room. Usually they give us a few minutes of chatter to cool down, but not tonight. It's well known if the coaches don't come in, it's either because we're doing well or they're leaving it to us to fix the areas we need to work on. Things must be pretty bad for them to actually follow us into the tunnel. And they are. For seven whole-ass minutes they lay into us. I swear most of the time they're looking at me.

When the head coach is done giving us hell, he and one of

the defensive coaches go back into one of the med rooms. The defensive coach gestures to me before the door is shut, and afterward, my name is shouted twice more. I gotta call my agent tomorrow and see if I can pick up any more sponsorship deals before my ass is canned.

This game fucking sucks.

Anna's return is conflicting. I'm relieved when she stops by because I don't have to worry about where she is and if she's safe. But she often brings chaos with her. It's wrong, but sometimes I enjoy escaping into a life without her. It's calm and peaceful when she's not around. But that's how this mess happened. I thought if I could ignore it and focus on myself, like a selfish piece of shit, then maybe her drug use wasn't really happening. Out of sight, out of mind. Some days it's just easier to forget about the baggage I carry. Especially when I feel so free with Freya.

Once Anna charged her phone, she sent me a message that she was going to stay at my place. It will be easier to keep an eye on her now that we have a small break from traveling. I'm thrilled to have the next four games at home, it means more time with Freya. More nights with her curled up next to me. More nights spent inside her.

When I get back to my building that evening, I stop in the bar to see my girl before going up to my apartment. It was only four days, but it seemed like a lot longer. I miss our sleepovers. There's nothing better than crawling into bed next to her, letting all the stress melt away. I'm so much more rested when she's by my side. I scan the bar and quickly find her peeling a lemon twist.

Almost as if she senses me watching her, she lifts her head

in my direction and trades those focused eyebrows for a huge smile. She tag teams with the other bartender so she can escape to say hi. The live band playing in the back has made our stairwell a lot noisier than usual. She hustles over to meet me by the entrance to our favorite dark hallway. I pull her into me and steal the full lips I've ached for all week. She tastes like spearmint.

"I'm sorry about the loss, you played hard, it was a tough game."

I can't even get into that right now.

"How many more hours until you're in my bed?"

She pretends to look at her invisible watch. "Six?"

I groan. "I can't wait that long. I need you sooner."

"It's a good chance for you to hang out with Anna. It's been a while since she's been around," she says, sounding more reserved than normal.

"I'll go check in on her but then I'm coming back here. Maybe tonight should be spent at your place instead. There's a lot to make up for."

She lightly scratches her fingernails down my arm. "Go drop your stuff off, and when you come back, I'll have a cold beer for you."

She walks backward toward the bar with a sweet grin on her pretty face. When she turns around, my eyes drop to her ass. *Damn.* I can still picture the subtle jiggle under my palm. Maybe I can salvage my mood and deal with all this another night. Tonight I want to lock away my thoughts about work and escape with Freya. My feet reluctantly turn to head up the stairs, but my hopes are dashed when I hear voices and footsteps the closer I get. *Why are the police in my apartment?*

"Rhys Kucera?" the man asks.

"Uhh, yeah, what's going on?"

"We received a call for a burglary."

The door to my apartment is open and there's even more police inside. *What the fuck is going on? Where's Anna?*

I rush inside. "Where's—"

Oh, thank God.

Anna's sitting on the couch speaking with an officer when she sees me, and she jumps up and runs toward me, bursting into tears.

"Rhys!" Christ, her hands are shaking. "Somebody broke in!" As soon as the words leave her mouth, the condition of my apartment comes into view. My eyes take in the mess. The couch is askew, drawers open and dumped out, some laying upside down on the floor. Something is beeping, and I look around and realize the noise is coming from the kitchen fridge, the doors have been left open for God knows how long. I'm probably going to have to throw out all my food.

"Rhys, I'm so sorry! I had a job interview a couple hours ago and forgot to lock up. By the time I remembered, I didn't want to be late to the interview, so I didn't turn around. This is all my fault. I knew it was unlocked! I'm sorry! I figured it was safe for an hour, I had no idea this would happen. As soon as I got home, I saw the door was open and your stuff was everywhere." She's almost hysterical. "I didn't know what to do, so I called the police."

I run my hand over my head. *Shit.*

"It's okay, it's not your fault. Are you okay?"

"I'm fine, but all your stuff, Rhys. I'm so sorry!"

"It's fine." I exhale. "It's fine. I'm just glad you weren't here when it happened."

The place is ransacked, my world feels like it's been flipped upside down. There's a broken mirror on the floor. The TV is still on the wall, but it's been smashed. *Cool.*

So much for having a relaxing evening.

Thankfully I had my laptop with me while traveling, but anything else of value here is long gone. The place is so trashed, I can't even tell what's missing yet. It's not like I can walk through here and notice if anything is out of place, there's debris all over the apartment. Stuffing my hands in my pocket, I slowly turn around in the space, unsure of where to begin the cleanup. It's not the damages that bother me, but knowing somebody, a stranger, was in here trespassing, rooting around and smashing my things. Everything feels dirty. Home is supposed to feel like a sanctuary.

I immediately turn around and leave the apartment so I can check Freya's doorknob. It's still locked. I breathe a sigh of relief. Her place is safe. She's always been safe for me. I have to notify her about what happened. I explain to the police I need to step away for a minute and head back down.

When I get back into the bar, she hands me a beer with a smile. I wish that's how tonight could have gone. Happy, chatting with her, and enjoying a drink. Too bad since I really could use that beer right about now.

I grab the back of her neck and pull her ear close to my mouth so she can hear me over the band. "My apartment was broken into. Your door still seems locked, but the cops are upstairs taking statements and checking out the damage."

She flinches and jumps away from me. "What?!" Her big beautiful green eyes are full of worry. I'm regretting telling her, I don't want to make her fearful of where she lives.

I lean in again. "I know, I gotta go back up there, I'll talk to you about it later. Just didn't want you to think I was flaking on you."

"Where's Anna?"

"She's upstairs talking with them."

She nods against me. This time she holds the back of my neck. "You still have my key? After the cops leave, I want you to go over to my place. You can stay with me tonight. I'll see if I can get someone to cover for me so I can dip out early."

I drop a kiss on her cheek, appreciative of her concern and

trying to take care of me. "It'll be okay. Don't worry, babe. It's only stuff."

I'm so fucking thankful neither Freya nor Anna were around when it happened. I don't even want to consider about what might have happened if she had somehow walked out of her apartment and found somebody in the middle of a burglary at my place. The thought only adds more stress. Now I have to worry about both of them.

I'm barely keeping my head above water.

After a couple hours with the police and my insurance agent, consensus shows I'm fucked. Once the police got whatever they needed and had my statement, I started putting my place back together. I'm a frugal guy, so there wasn't too much worth taking. A nice pair of shoes, a few smart home devices, my game console, a couple power tools, a blender, some hockey equipment—all things that can be replaced. The one thing that can't be replaced is my mother's wedding ring. I'm gutted. There aren't many things I have of hers. At the time I was in college and didn't have the money to store them. But her ring was important. It represented what she treasured most, her family. Dad left it to me, and I assumed it would become Anna's eventually since I had no plans for it. The thought of someone else having it makes me sick to my stomach. It could be anywhere by now.

I found a photo of the ring on my mom's finger, it wasn't great quality, but it let the cops know what to look out for. It's probably pawned by now. There's a couple shops nearby I could check tomorrow. I don't need anything else back. Fuck, I'd give everything I have left if it meant I could have her ring back.

"Where's your vacuum?" Anna asks, trying to help me clean up.

"It was stolen." I gesture to the hall.

"Who steals a fucking vacuum?"

Anna sits down on the floor and picks up the spilled garbage and putting it back in the trash.

My head is swimming with all the what-ifs I'm too distracted to answer.

I need to get some cameras set up around here. And in Freya's apartment too.

*Speaking of the Hellcat.* She gently knocks and pushes the ajar door open. She ignores the mess and focuses on me.

She walks right up and wraps her small arms around me, holding me in a tight hug for longer than usual. "What do you need right now?"

Behind me, Anna quietly scoffs, and Freya startles, pulling away and glancing behind me.

"Oh. Hey."

I cannot for the life of me understand out why Anna has such a problem with Freya. She seemed to like her after the night Freya took care of her. They should get along great knowing how similar their personalities are, but I suppose sometimes that has the opposite effect. I'm able to read Freya's body language enough to know she's uncomfortable.

"Hey, Anna, can you give us a sec?" I say.

"Sure! I'm going to take a shower. So good to see you again, Freya! Bye!" It's overly bubbly, which adds to the weird tension in the room. As if she thinks Freya won't still be here when she gets out of the shower.

I wrap my girl in my arms again, letting the shitty night fade away. *This is home.*

My face dips to her neck, and I breathe her in. "There's one thing I need. I really hate to ask, but do you mind if Anna stays with us tonight?"

Silence. Did she hear me? I pull from the hug.

"I'm sorry, Rhys. I'm not comfortable having her over."

I stand to my full height, looking her in the eye. *What the hell?* She can't be serious.

"What? Why not?" Why is she doing this now? I just want one thing to be easy today.

"Come on, I don't want to fight tonight." *Who's fighting?*

"There's no fight. Why would you let me stay, but not her? You have the room. She needs somewhere safe to go, and I'm not telling her to go back to whatever shithole she's living in. She's still shaken up from the burglary. All I'm asking for is one night."

"I get it. I just . . ."

Her stare remains fixed on a wall.

"Talk to me." I bend to get face-to-face, and she blinks, no longer dazed. My eyes are wide, searching hers for an answer. Why wouldn't she want to help my sister out?

"Anna's sober." I know she is because she called the cops to report the theft—she would've been way too paranoid to do that if she wasn't.

It's like something snaps, her hands ball into fists, and her jaw tics.

"I can't have her in my home."

*Is she for real?*

"Why? That's kinda fucked up, Freya. I need you to do me a solid."

"This is a limit for me. I told you at the restaurant that day, I can't go through this again. I can't. If this isn't going to work . . . Look, I'm happy to go to a hotel and pay for a room for her, but she can't stay at my apartment anymore. We can go with her to the hotel, we'll get two rooms. One for her and one for us. Would that work?"

My blood pressure rises along with the volume of my whisper-yelling so Anna doesn't hear us. I can't believe she's choosing *now* to push this grudge based on her history with her ex. It's bullshit.

"Anna isn't Kyle. You asked how you can help, this is the only thing I'm asking of you. The only thing!"

"I am, I'm willing to help you. We can all stay at a hotel. I just can't take her in."

"You're a safe space for her! She needs safe spaces. She trusts you—I trust you!"

"She stole from me!"

I freeze for a second. *What is she talking about?*

"She stole from you? When—what did she steal? Why are you just telling me this now?"

Her nostrils flare. Somehow, despite her body language, Freya's voice has returned to being level and calm.

"The night she detoxed, I went back to my room to change the sheets. There was almost three hundred dollars missing from under the mattress. So, no, Rhys, she can't stay with us. I know you love your sister, I get that you would go to the end of the earth for her—but I won't. I've been through this before. I am holding this boundary. I am sorry if this hurts you to hear because I care about you. God, I care about you so much. But I can't support your sister's addiction and enable her. Get her into the hands of professionals. She needs a recovery program. I can get you the names of some people if that's what you need. But I can't play a part in her addiction."

"She won't go to rehab." I feel like a broken record. Why did she pick tonight to bring all this up? "I can't do this with you right now."

"So you're going to continue like this? We can never have a future together if you can't hold boundaries for Anna and stop enabling her. You need to choose what is important in your life."

*Whoa. Back the fuck up.*

"How can you make me choose between my family and

you?" I demand. If she cared about me, she wouldn't give me an ultimatum.

"I'm not asking you to choose me! I'm asking you to choose *yourself!* You matter. Your mental health, your future, your safety, your happiness, your career, all of those things matter. I need you to be willing to make a change for yourself. Please, Rhys. I'm trying to save you from a future of pain."

I scrub my hands down my face, frustrated. She's not letting up. I really needed somebody in my corner tonight to help me forget about everything. It's been a rough fucking day. Why can't she help me out this one time? I thought she was the woman that would have my back no matter what. If the roles were reversed, I would have done anything she asked.

"She's my responsibility," I say. "I have to protect her. Am I not enough for you, Freya?"

"You are!"

Tears fall down her face, and I want to wrap her in my arms. Seeing her like this is breaking my heart, but my hands are tied, and she's giving me no choice. I can't abandon my sister.

She takes a few steps back. "One of these days, something is gonna happen to make you see this is not a safe situation for anyone. You are not helping her. The only way you can save her is to make her want to save herself. Hold your ground or, I promise you, she'll take you down with her. Her addiction will steal your sanity, safety, your self-respect, reputation, relationships . . . Her addiction is more than either of us can manage. Until she decides she wants a better life, I need to keep a distance from her . . . and you." Her voice cracks at the end.

I don't even know what to say to her. There are no words. She's talking about Anna like she's a dangerous fucking criminal. I pull out my wallet and pass her three hundred-dollar bills.

"I don't want your money."

She actually has the gall to look offended when she's stood here and talked shit about my sister for the last five minutes. She's pissing me off, and I'm pushing her away. Maybe I should just end this whole thing. If she can't accept me and my family, then it'll never work out. My eyes beg her to leave before I say something I don't mean and sabotage whatever is left of us.

"Please." I scoff. "We both know you never turn down money from me. That's our arrangement, remember?" It's a low blow. I can feel myself turning into an asshole, but I don't care. I've been through enough tonight.

"Excuse me?" She flinches. I want to take it back, but I don't. I need to take something off my plate, and she deserves better than I can offer her. She said it herself she can't be with someone tied to an addict. Between work, Anna, and her, something has to give, and it's her. I can't leave my job, and I can't leave Anna.

"You want a boundary, babe? Here's a boundary. I won't be with someone who keeps an active account on *Followers*. I need to be with someone who makes me the only man in their life. I've put up with all your fans, worked around your needs for long enough. What sacrifices have you made for me? Name one."

She crosses her arms over her chest and glares at me. I've never spoken to her like this, and even as I try to make it sound realistic, it comes out unnatural.

"Exactly. You can't. Did you really expect me to hang around while you whore yourself out on a weekly basis?"

Her gaze bounces back and forth between my eyes.

"Just some whore with a webcam? That's all I am to you?"

*Fuck, why won't she leave?*

I swallow before spitting out what I know will finish us.

"Freya, that's all you are to anybody."

The wince that flashes in her eyes is a punch to the gut. I

want to take it back, but I don't. I hate myself with every cell in my body.

My words hang in the air between us until she finally speaks. "Give me my key back."

I work to pull it off my keyring, and I hold it out with the cash.

She snatches up all of it, but throws the bills back in my face.

"Get fucked." That's the last thing she says before walking out.

"Guess we'll be getting a hotel," I mutter. I pull out my phone to look for vacancies for Anna and me.

As soon as she slams her apartment door across the hall, it sets me off. I clench my jaw and punch the air.

"Fuck!" I roar.

Anna steps out of the bathroom, blotting her hair.

"Whoa, dude." She freezes. "Did I interrupt something?"

"Do you have a bag? We're going to a hotel."

"I thought we were staying at Freya's?"

"Yeah, so did I." I hesitate to ask, but I have to hear it from her. "Did you steal three hundred dollars from her?"

"What?"

"Did you steal money from Freya?"

"No! Is that what she told you? See? I told you she's trying to break our family apart. And when did she say I *stole* this three hundred dollars, hm? Jesus, Rhys, I can't believe you would even ask me that."

"The night of your detox."

"Are you serious? I could barely walk, much less dig around her purse looking for cash. You need to find better girls to fuck. Lay off the crazy bitches."

It makes my teeth grind together. I may be upset with Freya, but that was out of line. Especially after everything she did for Anna.

"Don't ever call her that," I grit out, pointing. "She was there for you when I couldn't be."

Her jaw drops open. "She's accusing me of stealing, so sorry if I'm not her biggest fan! I've trashed my reputation enough, I don't need her lying about something I didn't even do."

"She had an ex that died doing the same stupid shit you are! It messed her up, so how 'bout you cut her some fucking slack."

My stomach suddenly wants to empty itself. I shake my head, the stress piling on, and finish scrolling through my phone to book a hotel reservation.

*I didn't think it would end this way.*

# THIRTY-FIVE

## Micky

I bring my knees to my chest, clutching the mug of lavender tea to me. The warmth spreads through my palms, and I try to find some comfort in it. It's been a week since I've heard from him. Did we break up and I just haven't realized it? I figured I would give him time to get his mind right. He didn't mean the words he said. He's struggling. He had a bad game, was tired from traveling, then came home to his apartment full of police after it'd been ransacked. And to top it all off, that's when I decided to hassle him about Anna. It's no wonder he snapped. Though, I expected him to apologize by now. Maybe I should be the one to make the first move.

We were both looking forward to his four days off, but we spent them apart. Now he's on the road again, traveling with the team, and I've been here. Missing him.

I wish he'd just deal with Anna. She's still living across the hall. I trust Rhys when he tells me his sister is a good person, I believe that she is. But she's also an addict, and it's the addicted person I can't trust. She's driven by a physical dependency out of her control. It's not a choice for her, it's a disease. Unfortunately, Rhys is getting the brunt of the side effects.

Never did I want to pit him against his sister, I only asked that he set up boundaries for both their sakes. A couple months ago, I would have relished pushing him down an endless flight of stairs. Not anymore. Seeing him happy, supported, and cared for is all that matters. The team has been a great family for him, but I love him too.

Instead of doing a livestream today, Birdie came over to keep me company while I moped and bitched, but when the Lakes flight was about to land, she had to head home. She misses Lonan like I miss Rhys. Even when we hated each other, we spoke more than we did this week. It's not the fighting that scares me, it's the lack of communication.

Feels like we're extinguishing the fire we worked so hard to kindle.

Where the hell is he? Their flight landed forever ago. Birdie says Lonan's been home for two hours already. It's getting late, and I'm beginning to worry.

Hey.

Are you home?

Can we talk?

The three little dots bounce around on the screen, and I feel a flutter in my chest. My heart is in my throat. Those dots are tethered to him, and I'm holding on for dear life. I set my phone on the coffee table in front of me, tapping my foot, watching and waiting for a text to come through.

Then the dots stop.

Watching the clock, I wait for a minute to pass. Nothing. He leaves me on read. What the fuck? Not even a *Hi, I'm alive*?

I've been pacing by the door for the last couple hours, anticipating our conversation, hoping to hear his heavy steps jogging up the stairs. Thinking back to my relationship with Kyle, I never felt about him the way I do Rhys. I gave, he took. I gave again. The longer that went on, the more unbalanced we became. I love that mutual respect and desire Rhys and I have for each other.

I want us to put this all behind us and move forward again. We can figure it out. What he said that night was an example of Rhys not knowing what to do. That's not how he talks to me. Even when he's calling me names in the bedroom, it's done with compassion. I fear he's being influenced the same way I was with Kyle. People tried to tell me, and I never stopped defending his actions. Even though I didn't listen, I would have appreciated having someone to walk with me during those dark days. I had the chance to be that for Rhys, but instead I walked away.

If he needs space, I'll give it, but having him spend the night with me sounds a lot better. We can have makeup sex and reconnect the way we need to. I check myself in the mirror and put on a couple swipes of mascara and the shade of lipstick I know he likes. The floral dress comes back out of the closet, the one I only wear for him. After knocking on his door, I run my hand over a small wrinkle in the dress, trying to straighten it with my hands.

I hear footsteps on the other side, but they don't match Rhys's stride. When it opens, Anna is on the other side. She gives me a smile, but it's not friendly.

"Hey, Anna."

"Hey, yourself."

"Is Rhys home?"

"He is . . . But he doesn't want to see you." Behind her, a girl wearing barely any clothes crosses the room and walks into the kitchen. Anna notices me looking behind her.

She points to the woman walking around Rhys's apartment. "I'm guessing Rhys hasn't introduced you to Anastasia yet?"

I'm so sick of her shit.

"Anna, I love your brother. A lot. If you love him half as much as I do, you will get your life together and enroll in a rehab program. I've been in his shoes, and I know how bad he's hurting. I am not your enemy here." She opens her mouth to speak, but I don't stop. "If you need help making the phone calls, I'll do it. If you need a ride there, I'll grab my keys. If you want to get sober, I am more than willing to jump through every goddamn hoop to get you into the best program available. But you are the *only person* who can make that decision, so make a fucking effort. You're his sister. Have his back the same way he has yours. "

"You need to stay out of our life. If I'm such a problem, then why did he choose me over you?"

"Because you made him choose, and I never asked him to."

She laughs. "No, it's because he's done with you!"

"Have a nice night, Anna." I turn to head back to my apartment. So much for getting dressed up.

"Oh, I will!"

The longer I go without seeing him, the harder it is to dismiss his behavior. I wrap my arms around my stomach. *Maybe it is over.*

Seeing Rhys on TV at work is a strange form of torture. Especially when the cameras do a close-up of him on the bench. He has that passionate, virile gleam in his eye. It's aggressive and focused. He used to look at me like that. I won't be able to keep working here if I have to watch him on an eighty-inch projector screen.

Amanda covers for me while I step away for a short break in our dark stairwell. It's not helping to keep my mind off us, but I feel close to him here. Rhys is supposed to come with me this week to the inspection, but it's not looking like that's happening. Pulling out my phone, I check on the commercial space, the future location of Sugar & Ice. These days, it's the only thing that distracts me and gives me something to feel hopeful about. I've been manifesting it all week. *Someday, baby, you'll be mine.*

The listing loads but this time red letters stand out, and I all but drop to my knees.

## PENDING.

*Pending?* Like, pending sale? How? It hasn't even officially hit the market! My back sinks against the wall, and I drop to the floor, grabbing my stomach. I feel like I've been sucker punched. Blinking to hold back tears, I scroll looking for more information, but can't find anything. No, no, no this can't be right. There has to be some mistake.

I feel like I'm drowning, all of my ambitions sinking with me.

Why didn't I try to move in sooner? I could have at least made a proactive offer. I'm so fucking stupid. And what about my inspection? Those motherfuckers didn't even give me a chance!

Every laugh that echoes from the bar sounds like it's aimed at me. The world is laughing at my expense. I want to scream or yell or punch something. But I'm hardly able to stand, as my limbs feel heavy and lifeless. Instead, tears roll down my face. This is one situation where I can't pivot. I can't afford a different restaurant space in this neighborhood; it will take me years to afford anything nearby.

I think of how hard I've worked. All the times I appeased the foul-mouthed masturbating assholes, the threats to dox me, the disgusting private messages, the intimidation tactics and warnings. All the long nights at Top Shelf, the extra shifts, the blisters on my feet. What's the fucking point.

*I did everything I was supposed to.*

My head drops between my shoulders, and I don't even try to wipe away my tears anymore. My sadness slowly morphs into anger. Who bought it? It's not fair they can just swoop in and steal it from me! Who the hell took it? I do some searches to see if anything gets a hit and then I see it. A Facebook announcement from Citra that they've bought up a restaurant space only blocks away. They're opening a tasting room and holding it as a new private-event space. What, because their enormous hundred-thousand-square-foot fucking brewery isn't big enough?

From this day forward I will never drink another one of their beers again. Fuck each of those sly shitbags that put in an offer before the bidding started. I'm not mad they got it, well, yes, I am. But what really chaps my ass is I didn't even get a fair shot.

Isn't this the cherry on top of the steaming pile of garbage that is my life. Why not just have the love of my life ignore me like I never existed in the first place? Let's also obliterate my dreams and aspirations while we're at it. *Fucking fabulous.* What else you got, world? How about you make a frozen pipe burst in my apartment? Perhaps an audit from the IRS, hm?

That was my chance. That was everything. The only thing

I feel is my raw throat and aching heart. Everything else is numb. I want to go home.

Leaning into the detachment, I dissociate from it all to preserve whatever dignity I have left. After fixing my makeup, I head back to the bar and throw back a couple shots.

*Fuck it.*

# THIRTY-SIX

## *Rhys*

"I don't know anybody who could handle their girlfriend showing their body off to other men." She shakes her head. "I mean, I couldn't imagine doing that if I had a boyfriend. It's so disrespectful to you."

"That's enough, Anna."

"Just saying . . ." she singsongs, scrolling her phone while flopped on my couch.

I feel like over the last week Anna has gradually been talking more shit about Freya. Besides Anna, my career always came first. Nothing else mattered. But now there's a lot more on the line—*mainly Freya*. I'm not giving up on us, but it's important I figure out my priorities without outside influence. Which is why Anna needs to stop adding her two cents.

"Hey, can I get a twenty? I want to get a burger from downstairs."

"I can cook you a burger." I've been trying to implement boundaries like Freya's suggested.

"With what? You don't have a grill."

"On the stove. Or I'll buy a grill." Probably should have one anyway.

"You'll buy a brand-new grill . . . but you won't give me twenty dollars for a burger? That's dumb."

"That's what I'm offering."

She scoffs and throws her hands in the air. "You don't trust me. See? She's made you not trust me! Why are you letting this chick still come between us?" Her fingers fly over her phone, texting someone. Probably that stupid fucking Anastasia chick she keeps inviting over when I'm not home. I told her she's not allowed to have anyone in my apartment.

"Who are you texting?"

"Oh my God," she groans. "You're not Dad, Rhys. Get over it."

If Dad was here, he'd be disappointed in both of us.

"Who are you texting?" I ask again. This time I snatch the phone from her and hold it over my head. She loses her mind. Snarling and grappling, trying to get it out of my hands. What in the fuck has gotten into her? She's in a full-on rage. Now, I really want to see who she's talking to. She keeps grabbing at my arms, it's hard to keep the phone steady to read, but I hold her gaunt frame away from me while I pull up her messages.

> Where u at?

> I want my money. U said saturday, it's tues.
> If u cn't pay we're going to have to find
> smthing else to xchng. Get it?

> > I'm getting cash now. Can you get me
> > another $40?

*Jesus Christ.*

"What the fuck is this!" I shout.

"Look, I just need the money. At least let me pay him back."

"She was right," I mutter under my breath.

"Are you fucking serious? You're going to listen to her over your own sister? It's me, Rhys! Who matters more? A piece of pussy or your own blood?"

"What is with you and these ultimatums about Freya? Why do you keep making this a *her or me* situation?"

"Because! She keeps driving a wedge between us! If you go back to her, I'm gone, and I'll never come back. There are plenty of men who are willing to help take care of me. I don't need you."

*I see the difference now.*

"Yeah, you do that." I chuck her phone against the brick wall, and it breaks into pieces and then she screams at me.

My phone rings, and I look down to see it's the police department. I've been waiting to see if they have found any information on my stolen things. Walking back to my bedroom to take the call and shut the door, I have to move farther into my bathroom to get away from Anna's screeching.

"This is Rhys," I bark.

"Hey Rhys, this is Officer Tomlinson. Wanted to know we found a few of your items at a pawn shop. Wanted to see if you could come in and retrieve them this afternoon. We also would like to ask you a few more questions to see if there is any more information you can provide."

"On my way."

"Was one of the items you found a wedding ring?" I ask the officer.

"Ah, yeah. Can you confirm the inscription on the inside?"

I traced my fingers over the engraving a hundred times. "Love is a fire."

"Yeah, we got it."

I let my head fall back and let out a shaky laugh. "Thank Christ." I exhale. I can't believe it. I don't care about getting back anything else, but they hand over a box of other items —my power drill, blender, and headphones, plus a couple smaller items. Afterward, I'm led into a small, cramped room with a bunch of computers and a few monitors on the wall.

An officer stands next to me and the evidence technician navigates the files of CCTV recordings. He pulls up a video file and presses play.

"This is the footage we have from the pawn shop where we recovered your possessions."

Two people enter the frame. The first guy spins around, and he's got the worst case of coke jaw I've ever seen. *That guy isn't snorting lines, he's snorting whole-ass paragraphs.* When the second person turns in the frame, I recognize them imme-diately, and my stomach drops out. *Anna.* She's got a hooded sweatshirt and sunglasses on, but it's her.

This is why Freya was so wary that night, she probably already suspected Anna staged the theft. I avert my eyes, I can't watch anymore. Swallowing hard, I pinch my lips shut. My lungs draw in slow, steady breaths, trying to stay calm. I stand behind the data technician while they watch her pawn her own dead mother's ring.

Mom's fucking wedding ring. And after I've been running myself ragged trying to watch out for her.

"That's my sister." I'm not covering for her bullshit. "The one you interviewed that night. That's her." My nostrils flare. "She's an addict," I explain.

"Do you know where your sister is at the moment?"

"Yeah. But first, she needs rehab. I've spent the last week getting her into a sixty-day program. Can I choose to not press charges if she promises to enter a treatment program?"

Not necessarily true, but as soon as I walk out of this

station I'm going to be making phone calls. It's the only chance I have to save her life.

The first two places I call all but laugh at me. I'm going to need to go out of state. That might be for the best anyway. The more distance she can get from the people here, the better her odds. However, that was my plan when I moved her to Minnesota with me, and look how well that turned out.

After a bunch of dead ends, I connect with an agency that helps with this sort of thing. Like a travel agency for treatment facilities. The woman on the phone is understanding of my situation, and she gives me tons of information I'm scribbling down as fast as I can on the back of a fast-food wrapper in my car.

After about an hour, we found a vacancy at a great facility in California. They have a high success rate, and they will provide a chaperone to essentially babysit her flighty ass and make sure she arrives on time and gets checked into the center. They have animal therapy, acupuncture, and it's right by the ocean.

"So what's the catch? Why do they have an opening?"

"It's expensive as hell." I appreciate that she doesn't sugar-coat it for me.

"How much are we talking?"

"If you're still wanting to go with a sixty-day program, you're looking at a hundred and twenty thousand."

Woof. It's only sixty days, and there's no guarantee it will even work? And if she gets kicked out, there's no refund. The woman on the phone tells me they'll only hold the spot for me for forty-eight hours, so she'll need to fly out tomorrow.

"Let's get her registered."

I practice speaking calmly the whole way home, but everything goes out the window when I get back to my apartment. I slam the door shut. Hard enough to rattle the shit on my shelves.

"Guess where I just got home from?"

"How the fuck should I know?" She's still trying to put the pieces of her phone back together. I'm sick of her attitude. "The police station!"

That gets her attention.

"Why?"

"Mom's wedding ring, Anna? Her wedding ring?! How can you sleep at night?"

"What are you talking about? I told you I had nothing to do with that."

I laugh without humor. She should be my brother with the balls it takes to say that to my face.

"You're on camera. You know they have security cameras at pawn shops, right? They have footage of you pawning my shit from three different angles."

I wait for her to apologize, confess, anything. Nope. She has nothing to say for herself.

"I'm an idiot. Freya was right, this is all you care about."

"Oh, fuck you *and* Freya."

"There it is!" Now that her mask is down, there's nothing left of Anna in there. I had the wool pulled over my eyes. My girlfriend tried to warn me a hundred times, and for some reason I thought my sister was somehow more capable than other addicts. It's so ridiculous now that I see it from her perspective.

"I don't need this. I'm already going through this stuff with my dealer. Do you know what he's going to do to me when I don't get him his money?"

"Let's hear it."

"I'm going to have to find another way to pay him if I don't have money."

"Yeah? You gonna fuck them for money?"

"You're one to talk. Isn't that like what you do with Freya?"

My hands ball into fists. "That's not the same and you fucking know it." I get in her face. "Don't you dare say her name again unless it's coming with an apology."

"Whatever, I'm outta here. I'll have my friends come get me."

"You don't have any friends! None of those people are your friends, they're in the same shitty position you're in and you're all just feeding off each other. Even if you did, how are you going to call them? They aren't picking you up, and I sure as hell am not driving you. If you had a way to leave, you'd already be gone. You have no money. You're here for the night, and tomorrow you're gonna get on a plane and check yourself into a treatment program."

She scoffs. "Fuck you."

"You can enter rehab or the police are going to show up and arrest you so they can begin proceedings to charge you with grand larceny. This is your choice. Figure it out."

After grabbing all the alcohol and over-the-counter drugs I have in the house, I walk to my bedroom and slam the door. I'm done. Freya was right, I didn't set the boundary and now everything is falling apart.

# THIRTY-SEVEN

## *Rhys*

I wake up to a strange noise, but immediately am distracted by a horrible smell. What is that? It smells like sulfur or . . . it's gas.

*Shit.*

When I open my bedroom door and step into the hallway, the heavy smell gets stronger. What the fuck is going on? I'm so disoriented. Where is it coming from? Top Shelf? It's barely light outside, it must be the early-morning hours. After nightfall but before dawn. Between my grogginess and the weird sensation, my brain is in a fog. *Focus, where is the smell coming from?* It's everywhere. *Where's Anna?*

I find her down on the floor with an empty bottle of cough medicine clutched loosely in her hand. Eyes seem half open or rolled back. Or both. I quickly slap the plastic bottle away and pick up her tiny body. *Where did she find this? How much was in it before she got a hold of it?* Jesus Christ. I might be sick. Not only from the image of her sitting there but my own exposure. I tap her face a little rough, her eyes blink and eyeballs roll back to face me. *Goddamnit, Anna. How could you be so fucking stupid?*

After dropping her in the outside hall, I go back inside to

check the stove. Beneath an empty pot is the hushed hiss of gas coming from the burner. I reach to turn the knob, but snatch back my hand. To turn off the gas, the knob must pass over the igniter again, which could cause a spark, right?

*Freya.*

I forget the stove and open the nearest window and the door to the balcony and shut the door behind me.

There's no answer when I pound on Freya's door. If I wasn't such a fucking idiot, I'd still have her key. I'm going to have to break down the door. *Never missing leg day is about to pay off.* Luckily there's a pair of my shoes still outside the door, I slip them on, then turn around and donkey kick, hitting just under the doorknob. I hear a pop, but the door doesn't open. I repeat the move, this time it bursts open wide.

Not wasting time calling out her name, I run to the bedroom. She's still sleeping. I grab her up, and it instantly pulls her from her slumber. She kicks and flails, trying to attack me—*as she should.*

"Stop! It's me! I'm not going to hurt you, chill out."

"The fuck are you doing? Put me down!"

"There's a gas leak, we gotta go." She's only in boxers and a camisole.

I grab the two coats off the hook next to the door before leaving and set her down in the hallway. I shove the coat into her hands.

"Put this on. Go," I command, nodding toward the exterior doors below.

Hoisting my barely conscious sister over my shoulder, I follow behind her. When we make it outside, I can literally and figuratively breathe again.

Fuck, I don't have my phone on me. There aren't any businesses open at this hour nearby. Pretty sure there's no where Freya could hide a phone in what she's wearing, and I smashed Anna's yesterday.

My eye catches movement across the street where an early-morning jogger in a reflective running jacket is out on their morning route. Cupping my hands over my mouth, I yell to flag them down. The runner is unsure of me when I hustle over to meet them in the road. Makes sense, I'm half naked and yelling at God only knows what time. The orange-tinged city streetlamps reflect off the small piles of dirty snow along the sidewalk. It's early.

"Do you have a phone on you?" I throw my thumb over my shoulder. "There's a gas leak and we need to call 911." I didn't have time to grab a shirt or jacket when we ran out. I'm thankful I had enough sense to grab Freya's for her. I work in the cold, I'm at least somewhat used to the temperature, she's not. It takes the guy a minute to process what I'm saying.

"Oh, shit, yeah, one sec." He pulls the cell phone from his running jacket and unlocks it, tapping the screen and dialing for me. He fumbles handing the phone over. At least he understands the sense of urgency here. He looks down at my sweatpants with a Minnesota Lakes logo on the pocket, and I see him make the connection.

"You're Rhys Kucera. You play for the Lakes."

I nod. The dispatcher answers, and I rattle off our address, reporting a gas leak and letting them know the gas is still on. We'll need at least one ambulance, possibly two. I need to have Freya checked out to make sure she hasn't been affected. I was so focused on getting her out of there, I can't remember if I smelled it in her apartment or not. My brain is so hazy and tired it's hard to think. The jogger stays with me as I walk back to the sidewalk by the girls. I button the extra jacket I grabbed around Anna's zonked-out body. She's still fully dressed from earlier, silver lining.

Freya is sitting on the curb, trying to tuck her legs into her long winter coat. Unlike the rest of us, she doesn't even have fucking shoes on, the soles of her feet are going get frostbite from the frozen sidewalk.

"Here, let me." I circle her ankles and help bring her feet up under her knee-length parka, at least this will keep them off the icy concrete until I can get her somewhere warm.

All I can hear are Freya's words.

*Someday she's going to take more than your stuff.*

She almost took the woman I love. If Anna had accidentally hit the igniter, or hell, even flipped a light switch, the building could have exploded. I shudder at the thought. How could I have let this get so out of control? I never imagined Anna would do something so dangerous.

It only takes a couple minutes before we hear the loud blare from fire trucks and ambulances. My new jogger buddy is more than happy to accommodate us and be part of the action. I'm thankful that the ambulance is the first one to pull up, two paramedics tend to Anna. She's breathing, but her O2 levels are dangerously low, her heart is racing, and oh, she's all fucked up on DXM. They explain where they are taking her and ask if I want to ride along to the hospital with them. I'm faced with the decision to go with Anna or stay with Freya. I shake my head, and they shut the doors, taking off down the road. From the corner of my eye, I see Freya's head snap up, confused.

The fire truck pulls up, and we explain the situation, and they head up into the gas-filled apartment. A second ambulance pulls up, and I pick up Freya to carry her inside the back so she doesn't have to walk on the frozen ground. We are each given thin, silver space blankets, and they fit our fingers with pulse oximeters to measure our blood oxygen saturation. It's not nearly as low as Anna's. The paramedics suggest we go to the emergency room, so that's what we will do. I wrap my arm around Freya and rub her shoulders. To my surprise, she doesn't pull away. She's hardly uttered a word since we got out here. Why couldn't I see what was right in front of me? This was avoidable, and I let it happen.

"I need you to go to the ER and get checked out."

"That's unnecessary. I'm fine. I can go to Birdie and Lonan's until everything airs out."

*Like hell.*

"Freya, I have to know that you're okay. We don't know how much you were exposed to. You've been sitting out in the freezing cold."

I can't believe I allowed Anna to put us in danger like that. I underestimated her addiction for the last time.

"What about you? You breathed in more than I did! You don't even have a shirt on."

"I'll go too." I move toward the seat in the ambulance.

"Wait, take the ambulance? Fuck, I can't afford an ambulance ride! No way."

She's not getting out of this one.

"You're going. If you don't want to take the ambulance, then I'm going to drive you."

She looks at me like I'm nuts. There's no way I'll budge. One of the guys on the fire truck runs over to give me a spare Minneapolis Fire Department sweatshirt. Fuck, that helps. Even if it's on the small side, it feels way warmer than my mylar blanket that's struggling to compete with the twenty-degree air.

"Fine, you can drive me. But this better be covered by my insurance." I'll cover it.

I hold up my right hand and try to hold back a smirk. I'll take all the shit she wants to give me with a smile on my face if it keeps her talking to me. Bickering is something I miss—I miss everything about her. This week I've let her down more times than I can count, but going forward, I will do everything in my power to protect her and show her I'm ready to show up for myself, her, and whatever I can salvage from our relationship.

The firefighters upstairs begin opening windows, and thankfully, one of them throws me down the keys to my truck and a pair of Freya's shoes. I owe them, the entire firehouse is getting tickets to the next game and some jerseys. It's not enough to repay them for risking their lives for my sister's bullshit.

After thanking them, I use the remote start to warm the truck up while we finish in the back of the ambulance.

I kneel in front of her. "Give me your foot."

She sticks out her leg, and I slide her boots on one at a time. We lock eyes for a second before she looks away, and it almost takes the air out of my lungs. *I needed that.* She misses me too. I saw it in her eyes, if only for a second. Once we each sign a waiver, stating that we are refusing the ambulance ride, we climb into the warm interior of my truck. My jaw immediately relaxes, and I lean against the heated seats. She does the same. I adjust the blowers to our feet, trying to warm up her bare calves.

"Mmmm . . . damn, this feels good." She moans, happy to be in a climate-controlled environment again.

"Don't make those sounds," I say through chattering teeth. "If you'll notice, I'm wearing sweatpants."

She answers too quickly. "I noticed."

*Was that a flirt?*

"Oh, yeah?" I rub my hands up and down my arms and hold my hands next to the vents. I can't stop the grin spreading across my face. *She was checking me out.*

"Not like that. Shut up."

"Uh-huh. Seat belt," I remind her.

We've been put into one of the emergency room bays. We've been given an oxygen mask to improve our O2 stats. They aren't too bad, but apparently all you have to mention is gas leak and they bring the good stuff. We sit in a large glass room with a sliding door, there's a privacy curtain I pull across the room. We're finally alone. I gotta say something. If she doesn't want to talk back, that's fine. But I need her to listen.

"Back in Maine, I had a hockey injury, the doctor prescribed these pain killers, and I got a little carried away. It felt like the pain was still there, and they made me feel better. Eventually my hockey performance became affected and I, luckily, was able to stop taking the drugs in order to keep up my college scholarship. I found out later Anna would take some too. I suspected she was becoming addicted, but I didn't say anything. I was too focused on getting back on track of my own goals.

"Then I left for college, and after Dad died, she used them to cope. I didn't know how to tell her to stop because I knew how bad she was hurting. And if that's what made her feel better, then why would I withhold peace when she needed it most? . . . Isn't that fucked up?"

She doesn't answer my rhetorical question.

"I left Anna to be defenseless against her addiction. I ignored it then, and ignored it here too. I looked the other way because I'm a coward and it's easier than accepting her addiction and dealing with it. Every time I pretended nothing was wrong or didn't stop her, she fell further into the hole. Her addiction started with me. I think that's why I struggled to get help. It felt like it was my mess to clean up since I was the one to cause it. I'm ashamed of what I did. I didn't ever plan on telling you that, and it's not an excuse, but I wanted to explain some of my poor reasoning and decision-making."

She removes the oxygen mask. "That's not how addiction works."

It's quiet for a minute, and I stand from my chair.

"I'm going to go see her."

She nods.

"I'm coming back for you, but first I have some things I need to say to her."

When I get to Anna's room, she looks ten times better than she did before. I don't even know what to say to her. I pull up a chair next to the hospital bed, and we look at each other. She becomes weepy, and I rest my hand on her leg.

"I love you, Anna."

"I love you too." She won't look at me. "They gave me Narcan. Ruined my high . . . that was my first thought when I woke up. Pretty messed up, huh?"

I clear my throat. "I'm done enabling you. I'm creating a boundary. Until you go to treatment, I can't see you, and I can't have you in my life."

"Rhys. Come on, I—"

"Stop talking. I need you to listen." I try to sound as calm as I can, inside I want to scream. From sadness, from anger, from guilt. "You're an addict. And your addiction almost killed us. It almost killed the woman I love. Your need to be high all the time has taken over your life. And I can't let you be a part of mine until you agree to treatment."

"I'm sorry. I'm so sorry. I'll start going to meetings, and I'll get a sponsor and all the things I'm supposed to do. Don't shut me out. Let me stay."

"No." It's breaking my heart.

"You can't say no! I'm your blood! There's nobody else. I'm alone!"

"I'm sorry, Anna, I can't."

"You can't or you won't? This doesn't even sound like you. This sounds like something Freya put you up to. If I can't stay with you, I'll have to start prostituting myself for drug money and find a busted crack house to live in. Do you know how bad the rats are in those places? It's disgusting. Is that what you want me to do?"

This is the manipulation Freya always warned me of.

"That's your choice, but you put all of our lives at risk tonight. Someone's going to get hurt."

"I'm the one that's hurt! The only reason I have this addiction is because of you! You're the one that let me have the pills. I never had a problem until you, this is your fault! You weren't there when I needed you most. You've never been there for me!"

"I know. You're absolutely right. But this is me showing I care. Take the rehab, Anna. Don't go to jail. Aren't you tired of living like this?"

She stares at me dumbfounded, tears welling in her eyes.

"This is a fight only you can do. Choose yourself, Anna."

"I can't do it," she sobs.

"You can. You're strong and you're so fucking resilient, you always have been. Hell, you could probably get through it with spite alone."

She chuckles and hiccups.

"This is a good treatment program, it's one of the best."

"I'm scared."

"I'm scared of what's going to happen if you don't go. I think we both know that's a much scarier outcome. This could change your life."

Tears stream down her cheeks.

"Are you going to keep seeing Freya?"

*I hope so.*

"If she'll have me."

"You love her?"

"Yeah."

She nods and looks at the floor.

"You've really changed, dude."

"I'm happier."

"I can see that." Her voice is sad.

I straighten out her oxygen tube wrapped around the bedrail.

"There's an agency that's going to stay with you and make sure you get to the facility safely. Your flight leaves around noon. I've already spoken with the person assigned to your case, and they'll meet you here in an hour. When I leave, I'll get your ID and clothes so you can get on the plane without any issues."

Her lip trembles. "Are you saying goodbye?"

"Yeah, this is goodbye. You're my sister, I love you, Anna. I will always love you. Make Mom and Dad proud. Make yourself proud. Do the work, and fucking fight for yourself." My eyes well with tears. I know she will struggle with this. But the only way to get my sister back is if I send her away first.

Her tears fall faster. I'm proud of her for making the right choice.

"I love you too."

# THIRTY-EIGHT

## Micky

*Don't get your hopes up.* I can't assume he's getting her help, or I'll be disappointed if it's not true. Disappointed is an understatement. I'll be heartbroken and devastated. Not just for Rhys, but for Anna. I don't want her to face the same fate as Kyle. I want her to have a relationship with her brother; they're all the family they've got, and they need one another. But if Anna stays with him, I'll need to step away. I can't make him leave with me, but I can't stick around and put my physical safety in jeopardy. There can't be a repeat of tonight. Which means I'll need to find a new apartment . . . and a new job.

Between Rhys and Sugar & Ice, I've cried enough this week. I don't know if this thing we have is over or not. He seems as far away from me as he's ever been. At least when we hated each other, we felt anger. This is like I don't even exist to him. The ambivalence is suffocating.

I put the oxygen mask back on my face and breathe in more. It's kinda nice. Can't believe he made me come here. Fresh air would have sufficed.

I know it was an emergency, but feeling his hands on me again when he picked me up was like being wrapped in a warm blanket. It's amazing how much a person can miss a sensation like touch. *His touch.*

Tilting my head to the ceiling, I close my eyes. He better come back for me. I have no way of getting home and don't have my phone. *How long do we have to be here anyway?* A house inspector is supposed to go through the space and make sure it's safe for us to reenter. They said it would be a few hours before Rhys's apartment would be safe to return to. They want to make sure there isn't a leak in either of our apartments or at Top Shelf.

Once work found out, they told me to take the next couple days off. Fine by me. It's not like I'm on some financial deadline anymore. I wouldn't mind a little vacation from my life. Hideaway in my apartment. Stay in bed with a good book. Only leave the room to answer the door for food delivery. Sign me up.

The glass door to our emergency room bay opens. I crack open one eye, and Rhys slides it closed behind him. Metal chair legs scrape over the floor as he pulls it next to the hospital bed.

"Lemme get a hit of that."

Without opening my eyes, I hold out the oxygen mask. He scoots his chair closer to the hospital bed and inhales.

"Hey, I want to talk to you."

Great. Here we go. The we-need-to-talk talk. I dig deep and put up the biggest wall I can, I will not cry in front of him when he breaks up with me. Who breaks up with someone in the emergency room?

*Assholes, Freya. Assholes.*

I open both eyes and sit up straight, ready for the grand finale of my shit week to rain down on me. I'm a solid wall of deflection, he will not see me break.

"I never meant to hurt you."

"You didn't. I'm fine." A scuff on the floor makes for a helpful distraction while I focus on keeping myself together.

"No, you're not. Look at us, Freya. You're in the hospital because of me. I should have listened to you. You told me this would cost me more than my things, and you were absolutely right. It almost cost me you. You were right about everything."

*Fucking duh.*

"The police called, they found some of my things, and had footage from the person trying to pawn it. It was Anna. Some other guy was there too, but she staged the burglary. I gave her the choice between a treatment program or getting arrested and facing jail time. I don't know what tonight was, some desperate attempt at a final high. I think she felt trapped." He clears his throat. "I just said goodbye. She has a chaperone that is going to meet her here and escort her to a treatment center in Big Sur. I told her I was done yesterday, I just didn't realize she would have gone to such extremes once she found out she was unable to manipulate me anymore."

*Holy shit.* Even if he's about to tell me to pound sand, I'm so fucking proud of him. This is the hardest step; it takes so much bravery to stand up to the ones you love. I don't know what to say.

"As soon as I said that stuff to you about the money, I wanted to take it back. It was an attempt to push you away, I was spiraling and didn't want to suck you into my vortex. You deserved someone who could give you what you needed and at the time I had no idea how to become that for you. I didn't mean any of it. I was hurting, but I never should have taken it out on you, that was fucked up. I fucked up. Please don't go back to hating me again."

"I wanted to talk to you when you got home from Colorado. I went to your apartment, but Anna said you were home but didn't want to see me. There was some girl there, Anastasia."

He scrubs his hands down his face. "I didn't get home until almost midnight, I had to go straight from the airport to another meeting. I wasn't home. I have no clue who that girl is, someone Anna was hanging out with. The only times I've ever spoken to her were when I kicked her out."

"How come you weren't returning my text messages?"

"I tried, but I didn't know what to say. I didn't want to be like Kyle and make promises I couldn't keep. So in between hockey games and all the police shit, I had some other things I needed to take care of."

It's hard to look at him, I peer down at my lap. Reaching into my view, he covers my hand with his and massages my palm.

I want to wrap my arms around him and support him, reassure him that he's doing the right thing by Anna, but I'm still mad. And hurt. "You did a really hard thing today. I'm happy she's getting help."

He nods. "Me too."

"I thought you were breaking up with me."

He hunches over with his elbows on his knees. The thinly padded seat next to the hospital bed squeaks. "I let you jump to that conclusion, and I shouldn't have."

When I glance over, he's looking up at me through his lashes, and my stomach flutters.

"Can you forgive me?"

*With every part of me.* "I forgive you."

His shoulders relax, and he drops his head in relief before returning his gaze. I avert my eyes, attempting to keep the loose emotions in check, and frantically trying to peel off all the armor I put up at the beginning of our conversation.

"Darling, I was always coming back for you. I should have said it that night."

"Do you love me?" I need to hear him say it.

"I love you. I am *madly* in love with you," he says.

Those words instantly mend every crack of my jaded heart.

"I love you too." I laugh and sniffle again. So much for not crying. I didn't anticipate the tears being happy ones.

He shoots to his feet and slides his hands into my hair, locking his lips on mine, and it takes all the air out of my lungs. His kiss makes me complete again. In my fists, I grip the too-small sweatshirt on his chest. My pulse quickens and everything else floats away.

"Leave with me," he says against my mouth.

"Of course I'm leaving with you." His lips curl into a smile. "I don't have a car."

He delivers a small smack on my ass. When our kiss slows, he pulls back and looks at me with serious eyes.

"Do you mind if we get a hotel room? I'm not ready to go back there yet."

He tries to hide the sadness in his voice, but I know it's there. He's been through a lot in the last twenty-four hours.

"Of course."

# THIRTY-NINE

## Rhys

O n the way to the hotel, my phone rings, it's my agent.

"Hey, Carrie."

"Hey, Rhys, glad I caught you. Do you have a minute to talk?"

I peek over at Freya. "Yeah."

"Great. First of all, how are things going?" I'm not interested in small talk.

"What are you calling about, Carrie? Does this have to do with my contract?"

I can feel my girl's eyes on me.

"Yeah. I got a call from the Lakes this morning"—*Fuck. Here it comes*—"and they want to offer an extension."

*No way.* "Seriously? How long?"

"Four years."

I got us a room at one of the nicer hotels. Nothing too outrageous, but enough it feels like a getaway. I want to spend tonight wrapped up in each other. No outside noise, no distractions, no family drama. When we get to our room, the first order of business is getting in the shower. Once she strips out of her tiny shorts and camisole, I withstand jumping on her. God, *that ass*. I want to sink my teeth in it.

"Mmmm . . . shower was a good idea," she groans under the hot spray. I step in behind her, and we share the luxury shower. *Good call on the hotel.* I lather the shampoo in my hands, running it through her soaked strands. The faster we get clean, the faster we can get dirty again.

"Is that a coffee thermos or are you just happy to see me?"

"Coffee thermos."

She giggles. I love that sound. After rinsing her hair, I start on mine. Then carefully wash every inch of her slippery body. She returns the favor with the same lingering touch. It's caring and tender . . . until she gets to my cock. Then it's teasing and hungry. I cup her face in my hands.

"I love you," I say gruffly.

"I love you too," she whispers back.

My lips take hers, and I walk her backward to the tile wall, allowing my touch to roam her skin, this time selfishly.

Her lips leave mine and move from my pecs to my abs to my . . . *I know where this is going.*

"Good fucking girl," I praise as she gets down on her knees. I put my thumb in her mouth, and her jaw opens for me. *Gorgeous.* Mascara is smeared on her face, she's so sexy. This time when she takes me in her mouth, I let her control the speed and tempo. Black painted fingernails dig into my ass, and I brace myself with an arm against the wall. Her tongue flicks over me before she swallows me down her throat.

*"Shit."*

My free hand cups her face, and I stroke her cheek while she bobs over me. Feral eyes look up at me with charcoal-streaked water dripping down her cheeks like tears. Rivulets of water making streams over her creamy breasts. God, I love her messy. Big eyes gaze up at me, and she's so sweet with her mouth full.

She moans around my length, and the vibrations send a jolt through me. I steel my arm against the wall to prevent my knees from buckling.

"Is that so?"

Her eyes crinkle at the corners, smiling back at me.

I nudge her knees apart with my foot. "I want you to focus on how empty it feels between your thighs and how hard I am for you."

She groans and picks up speed.

"You crave it, don't you? Fuck, I wish you could see how hot you are like this. So needy." I brush wet strands of hair out of her face. "So willing to please."

Pulling off me, she arches her back and tilts her head up to me. "Control me."

She submits willfully. Like a lioness inviting me to be her king. She'll always the hold the power. *I'm forever hers.*

It wasn't part of the plan, but I can't resist her request. I'll give her anything she wants. I exhale through my nose, and my fingers get lost in her hair as I set our pace.

"Deep breath, darling."

She inhales, and I slowly push down her throat. She wiggles. "Keep those thighs apart."

I pull out, she coughs, and I slide back inside, pulling her hair taut and bobbing her pretty lips over my cock.

"I can't wait to eat your pussy after this. I've missed you on my tongue." Her eyes grow wide, and she drags nails down my thighs. My abs flex, I won't be able to hold on much longer. "It seems you miss it too."

Her eyebrows push together, determined as she sucks.

"You think you deserve this?"

She nods, wanting my cum. "Of course you do. You're my perfect little slut. I can't imagine my life without you in it."

Her whimpers are all it takes to send me to the brink.

"Swallow every drop," I warn.

I grab the back of her head and fuck her mouth. *Shit, she takes me so well.* It's exactly how I like getting my dick sucked. *How did I get so lucky?*

There's an unholy gleam in her eye, almost like she's daring me to fuck her harder. She gently tugs on my balls, and it feels like a frayed cable that finally snaps. My hips jerk, and I clench my jaw, shooting down her throat. She swallows me down.

"Fuck, Freya. Just like that. *Good girl.*"

Clutching my outstretched hand, she stands, allowing me to press my forehead to hers while I catch my breath. I turn the water off and grab a towel, then swipe the smoky streaks from her face with a washcloth.

In front of the mirror, I pull her back to my front, looking at the both of us. My fingers skim down her arm and unwrap the towel from her body. She stands naked, her nipples hard and skin pebbled with goose bumps.

"Don't move."

I love hearing her breaths become shallow as she's forced to stand still while I grope and tease her body. After dropping to my knees behind her and flattening my tongue, I move my head side to side, picking up every drop of her arousal. When I spear two fingers inside, she lets out that first gasp I love so much. I bring my lips to her clit until she clamps down on me like a vise. I let her finish climaxing before I rise to my feet and admire her flushed face in the mirror.

I massage her fleshy round cheek before I bring down a firm slap.

"Get your ass on the bed. I'm not done with you yet."

Following Freya, I climb over her and brace myself on my

elbows, bracketing her beautiful face. My gaze settles on her. Unable to look away, unable to move. The love I have for this woman is never ending. I try to swallow down the emotion climbing up my throat. My mouth brushes over hers, resulting in her faint sigh. I want to experience these moments for the rest of my life.

My tongue traces her full lips, and I suck the lower one between my teeth. Her hands travel down my body, and she grips my length, lifting her ass to slide me through her folds, showing me how wet she is. I smile and nip at her mouth again as I take her body.

"Fuck." *It's been too long since I've heard her mutter that desperate little curse.* "I love the way you feel inside me," she mewls.

She knows how to feed my ego. Her hips snap in rhythm with mine. I sit up on my heels and drive into her harder.

"Like that. Fuck, yes. Like that," she begs. Her knees quake. "Oh god . . ."

"Shhh . . . you're doing just fine. Just relax. You want to come on my cock, sweetheart? Do it."

It's like she's been waiting for permission, as soon as the words leave my lips, she's gripping the sheets and crying out.

I roll us so she's on top and pinch her nipples. Leaning back, she braces her hands on my thighs as she gyrates her hips. Her fiery hair falls over her tits, and I wrap it around my fist, pulling her head back. Her chin raises to the sky, and she draws in a sharp breath at the sudden pressure on her scalp. I don't want to miss one bounce as she rides me. My thumb finds her clit, and she switches to grinding against me.

Loosening the hold on her hair, she sits up on her knees so I can thrust up into her while she grabs my shoulders.

"Goddamn, you're taking me so well." I smack her ass, and she jolts.

"Fuck me from behind."

My pleasure.

She climbs off and gets on all fours. I bestow another spank to the other cheek, watching it pinken as I knead her ass. I slap my cock against her clit before I push inside again.

"Fucking hell, baby." My eyes feel unfocused. "You"—I thrust into her again—"belong to me."

"Promise?" she pants.

I slide my hands down her smooth back and over her curved ass. "Try and stop me. You're mine forever."

My hands take control of her hips, and I give her what she wants. I fuck her. Each time I drag out and then hammer into her again, she gasps.

I reach around and collar her throat with my hand while I kiss her up her back as I drive into her over and over again. She's heaven.

Her choked cries settle, and she stiffens, ready to peak again.

"Not yet, you're going to come with me on this one."

"I can't hold off."

"You have to. Show me how well-trained that sweet pussy is," I demand.

Wrapping an arm around her stomach, I lift her back to my front. Still keeping one hand on her neck, I move the other from her abdomen to between her folds. Massaging her as I work her from behind. Her hands brace against the wall as she gets closer to the finish line. "You're doing such a good job waiting. I can feel how bad you want to come. You're *so* ready . . . Is it torture?" She groans, and I chuckle at her frustration.

"Please, Rhys . . ."

I run my nose along her neck.

"Can you hear how wet you are when I fuck you?"

She sobs her *yes*.

"Look at what a behaved little hellcat you can be." I

motion toward the mirror on the side of the room. "See how obedient you are for me? I love that."

She nods. She's about ready to lose it. Her body is filled with unhinged lust, it's a miracle I've held on this long.

"Ready?"

"Yes!"

"Count yourself down from ten."

"No, no countdown! I need it now."

"Do it, Freya. Or you won't get to come on this cock."

"Ten, nine." She counts.

"Slower." I grin, she works so hard to please me, and I get off on taming her.

"Eight . . . seven . . ."

"There you go. Good girl."

"Six . . . five . . . four . . ." Her whimpers grow louder with her counting.

Fuck, I'm about ready to lose it.

"Three . . . two . . ."

"One," I growl in her ear.

She clamps down on me like never before as her orgasm fires through her. It sets off my climax. My name is on her lips as she comes, and I wrap my arms around her while she bucks on me. My head tucked into her neck, breathing her in, I shudder as she milks my cock.

"That's it, darling. You did so fucking good."

I gingerly lower us back down to the bed and envelop her in my arms, she trembles against me with little aftershocks.

She's so fucking perfect.

After we both get a moment to catch our breath, I bring back a warm washcloth from the bathroom.

## FREYA

"I want to discuss the *Followers* thing."

*Come on, why'd he have to go and bring that up?* The storm cloud of reality moves over me. A reminder that I've lost the thing I'd been working so hard for. And if he's about to ask me to stop my *Followers* account, it'll be a decade before I have enough money.

"Rhys, I don't want to get into it right now." The topic makes my chest tight. The last time we spoke about this, it didn't go well. I spin the plastic admittance bracelet still around my wrist. I want to stay in the bubble of happiness we're in.

"Why not?" He looks distant.

"I just don't want to talk about it. It's a sore subject for me. I found out this week . . ." *Christ, I still can't say it out loud without getting emotional.* I exhale slowly. "Someone bought the space. It's over. I missed it. There's a few other locations that would work, but the rent is a lot higher, and it would take a lot more money and time before it could get off the ground. I haven't decided what I'm going to do yet. But either way it will be put on hold for a few years."

Finally, his eyes reach mine again. "I bought it."

*What?* It takes a second for his words to register, and once they do, I can't breathe. My thoughts race. *No, that's not what it said online. This doesn't make any sense. What does he mean, he bought it?*

"I don't understand. I read online that Citra bought it."

"No, I met with Citra a few weeks back when I heard a rumor they were moving in on it. We went toe to toe with bids, but during that time, the city inspector came back with a mile long list of repairs that needed to be completed before any new business could occupy the building.

"According to some old contract that had been put in

place when the guy bought the place, all fixes were the responsibility of the landlord, not the tenant. I think he thought he could somehow get by without the renter finding out. Anyway, Citra dropped out when they saw the projected timetable for moving into the space.

"The owner didn't want to be buried in repairs, and I knew you were already anticipating paying for the renovations anyway. I had it written up that I would be responsible to make whatever restoration changes necessary to bring it up to code if he sold me the building in it's entirety."

I push up on my knees, facing him completely slack jawed. "Oh my God!"

"He took the offer and we cut a deal." He shrugs, like it's no big thing.

"So, Citra didn't—"

"Citra found another property that opened up on the same street, but a block closer to the brewery. That place with the outdoor patio? *That's* the restaurant they are taking over."

My hands cover my mouth. I'm speechless as we peer at each other, unblinking. *Oh. My. God.* My heart pounds. My emotional dam is about to break. *Am I dreaming?*

"Rhys . . ." My eyes are swimming with tears. The stress, frustration, and defeat weighing on me seem to melt away.

He continues. "I don't care if you keep doing *Followers*. Hell, I'll start making sex tapes with you if you want. We can start right now. But I need to know that you're doing it because you *want* to, not because you need the money. So, I took that part out of the equation."

"I can't accept this. It's too big." *Shut up, Freya. Just take it and pay him back or something. Round the clock blowjobs. Whatever. Settle it later.*

He laughs. "I know you can't because you're stubborn as fuck. That's why I'm listed as an investor. This is me investing in you. I believe in you. And actually, Citra does too. I told them about your concept, and they seemed impressed. They want to talk about some collaboration opportunities with a microdistillery they have plans for. I told 'em they'd have to talk to the boss."

My smile grows ear to ear. My vision blurs, thanks to all the moisture in my eyes.

I climb on top of his waist and straddle him. "Oh my God. You're serious?"

"Of course I'm serious. Anyone who's ever met you knows how dedicated you are to this. If anyone can do it, it's you. But we close in a couple weeks, so you may want to put your notice in soon. You're about to be very busy, 'cause you were right . . ." He shakes his head and smirks. "That place is a total fucking fiasco. There's so much work to do."

Tears fall at their mercy, and now I'm doing this weird cry-laughing thing. I can't believe this man. I'm speechless. My mind is spinning with the news. This is the greatest gift I've ever received, the most heartfelt and thoughtful thing anyone has ever done for me. He's literally making my dreams come true. He wipes my tears away.

"What made you do this?"

"Love, mostly. But also because you are creative, ambitious, and intelligent. Like I said, it's a solid investment. I'm *diversifying*."

He wraps his arms around me and pulls me closer to him. His eyes drop to my lips, and I grab him and kiss him with everything I have. This is everything I've ever wanted. He wipes away a couple more tears, and I rest my cheek on his chest. He rests his chin on the top of my head. I hug his torso for dear life.

"I love you so much."

"I love you so much too. It's me and you."

"Stay with me tonight." He doesn't ask. "Stay with me every night."

"There's nowhere else I'd rather be."

"Here are the keys. Congratulations, Rhys and Freya."

"Thank you! Come see us at the grand opening. First drink on the house."

Rhys hands me the keys, and I insist we drive straight there. I can't wait to get started on the demolition. Birdie and Lonan are meeting us there so we can get some before pictures of the space; something that will remind us how far we've come.

When I step out of the car, my best friend is already there waiting for me.

"Micky! It's happening!" Birdie runs up and holds me in a tight bear hug.

"I know! How many years have I been obsessing over this?"

"Too many. Half the reason I didn't move back in with you was because I couldn't handle one more night of you reciting cocktail recipes and monthly revenue statements in your sleep."

Rhys unlocks the front door for us.

"Shut up." I laugh, elbowing her off me.

Lonan pulls her into his side. "Hey, now, I thought I was the reason you didn't move back in with Micky."

"Of course, baby." She holds her hand to block her lips and stage whispers, *I didn't want to hurt his feelings* out the corner of her mouth.

He grabs her sides and throws her over his shoulder as they step inside and wander around. "We're going to go explore," Lonan says.

"No fucking in my kitchen!" I call after them.

Rhys comes up behind me and wraps his arms around my stomach. I lean back into him.

"We have a lot of work to do," he says.

"You know this would never have happened without you, Rhys."

"Nah, you would have done it. You're too stubborn to give up."

"I love you." I turn around in his arms and press my lips to his.

Roaming hands find my back pockets, and he lifts me by my ass so I can wrap my legs around him.

"Let's go do our own exploring. I want to fuck you on Richard Nixon's face."

"No!" I giggle. "Not until we get this place cleaned up . . . and maybe get our tetanus shots up to date."

"That's valid. I still can't believe I love you enough to buy you this dump."

"Just you wait, this will be the most sensational dump you've ever seen."

"Please be talking about the bar."

Laughing, I give him a playful nudge on his shoulder.

Birdie comes around the corner looking upbeat. "Ovens look to be in pretty good condition. Probably won't need to replace them for at least another five years." It's nice to have a legit chef take a look at the equipment for me. "I got some shots of the kitchen, but let's get a few pictures out here with you in them. This is a big day for you, it needs to be captured."

"Go stand by the archway over there." I go over and we take a couple selfies with all four of us. "Okay, now just you."

Rhys must be bored out of his mind. He's being a good sport, standing off to the side, waiting patiently, and occasionally flashing that handsome smile at me.

"Rhys, get over here, you need to be in these too. We're a partnership. You're my angel investor."

He walks over and stands behind me in the photo.

"Great, these look excellent. Stay like that, I'm going to change angles."

"I think we have enough, Birdie."

"One more. Okay, turn toward me, angle your head down just a little bit."

"Okay, last one. The guys are probably hungry." They're always hungry. When my feet pivot, I do a double take and Rhys is down on one knee.

*He's not . . . ?*

*Oh my God. Is this happening?*

"What are you doing?" My hands start to shake. "Is this the thing? This is the thing, right? The thing where people ask other people to marry them?"

He ignores my question and beams at me. "Freya Girl . . ."

"Fuck! Are you sure?!" I blurt out.

He laughs. "I haven't even asked you anything."

I'm so flustered.

He pulls a ring box, and that's when the tears fall. It's his mother's ring. It's beautiful. I'm speechless.

"I'm convinced the only reason this was found is because it was meant to live on your finger," he says, removing it from the ring box.

I choke back a sob and smile.

"Before I ever saw your face, I knew we had something. There was a spark from the beginning. I couldn't stay away from you, no one has ever held my fascination like you do. I needed more. And I'm so glad I did. You entered my life like a fireball. The more I tried to resist it, the bigger it grew. Until one night you were standing in front of me, and when I looked in your eyes, I knew instantly you were everything I needed. You consumed me. Our love is a fire, Freya. It's strong and wild, and knows no bounds."

I laugh, my eyes swimming with tears, not caring there's an audience behind us.

"I promise to fuel it, be careful with it, and never let it burn out. You love me in the rarest of ways, and I want to love you for the rest of my life." His glassy, emotion-filled eyes make me melt. "Will you marry me?"

This man is my world. I drop to my knees in front of him and move my lips to his. "Yes. I will never be done falling in love with you," I whisper against his mouth.

# EPILOGUE

## Micky

*One Year Later...*

"Can we get a dog?" Rhys asks with sad eyes.

I crouch down with my box cutter. "As long as it's a *dog* and not a *puppy*. Neither of us can handle a puppy right now." I grunt, pulling up the last of the carpet padding.

"That's fair. I think it would be nice to have the pitter patter of little feet around here."

My eyes go wide, and I look over my shoulder at him, shooting daggers. We are *so* not in a place for that mess right now. "You keep saying that shit and you'll conjure a pregnancy. I'm not ready for that. I'm barely prepared to babysit for Birdie and Lonan when they have their baby."

"Alright, alright . . . So, are you nervous about the soft opening tonight?"

A smile spreads across my face. Tonight Sugar & Ice opens its doors. Last week we did a dry run with the Minnesota Lakes. I appreciate Rhys getting the whole team to show up, though with all the drinks I poured for them at Top Shelf, they were happy to oblige. I figured it would be a great test for the staff to see if they were ready. At first, they were nervous seeing a room full of athletes, but they didn't get flustered, everyone acted professionally, and things ran smoothly. I had the guys throw some curveballs at them with drink orders and questions about pastries. Everyone on the floor was phenomenal.

"Nope. They're going to kill it."

"It's going to be a hit, I'm so proud of you."

"Funny, I was just thinking the same about you. This house is going to help a lot of people transition into the real world after rehab. You're one hell of a human, Rhys."

After his first property investment with the cocktail lounge, Rhys found a hidden passion of his. He's on track to opening six new sober-living homes within the next two years across the United States. Twenty percent of profits from Sugar & Ice go toward Kucera Housing, and we plan on having quarterly fundraising events to bring more awareness to his project. A bar funding sober-living housing? *Why not?*

It's given him something tangible to work toward, and he finds the work fulfilling. He's inspiring, I'm so proud of him and everything he's accomplished. Today we're helping with the demo on one of the local sober-living builds that will open next fall. We use contractors for most of the work, but when it comes to the demolition, Rhys likes to be involved anywhere he can annihilate something with his hands.

I take his outstretched hand and rise to my feet where he pulls me into his chest.

"I love you, Freya Girl."

"I love you too. Have you spoken to Anna today?" She's been living in the first sober house he opened and has been helping with the planning of new locations. It's given her something to focus on, and she's as passionate about it as Rhys. She relapsed the day she was discharged from her sixty-day program, but immediately went back in and has been sober for nine months and twelve days. Rhys keeps track.

When I suggested to him we involve her in our projects, she jumped right in, and has provided phenomenal insight to different amenities we can add to make the residents more successful, as well as helping organize events and classes. She's even enrolled at the university to become a licensed counselor with an emphasis in addiction. She and I have grown a lot closer.

"Yeah. I made a reservation for us to grab dinner with her next week."

"Awesome. I want her to help me with choosing paint colors for the kitchen on forty-second. Ooh, we can turn it into a girls' day! I'm going to book us manicures and blowouts."

"I could go for one of your blowouts." I laugh and kiss his lips speckled with sheetrock dust.

"Oh, forgot to tell you. Guess who's announcing his retirement tomorrow?"

"On the team? Who?"

"Sully. It's gonna be his last season."

"No shit!? Who's going to be captain?"

"They haven't released it yet, I'm sure there'll be a lot of meetings to figure it out before the time comes." He claps his hands together, wiping them on his jeans. "All right, Hellcat. That's enough teardown for today. We gotta get home so you can start getting ready."

The soft launch tonight is invite-only. Mostly neighboring ad executives and creative agencies. Our close friends, which includes the entire Lakes team. Obviously, we invited Citra, since we have two small batch kegs of a special brew especially made for Sugar & Ice.

*It's magnificent.* The exposed brick and dark walls are moody and intimate, perfect for the speakeasy vibe. It looks like it came right out of the 1920s. It was easy coming up with a password for guests to get in: *Hat Trick Swayze* in honor of the love of my life who made it all come true for me. Sugar & Ice is better than I ever could have imagined. The space was meant to be. Like Rhys and me.

"So how long did the renovations take? This building used to be such an eyesore but it's incredible in here!"

I've been chatting with one of the women I met at the ad agency. She's an executive assistant to one of the chief officers. When I called to send out an invite, she and I lost track of time chatting. She's very interested in supporting women-owned businesses, and I am flattered she's taken such an interest and has done so much to spread the word about Sugar & Ice to the leadership over there.

"It was about a year altogether. It's been quite an adventure. Oh! I want to introduce you to my friend, Birdie. Birdie, get over her!"

"Birdie, this is Raleigh. Raleigh this is Birdie. Raleigh works over at Method Marketing."

"Oh! Micky told me about you. You have made quite the impression on her. You'll have to come out for drinks with us sometime. Well, drinks for you, I'm due in August, so I'll be designated driver," Birdie explains. *I'm so excited to be the godmother!*

"Congratulations! Do you know what you're having?" Raleigh asks.

"A boy, but we haven't thought about names yet."

"Boys are great. I have a four-year old son, Arthur. I promised I would bring him home some of your desserts,

Micky. Not sure how many will actually make it all the way home, though."

"I already put together a box for you, just tell them your name by the register before you leave tonight." I nudge Birdie. "Looks like the rest of the boys are finally arriving." I nod to the entrance doors.

"God, they are always late," she mutters and then holds her arm in the air so he can spot us.

"You're so sweet to set something aside for me, thank you!"

"Lonan!" Birdie shouts. He makes eye contact and heads in our direction. He's looking at Birdie like she's one of the items on the patisserie menu.

Raleigh turns to follow our gaze at the front door where Sully and Conway are shaking hands with the bouncer. When she spins back to face us, her face is pale, and she looks like she's seen a ghost.

"Girl, are you feeling okay?"

"Actually . . . um . . . I'm so sorry. All this talk about kids reminded me I was supposed to get back to the babysitter like twenty minutes ago. I gotta run." She grabs her purse and backs up. "Congrats on the soft open, this place is amazing! It was so good to meet you, Birdie."

"Don't forget your—" She's already slipping out the door before I can remind her to get the box of pastries.

*Well, that was fucking weird.*

# RHYS

She's a force, working the room like a champ. The place is packed, and there's a line out around the block. I never doubted her for a second, but neither of us anticipated a crowd like this. Her smile is contagious, but behind that grin she's exhausted.

"You look great out there. How are you holding up?"

"I'm beat." She leans forward to rest her head against my shoulder. "You know what the best part of being the owner is?"

"What's that."

"Getting to leave whenever I want. I love my staff, they know what they're doing, and if anything goes wrong, I can always come back downstairs and handle it."

I chuckle and give her a squeeze. "Finish what you gotta do, then meet me upstairs."

While building Sugar & Ice, we remodeled the upstairs loft as well. *We were already used to living above a bar, why not live above our own?*

I strip off my clothes and run a bath for us. It's become a ritual for us after a rough day. *Or rough sex.* After setting towels on the side of the tub, I climb inside. When she enters, her features soften, and she lays a hand over her heart. "Oh my God, you're the best. This is exactly what I need. My feet are killing me."

I never get tired of watching my wife strip down for me. *My wife.* We opted for a small elopement in Hawaii.

Freya settles into the hot water and reaches up to wrap her arms around the back of my neck. I nuzzle into her shoulder and leave a trail of kisses. She releases a soft moan. We soak in the still silence, enjoying the first peaceful moments of the day.

"It's so quiet," I comment.

"It is."

"Wanna make a bet on who makes noise first?"

THE END

# OTHER BOOKS BY SLOANE ST. JAMES

# ACKNOWLEDGMENTS

Okay, let's jump right in! As usual, I have a lot of people to thank.

First, my husband and my kids for their love and patience. I love you all so much. You make my life beautiful. And chaotic. But mostly beautiful. *Funny story, after writing about the lost wedding ring, my son flushed my own wedding ring down the toilet and it was never recovered.*

To everyone who picked up this book, thank you for taking a chance on a new author. I'm incredibly appreciative from the bottom of my heart.

Big thanks to everyone who read *Before We Came* and then came back to read this one. All of my ARC readers and reviewers are amazing, but I want to give a special shoutout to Alejandra, Christina, Leia, Nichole, Sarina, and all my betas. Thank you for sharing my books, you have directly affected my confidence as a writer. I'm blown away by your positive messages and reviews. I read every single one.

My beta readers: Mark, Nicole, Shannon, Emma, Megan, and Katie — you all are my biggest supporters and my hype squad. Thank you for making me step back from this book when I needed to focus on my mental health. Sorry for the nonsensical, manic email I sent that one day I was spiraling. I love you all!

To my fantastic editor (and awesome human), Dee Houpt, who transforms and polishes my manuscript until it sparkles. You make me fall in love with my own books.

My formatter, CC, who is a rockstar. You make my paragraphs, chapters, and text messages look beautiful on the page. I cannot wait to hold this one in my hands.

Special thanks to SJ Tilly for enthusiastically letting me reference Second Bite in this story.

And finally, to my corporate day job for always motivating me to sell more books so I can get the hell out of there.

There was a lot on my mind when I wrote this book. I started writing in January 2023, that same month I made the difficult decision to have a prophylactic double mastectomy in May. I made the surgery my deadline. During those five months, I was dissociating from a lot of the things happening in my life. When I didn't want to think about losing my breasts, I worked on Strong and Wild. That worked until everything sort of came to a head in April when I couldn't focus on anything but the ambiguous grief I had over losing a part of myself.

Once that hit, I kind of lost my marbles. My writer's block and imposter syndrome teamed up with each other and I lost all faith in the book. I sat down with my manuscript and tore it apart limb from limb and rearranged all the pieces. Nothing was working.

At some point I texted my betas and told them I was going to scrap the whole thing. They told me to take a break and come back. I was running out of time to finish before surgery, but I still took the break. I'm convinced that break is the only reason I was able to complete it.

The last week of April, I began getting these tiny bursts of inspiration. I sat down with it and got to work. For the next two weeks, I stayed up late every night after my kids went to bed and worked tirelessly on it, trying to give Micky and Rhys the justice they deserved. Micky is an extension of myself and I needed to take care of her.

As I write this, I'm exactly one week away from my

surgery. I hope that when I do a re-read in a few weeks, I'll be able to see the forest for the trees.

If you or someone you know is struggling with addiction and you need help finding a program, reach out to the Substance Abuse and Mental Health Services hotline 1-800-662-4357. Someone will answer 24/7, 365 days a year.

If you enjoyed reading this book, please help spread the word by leaving a review on Amazon, Goodreads, Bookbub, Facebook Reader Groups, Booktok, Bookstagram, or wherever you talk smut.

And now I'm going to shamelessly beg:
Please, tell your friends and followers. Recommend this book and share the hell out of it.
If you already have, you have my endless gratitude. I hope you sleep well knowing that you are making some woman's mid-life crisis dreams come true!

I love to connect with my readers!
SloaneStJamesWrites@gmail.com

Want to join my ARC team?
SloaneStJames.com

Facebook Reader Group:
Sloane's Good Girl Book Club